# LONG STORY SHORT

# LONG STORY SHORT

*Serena Kaylor*

WEDNESDAY BOOKS
NEW YORK

First published in the United States by Wednesday Books, an imprint of St. Martin's Publishing Group

LONG STORY SHORT. Copyright © 2022 by Serena Kaylor. All rights reserved. Printed in the United States of America. For information, address St. Martin's Publishing Group, 120 Broadway, New York, NY 10271.

www.wednesdaybooks.com

Designed by Devan Norman

Library of Congress Cataloging-in-Publication Data

Names: Kaylor, Serena, author.
Title: Long story short / Serena Kaylor.
Description: First edition. | New York : Wednesday Books, 2022. | Audience: Ages 14–18.
Identifiers: LCCN 2022005301 | ISBN 9781250818416 (hardcover) | ISBN 9781250818423 (ebook)
Subjects: CYAC: Camps—Fiction. | Theater—Fiction. | Acting—Fiction. | Belonging (Social psychology)—Fiction. | LCGFT: Novels.
Classification: LCC PZ7.1.K388 Lo 2022 | DDC [Fic]—dc23
LC record available at https://lccn.loc.gov/2022005301

Our books may be purchased in bulk for promotional, educational, or business use. Please contact your local bookseller or the Macmillan Corporate and Premium Sales Department at 1-800-221-7945, extension 5442, or by email at MacmillanSpecialMarkets@macmillan.com.

First Edition: 2022

10  9  8  7  6  5  4  3  2  1

THIS IS FOR MY PARENTS.
THEY TAUGHT A LONELY, AWKWARD GIRL
THAT WORDS HAVE POWER
AND SOMEHOW CONVINCED HER
SHE COULD DO ANYTHING SHE DREAMED OF.
SO SHE DID.

We've all seen it. That play with the guy and the girl and the priest. The one where they're stupid enough to believe in "love at first sight" and reckless enough to die for it. Romeo, who was quick to murder a girl's cousin but wasn't calm and collected enough to check Juliet's pulse. Who couldn't take five seconds to calculate the duration of the potion he was so willing to let his young wife drink. Romeo, who didn't display an ounce of sense, and yet people will walk around crowing:

"Romeo, Romeo. Wherefore art thou Romeo?"

All the while not realizing that "wherefore" doesn't mean "where."

It means "why."

As if he had a say in the matter.

As if there were an opportunity to change.

# Chapter One

"YOU KNOW, YOU'D BE A LOT PRETTIER IF YOU smiled more."

I pushed the asparagus around my plate, ignoring him. Dinner parties with my parents' colleagues were always painful, but nothing was more painful than having to spend time with the Robertsons.

Stevie Robertson cleared his throat and repeated himself because he was an idiot.

I dragged my eyes off my plate, leveling him with a glare. It wasn't necessarily his *fault* that he was an idiot, but I didn't imagine he'd enjoy my attention now that he had it.

I adjusted my glasses, evaluating him as if he were a specimen under a microscope. He shifted nervously, a brainless little collection of cells, wearing a formfitting jacket that he insisted on keeping on throughout the entire dinner. A little bead of sweat slid down the collection of baby fuzz he was attempting to grow on his upper lip.

He broke eye contact and gulped a few swallows of water. Spittle shot across the succulent centerpiece separating us, and the candlelight wavered as he violently coughed. I leaned away from the splash zone, moving a candlestick slightly to the left as he loosened his tie and sputtered into his napkin.

"*Stevie!* Stevie, sweetheart, are you okay?" He waved off his mother, clearly having gotten his taste for theatrics from her, before turning a delightful shade of purple.

Now I smiled.

With Stevie occupied with things like breathing, I tried to calculate how angry my parents would be if I excused myself to go to the bathroom and slipped up the stairs to my room. Dr. Horowitz was always saying I should attempt to interact with people more, and that I spent too much time inside my head. I wrinkled my nose as Stevie mopped his face with his napkin, harsh little sounds continuing to sputter out of his trachea. I imagined the good doctor would give me a pass on *this* particular situation, as I had more important things on my mind.

Things like, I don't know, my entire future, success, and happiness.

I flushed under the candlelight, attempting to regulate my breathing. My mind was brimming with logical progressions and pathways, all trying to find the answer to this problem. A solution. A life raft. The *appropriate* way to handle the letter I got today. The very official-looking letter that was now carefully pressed, lovingly refolded, and hidden upstairs in my desk drawer until I was brave enough to announce it.

*Dear Ms. Quinn, I am delighted to inform you that your application for admission into the University of Oxford as an undergraduate student in the Department of Statistics has been successful.*

Tears pricked at my eyes, and my lungs complained as if there wasn't enough air in this smothering room.

In this smothering city.

All that work, all those hopes stacked so perilously high, and

I'd actually *done it*. I'd gotten into the university that I'd loved almost my entire life. This obsession that grew and grew alongside me, until it was so powerful it threatened to swallow me whole.

When I was a child, I was enchanted by the fact that Oxford University looked like a castle. As I got older, I became fixated on the idea that the entire city of Oxford, a place built by this paragon of learning, was likely filled with people who were similar to me. People who loved books more than people, and nobody thought that was weird.

Dr. Horowitz liked to claim that I didn't *actually* love books more than people and that was simply a defense mechanism. We've agreed to disagree.

It all came to a head a few months ago. I was tirelessly plowing through my online community college courses at an alarming clip, and my finger just kind of slipped. Right over the submit-your-application button on Oxford's website. *Whoops.*

Their statistical genetics program was unapologetically brilliant and unorthodox, and there were labs that approached curing cancer as if it were a simple math problem. I knew it would challenge me and change my entire life, and everything was finally within my grasp. I was going to do it. I was going to move to England.

Well, maybe.

I forced down another bite of oversalted asparagus as my pounding heart threatened to crack my ribs.

"Beatrice, are you enjoying the asparagus? I made it especially for you." My mother smiled from the head of the table, but it didn't reach her eyes. She spent most of her life laughing, dancing, and enjoying the little things. She did not, however, enjoy Mrs. Robertson. Unfortunately, they had similar areas of research; so, every few months they would force our families together to subtly stick it to each other from across a beautifully arranged table.

I nodded, trying to keep the pained expression off my face. I'd done the math already. *I always did the math.* I had a precise timeline estimating how long it would take to arrange student visas, housing, and books, and there was a very small window before I would be forced to tell them. Wasn't getting into college supposed to be a happy occasion? A cause for celebration?

I slumped deeper into my chair. I'd announced that I was going to apply to Oxford, and my parents had chuckled and told me that we could maybe talk about it in a few years, picking their papers back up and dismissing it. Dismissing *me.* One of the things people forget about homeschooling is that even if you do graduate high school at fourteen, parents don't typically let you move out any sooner. Now, at sixteen, I was still here—just moldering away like some middle-school science project. Some fungus that nobody wanted to touch until it had matured beyond a certain point.

I jerked as everyone clapped, and Stevie smirked across from me, straightening the lapels of his jacket. I looked to the other end of the table at my dad for context clues. He smiled, his bright blue eyes crinkling at my usual cry for help. "Stevie is going to Stanford, Beatrice. Isn't that exciting?"

"Oh." I nodded. "Congratulations."

He preened despite my lukewarm praise. "Don't worry, Beatrice. I won't forget all the little people once I'm a university man."

I considered stabbing him with my butter knife as his mother leaned over, her cloying perfume invading my personal space. "Stanford's *basically* Ivy League," she purred, patting my arm and violating my rules against casual physical contact.

"But it's not actually? Right?" I looked to my dad for confirmation as he choked on his wine. He gave Mrs. Robertson an apologetic smile, his golden good looks softening my words.

Mom frowned at me. "Stanford is a wonderful accomplishment. You should be very proud of Stevie."

"Oh, we are!" Mr. Robertson bellowed, with all the subtlety of a man who insisted people call him The Captain even when off the water. "He's a brilliant boy, and anybody would be lucky to be in his position." He raised his glass in his son's direction and tossed the contents back before anyone else could join him.

"What are you up to these days, Beatrice? Still doing those little online classes from your bedroom?" Stevie grinned across from me, a greasy stain spreading across his striped teal tie.

"That's right, Steven. I'm still doing my little online classes." I took another bite of limp asparagus, forcing it down with his words.

"Should we really call advanced-level physics little?" Dad mumbled.

"Don't worry, my dear!" Mr. Robertson yelled, although I was only a few feet from him. "You keep working hard, and studying, and you might get into a good school too!" He gave me a wink and slapped his son on the back. "I'm sure Stevie here can help if you need any tips on applying."

Stevie laughed, and I stiffened, the sound crawling up my spine. "That's not necessary."

Mom stood up, refilling wineglasses. "Beatrice is right. She's only sixteen. We have plenty of time."

I flinched as Mrs. Robertson touched my arm again. "It's best not to leave it to the last minute. You might think you have all the time in the world, but there's a chance you might get wait-listed at your first-choice schools, and then you're waiting another year before applications open up again."

I wrenched my arm away from her, and the words slipped through my teeth before I even realized what happened. "I'm going to Oxford."

She chuckled. "Well, if you want to go to Oxford, you'd better give yourself even *more* time."

"No," I said, correcting her, the words tangling on my tongue. "I got into Oxford. For the fall semester."

"Wait," Mom said, her fork clattering against her plate. "What did you say?"

I dug my fingers into the thick pleats of my skirt, eyes carefully fixed on my lap. "I applied to Oxford. I found out this afternoon that I got in."

The clink of glasses, chewing, and ambient dinner sounds slowed to a crawl as the silence hung heavy in the air.

"*You?* You got into Oxford?" Stevie demanded as all eyes pinned me to my chair.

"You didn't know she was applying?" Mrs. Robertson asked, her tone gleeful.

I cleared my throat, looking up from my plate. "I was curious to see if I could get in." I folded my napkin next to me, my appetite gone. "Apparently, I could."

"Beatrice Quinn, I would like a word with you." Mom smiled at our guests, but it was all teeth. "We'll be just a moment."

Dad stood up and shrugged. "Teenagers, right?"

The Robertsons chuckled as my face flamed red. I resented the implication that I'd done something reckless or immature. I'd applied to *college*. I marched past my parents toward their office on the other side of the house where they ran their practice. I paused outside the double doors, their brass plaque winking in the light:

Sophia Quinn, Ph.D., and Edwin Quinn, Ph.D.
Marital Counseling and Sexual Health

I rolled my eyes for what was probably the millionth time and once again reminded myself why I'd never really fit in here.

Berkeley, California, where even the academia had an emotional component to it.

Sometimes I wondered if I had any emotional components at all.

# Chapter Two

THEY BARRELED IN AFTER ME, YELLING OVER each other before the door had even closed. "You applied to Oxford?" Mom demanded, bangles flying as she tossed her arms over her head. "Were you even going to tell us?"

I frowned. "I'm telling you now."

Dad massaged his temples. "Oxford, *again*? Honey, I haven't heard you mention that place in months. I thought you'd lost interest. Don't they require, I don't know, an interview or something?"

I nodded, my stomach clenching at the thought of the Zoom call a few weeks ago, my legs trembling under the table, just out of sight.

Mom narrowed her eyes. "Is this why you've been acting so strangely over the past few weeks?"

I shifted in place as she sank into her overstuffed leather chair.

She laughed. "I thought . . . I don't know what I thought. That maybe you were being so secretive because you'd made a *friend*?"

Heat blossomed across my cheeks. She always asked about

dating, her and Nana Quinn both. You'd think that after sixteen years she'd know her daughter well enough to know that was probably never going to be a pressing issue. When it came to my nana, I'd typically make up some story about how that last guy I ran into—while attempting to read and follow my mother around the local co-op—had asked for my number.

People are supposed to be kind to the elderly.

I shook my head, trying to get back on track, when Dad sank into the matching chair next to Mom.

"Beatrice, you must understand this is a shock. You're still so young, and the idea of you moving out of this house or out of the country is a lot to take in."

I nodded, trying to understand their perspective as I sat primly on the couch across from them, which was usually reserved for their clients. My fingers dug into the buttery, worn leather. "I didn't know if I was going to get in, so there wasn't any point in making a big deal about it. I only found out today, so I thought we could start making plans."

They sat with twin looks of disbelief aimed in my direction.

I sat up straighter, my glasses sliding sharply down my nose. "Okay, well, as I was saying, it is time to move beyond my current level of education. The decision to go to Oxford was threefold. First, I felt that—"

Mom leaned forward, her dark hair tumbling over a turquoise peasant top. "Sweetheart, I need you to hit pause on the speech and get real with us. I don't think this is a good idea."

I bit my bottom lip. I *hated* when she asked me to "get real" with her. It implied that she thought my actual personality was fake.

"All right," I said, resisting the urge to roll my eyes. We were briskly moving toward the debate part of this conversation. That was fine; I was prepared. "Please, tell me your concerns."

"For one, you're only sixteen!"

Dad placed a hand on Mom's knee, and she stilled. His sandy blond hair and tan implied he was more at home on the beach than in all the classrooms it took for him to obtain his doctorate.

"Sweetheart, it will be a lot of new experiences for you, which you don't always enjoy or respond well to. You've been home-schooled or taken online classes your whole life, and now you will have actual classmates. It will be another country with new laws, foods, and customs. You will be living alone or, more likely, living with a stranger. Any one of these things would be a difficult transition, but *all* of them? It's a much better idea to start small. Let's sign up for a few in-person classes at Berkeley and see how that goes first. They have an amazing statistics department."

"Yes, honey, the last time you took an in-person class, you refused to say a single word, even when called on. The teacher thought you were purposefully ignoring him," Mom said, her knowing look scraping against every nerve I had.

I almost wavered, smoothing out the creases on my lumpy blouse, unable to hold their concerned stares as they outlined all my flaws. My *difficulties* with change. With people. With the world outside my bedroom. I knew it frustrated them and they didn't get it, or get *me*. I was never going to be some picture-perfect social butterfly, but I just wished they'd remind me of that less often.

"Look, I'm older now, and I doubt that Oxford will be that much different than the online classes I'm currently doing. They give you a topic or assignment, you study it, and then you take a test or write a paper. What am I missing?"

"Everything else!" Mom blurted as she jerked out of her seat. Her features sagged as she walked over and sat next to me, gently taking my hand. "You are missing everything else! You're a brilliant, incredible young woman, but everything is about your work.

You barely come out of your room. We don't want you to fall off the face of the earth and be found in a cramped apartment under a pile of books, like on one of those creepy *Hoarders* episodes."

I pulled my hand out of her grip. "As lovely as that visual is, there's nothing wrong with dedication. All those books are the reason I have an acceptance letter to Oxford."

She sighed, and one of those long, unspoken looks stretched between her and Dad. My stomach cramped. Something about that look seemed final, and I hadn't even outlined all my arguments.

"I'm sorry, honey," she said. "I just don't think you're ready for it, and I'd be a lot more comfortable if you could defer a year. You'll be seventeen then, and we'll have some time to figure out the rest. We can take a look at some local programs, all right?"

My mind blanked, as if I had too many tabs open and the system just crashed. I stood up, pacing across their thick, shaggy rug, attempting to find the fluttering threads of my argument. That *couldn't* be it. There was always another pathway, another solution. Another defense I hadn't found yet. I spun toward Dad, knowing he was my only hope.

"You know what this means to me. When have I ever asked either of you for anything? Do you know how statistically impossible it is that I got in? Who knows if they would even let me defer!"

Dad grasped my hand and pulled me into the chair Mom had vacated. "Okay, let's figure this out." His calm voice washed over me, as if we were a couple who needed mediating. "You want to start college in the fall, and your number one pick is Oxford?"

"My only pick is Oxford."

"Sophia, your concern is that while she's mentally prepared, she's not emotionally prepared to live so far away from home?"

Heat crawled up my face again, and I pulled the collar of my blouse closed as a dusky red blossomed across my chest.

"I'm concerned my daughter is just going to disappear in England. If you add on graduate degrees, she might never come back here. To be perfectly honest, I don't trust her to build anything but half a life for herself over there!"

I laughed, the words a knife in my gut. "Heaven forbid a daughter of yours have no interest in boys, or clothes, or whatever ridiculous things you think make up a real person."

She leaned back as if I'd slapped her. I knew I wasn't making a strong case for my maturity here, but it was too late for me to care. I'd heard this complaint too many times before. It was embarrassing when your own parents thought you were a loser, but they didn't get it. I didn't seek out the company of others, nor did I feel that I was missing out on anything.

I was *fine* with being alone.

"That's not what I'm saying," she said, her words heavy with an emotion I couldn't identify. She crossed the room and crouched in front of me. "You were so advanced and so bored in preschool and, yes, different. Special. I didn't want you to be labeled, judged, and diagnosed into some box. I thought homeschooling would give you the freedom to achieve your potential. I thought that was *best* for you." She brushed my thick brown hair out of my face, the mirror of her own. "Now I'm not so sure we did you any favors."

My response caught in my throat as Dad squeezed my shoulder and moved toward the door. "We should probably get rid of the Robertsons. Based on the state we left them in, they've probably gone through all the wine and continued to toast Stevie in our absence."

Mom smiled. "At least Beatrice gave us an excuse to end the evening early."

"So glad my disappointment has a silver lining."

Her face pinched. "You can stay here if you'd like."

She eased the door closed, and I sank onto the couch, my vision blurring.

"Breathe." *Helium. Neon. Argon. Krypton. Xenon. Radon.* The pattern felt comforting as I fell back on familiar habits. *Helium. Neon. Argon. Krypton. Xenon. Radon.* My lungs expanded, and the anxiety blunted to a dull edge.

I knew I was overreacting, but I'd never wanted anything so badly before. The sheer wanting of it threatened to choke me.

Was that it, then? I was going to sit here another year, taking local classes and placing my life on hold? Waiting for some divine signal or sign that once I achieved a certain amount of time on this planet, I was suddenly equipped to handle change? Another wave of anxiety rolled over me, and I erupted out of the chair. I stalked past floor-to-ceiling bookshelves, my fingers twitching over the beautiful leather-bound books and me holding back angry tears by sheer force of will.

The door opened behind me, and I turned as Dad slipped through.

"I can't stay here another year just *waiting*," I said, my voice breaking.

He sagged against the doorframe and nodded. "I know, kiddo. I just wish you'd given us a little more notice. This is a really big thing to spring on us."

I nodded as Dr. Horowitz's voice played in my mind: *Beatrice, you live too much in your own head and then expect people to be on the same page as you.*

"If you had a few days to get over the surprise of it, do you think you could help me convince Mom to let me go?" I asked. I was so careful not to get my hopes up, but I couldn't help the fluttering in my belly as the words spilled out.

"Beatrice, we both have a lot of concerns about this plan. You're taking the stress of going away to college and doubling it in a way where we would be nowhere nearby to help. I'm not exactly on your side here," he said, moving forward and placing his reassuring hands on my shoulders.

I sank with the weight. "You're the only one who's ever on my side." I knew my mom loved me, but her best intentions always dangled with strings attached. *Oh, you need more clothes? Let's go shopping and I will pick out what I think you should look like. You like spending time alone in your room? That's just because you haven't been forced into the right social group.*

"That's not fair, and we're only trying to make the decision that's going to be best for you," he said, the pressure of his fingertips grounding me.

Dad jumped as Mom swung open the door, announcing, "They're finally out of the house! They almost blustered their way back here to offer Beatrice more congratulations and advice."

I scoffed, pulling away from Dad. "Congratulations for what? Spending another year fiddling with my little online classes?" I flopped onto the couch.

She looked up, commiserating with her higher power. "I'm furious because you knew how we felt about you leaving at this age, but I'm also proud of you. I can't believe you got into Oxford." She shook her head. "Not that I wouldn't believe it; you're the most brilliant kid I know. I'm just shocked. It's a *huge* deal."

I tensed as adrenaline flooded my nervous system. *Was she coming around? Could I resume my three-pronged defense?* "How am I supposed to respond to that? Thank you for being proud of me? Even though it doesn't matter and I'm not going to go?"

"I just want you to be happy," she said, defeated. "Of course I want you to excel at your classes, but it's not just that. I also want you to fall madly in love, find a best friend you can pour your heartbreaks out to, and have people you can go on adventures to Spain with."

"Who says that won't happen anyway?" The lie tasted sour on my lips. I'd never been good in social situations, and it probably hadn't helped that I'd only really been around adults my entire life. Usually by choice.

"I know you had a difficult time with kids your own age a few years ago—"

"You told Dr. Horowitz you wouldn't bring that up anymore," I said, anxiety rising to a level that threatened to flood my entire body and wash everything away.

She sighed, worrying the rings on her fingers.

"Well, what can we do?" Dad asked, breaking the tension and giving me a reassuring smile. "You want Beatrice to come out of her shell, right?"

I flinched, suppressing the urge to clarify that creatures stay within their shells for a very good reason. Mom nodded, joining me on the couch.

"Well, we have an entire summer to make that happen, and if she shows us that socializing isn't a problem, that she makes some friends and can find interests other than studying, then maybe we can send her to Oxford in the fall?"

I froze. What was the name of the girl who lived next door? Stacey? Casey? She was about my age, and I was about to haunt her footsteps. I winced, trying to remember where I'd put those *Gossip Girl* box sets.

"It would have to be something completely out of her comfort zone," Mom said.

"A job?" He shook his head, immediately discounting the idea. "No, it should be more social."

"How about an internship at a museum or library?" I said. "Those have lots of people."

Mom rolled her eyes. "I want you to be around people your own age. Try again."

Dad snapped his fingers, a smile spreading across his lips. "Camp! I went to camp every year growing up, and some of the best memories of my life were made there!"

Oh no. Not a chance in hell. I was not an outdoorsy kind of girl who could hike and swim and look beautiful and golden in the sunlight. I burned, freckled, and had a habit of sweating in surprising places. I was also not the type of girl who enjoyed large crowds, or small crowds, or people in general.

If you wanted a ten-page paper on the comparative camping techniques of various cultures, I was most certainly your girl. I would even include graphs.

But *camp* camp?

I cleared my throat, ready to suggest some fresh new hell they could put me through, but Mom jumped in first.

"Camp." She bit her lip. "You might be onto something there, but I don't know. Wouldn't it be too easy for her to sulk in the woods or keep to herself?"

I frowned, as I was once again talked about like I wasn't even in the room. It hardly mattered that she was probably right.

"Wait!" She turned toward my dad, her hands fluttering like small birds. "Remember our old clients Jack and Theresa Carson? The couple with the intimacy issues and the godawful daughter?"

"Angelica? The girl you'd make me entertain while you all were in session? The one who only ever wanted to play a game she called Pop Star, where she would sing nonstop, and my role was to pretend to enjoy it?"

"Sorry, sweetie," Dad said, wincing. "What about them?"

"Well, Angelica was determined to be famous, so they sent

her to this acting camp in LA!" She threw her arms open as if she'd accomplished something spectacular. "Theater camp!"

My body attempted to laugh and gag at the same time, my protests cut short by my lack of oxygen. *Theater camp?* An entire group of people assaulting me with their talents like Angelica Carson?

"She'd be forced to be an extrovert," Dad said, hiding a small smile. "Nobody escapes theater camp without spending some time on the stage."

They clearly didn't know their daughter very well. "There is no way I'm going to prance around on a stage with jazz hands and sing with ridiculous boys about *summer loving.*" The idea alone was absurd.

Mom shrugged. "All right, then you're not going, and we can all suffer through dinners listening to Stevie Robertson brag about Stanford over the next year." She stood up, moving back toward the door.

"What?" I said. "That's it? It's camp or nothing?"

"To be fair, honey," Dad chimed in, "we tried suggesting an idea that would make us feel better about you going. An idea that contained stepping-stones like spending the summer away from here, being in a new environment, and even having a roommate. You refused to consider that idea."

I blinked, recognizing I was walking a fine line of going back to a hard no. "It's not as if they're the same experience," I said, scowling.

"No," he said, trying to suppress a smile. "At camp, you'd be able to call us up and fly home earlier if you realize that you don't enjoy this type of experience. Going to Oxford is a little more permanent."

The rest of Oxford's incoming freshmen would be spending

their summer taking classes or moving to England to orient themselves with the campus. My summer was going to include tights.

I really didn't have a choice.

"It'll just be a little push, Beatrice," Mom said knowingly. "Getting out of your comfort zone is probably just what you needed all along."

"They call it sink or swim because failure is fifty percent of the available options," I said.

She shrugged, knowing she had me over a barrel. I did a quick pros and cons list in my head, but there was no contest. This was for Oxford.

"*Fine,*" I forced out through my teeth. "Let me keep a little dignity, though. There will be no singing, dancing, or contemporary issues to act out. I want something serious and academic, like Shakespeare. Preferably one of the tragedies."

Dad smiled. "Shakespeare could probably be arranged."

# *Chapter Three*

MY FROWN REFLECTED IN THE GLASS WHITE-board that took up one large wall in my bedroom, and only deepened as I reviewed my work. The packet from the Connecticut Shakespearean Summer Academy was spread across my desk, with all the concerning information copied onto the board in front of me in glossy, corrective red. A sea of problems I had no idea how to fix. I tried to focus on the facts, the schedule, and the rules and regulations. *Campers will be required to adhere to the schedule and duties of their respective concentrations.* Which, of course, meant that there would be no hiding backstage or trying to blend in with the production crew. I would be at rehearsal with the *actors*. The people who were out there thinking it was totally normal to get in front of scores of people and . . . perform. I shoved my glasses back into place and reviewed the outlined schedule again. Everything revolved around the stupid play, and there wasn't any designated time for independent study or even a book club. Not really the academic Shakespearean camp I had in mind. They were all going to be like awful Angelica, and all of them an absolute chore to talk to.

"Knock, knock," Dad said, easing the door open.

"You don't have to say the sound; you can just knock."

"I could knock all day, but if you were reading you would never hear it," he said, the corner of his mouth twitching.

I sighed, capping the marker. "What can I do for you, Dad?"

"Well, progeny of mine, I was wondering if you would deign to come have dinner with your poor parents who will be devastated when you're gone next week?"

I snuck a glance at the whiteboard. "I'm not really hungry."

"Good thing I wasn't really asking," he said, reaching out a hand.

I shuffled over, and he tugged on my tangled braid and propelled me down the stairs. "You need a break, kiddo."

"I'm just trying to map it all out in my brain so I know how it will go," I said, walking into the dining room. The patio doors were thrown wide open and a warm, fragrant breeze wrapped around me. I blinked as the rosy tint of dusk stained everything it touched. Time passed a little differently in my room, and I didn't realize it'd gotten so late. Or that spring had given way to the cusp of summer and the past three months had flown by and I was days away from leaving for camp. One hundred and sixty-eight hours. Six hundred four thousand, eight hundred seconds.

I breathed a little deeper, filling my lungs.

"Map out how what will go?" Mom asked, setting dishes on the table.

"Beatrice thinks she can force a month away at camp with hormonal teenagers into an organized little box," Dad said, grabbing a covered dish from Mom. The scent of rich spices floated through the air, and I sat down in my usual seat. A plain slice of mushroom pizza already on the plate in front of me.

"What's in the pot?" I asked, picking up a knife and fork.

"Vickie from next door gave me this great plant-based recipe with lentils," Mom said, serving a hearty portion of something brown on Dad's plate. "Want to try?"

"I'm okay," I said, shoving the familiar bite into my mouth. Bread, cheese, light tomato sauce, and mushrooms. Nothing fancy, and the exact same every Friday night.

Honestly, it was probably the easiest way for me to keep track of what day it was. Chicken and asparagus on Monday, fettuccine alfredo on Tuesday, roasted eggplant on Wednesday, veggie burger Thursday, mushroom pizza Friday, and the weekend was just a free-for-all of animal crackers and grilled cheese sandwiches as my parents ate out or socialized with friends.

It was structured and reliable. The components never changed, and it fit my routine. It made sense to my brain.

"So," Mom said, smiling brightly. "Do you think you're ready for camp?"

I shrugged. "I've gone through Shakespeare's entire catalogue twice, so I think I'm ready for any possible discussions regarding his work."

"You should see the whiteboard," Dad said, mopping up lentils with some bread. "There's so many lists, and no less than three graphs."

I rolled my eyes as Mom put down her fork.

"What were the lists?" Mom asked.

"I saw one on the rules of modern-day friendship, and another on ways to casually end a conversation."

"How much red ink?"

"*All* of it."

They both turned to me, and bland pizza scraped down my throat.

"What?"

"Honey, we don't have to do this if you don't feel up to it," Mom said, sliding her hand across the table.

I ignored it. "Clearly we do because you won't let me go to school otherwise."

"Beatrice, I can't even get you to try a different meal for Friday night dinner. What do you want from me? How would I even know if you'd fly over there and be able to feed yourself?"

"Sophia, let's not get into it again," Dad said. "Beatrice has agreed to this experiment, and despite the concerning amount of red on the whiteboard, she's moving forward with it."

I nodded. Problems only became blue ink if I'd found the solution, but I knew that I could solve this. I always could.

"Edwin, do you think they'd call us if she wasn't eating?"

"Mom, enough!" I pushed back from the table, the limp pizza forgotten. "I'm not going to *starve*. I'm capable of feeding myself, of getting through four weeks of just about anything, and moving away to England just so I never have to have this conversation again." I punctuated this by taking a forkful of lentils from the dish in front of me and shoving it in my mouth.

I immediately started coughing as spices coated my tongue and made my nose water. My whole body felt flushed and heavy—from anger, fear, or the stupid lentils—I couldn't tell. Camp hadn't even started yet and my carefully structured life was already unraveling.

Dad patted me on the back. "See, Sophia? She's becoming more adventurous already. Now, sweetheart, why don't you tell us about some of the things you're worried about? We both went to camp when we were your age, and we might have some insights."

"How about that they take your phone when you get there, and you're trapped like a prisoner?"

Mom rolled her eyes. "It's not to trap you; it's so all the campers are more present. You already know you get to talk to us and Dr. Horowitz on Sunday, and there's no reason to have it otherwise."

"What if there's an emergency?" I challenged.

"Like wanting to come home early?" she asked over her wine-glass.

"Of course not," I said, not willing to even consider the possibility of failure. I took a gulp of water, popping loose the top button of my blouse. "Okay, since you brought up concerns, I've been meaning to ask you about something. There are concentrations other than acting at the camp, and I think there's one that might be a better fit for me. It would still require me to go and be away from home, but—"

"What are the other concentrations?" Mom asked, suspicion staining her words.

"Well, there's acting, as you know. There's costume design, but I think you have to be able to sew on more than a button to join." I took a deep breath. "Then there's production, which is lighting, directing, and backstage work. I think I would really flourish in that type of environment."

"Absolutely not," Mom said, pushing her plate away from her.

Dad reached over and placed his large, warm hand over mine.

"Beatrice, we wanted you to branch out and really get out of your comfort zone. Painting sets in the background isn't going to cover that."

I pushed the palms of my hands into my eyes until the world blanched. "I just don't know what you expect from me. Am I just supposed to walk around *taking it in* for a month? Show up on the stage in some capacity and Oxford is mine?"

"You're absolutely right." Mom stood up, walking over to the console table currently supporting a host of potted plants in various stages of death. She rummaged in a drawer and pulled out a legal pad. "We haven't given you enough structure. You need markers of success and goals to achieve while you're there." She sat the pad in front of her and scrawled *The Teenager Experience Experiment* at the top with a flourish. She grinned at Dad over the top of her wineglass. "Now, what are normal teenager experiences?"

I noted that she did not ask me, the only teenager in the room, but was self-aware enough to know that was probably the best call.

"Why don't we start small," Dad said, smiling gently. "Let's start with friends."

### 1.) *Make a friend*

It wasn't as bad as it could have been. "How do you know if someone is your friend?" I asked, unable to meet their eyes. I kept my attention fixed on the perfect pleat running down the length of my khakis.

I felt the sigh before I heard it but refused to look up.

"They don't always tell you, because it's usually an assumed thing, sweetie. It's a person who enjoys spending time with you, usually seeks out your company, and that you feel comfortable with," Mom said.

"I'm sure if you did ask, they would tell you too," Dad said, and some of the tension released in my shoulders.

I nodded. This was a specific problem to attack. I could work with this. "Fine, what's next?"

"What about deepening some of those friendships? Share a secret!" Dad said, nudging me.

### 2.) *Share a secret*

I grimaced. Nothing like forcing a little emotional intimacy on somebody to kill whatever fledgling relationship I'd been able to produce.

### 3.) *Walk up to someone and make small talk*

Dad nodded as Mom's pen scraped across the paper. "That's a good one, and good practice. Why not one where she can't talk herself out of doing something social?"

*4.) Accept an invitation you don't want to*

Well, I'd certainly have plenty of opportunities to check that box off.

"Oh, and maybe something to make sure she gets outside," Mom said, putting pen back to paper.

*5.) Do an outdoor activity*

My stomach clenched as I thought of the brochure with kayaks and sunburnt campers running around along the lake. It was like observing an exotic culture or an alien species.

"What's the age range on this camp again?" Dad asked.

"Fifteen to eighteen," I answered automatically, the details already burned into my brain.

He scrunched up his nose. "Is that too mature for pranks? That was one of my favorite parts of camp growing up. One of my bunkmates stole every pair of my underwear and strung them all up on flagpoles across campus," he said, laughing.

My lungs constricted, and I took a deep breath in and out. *Helium. Neon. Argon. Krypton. Xenon. Radon.*

"I can't imagine what you did in retaliation," Mom said, tears in her eyes. "I love that idea, and she could use some light-hearted fun!"

*6.) Pull a prank*

*7.) Execute a dare*

I took another deep breath in and out, each task settling heavily on my chest.

"How about something simple like a hug? It might be a good idea to practice that too?" Dad said, giving me his encouraging smile. His *trust me, you'll really enjoy this* smile.

### 8.) *Hug three people*

My body responded before my mind could even catch up, and I bolted upright, the chair flying out behind me.

"That's enough."

Mom frowned, a question hovering in her eyes, and I stuck my hand out before she could ask it.

"Each one of these tasks will require extensive research and preparation, and I leave in a week. I need to start on my homework." I stuck my chin out, the bravado covering the panic that I couldn't give way to. My limit had been met, and my brain refused to accept any new information until I at least had some sort of handle on all of this.

She sighed, tearing the sheet free. "I was hoping you'd look at this like an adventure."

I peeled my lips back into the best smile I could produce under these circumstances. "I love adventures." I plucked the sheet from her fingers and ran up the stairs before they could utter another word or platitude. I closed the door and braced myself heavily against it. My breathing was already easier as the familiar sage-green walls settled me. The angry red bullet points stood out from the whiteboard, and that familiar wave of anxiety rolled over me. *Xenon. Neon. Argon—* No, I didn't have time to freak out. I didn't have time to feel sorry for myself.

I was overwhelmed before because I didn't know what I was supposed to do, but now I had a very detailed checklist. A ridiculous checklist where I was hugging strangers and forcing small talk on them, but a checklist all the same. I stalked over to the whiteboard and cut through the red with my eraser. All that work and all those concerns with no solutions gone in an instant. It was time for a different approach. I pressed the red marker back to the wide expanse of white.

### The Teenager Experience Experiment

I rolled my eyes at the name and only hesitated for a moment before writing below it:

### 1.) Make a friend

I nodded before booting up my laptop and pulling up the website for *Teen Life Magazine*. "Okay, Beatrice. Let's turn you into a teenager."

# Chapter Four

**I SIGHED, LEANING MY FOREHEAD AGAINST** the grimy glass of the van window. The Connecticut countryside flew by in puffs of sheep and bushes, and fields as far as the eye could see. Despite being usually comforted by a lack of stimuli, my brain felt like it was overheating from the abrasive newness of it all. Back home I would've been working on some independent study project or relaxing with one of my favorite nature documentaries. Instead, I was sitting in a van that was likely built during the Reagan administration and hurtling toward what would be the most uncomfortable four weeks of my life. I would've nearly turned around in the airport and booked a flight right back home, if the gruff old man sent from the camp to collect me hadn't grabbed my belongings.

Correction—the gruff old man sent from the camp to collect *us*.

I turned in my seat and evaluated the girl sitting behind me over the rim of my glasses. Every inch of her was polished. Not a crease in sight or a hair out of place. She'd drawn little wings on her eyelids and was carefully painting a dusky shade of rose onto her lips. I was pretty sure if my face was close enough, I'd be able to see my reflection in the fire-red curls that were artfully tumbling down her shoulders. I bit my lip and adjusted my own frizzy mass of hair into a riotous bun, the least methodical thing about me.

Twisting back around, I shifted on the uncomfortable seat. I should try out some of the instant-friendship conversational topics that I'd developed under Google's guidance. *Hey, don't I know you from somewhere? Did you catch that last sports ball game? Dogs are the best, am I right?* The sheer quantity of options had left me overwhelmed. It was as if countless articles were implying that you could talk to people about anything and the entire world was dying to engage. My glasses slid down my nose, and I tried to slam the door on the memories of the home-schooling social events that Mom used to drag me to. Children crying, moms yelling, someone pulling hard on my braids as I explained how theoretically impossible Santa was. It only got worse as I got older, and my brain packed up all those memories into a tightly sealed box. In the end it led to everyone ignoring me, and things were better off that way. That was certainly my preference as well.

Still, the point remained that I had to show some evidence of success at the end of the month on Parents' Day, and based on the list provided to me, I had my work cut out for me. If my only task was to paint the illusion of having friends, I had brought a little extra money and could have rented a few for a day. Me smiling brightly at my parents while cheerful, normal teenagers laughed next to me and told them, *Beatrice? She's the most outgoing person I've ever met! She was always the first person to sign up for tag or whatever it is we like to play!* I wrinkled my nose. Was tag a thing? What else do you do outdoors? My shoulders slumped as the summer stretched out in front of me. I couldn't even imagine a believable script. Stuffing my hand in my pocket, I pulled out the wrinkled sheet of legal paper that was going to dictate my life for the next four weeks. The eight bullet points already played in my mind on a continuous loop.

### 1.) Make a friend

Well, there's no time like the present, and people are less scary one-on-one. I took a deep breath and visualized the research I'd done. I knew what my target population liked. I was just going to pretend to be one of them, and they'd accept me into their group and my parents would be satisfied. I cleared my throat, always determined to get an early start on my homework. The redheaded girl looked up at me. "Hello. My name is Beatrice Quinn," I said. "I'm from Berkeley, California." I started to hold my hand out before letting it drop awkwardly to my lap. *Was it normal to shake hands?*

Her eyes scraped uncomfortably over me from head to toe and she arched an extremely symmetric eyebrow. She pulled out a magazine before mumbling, "Darla."

I breathed a sigh of relief. This was progress. "Hi, Darla. It's nice to meet you. Did you have a comfortable journey getting here?"

"Mmm." She opened the magazine and flipped through it.

I stumbled over what would be the next appropriate sentence as she slid down in her seat and angled her body away from me. I didn't have a ton of experience to fall back on, but this did *not* seem to be a person who had any interest in talking to me. I turned back around in my seat, my chest tightening. *Did I say something wrong? Was it really this hard? Is it getting hotter in here?* No wonder my parents were worried about me. If she'd been one of my parents' colleagues, we would have had a civil chat about their journey, the weather, and techniques to overcome jet lag.

I really didn't have any idea how to behave with my own generation.

I tried to exhale the slight feeling of nausea and wished desperately that I could roll down a window.

I could do this. I *would* do this. I was going to check off every one of those stupid tasks, escape this summer relatively unscathed, and finally get to Oxford. I squared my shoulders. *You're prepared; you've done the readings and the research. You practiced winking in a mirror, and how to laugh on command. You know the key to tackling a difficult problem is always more research. You just need to find out what this particular specimen likes and dislikes.*

I stretched out, twisting my body, and squinted at her magazine cover. She flipped through the glossy pages and rows of neon-pink shorts, strappy sandals that wouldn't break the bank, and something about techniques to nail that first-date kiss swam into focus.

I spun back around, sucking in a shaky breath, and squished my cheek against the cool glass. This was a terrible mistake. I needed to go home. I needed to catch the next flight out, and just go back to Berkeley. *I need to go home. I need to go home. I need to go home. I need to go home. Helium. Neon. Argon. Krypton. Xenon. Radon. Helium. Neon—*

The van hit a pothole, and the window smacked me in the face.

I heard a snort from behind me, and the decrepit driver jumped in with a "Watch yerself. We're pulling up to the camp now."

I probed the tender spot on my temple as we pulled up to a squat wooden structure. It looked like a little log house, and the sign outside simply stated: "Camp Director."

"Yer responsible for yer own bags," our chauffeur mumbled

as he jumped out, producing a wet cough and showering the bottom steps with phlegm.

I winced, kicking at the battered suitcase at my feet before shoving it out onto the ground. I stepped out into the blazing sunshine and blinked. The smell of fresh-cut grass tickled my nose as humidity settled over me like a wet blanket. The cabin sat on the edge of a wide stretch of green, framed by three large buildings. A path crisscrossed through the quad, connecting several other wooden structures before extending into the woods in opposite directions. I paused, teetering on the edge of demanding to be driven back to the airport, as Oxford, always Oxford, swam to the front of my brain. The back of my blouse grew damp before I stepped forward and pulled open the cabin's rough-hewn front door.

The temperature was only marginally cooler inside, and the interior looked a lot like the outside: rustic and a little worn. Everything was wooden, from the walls to the furniture, and a rickety window unit rattled away in the corner.

"You know the ropes, Darla. Here's your packet, and you're in number three this year. I'll see you this evening."

"Thanks, Ms. Reid!" Darla grasped at the packet, wheeling her suitcase out of the room in front of me. The person she was speaking with followed her out and crossed her arms as she gave me a once-over.

All I could do was stare at the impressively built woman standing in front of me as Darla almost knocked me over in her enthusiasm to leave.

"This must be the little genius, then." Her voice was as no-nonsense as her stoic expression and starched white shirt. A bright red whistle dangled from her neck.

"Excuse me?"

"Come, let's have a chat."

I abandoned my suitcase and followed after her. She eased

herself down behind a massive desk and nodded toward the chair in front. I sat down primly, folded my hands in my lap, and tried not to stare. She looked to be in her mid- to late fifties, and I wouldn't be surprised if she was almost six feet tall. Her graying hair was pulled back severely, and her face was scrubbed clean of makeup. She looked serious. Formidable. She looked like you could drop her in the woods and she would survive until she died of natural causes.

She allowed my assessment before finally speaking. "My name is Martha Reid, and I will be your camp director this summer. Your parents have outlined your situation for me, and I'm completely on board with helping you keep up your end of the bargain."

"I can't believe they didn't think I was capable of doing that myself," I said, the surprise hurting more than I'd expected.

"This experience will be good for you. You look like you could use a little time outdoors or with young people that are different from you. I'm simply informing you that if your parents ask about your level of involvement here at camp, I'm going to tell them the truth."

Her tone wasn't malicious or condescending; she was simply stating the facts. That, I could appreciate.

I wilted in my seat. "Fine, let's get this over with. What do I do now?"

She gave me a look that might have been a smile and pulled out a packet with my name on it. She slid it across the desk, and I tore into it. There were already too many unknowns before I got here. Now there were Darlas and mysterious things I had to be involved with or I was going to get ratted out to my parents.

"You are one of the last to arrive, and the camp officially starts with this evening's meet-and-greet mixer. Before you ask, Miss Quinn, your attendance there is nonnegotiable."

I frowned. I was hoping to have a little time to work up to something like that. Maybe I could fake cramps, or a migraine, or a bear attack.

I shoved that to the back of my mind and rifled through the papers.

"You will find your room assignment at the front. You're in cabin four with . . ." She paused, scanning some papers. "Mia Parker and Shelby Walsh. They're also in the acting concentration and were both here last year, so they can help you get oriented."

"Sounds perfect," I mumbled.

This time she did smile as she stood. "Feel free to stop by if you have any problems, and I'll look forward to seeing you at the mixer this evening." She tossed me a pointed look and gestured toward the front door.

"Oh! Before I forget, I'm going to need your cell phone," she said, her hand outstretched.

I fumbled around in my bag. "What if something comes up and I need to get in touch with my parents?" *What if I decide tomorrow that I need to get the hell out of here?*

"If you have any emergencies you can come see me; otherwise you'll have to wait until Sunday."

I'm sure she wouldn't be surprised at all if I came to her tomorrow and said I needed to leave. I'm sure my mom wouldn't be either. I dropped my phone in her outstretched palm, and she ushered me outside.

"If you take that path around the side of the building, you'll see a row of smaller cabins off to the right. The boys' cabins are to the left, and I don't think I need to tell you that I better not find you in one of them."

I snorted at that superlikely scenario.

"The main buildings are all in the middle: cafeteria, auditorium, laundromat, and some classrooms and buildings for students in our production and costume design programs. The counselors' office is next to the cafeteria, and if you need help you can pop in there or just flag down anyone wearing a camp T-shirt. There's a detailed map in your packet."

I bit my lip, wishing again that I'd been given the choice to paint sets and fade into the background.

Ms. Reid awkwardly patted my shoulder. "If you keep walking past the cafeteria and follow the path to the woods right behind it, you'll see our reproduction of the Globe Theatre. It's roughly half the size of the original, but it's very detailed and historically accurate. There's also a lake for swimming and kayaking that a young person such as yourself may enjoy."

I nodded, attempting to produce some semblance of a smile.

"My door is always open," she added before turning and heading back into the building, her duty complete.

This information rattled around in my head as I dragged my suitcase down the dirt path in the direction of my new home for the next few weeks. I trudged toward where the cabins started, just at the edge of the woods, and focused on one step in front of the other. Laughter carried on the soft breeze blowing in from the trees, and my heart pounded as I moved to the side of the path as groups of girls breezed past me without a second look. They all looked so comfortable with glowing skin, easy smiles, and linked arms that spoke of a closeness I'd only read about. It made sense. We, as a species, were pack animals. From a survival standpoint, those who broke from the herd were always more vulnerable to attack. I kept my eyes down as they walked past, and my mind whirled, cataloging all the changes: the people, the location, the things that were going to be required of me, and the very real possibility of just failing completely. I didn't doubt that Mom would stick to her word and not allow me to leave Berkeley if I couldn't make a success of just one summer here. She'd give me a hug and one of her sad smiles, and everything would stay exactly the same.

Failing was *not* a choice.

Pulling up to the first cabin, I counted three more down the line and frowned at my new home. They were all ugly, stumpy log buildings, with screens in place of windows, and a small, jaunty porch hanging off the front of each one—almost like an afterthought. I yanked my suitcase up the front steps and pulled it through the screen door with me. It caught on an uneven floorboard, and we both went sprawling into the cabin.

"That's a hell of a way to make an entrance."

# Chapter Five

I SCRAMBLED TO MY FEET, STRAIGHTENING my glasses, and the blurry figure lounging against a doorway to the left came into focus.

She was an explosion of color.

She had deep brown skin, laughing eyes, and brilliant blond curls that surrounded her like a halo. I froze as my brain processed the leopard-print leggings, denim miniskirt, and dangling rainbow beads hanging from her ears. She gave me a moment to stare before stepping forward and extending her hand.

"I'm Mia Parker," she said, smiling. Her soft southern drawl washed over me.

I wiped my hand on my pants before shaking her hand, trying not to glance down at my khakis and plain white polo shirt. It was hard not to feel like a child standing next to her.

She raised an eyebrow as the silence stretched between us.

"Oh, *sorry!* I'm Beatrice Quinn," I stammered, my words tumbling out of my mouth and all over each other. I swallowed against the lump in my throat and resisted the urge to look at the floor. *Could you be any more awkward?*

"Well, there are two beds in each room, and I'm in this one."

She gestured to the left. "You're welcome to join me, or you can bunk with the ice queen over in that one."

"The ice queen?"

Mia grinned. Lean, elegant fingers capped with baby-pink nails grabbed my suitcase and yanked it toward the room on the left. I followed her around a faded plaid couch and scuffed coffee table. A Formica kitchen table with piecemeal chairs and a minifridge rounded out the remainder of the common living space. Ducking my head into a small bathroom jutting off the living room, I wrinkled my nose at the faint smell of mildew clinging to the air. The wood paneling had even spread in there, like a virus, and the plaid shower curtain matched the curtains fluttering over each window.

"Stop stalling," I muttered under my breath.

I hovered in the doorway of the bedroom on the left, feeling like an outsider, before making a conscious decision and stepping over the threshold.

"Did you say something about a queen?" I blurted out.

"*Ice* queen," she said. "That's my affectionate nickname for Shelby. We were roomies last year too, and girl totally earned that. You'll know what I mean when you meet her." She shoved my suitcase against a sparsely made twin bed and with a running jump sprawled out on an identical one. A wobbly ceiling fan creaked merrily above us.

I eyed the mattress with suspicion and pressed a palm against it. The springs bit into my hand and it started trickling in, amongst all of my many, many concerns, how much I was going to rough it.

I smoothed my shirt and turned to my new roommate. "First-class accommodations?"

Mia snorted. "The beds suck, and so does the lack of air conditioning, but the theater is *ammmmaazzzziiinnngg!*"

I winced. She'd infused more energy and enthusiasm into that one sentence than I'd ever had in my entire life.

"Are you okay? You look like you're going to be sick."

I eased down onto the bed across from her. "I'm not exactly here by choice," I said abruptly. My stomach twisted into knots and I debated whether I should even unpack.

She rolled to face me, a line appearing between her perfectly sculpted eyebrows. "From the top, please."

Her expression was so open that my rehearsed script about picking up new hobbies and wanting to see more of Connecticut just flew out the window. I needed advice. I needed someone to help talk me off the proverbial cliff and tell me that it wasn't going to be as bad as it was beginning to look like it'd be.

"My parents don't trust me to go off to school in England, and they're hoping that a summer outside my comfort zone will force me to learn how to socialize." Was now an appropriate time to practice that wink I'd been working on?

A brief smile flitted across her lips before her expression smoothed into innocence. "Socialize?"

"Yes," I said with no hesitation. *Just rip it off like a Band-Aid.* "My parents think I'm too much of a loser and want proof I can interact with people my own age."

"What about school?" Mia swung her legs off the edge of the bed and leaned forward.

I shrugged. "I was homeschooled."

"Shut *up*! What about dating?"

I pressed my lips together, on the verge of saying, *Well, once I came close,* but that wasn't true and none of that had been real. "Well, I know the kids of some of my parents' colleagues, but it's never really been much of an . . . issue." The word fell heavy from my mouth.

Mia shot up and plopped down next to me, her body vibrating

with excitement. "Well, take my word for it, there are usually some major hotties here, if you're into that sort of thing. There was this gorgeous guy named Stephen here last year, but he's aged out now that he's nineteen. He had these soulful green eyes, and such beautiful lips." She swooned against me, fanning herself. I stiffened before forcing myself to relax into the contact.

She jumped up, an endless well of energy. "Wait! You've never been in a play before?"

"Well, I've read and analyzed a bunch, but I've never tried to perform any. I'm one hundred percent certain that acting would be impossible for me."

"I don't know," she said with a wink, and I made note of her technique. "You have this great smoky voice and a really expressive face. I bet you'd do better than you think."

Mia tossed the words over her shoulder without a second thought and I knew it wasn't a big deal to her, but the compliment both warmed and discomforted me. I focused on my shoes, trying to come up with the appropriate response. The right words. A normal reaction.

"Well, at least we know she isn't any competition for Juliet," said a clipped voice from the doorway.

All I could think was *monochromatic*. Her skin was sickly-Victorian-child pale, with white-blond hair and ice-blue eyes. She was the little doll my parents had given me on my seventh birthday, which I immediately shoved under the bed.

"Wait, Juliet? They're doing *Romeo and Juliet* this year?" Mia frowned.

The new girl shrugged. "I heard some counselors talking about it, but Juliet is mine. I didn't come all the way out here to play somebody's mom."

Mia rolled her eyes and gestured to my new least favorite person. "This is Shelby, in case you couldn't tell."

I gave her a slight nod. "Beatrice."

Her eyes traveled over me from head to toe, taking in my battered loafers and pressed khakis. I was nothing that concerned her. "Hi," she said, her tone bored. She turned on her heel and swept out of the room.

I nodded thoughtfully. "Ice queen."

She grinned. "I like you, Bea. I have a feeling we are going to get along just fine."

I smiled back. *Bea.* I had a nickname. Based on my research, this was a good prognostic indicator of friendship. Trying not to get my hopes up too high, I dragged my suitcase up onto my bed. "I'm assuming *Romeo and Juliet* is the only play they'll be putting on this summer?" I pulled open a drawer in my tiny dresser and scanned for spiders before shoving my underwear in it.

"Yeah, we just do one, so we have time to get all the acting, costumes, and sets perfect," she said, shaking her head. "I don't know why they chose that one, though. We must not have that many people in the acting section this year."

"How many are there usually?"

She shrugged. "About twenty in acting, and maybe thirty apiece in production and costume design."

She lingered on my side of the room, poking through my belongings as I hurried to put them away. I pulled out a stack of books and quickly shoved them under my bed.

She frowned. "Did you bring homework?"

I kicked the stack farther under the bed, not meeting her eyes. "They're just some books on Shakespeare that I thought would come in handy while I was here."

A delighted smile spread across her face. "You know we don't have any tests or anything, right?"

I hadn't known that. I nodded a little too forcefully. "Of course."

"This is *theater* camp! It may be Shakespeare, and the writing may be dated, but the basic plot is still current. Boy meets girl, boy falls in love with girl, and six people die in their attempt to be together," she said, laughing.

"This is why I was homeschooled. High school sounds way too dangerous."

She yanked my plain black one-piece swimsuit out of my suitcase and frowned. "You've never been in love? Or maybe even—lust?"

"Of course not. I've been too busy with school the past few years, and I can't say I've ever met anyone that came close to inspiring *those* types of feelings." I gave her a lopsided smile, aiming for that casual cool-girl persona I'd researched. "With advanced physics and extra credit, who even has the time?"

She chucked the swimsuit at me, smiling. "You won't be playing Juliet with that attitude."

"I don't want to play any character," I said, refolding the swimsuit with care. "Acting is just ridiculous."

Her smile fell and I bit my lip. That expression was wrong, and something had happened. *You've made a mistake.* I froze, rewinding the past few sentences in my brain.

Wait.

Ah, that was it.

Oh no.

I could be such an idiot.

I reached up, my hand faltering before I touched her shoulder. "Mia, I'm sorry; that was such a stupid thing to say. I'm not very good at all this, and of course acting isn't ridiculous. *I'm* ridiculous." I sank down on the bed, forcing the rest out before I lost my nerve. "I'm sorry you're stuck with me as a roommate, and I'm sure you were expecting someone a little more normal."

The bed sank next to me after a moment. "Well, nobody is

really expecting normal at theater camp." She continued to face forward. "But we do expect people to not look down on the thing that matters the most to us."

I died a little more. It wasn't until I saw her face fall that I realized how much her opinion mattered to me. I wanted to re-wind back to when I was *Bea* and she said she liked me. She was nothing like Angelica, who always made her presence a burden.

*I was the Angelica here.*

"I'm so sorry; that was a thoughtless comment. I'm just . . ." I paused, trying to find the words to make sense of everything flooding my circuits. "I'm scared I'm going to say something stupid again, and I don't know how to prevent it, and I don't even always realize it until it's too late. I'm scared I'm going to ruin the chance for us to be friends."

She looked at me, the angles of her face softening. "I can see that, and since I'm such a magnanimous and generous woman, I forgive you."

I almost wilted in relief. "I promise to keep the complaining to a minimum and will try not to alienate any more people."

This time her smile reached her eyes. "I have nothing but faith in you, especially since I'm an excellent instructor in both acting *and* socializing."

"Oh really?" I said, trying to find the relaxed tone of our ear-lier conversation. "Well, what are your credentials, Ms. Parker?"

"Why, Ms. Quinn, I thought you'd never ask. I have been in eleven plays since fourth grade and was the lead in three of those. From a social standpoint, I've had four boyfriends and two girlfriends." She leaned closer, her eyes sparkling as brightly as the gold glitter dusting her eyelids. "And that was just high school."

I blushed, reminded once again how natural and effortless everyone else was in this environment. *Act out a scene in front of*

*a hundred peers and all their parents? No sweat! Have social in-*
*teractions that don't include insulting the life's passion of someone*
*you desperately want to be friends with? No problem!*

"You don't have to go through the trouble of helping me not
make a fool of myself, but I'm grateful that you're willing to try."

She swayed into me, knocking me off-balance in more ways
than one. "You're such a sweet, quiet thing, how much trouble
could you get into?"

I wrinkled my nose. "I'll remind you of that later."

"Now, let's stop being Debbie Downers and look on the bright
side! You get to spend the next four weeks with the best roommate
ever, and you might even get to first base if you're so inclined!"

"Whatever that even means, it probably isn't going to happen," I said, an eyebrow disappearing up into my hairline.

Her loud peal of laughter filled the room, warming me.
"Never say never!" She jumped up and rifled through her own
dresser. "Now, what are we going to wear to this mixer tonight?"

"I have to change?"

"Yes, you have to change. Here's your first socializing lesson—
first impressions are important. What do you think that current
outfit says about you?"

"Why does it have to say anything about me?" I asked, chewing at nails that had already been worn down to nubs. A headache was forming at the base of my skull. "Can't people just talk
to me, and then I can tell them about me?"

She pulled out a neon-green dress and held it against her
six-foot frame. "Haven't you ever heard of self-expression?" She
turned to me and bit her lip.

My stomach churned, and the protein bar I'd choked down at
the airport was beginning to revolt in my stomach. "Well, what
does a bright green dress say about you?" I asked, swallowing
nerves and bile.

She grinned. "I'm so happy you asked. It says that I'm outgoing and unpredictable. It tells the boys and girls that I'm fun and they shouldn't waste their time with all the plain black dresses dominating the cafeteria."

"I don't think my clothes should be speaking to strange people. I'd rather they minded their own business."

She sighed in defeat. "Well, it's a party, so you have to look a little dressier than that. What do you have along those lines?"

I considered the clothes I'd packed. "I guess I have some black pants, and maybe a few button-down shirts."

"Pull them out, and we'll see what can be done with them," she said, shimmying into her dress.

I felt the blush spreading across my face as I dug around for the requested items. I'd never cared much about clothes, replacing them only when I'd outgrown them. I hadn't realized just how unprepared I was for all of this. I found the black pants and pulled out a starched white button-down shirt. Mia talked me into putting them on, and we stood side by side in front of the full-length mirror on the back of our door.

I smoothed out the shirt. "What do you think?"

She bit her lip. "It's a little on the waiter spectrum, but we can always dress it up a bit." She nudged me and gave me an encouraging smile. "We're going to have a blast tonight, and you're going to have a whole new outlook on being here."

"That sounds ominous."

She opened a sparkly silver case on her bed. Rows and rows of makeup and jewelry in neat little trays expanded out across the bed, and I was tossed miles out of my comfort zone. She waved me over, taking hold of my stiff shoulders and pushing me down next to the case.

"I don't know about this. I've never really worn makeup before."

"*Please*, Bea! It's going to be so much fun!" She gently pulled off my round wire-rimmed glasses. "I promise I'm really good at it."

"It's not your skill set I'm concerned about."

"Well, if you're looking to improve socialization, I can tell you that this is how girls get ready together."

"Really?"

She laughed. "No joke. It's a very serious ritual."

I sighed, and she knew she'd already won. She paused for a moment, her fingers stretching into the space between us.

"May I?"

I nodded woodenly before I could change my mind. Her clever hands unraveled my hair, and I breathed through the contact. There was no hesitation as she tilted my face, blending and powdering as the dwindling sunlight stretched out across the floorboards. As her breath warmed my face and her low humming filled the room, all I could think was that this was the closest I'd been to another person in a very long time.

# Chapter Six

**"OOOF!" I STUMBLED FORWARD ONLY TO BE** yanked back up by Mia.

"Have you honestly never worn a pair of heels before?" she asked, struggling to keep me upright.

The moon was bright, washing the path with silver and guiding our way, and a thin sheen of sweat coated my palms as the cafeteria came into view. It was a large, imposing log structure, with a grassy quad that sprawled right up to the front door. The faint sound of music filled the heavy night air, and groups of campers milled around in pockets in front of the entrance. A girl broke away from one group before enveloping another girl in a giant hug, her exclamations carrying above the bass.

There was no way I'd get through tonight without falling.

"Yes, I've worn heels before, but not ones that are five thousand feet tall," I said, arms spread wide, attempting to stabilize myself. The bright red heels on my feet matched the red lipstick and bangles that Mia had insisted *tied the outfit together*. I swiped my clammy palms on my pants, trying to pretend that I belonged here. That this wasn't the first time I'd ever worn lipstick.

Mia winked down at me, clutching my elbow and propelling

me across uneven ground. Her body already moving to music we could barely hear, as if she could just sense it. People shifted and looked in her direction as we passed them, drawn to the way her hips moved, the secret smile across her lips.

I squinted in the darkness, recognizing Shelby standing in one of the little groups. She smiled, and I blinked as her face completely transformed. She looked younger, and softer. Her small, delicate hands traced the lines of her pale pink slip dress, and the group around her inched in just a little bit closer. She'd made it clear that she had no interest in getting ready with us or spending any time with us whatsoever. Darla from the van hovered at her elbow, hanging on her every word, and three overdressed-looking guys stood with them, their collars popped up against an imaginary wind.

Mia steered me away from their group. "I have no interest in listening to Shelby talk about her latest modeling job or yogurt commercial. Keep going inside and don't trip in front of them, or you'll never hear the end of it."

Her grip on my arm tightened, and she guided me toward the front door.

"Do my eyes deceive me, or is that the inimitable Mia Parker?"

I stumbled as Mia squealed and released me. I grasped for the side of the building, teetering over the gravel like a toddler taking their first steps.

"Love muffin! I was wondering when I'd finally run into you!" She lunged toward a guy standing next to the door. His blond hair swooped over his forehead and across one eye, and his smile was as sharp as the cut of his suit.

He leaned down and deftly plucked her off the ground. Her laughter rang out across the quad as he spun her around. "You look ravishing, Mia darling."

"Not as ravishing as you."

"What? This old thing?" he said, aware of his charm. He placed her back down and took my measure as I leaned on the building for support. "And who is this adorable creature you have with you?"

"Hi." I mustered up a strained smile and gave him a weak wave. "I'm Beatrice."

Mia's enthusiastic admirer walked over and grasped my hand before giving it a brief kiss. "I'm Nolan, Mia's camp best friend. I'm sure you've heard all about me."

"You conceited beast. She most certainly has not, but she will if you behave this year like you did last year," Mia said, helping me off the wall.

He turned, a wicked smile blossoming across his face. "I'm sure I don't know what you're talking about."

Mia nodded in the direction of Shelby's group. "Somehow, through some strange twist of nature, Nolan is Shelby's twin."

I blinked in surprise, recognizing the same coloring and cheekbones that were present on the girl a few feet away.

"Clearly I got the best combination of genes," Nolan said, straightening his lapels.

"She's our roommate," I said, reaching for the right response. "She seems . . . nice?"

"No, she's not; she's awful," he said, smiling fondly in her direction.

I blinked, unsure where to go from there. Was that a joke? Should I agree with him? "Are you going to audition for Romeo?" I stammered, searching for a safer conversation.

"I can understand your confusion. At first glance one would think I had that certain leading-man quality, but the truth is I'm in it for the clothes." He spun so I could take in his outfit. The navy suit hugged the graceful lines of his form, and he tweaked his bow tie for emphasis.

Mia rolled her eyes, giving him a little shove. "Nolan is in costume design, and a terrible influence. He's also a regular like me, and we've spent the past three summers here."

"Together forever," Nolan said, straightening the cap sleeves on her dress.

"Oh," I said, nodding. "So, you two are . . ."

Mia's burst of laughter cut through the night, and a delighted smile stretched across Nolan's face. "Not so much in that sense, no."

I flushed, struggling to keep up as all my social cues got tangled and I tried to make sense of relationship dynamics and behaviors that I did not know enough about to recognize. "Oh. Um. Sorry. Are you looking forward to . . . making the costumes?"

"Well, you do one brocade dress, you've done them all. This place is all about the behind-the-scenes fun, if you get what I mean."

I bit my lip. *Dear god, what now?*

Mia laughed and elbowed him. "I'm honestly surprised they let you come back."

"Oh, you know how persuasive dear old Dad can be." His expression hardened briefly as he plucked invisible lint off his jacket. "This year has some big shoes to fill," he said, turning a thousand-watt smile in my direction. "We did A *Midsummer Night's Dream* last summer. A lot of our fairies wore mostly glitter and little else."

I blinked as my brain added costumes to the list of things I should be worried about.

"Well, it's only right that we get to spend our last summer together. I'm off to NYU in the fall," Mia said, beaming.

"You didn't! For acting?" He squeezed her into a bone-crunching hug.

She laughed. "You know it! It's that starving-artist life for me!"

"Congratulations!" I said, a little shocked. I knew she liked acting, but to dedicate your life to it is another level. "You must be really good."

"Oh, she is," Nolan said. "She'll get a TV pilot before she even graduates with a degree."

"Stop it," Mia said, grinning ear to ear. "You'll have your own show at Fashion Week soon enough!"

"Especially since I'm off to the Rhode Island freaking School of Design," he said, brushing off some lint from his cuff.

Mia squealed, drawing looks from the surrounding groups. "Shut *up*!" She pulled him down by the lapels and squished him into another hug. "Scratch that; you'll have an entire line by Christmas."

"Give me time, I'll get there."

I nodded, always a beat behind as the conversation moved forward before I could organize my thoughts enough to contribute.

Nolan turned an encouraging smile on me. "Let me guess, you have your heart set on Juliet too?"

"Not even a little bit," I said, a sour taste coating my tongue. "I'm hoping for the smallest possible role, and in a perfect world I wouldn't have any lines at all."

Nolan brushed the hair out of his eyes. "Don't sell yourself short, my little wallflower. Modesty is overrated." He wiggled his eyebrows and the corner of my mouth turned up.

He offered an arm to each of us and nodded in the direction of the front door. "What do you think, ladies? Shall we?"

I slipped my hand in the crook of his arm, leaning against him, as he guided us through the door.

I blinked as my eyes slowly adjusted to the dim lighting and the bass seeped into my skin and traveled down to my bones. The only lighting came from strobe lights on the dance floor, and paper lanterns and fairy lights spread out on tables filled with punch, cupcake towers, and cheese plates. There were picnic tables stacked on one side of the long room, and a DJ booth occupied the other end. Groups of people, their bodies pulsing to the music, spread before us. The air was close and hot and my glasses started to fog at the edges as beads of sweat prickled against my scalp.

My stomach growled, and I was dying to grab a plate of food and sit in a dark corner the rest of the evening. I veered off toward a cupcake tower.

"Oh no you don't." Mia grabbed me, dragging us into the fray. "You've earned a cupcake when you've danced to at least three songs and met five new people."

My breathing hitched. The last time I danced was at a cousin's wedding, and it was with my dad. "You know I have no idea how to do either of those things, right?"

She laughed, pulling me along to a small group near the DJ. "I had a feeling. Don't worry; I've got you." She grasped my hands, moving me side to side. My movements were jerky and unsure. I gripped her hands tight as my heart sped up, keeping time with the thundering beat.

Nolan moved around us, his body rolling with the tempo as he shot a devastating smile at the DJ.

"I've met Nolan. That has to at least count for a cookie?" I pleaded, shouting over the music, my breath coming in heavy gasps.

"Why are we giving people treats for meeting me?" Nolan yelled in response.

"Bea has some socializing difficulties, and she gets a treat when she plays nice with others."

He raised an eyebrow in my direction, as if I'd become slightly more interesting. I bowed under his gaze, my hand grasping for the wrinkled paper in my pocket. I stepped toward him, wobbling, and his hands reached out to gently cup my elbows. I leaned in, heat already radiating off him. "I don't have a lot of experience with other people or being away from home. My parents sent me here to learn how to be a real teenager before they'd agree to send me away to Oxford."

He pulled back, his eyes laughing. "How exactly do they know when you've become a teenager or not?"

I'd gotten this far, and was at a party wearing lipstick, by trusting someone else to help me with all this. They might as well see what they're getting into. I pushed the wrinkled paper into his hands before losing my nerve, and Mia peered over his shoulder. He lifted it up into the air as green lights from the DJ booth flashed across it. I shifted in place, each task already carved into my brain.

The beat changed with the next song, and my chest tightened as more campers spilled onto the dance floor. Nolan looked up and arched an eyebrow as Mia snatched the list out of his hands and pored over it.

"It's a little tame and leaves a lot of room for interpretation. You could probably make a case for technically doing every one of them here tonight," he said.

I shrugged, torn between my desire to end this entire farce right now and my hesitation to ever do anything halfway.

"I can't believe they made you a list," Mia said, looking up, an expression that made my stomach cramp written across her features.

"I can't believe they think *these* are the things you need to do to have a teenage experience," Nolan said, grinning.

I flushed, taking the list back from Mia and stuffing it in my pocket. Nolan steered us off the dance floor toward a quiet corner and straightened his lapels. "Okay, so which task should we check off tonight?"

Relief flooded me as Mia rubbed her hands together. Cards on the table, I wasn't sure they would think it was worth it to stick it out with me. I knew what I was. I wasn't funny, at least on purpose, or outgoing or exciting. If anything, I would just hold them back. I bit my lip.

Hard.

When I was certain I would sound normal, I said, "Well. This is supposed to be a mixer, right? I guess Mia's right and I can meet someone and make a friend. Pretty sure if we tried any more dancing, I would fall off these shoes and break a leg." *Should I ask them now if we're friends?*

"Aww, you're using our slang already—" Mia said.

"Who should be your next conquest?" Nolan mused, linking one of my arms and turning me to face the room.

"Oh! What about that group of guys over there!" Mia said, excitement thick in her voice.

I squinted at the three guys she was talking about. They all looked like they had just walked out of a magazine. Their clothes looked trendy and expensive, and they were all tall and—well built. My eyes fell on the tallest of the three, and I strained to make out any details in the dim lighting. His hair was curly and black, and just long enough to spill over onto his forehead.

I jerked as he barked in laughter, revealing a streak of perfect teeth. It knocked the sense back into me. "No thank you. How about I introduce myself to Shelby again? I doubt she remembers the first time."

Nolan laughed, but Mia pulled out a tube of lipstick from her clutch. "Who's the guy standing next to Nikhil?"

"Which one? Troy, whose heart Shelby absolutely crushed last year, or tall, blond, and friendly looking?" Nolan asked, tilting his head as Mia carefully painted her mouth purple.

"The blond one," Mia said, bouncing on her tiptoes to see over the crowd.

"I heard someone say it's Nik's best friend from the city. Ben or Brad or something."

Using my impressive deductive skills, I whispered, "So Nik is the tall one with—the hair?"

Nolan slung an arm around me. "Oh, honey, the hair is just one of many impressive descriptors. His name is Nikhil Shah, as in his parents are Rishi and Miranda Shah."

They looked at me with knowing grins, and I shrugged. "Who?"

Nolan rolled his eyes, but Mia leaned in close. "They're both superfamous stage actors. Rishi did a lot of popular indie movies in the late eighties, but then he met Miranda in London and they conquered the West End together. They moved to the states about five years ago, and both of them work on Broadway now. They helped found this camp." She spread her arms out as she danced in a circle.

"Really? So, they're to blame for all of this?" I tried not to sound impressed.

"They're like, ridiculously talented, and Nik always gets the lead in whatever play they pick. He'll definitely get Romeo since he ages out after this year!" Mia yelled over the music.

I rolled my eyes. "They built this camp to make sure their son gets whatever role he wants? That's really kind of sad." I crossed my arms, comforted to have found a flaw.

Mia shook her head. "Save the judgment until you see him act." She smoothed out her dress and grinned. "I think we should go over and say hi."

"No, thank you. I said I would meet *one* other person. They're scarier in groups."

"Come on," she pleaded. "I know Nik and Troy from last year, so they aren't strangers! I want to meet Ben-Brad."

I looked to Nolan for help, but he just smiled, his body still moving to the beat.

I raked my hands through my hair, unused to the mass hanging loosely down my back. I knew from my research that friendship sometimes meant you did things you didn't want to do so the other person could be happy. It was probably the least I could do. "Fine, I'll stand next to you both, but that's about all I can promise."

She squealed, jumping up and down. "Thanks, Bea!" She grabbed my hand and sashayed toward them as I wobbled behind her. I shot another desperate look at Nolan as he brought up the rear, but his delight at this turn of events was evident. I wasn't getting out of this. The guys turned toward us as we approached, eyes drawn to Mia as the lights danced over her green dress. Every step was perfectly timed with the beat. They'd felt her magnetic pull, just as I did, and I reluctantly moved into place next to her.

"Hi, Nik, good to see you!" she said, eyeing up Ben-Brad, who couldn't take his eyes off her.

Nik looked between the two of them, amusement written across his features. "You too, Mia. Have you met my friend Ben yet?" His voice slid over me like honey. Honey with an English accent.

Up close I could see the square jaw and the delicate shape of his lips. I swallowed the lump in my throat.

"Nope, not yet," Mia said, extending her hand toward Ben. "I'm Mia."

He blushed, taking her hand. "Nice to meet you, Mia."

He reminded me of the golden retriever we had when I was a kid. I relaxed a fraction, trying to bring my shoulders back down from my ears.

"Hello again, Shah," Nolan said, nodding toward Nik.

Nik grinned, pulling him in for a thumping hug that reminded me of a documentary I'd seen on Neanderthals. "Nolan, I was wondering if you would show up again this year."

"You know me; how could I resist the delights of pastoral Connecticut?"

I pushed my glasses up, shrinking my body into the shadow of Nolan's personality. I had no idea how to stand there casually, smiling and laughing, and *normal*. Nolan's elbow shot out and jabbed me in the ribs, and I stumbled. Oh, right. Socialize. I was never going to get a cupcake at this rate.

"And you are?"

I jumped, peeking out from behind Nolan. Nik tilted his head as if I was a question he wasn't sure he had the answer to.

"Beatrice Quinn," I murmured, searching for my composure. "Actually," I said, straightening my spine, "I go by 'Bea.'"

I was a cool girl. A girl with a nickname, and maybe even some friends.

"What program are you in, Beatrice?" he said, a small smile extending up to eyes that shone black. The fairy lights from the refreshment table slid across his sharp cheekbones.

I stiffened as he deliberately drawled out my name.

"Acting," I said, sliding my tongue against teeth that were probably stained with lipstick. Mia and Ben were caught up in their own private conversation, and Nolan was no help either. His blond hair swayed like a curtain as he leaned over and whispered into Troy's ear.

"Hmmm," Nik said. "Are you prepared to fight for Juliet tomorrow?" His gaze drifted over the crowded room.

"Why would I fight for something I don't want?" I said, my tone sharper than I'd intended.

His attention returned to me, and his lips pursed in surprise, or amusement. I wasn't sure which. He raised his hands in surrender. "No need to get bent out of shape. I assumed that a girl who ended up at an expensive theater camp for the summer would have her heart set on being the lead. The lovestruck ingenue.

The dreamy girl in the tower looking for her Romeo," he said, his tone polite but bored.

A girl in a tight white dress walked by and wiggled her fingers in Nik's direction. He smiled appreciatively, tracking her progress across the room, and I was unceremoniously forgotten.

My cheeks burned, and I lifted my damp hair off my neck. I didn't expect anyone to fall over themselves to befriend me, or even go out of their way to talk to me. I knew I was a work in progress and all my edges were a little too rough to fit comfortably with other people. I was *trying*, though. I was trying harder than I'd ever tried in my life, and it humbled me to the core that I was so boring that this boy couldn't even fake a polite conversation for more than fifteen seconds.

His attention drifted across the room before settling back on me, and he started as if he'd just remembered my existence.

"Umm, was there a different role you were planning on going out for?" he asked, pushing his curls out of his eyes. "*Romeo and Juliet* has a number of different roles that you might feel better suited for. There's the Nurse, or maybe Lady Capulet or Lady Montague?"

He talked to me like I was a child, or clueless. I'm sure he knew all about "lovestruck ingenues," and I wasn't going to be mistaken for a member of his fan club. I was never going to be that girl ever again. This time I had the benefit of experience, and I'd met his kind before.

I pushed my glasses up, struggling to keep my mouth shut.

I tried to swallow the words back down, but they slipped out anyway. "You know, I'm not really interested in theater, but since I'm forced to be here, I was thinking maybe Romeo? Then again, I may have heard you always get the male lead for some reason."

Mia ripped some of her attention away from Ben to give me a

*what the hell do you think you're doing?* stare. I stared back at her, my eyes wide and innocent.

Nik's gaze narrowed, and that condescending little smile disappeared. I assumed people had made enough comments in the past that he knew exactly what I was implying. A smirk I wasn't polite enough to hide spread across my lips.

"Oh, you think you could do a better job as Romeo? Seduce any girls off their balconies lately?"

"Is that all it takes?" I asked, evaluating him over the tops of my glasses. "Seduce enough girls and you're perfect for Romeo?"

His nostrils flared, and I reflexively cataloged the emotions that could match that face: anger, envy, irritation, terror, a bad stench wafting through the room.

I smiled carefully. I really hoped it was anger.

Mia slung an arm around my shoulders. "Hey! We're all friends here, right?" she said, barreling into the conversation. "I'm pretty sure Bea's going to be my favorite roommate ever. She doesn't really like acting, but she is *crazy smart* and going to Oxford in the fall."

I winced at her attempt to defuse the situation. I did intend to make friends, but not with this smug, superficial boy.

He looked me up and down and stepped into my personal space. "Oxford, huh? Why don't you tell us all, Beatrice Quinn, why you would come to an acting camp when you obviously feel it is so far beneath you?"

I craned my neck up at him, my face warming either from the heat radiating off him or from so many eyes on me. I refused to step back, even as I felt the shame of my earlier remark to Mia. I'd had so many preconceived notions coming into this camp, especially about the people, and I'd been nothing but wrong since my arrival. "I don't look down on it. I just have no interest in it, and my reasons for coming here are none of *your* business."

"I was just trying to make conversation."

"Well, we all learn from our mistakes." I crossed my arms.

How dare he try and make me feel like I was the one who was being rude. As if I would ever want to be the Juliet to *his* Romeo. He clearly didn't need any more groupies, and I wasn't about to help inflate his massive ego any more.

We glared at each other until a pale, delicate arm shot out and trailed down his biceps.

"Here we go!" Nolan said gleefully.

"There you are, Nik! I've been looking for you everywhere. I thought you were going to meet us outside," Shelby said, her mouth pinched. She nodded at Nolan, who blew her a kiss. "Brother."

"I was just meeting one of our newest campers," Nik said, his eyes measuring every ounce of me.

"Yeah," she said. "She lives with me and wants to play the Nurse or something."

"I do not want to be the Nurse," I said, smoothing my button-down. "I'd rather play—Rosaline. She has no lines, and never even appears onstage." I turned to Mia, beaming.

"Yeah, but isn't Rosaline supposed to be really hot?" Nik whispered to Troy.

The music ended right when he spoke, and I was close enough to hear every word. Shelby giggled from behind her hand, and I felt my face catch flame. I took a step back. Then another.

"Bea, are you okay?" Mia asked me as I retreated farther away from the group, her head tilted in my direction.

Only the people closest to Nik heard, and I doubt he knew I heard him too. I gave Mia my brightest smile. My jaw aching from the force of it. "You know, I think I've gotten in all the socializing I care to tonight. I'm going to head back, but you stay and have fun." I didn't say good-bye to anyone else, and I walked out the door as quickly as I could.

I peeled the shoes off my feet, the dirt path smooth and cool as I power walked back to the cabin. *Helium. Neon. Argon. Krypton. Xenon. Radon. Everything's fine. You're fine.*

I viciously scrubbed all the makeup off my face in our painfully small bathroom and put on my threadbare pajamas, the NASA logo peeling in several places. I pressed two fingers into my sternum, trying to rub out the ache that had suddenly appeared. I had no idea what I was doing, and tonight made that *painfully* clear. Even with the destruction I was sure I'd left in my wake, I still couldn't gauge how bad it was. Was that Chernobyl-level awful, or just slightly eccentric Beatrice? Did everyone hate me now? Did I care if they did? I squeezed my eyes tightly against memories of kids crowding around me, laughing, until I broke away—

The screen door slammed, and I tensed before Mia appeared at the threshold. She hesitated, hovering just on the other side.

A worried little crease materialized between her eyebrows, and she held out a bright and sticky assortment of cupcakes like a peace offering. "Want to talk about it?"

The ache in my chest eased a little, and despite my inexperience, I recognized the gesture for what it was. She didn't owe me anything but still left a party with her friends to see how her awkward roommate was. Even after I made an ass of myself. I patted the bed next to me, and she sat down with the cupcakes. Grabbing a big purple one, I shoved it into my mouth—swallowing down cupcake and whatever unrecognizable emotion had lodged itself in my throat.

"Mia, I didn't tell him that I looked down on acting."

She nudged her arm into mine. "I know. I didn't hear all of it, but I heard enough to realize that. Do you want to talk about it?"

"Where should I start? Should we talk about how my room-mate deserves the Nobel Peace Prize for her attempts to defuse the situation, or how Nikhil provoked me into being a bitch and then called me ugly?" I was surprised at how even my voice was. I was even more surprised how much it stung to say it out loud.

She choked on her own cupcake and looked up in surprise. "Both, please."

After retelling his comment enough times, and Mia's over-dramatic impressions in a ridiculous English accent, my feelings no longer felt quite so hurt. It was all just fuel for the fire. The anger settled across my shoulders a lot more comfortably than the brief period of time I'd evaluated his cheekbones.

"Okay. Hand it over," she said, licking the icing from her fingers.

"Hand what over?"

"The list!" she said, and I hesitated for a moment before passing her the paper sitting on my nightstand.

She dug into her bag and stuck a red Sharpie in her mouth while she smoothed the paper out on her leg.

"What are you doing?" I asked, my throat tightening.

She pulled the marker out of her mouth and grinned. "I'm going to check off your first box!"

I dug my fingers into my legs, leaning over as she checked off task number one, *make a friend*, in thick red ink. She recapped the pen with a flourish and handed the list back.

I refolded the paper, the red ink bleeding through to the other side and reminding me that not only was I almost 13 percent closer to my goal, but someone had actually called me her friend. Clutching the evidence in my fingers, I looked up at her, a small smile spreading across my lips. "Friends, huh? I wasn't sure I'd even recognize when to check that one off."

She grinned. "There's no secret ceremony or handshake. I like you, so you've made a friend."

"Likewise," I said, nodding and trying to play it cool. I gently replaced the list on my bedside table like this was something that happened to me regularly. Like I had friends other than her.

I leaned back on my uncomfortable bed, the springs biting into my back, and moonlight filtered in through the screen above. Tomorrow was going to be a long and extremely unpleasant day. After a life of carefully avoiding extremely public situations, I was going to be forced to be the center of attention. All eyes on me and my many flaws. I closed my eyes tightly; it would be better this time. I was older now. I knew how to blend in better.

Before I drifted off, eased by the rhythmic cadence of Mia's breathing, I didn't focus on how it felt a little strange, but comforting, to no longer be quite so alone. I didn't dwell on how this was the first night in a long time that I felt completely unsettled. Unsettled and awake. Most of all, I tried not to think about beautiful boys with poisonous tongues.

# Chapter Seven

**OPEN YOUR EYES, BEATRICE. YOU CAN'T PRETEND** *to stay asleep for four weeks.*

*This is happening.*

I sighed, peeling my eyes open and squinting in the sunshine that spilled merrily in through the window. I flung the blankets back over my head.

Connecticut.

Theater camp.

The auditions.

Mia moaned from across the room. "Why do you keep tossing and turning? What time is it?"

I stuck a hand out from under the covers, fumbling for my watch on the nightstand. "Seven thirty," I said. "If you want to talk about waking people up, let's talk about your snoring."

"Shit! Get *up*, Bea! Auditions are in thirty minutes and I'm not showing up there without a shower and food!" She yanked open our bedroom door and knocked loudly on the bathroom door. I flung back the covers when I could no longer block out the barbed insults between Mia and Shelby. I assumed Mia won, because the shower turned on and Shelby was still yelling. I rubbed the sleep out of my eyes, wincing as the events of last night over-loaded my brain. So much for flying under the radar. I just had to say something. I couldn't just stand there like a normal person and smile blandly as people talked around me. *Thank you for explaining* Romeo and Juliet *to me; maybe I will consider the role of Lady Capulet. Good luck on your own auditions; I'm sure you will get Romeo for completely well-deserved reasons.*

I couldn't regret it, though. Nik had pushed every button I had, and I wasn't the sort of girl who would just roll over while someone trampled all over her.

At least, not anymore.

I put on my glasses, the world sharpening, and picked apart today's schedule: If you subtracted our lunch break and all the time the other people would be on the stage, maybe I would only have to suffer through about twenty minutes of acting. I could handle that.

I could *probably* handle that.

"I don't know what you're worried about. It's not like you're going to get a big part or anything," Shelby said, hovering in the doorway, red blotches spread across her cheeks. She raised an eyebrow, daring me to contradict her. Pin-straight hair tumbled down her shoulders and over a fluffy pink bathrobe speckled with bedazzled tiaras. I knew her type. I knew she was lashing out because I was conveniently nearby, and it was certainly not the first time somebody had tried to bully me. I could try and stand up for myself and tell her how I had no interest in getting a big part, but I was exhausted. Bone-tired from trying to guess the appropriate response to every question, every situation, and second-guessing every instinct. Every step plunging me further and further outside my comfort zone.

I settled for a personal compromise and walked over and shut the door in her face.

Remnants of her cloyingly sweet perfume lingered, and I sneezed as chemical roses climbed up into my sinuses. I tried not to feel immensely satisfied when I heard her door slam from across the hall, but it put a little bounce in my step as I walked back to my dresser.

I eased the warped drawer open, wrinkling my nose at the stale smell and the contents. I didn't want to admit it, but Mia's opinion on the importance of clothes and first impressions had burrowed under my skin. Deep under my lumpy hair, giant glasses, and limbs so long that they could only ever be described as gangly. Before our conversation I had only thought of clothes as being utilitarian. I wore khaki pants and a polo shirt, or a button-down if I was supposed to dress up, every single day of my life. It saved time and thought, and it was practical. My mother liked to refer to this as my "uniform," which I hated. Mostly because that term was usually coupled with *Honey, don't you want to dress this up a bit?* or *Honey, don't you think this looks a little boring?* I waited for that same irritation to surface when I got ready with Mia last night, but it never came. She approached it logically. The rules and regulations for parties are that you have to dress up and other teenagers sometimes recognize you as a possible member of their pack based on your appearance. It was information I'd not realized before, and maybe if I'd brought some other clothes they might have thought I was one of them.

I stuck a hand in the drawer and blindly pulled out a pair of khakis and an olive-green polo. There was no use trying to pretend I was someone else. I was going to see these people every day for the next four weeks. They would know soon enough.

Mia raced back into the room, clutching a towel, with a sunshine-yellow shower cap perched on her head. "Tag, you're it!" she said. "Hurry up; we still need to eat too!"

I grabbed my things and went into our cramped bathroom.

Steam and scented products hung heavy in the air, and the world blurred as fog crawled across my lenses. The water was lukewarm at best, and I was dressed and ready to go in about ten minutes. I walked back into our room as Mia was finishing up her makeup, and she eyed me up and down. I tucked my polo into my pants and slipped on my battered loafers. I could feel the weight of all the things she wasn't saying hanging heavy over my head.

"What is it now?" I sighed.

She bit her lip. "Nothing. Are you ready to go?"

I shrugged and sat back down on my bed as I waited for her to finish up. She was wearing a short denim skirt that I was pretty sure she couldn't bend over in and a gauzy white top. We were spending the day in the same place, but we couldn't have looked any more different. I smoothed out a wrinkle on my khakis.

She grabbed her makeup bag and marched over to me with purpose. "Do you want me to give you some war paint?"

I groaned. "They are going to realize I don't wear makeup, or dress trendy, or do anything with my hair soon enough."

She grinned. "Shut up; I'm just going to do the eyes. You're adorable, and I think you are underestimating the charm of the bed head look."

I snorted and shut my eyes, trying my best not to blink and mess up her work. My eyelashes fluttered as her breath warmed my face.

"There!" she said with a final flourish. "All finished, no thanks to you."

I took the offered mirror to be polite. The effect was subtle but disorienting. The golden-brown color she had artfully painted on emphasized my eyes, but it sat uncomfortably on me. This was a girl who had phone numbers in her phone that weren't just relatives'. She smiled easily and knew how to have conversations with strangers that didn't end in confusion or anger. I didn't know her.

"Interesting," I murmured, placing the mirror facedown on the bed.

She laughed, but it changed to alarm as she glanced at her watch. She pulled me off the bed, and we ran for the door.

The heavy early morning air promised another smothering day as we hurried down the path to the cafeteria. We sprinted inside, and I did a double take under harsh fluorescent lights. The dim lighting and paper lanterns from last night had thoroughly disguised the bland yellow paint and linoleum tiles. The walls were papered with faded posters from past plays and pictures of happy campers laughing and hugging. All promising the possibility of normalcy. Friendship.

"What are you frowning at?" Mia asked, her hands full of two doughnuts and a cheese Danish.

"Propaganda," I said, turning away from the posters. I made a beeline for the coffeepot.

"It looks like they're already deciding where the cool table is this year," she said, nodding toward the other end of the cafeteria where fifteen large picnic-style tables sat.

I frowned at Shelby holding court in all her glory. She sat on top of one of the tables, legs swinging as she smiled down on Nik. Eight other people, all perfectly dressed, and all eyes on them, were spread across the surrounding benches. I turned back to the coffeepot as the table erupted in laughter and I flinched. Maybe Nik was retelling his hilarious joke from last night. _Yeah, but isn't Rosaline supposed to be really hot?_ I fumbled with the lid of my travel coffee cup.

I offered Mia the pot, but she was still staring at their table, specifically the area that Ben was currently occupying.

I nudged her in the ribs. "You're starting to drool." I wrapped my hand around my cup, the warmth seeping into my palm with a comforting familiarity.

She grinned and looped her arm through mine as we walked toward the exit. "Oh my stars, he's so adorable. Maybe I'll get lucky, and Nik will choke, and then we can be Romeo and Juliet together." She danced along the path, her movements as sure as walking. Was it that certain that Nik was going to be Romeo? It seemed ridiculous that just because his parents started this camp it was assumed that he would get the lead role. I squashed my anger down and tried to concentrate on Mia's plans for Ben as we hustled across grass damp with morning dew to the auditorium next door. It was an impressive structure, much bigger than the surrounding buildings, and the cool kiss of air conditioning slid over my skin as we pulled the heavy door open. I sucked in a breath at the giant stage with red velvet curtains pulled off to each side and tried to suppress the butterflies that had erupted in my stomach. Dozens of rows of plush chairs spread out before us, and I pulled Mia into a row in the back—my survival instincts on high.

"I thought there was this replica of the Globe Theatre that we were supposed to use."

Mia nodded, talking around a mouthful of doughnut. "It's so amazing, but it's kind of open to the elements. We do a lot of our practicing here where it's air-conditioned and move over there once we start doing costume rehearsals."

I nodded, slouching down farther in my seat as campers filed in and found their seats. "So how does this audition thing work?"

She grinned and pointed forward. "You're about to find out."

A man walked out onto the stage, and all the talking came to a standstill. He was in his late forties, with short salt-and-pepper hair, brown skin, and a burgundy sweater-vest that I kind of admired.

He cleared his throat. "As many of you already know, my name is Isaac Gregory, and I will be your senior director. During the rest of the year, I teach Shakespearean literature at the University of Connecticut, but I double-majored in theater during my undergraduate studies."

"Mr. G is really nice, but definitely a perfectionist," Mia murmured. "Last year, some of the girls pretended having a lot of trouble with their lines so they could request more practice time with Nik." The smile died on her lips as soon as she spoke.

"Let me guess, you found yourself having a lot of trouble too?" I asked, refusing to give him the power of being a taboo subject.

She smirked, relief in her eyes. "Who, me? I don't need such obvious tricks to meet people."

Our conversation died out as Mr. G began speaking again. "Once the roles have been assigned, you will also be working with campers from the production and costume design concentrations, and I expect you to show them the same courtesy that you show me. With that said, we're just going to jump into the part you've all been waiting for. The auditions!" The auditorium burst into cheers, and I slouched lower into my chair.

Mr. G grinned and waved his hands to quiet everyone down.

I pressed a hand to my stomach. *You are* not *going to vomit.*

"Don't worry if you mess up; you will have several chances to read. I know the dialogue can be tricky, and I don't expect perfection on the first try." He clapped his hands over the hushed conversations. "Now, we have a lot to cover, so we're going to go ahead and get started. I will call your name on the roster and give you a part and a scene. The first time you come up, I want your name, where you hail from, and your favorite role you've ever played." He smiled again and made his way down to the front row as an excited buzz filled the air.

"I'm dead, aren't I?" I murmured, cradling my face in my hands.

"Don't worry, this thing will go on all day, and after a while people stop paying attention. By the time they get to you, no one will even be watching."

"Can I please have Beatrice Quinn and Gwen Lim to the stage."

Mia froze next to me, and I felt the beginnings of a full-scale panic attack.

"No, no, no, no, no. I can't be first. Mia, I can't be first!" I hissed, hysteria bleeding into each word.

She clamped down on my arm, fingernails digging into my skin. "You have to pull yourself together. Now. Do you want to go to Oxford or not? Are you going to let *this* ruin your chance to go?"

I took a deep breath, trying to fill my lungs. I eyed the exits, but running now would only make it worse when I was forced to come back. "I don't know! I can't go first!"

"Beatrice Quinn?" Mr. G asked, looking around.

"You've got this!" Mia whispered.

I stood up on shaky legs and moved up the aisle toward the stage. *Helium. Neon. Argon. Krypton. Xenon. Radon.* I felt like I was being led to my execution. A lamb to the slaughter. How does someone even act? Just pretend to be another person? A more advanced game of make-believe? I didn't even do that well as a kid. I passed the front row and took a script from Mr. G, shrinking under his encouraging smile. *Helium. Neon. Argon. Krypton. Xenon. Radon.* I took the side steps up onto the stage, two at a time, and met a smiling girl in the middle. I pushed my glasses up, my skin slick under the gaze of dozens of upturned faces.

Mia waved from the back, her smile wide. I jumped as the girl next to me started speaking.

"My name is Gwen Lim, and I'm from Raleigh, North Carolina. I've been doing theater for years, and it's really hard to pick my *favorite* role of all time. If I had to choose, I think it would be when I played Kim McAfee in *Bye Bye Birdie*. I love to sing too."

She beamed at the audience, and I wanted to punch her.

I grimaced, wiping my clammy palms on my pants. "My name is Beatrice Quinn, and I'm from Berkeley, California. I've never been in a play before."

It took Mr. G a second to realize that I had nothing else to say, but he recovered quickly. "How wonderful that your first experience will be with the Bard!"

Shelby's little group all sat over to one side, and they laughed. Call me crazy, but I'm pretty sure I heard someone throw out the word "virgin."

Perfect.

Nik sprawled artfully in the front row, a smirk spread across his lips, and I wanted to sink into the ground. He knew I was going to be awful, and he was going to enjoy every single second of it. I wilted under the stage lights and prayed for a fire drill. Or a natural disaster of some sort.

Mr. G cleared his throat. "All right, we are going to do act two, scene five, which is an important and pretty comical scene. In this scene, the Nurse is just getting back from meeting with Romeo, and she's explaining to Juliet that Friar Lawrence will secretly marry them. Gwen, let's have you read Juliet, and Beatrice will play the Nurse."

Gwen preened next to me and flipped open to the appropriate scene. She closed her eyes and took several deep breaths, as if she was becoming possessed. Her eyes flew open, and I took a step back as she flung her arm out and against her forehead.

*"The clock struck nine when I did send the Nurse.*
*In half an hour she promised to return.*
*Perchance she cannot meet him. That's not so. . . ."*

It was like watching a car crash. Even as I thought it, knowing I was about to make a fool of myself too, I felt the ridiculousness of it. I didn't understand why people did this.

It was just so *fake*.

Mia gave me another thumbs-up from the back, and I tried to focus on her encouraging smile. I knew I looked miserable, but nothing in the agreement with my parents said that I had to enjoy this. I squinted as she swung her arms overhead and pointed behind me. It slowly dawned on me that Gwen was no longer speaking, and I turned into the force of her glare.

"Oh! Sorry," I said, forcing the words out. *"Peter, stay at the gate."*

I shifted under the weight of everyone's attention, feeling like I was going to tip over at any moment. My glasses started to fog at the edges.

Gwen's eyes narrowed at my monotone delivery, but then she decided to be dramatic enough for the two of us. She walked over and clung to me like a barnacle.

> *"Now, good sweet Nurse—O Lord, why look'st thou sad?*
> *Though news be sad, yet tell them merrily.*
> *If good, thou shamest the music of sweet news*
> *By playing it to me with so sour a face."*

I felt this gave me liberty to look as wretched as I felt. I carried on, my words forced and tumbling all over each other:

> *"I am aweary. Give me leave awhile.*
> *Fie, how my bones ache. What a jaunt have I."*

Mr. G cut Gwen off before she could go any further and tilted his head at me. "Beatrice, are you very familiar with this play?"

I frowned. Did he want an assessment of the scene? Was this the point where I was supposed to figure out my character's motivation?

He pointed at my hands, and I looked down. The script was rolled up tightly in them. Unused. My knuckles were white with strain, and I understood. I hadn't been using it and I didn't even realize it. Well, if I was going to be a freak, I might as well put all my cards on the table.

I cleared my throat. "I have an almost photographic memory, and I read through his plays again before I came here."

His eyebrows shot up. "That's a very useful talent for an actor to have! I am going to stop you two right here, and I would never have had Beatrice go first if I knew that this was her first try at acting. Sit down, and try and relax. I will call you up again in a little while."

I nodded, staring at my feet and letting them propel me around Gwen and all the way back to my seat. I sagged down next to Mia, trying to make myself as small as possible. "Oh god, Mia. He thinks I'm going to get *better*."

"Forget about that! When were you going to tell me that you were a supergenius?"

"What? Oh, that. Who cares if I'm able to tell you the line, if it's excruciating to hear it from me?"

She gave my arm a sympathetic squeeze. "It was your first time doing it, and a lot of it really does have to do with nerves. I'm sure it will get better."

I blinked in disbelief. "Highly unlikely."

"Mia Parker! Could you please come up and take over as the Nurse," Mr. G called.

Mia flashed me an excited grin and bounded up the aisle. She plucked a script out of Mr. G's hands and floated up the stairs to center stage.

"My name is Mia Parker, and I'm from Atlanta, Georgia. I

have no idea what my favorite role has been. Maybe Lady Augusta Bracknell from *The Importance of Being Earnest*? I have a lot of fun with comedic roles." She grinned at the audience, all confidence and charm.

They picked up where we left off, and it was objectively a lot less awful to watch. Mia transformed with every word. Her posture changed, and she hunched over and spoke with a cracked and halting voice. She even made Gwen look halfway believable, and that had to indicate some sort of real talent. Soon the scene wrapped, and Mia sat back down next to me.

"You were mesmerizing," I said, staring at her. She beamed, and I felt a twinge of envy. What must it be like to feel so confident in your own skin that wearing another person's seemed like nothing at all?

"Nikhil Shah!"

My head shot up. At least here would be some entertainment and I would be able to watch an actor so bad that he could only get parts at his parents' camp.

"This should be interesting," I snorted.

Mia frowned. "I know we hate him, but I'm afraid you're going to be disappointed."

I ignored her as he climbed up the stage. He wore low-slung jeans that probably cost as much as my entire wardrobe and a fitted black T-shirt. I hated that I noticed how he looked, and I hated that he hurt my feelings last night. I wanted him to be terrible. I wanted to see flaws.

Mr. G stood up and addressed the audience. "All right, Gwen, you're going to stay up there as Juliet. I'm going to have Nik read one of Romeo's most famous monologues, and then we'll move into the balcony scene with the both of you. Nik will start us off on act two, scene two." He indicated for Nik to begin and I leaned forward, my hands curling over the seat in front of me.

"Hello, my name is Nikhil Shah." He nodded toward the audience. "I suppose you could say that I'm from a lot of places, but I've been living in New York City for the past few years. If I had to choose, I would say that my favorite role of all time was Hamlet."

He looked down at the script for a moment, and it was almost as if I could pinpoint the moment he became somebody else. I'd realized my mistake before he even opened his mouth.

*"But soft! What light through yonder window breaks?*
*It is the east, and Juliet is the sun.*
*Arise, fair sun, and kill the envious moon,*
*Who is already sick and pale with grief,*
*That thou, her maid, art far more fair than she."*

I swallowed past the lump in my throat. His voice washed over me, and he was young love embodied. He was secret meetings in a garden. He was yearning and relief and every sticky feeling I've ever had rolled up into one.

All the hairs on my arms stuck straight up, and I hunched back down in my chair.

"It's not fair," I whispered to Mia, my voice hoarse.

She reached over and squeezed my hand.

# Chapter Eight

"BEATRICE, YOU'RE JUST RECITING THE WORDS in the same tone. Can you hear that? Try and imagine that this is a conversation that you're personally having." Mr. G's voice cut through the scene and my third attempt on the stage.

I froze under the lights, my skin slick with sweat, and I was using every available ounce of energy I had to continue with basic bodily functions. Like breathing.

"Mr. G, maybe she just always sounds like a robot."

"Shelby, if I want commentary from the audience, I will ask for it," he said, turning around to frown at her.

*Helium. Neon. Argon. Krypton. Xenon. Radon. You will not pass out on this stage. You will not pass out on this stage. Helium. Neon. Argon. Krypton—*

"Ben, go ahead and have a seat. Nik, come on up and take over as Romeo." Mr. G turned his strained smile on me. "Beatrice, you're doing great; we're just going to mix it up a bit. Try and relax, continue as the Nurse, and follow Nik's lead."

They were literally trying to kill me. They could tell I wasn't one of them and were just trying to finish me off before they'd be forced to cast me in a role. I wiped beaded sweat off my upper lip with the back of my hand. Maybe I should just try fainting. That would at least put an end to all this. Nik ambled across the stage as my vision started to tunnel.

"Beatrice?"

I tried to focus on Mr. G's face as his voice cut through the ringing in my ears.

"Are you ready to start?"

I must have nodded because Nik's face came into view, and he leaned closer. As if we shared a secret. As if he couldn't see my braid plastered to my neck, and the whites of my eyes.

"*What wilt thou tell her, Nurse? Thou dost not mark me.*"

"*I will tell her . . .*" The words scraped up my throat and were released on the faintest of breath. Nik leaned closer, his frown growing. "*I will tell her, sir, that you do protest, which, as I take it, is a gentlemanlike offer.*" The lights grew hotter with each word, and I knew I was moments from passing out. I couldn't spend another second up there and on display for all of them to pick apart. It was either throw in the towel or collapse in a lump of sweat and stubbornness.

"*Bid her devise—*"

"I need to get off the stage now," I said, cutting off Nik. He frowned again as Mr. G's head popped up.

"What was that, Beatrice?"

"I am leaving the stage now."

Faint laughing spread across the auditorium as the heat from the spotlight became unbearable. I didn't even wait for his permission before marching to the side of the stage, lunging down the steps, and making my way back to the blessed darkness of the back row.

"Well, that's quite all right, Beatrice. In fact, I think it's about time to call it a day." Mr. G pulled himself up onto the lip of the stage. "You all did an incredible job today, and I know sitting here for hours was tedious. I'll let you go a little early so I can get working on the cast list!"

The auditorium erupted in cheers, and I wilted in my seat. The sweat dried in sticky streaks down my neck, and I shivered.

"That wasn't so bad, was it?" Mia said, a pained smile stretched tight across her lips.

"Were we not at the same auditions?"

She bit her lip. "You just need to get used to it. It can be really scary when you first start."

I shook my head. "I don't intend to do this enough to get used to it." I knew I wasn't cut out for this and I thought I could maybe get by in the background somehow, but I couldn't be on this stage. I *refused* to be on this stage ever again.

Campers brushed past us, and I nudged her toward the exit. "Go on ahead; I want to speak with Mr. G for a moment."

"About what?" she asked, her eyes narrowed.

I shrugged. "It's just logistical stuff; don't worry about it."

She moved toward the doors, that deep crease back between her brows. "Okay, but don't take too long. It's almost time for dinner, and I'm getting hangry. Those little sandwiches they passed out for lunch didn't even take the edge off."

I nodded, waving her on, and moved against the tide to the front of the auditorium.

"Mr. Gregory?" I asked, marching up to him as he was packing up all his scripts.

"Yes?" he said, turning in surprise. "Ah, Beatrice. How are you enjoying your first taste of theater?"

I felt bone-tired, like I'd just run a marathon. "I'm sure we're both aware of how awful I am."

"Nonsense! Stage fright is a very real thing, but it usually fades. Be patient with yourself—"

"Mr. Gregory!" I said, barreling over his practiced lecture for unskilled campers. "I don't see me getting any better at this, and I don't think you want to risk putting me in a speaking role if that's the case. To be honest, I'm only here to placate my parents and convince them to send me off to university in the fall. Is there any way I can do something backstage?"

He gave my shoulder an awkward pat. "I'm sorry, Beatrice, but you're in the acting concentration. Backstage work is a completely different area, with different staff making those calls."

I covered my face in my hands. "I'm doomed. I'm going to ruin this whole thing, no matter how small my part. I can't speak without fainting into one of the sets, and I'll just have to get used to being humiliated every rehearsal." My breath started coming in faster gasps, and I collapsed into one of the chairs and put my head down before I plummeted into what was looking to be a truly spectacular panic attack.

He cleared his throat and tried to hide his discomfort. "Let's try and calm down and see what can be done about this." He sank into the chair next to me. "What would you say your strengths are?"

I slowly sat back up, already defeated. "Well, I'm good at research. I guess I'm good at memorization too, and I already know the play." The list was small and unimpressive.

He tapped his chin. "There's an idea. Usually, we just throw a script at someone during each rehearsal and make them the prompter. I suppose I could make it a permanent position for you, but I don't think your parents will feel that they're getting their money's worth."

It was a life raft. "I'm sure they would be fine with that! I mean, they know I don't have any theater training! I would really appreciate it and would really, *really* like to stay away from the stage."

I tried to look pitiful and desperate, and he seemed to reconcile himself to the idea. "Very well. When I do the casting, I'll list you as prompter. There is one condition, though."

I sagged, relief coursing through my system. "Anything."

"You will also be the universal understudy. Attendance was a little light this year, and having someone who already knows all the lines will stop people from having to double up and learn multiple parts. I will excuse you from having to act during rehearsals, but you will have to accept the fact that you may still end up on the stage."

I tensed a little, but it still seemed like an excellent deal. Nothing short of death would keep these people from making an exhibition of themselves. I stuck out my hand. "Deal."

I escaped before he could change his mind and pushed open the heavy door into a wall of humidity. I chewed on my ragged cuticles, my mind already building a defense. The relief I felt at wiggling out of a speaking role was palpable, but I wasn't entirely sure how my parents would react once they realized I'd pulled a fast one. To be fair, I would have ruined whatever part had been tossed my way, and it wasn't as if acting were even on the list of tasks I had to accomplish.

"Bea!"

"Miss Smarty-pants!"

I squinted in the blinding sunlight, and Mia and Nolan waved from blankets spread out on the quad. The thick grass was a green you rarely saw in my area of California, and it sprang beneath my shoes like Nana's shag carpet. The crushed blades released a sharp, sweet smell as I stepped over sunbathers in various stages of undress. My face was red by the time I reached Mia and Nolan, and it wasn't from the heat.

"Look who I found!" Mia said, her face turned up into the sunshine. They looked like they belonged in a magazine.

"Smarty-pants?" I asked Nolan as I collapsed down into an empty spot by Mia.

He grinned, brushing his hair out of his face. "I call 'em like I see 'em. How was your first day in the illustrious world of theater?"

I slumped over, burying my face in the blanket.

"Oh, come on," he said, leaning over to rub my back. "It couldn't have been that bad."

I looked up at him through my curtain of hair. "Wanna bet?"

"I probably wouldn't bet her," Mia said.

"It couldn't have been any more dramatic than your showdown with Nik last night."

I picked grass off the blanket, clearing a tidy little circle around myself. "That wasn't that dramatic. We just aren't very compatible. My parents said I need to make friends at camp, not make friends with everyone at camp."

Nolan laughed. "If I had to make only one friend at camp, I'm pretty sure it would be him."

"Hey!" Mia said, swatting him. "What am I, chopped liver?"

"How about we talk about the field trip tomorrow?" Nolan said, eyes sliding over my pained expression.

"What field trip?" I demanded, desperate for anything that wasn't acting-related.

"It's basically our only chance to get off the compound the entire month," Mia said. "They always have it the first weekend we get here, in case we forgot anything. It's a pretty small town, but it's an opportunity to do some shopping and maybe see a movie."

I shrugged, losing interest. "I don't think I need to pick anything up."

Nolan raised an eyebrow. "You sure about that? You're going to dress business casual the entire summer?"

"There's nothing wrong with my clothes," I said with none of the confidence I used to have. *Would buying a skirt or something make any of this easier?*

"What she needs is a new bathing suit. You should see the dinosaur she brought with her."

"Mia!"

"I can only imagine," Nolan said, eyeing my khakis.

"Ha. Ha. Everyone gang up on Beatrice. I don't see how a new bathing suit is going to change anything. Good luck getting me into it in the first place." I folded my arms across me like a shield.

"Come on, Bea," Mia said, nudging me. "It'll be fun! We'll all get to hang out for the day, and maybe I'll end up sitting near a certain adorable blond on the bus."

"You have such a one-track mind."

"I don't know about y'all, but I heard yes." She beamed.

I knew it was pointless to argue and that come morning I would find myself sitting on an activity bus, heading toward the coast. I was just flattered that they cared enough about my attendance to bother arguing with me. I flipped onto my back and stretched out in the sunshine like a cat.

"Is this what camp is like?" I asked. "Torture in the mornings, lying on blankets and trying to recover in the evenings?"

"So young, yet so cynical," Nolan said. "It's just the first day, love. We'll make sure you get your money's worth."

His sly tone made me pause. I squinted at his silhouette, backlit as the sun dipped lower on the horizon. "What would you consider me getting my money's worth?"

Mia stretched out next to me. "Let's see—illicit parties, playing in the lake, pranking other campers. Oh! When they project movies onto the side of the cafeteria, and you find someone cute to snuggle up with!"

"Maybe I'll end up getting kicked out for one of those activities," I said, turning the possibilities over in my mind. "My parents can't get mad at me for having *too* much fun."

Mia pinched my arm. "What, and leave me alone with the ice queen? Some friend you are."

"You two are the ones trying to corrupt me. I can't be held responsible for the consequences of your actions."

She chuckled, and I tried to hold on to the moment with both hands.

Nolan stood up, grabbing the edge of the blanket. "All right, off we go. I'm hungry for sketchy meatloaf and drama."

I groaned, letting him pull me to my feet. Mia jumped up, linking her arm through mine. "Do you think it would be too forward if I just sat down next to him?" she asked, propelling me toward the cafeteria.

"Who?"

"Ben!"

"Ummm." My brain locked up as I ran that scenario in my mind, focusing on the part where I would also be sitting at that table.

Nolan appeared on my other side and took my other arm. "You know she doesn't really understand the dynamics of the cafeteria."

"What?"

"You're right," Mia said, wrinkling her nose. "These things can get very complicated."

"We are just talking about eating, right? How complicated could it be?"

Nolan tossed the blanket over his shoulder. "We all know you're very smart, love, but you're going to have to defer to experience here. It's actually quite political."

I snorted, shaking loose of them. Maybe since I was homeschooled, I was a little more mature than my friends, but I could hardly think that the process of consuming sustenance could really be any cause for concern or drama. I marched straight through the double doors.

My steps faltered as the noise seemed to die down with every step forward. Was it just me or did the talking seem to stop when I walked in? It had to be me; these kids never shut up. I straightened my polo, and my glasses slid down my nose. It was almost as bad as being onstage again, and I shuffled back until I bumped into Mia.

"Ow!" she complained, jabbing me sharply in the kidney. "The food is the other way!"

"Did everyone stop talking?" I asked, moving around them so Mia and Nolan were in front. "It feels like everyone is looking at us."

"As they should," Nolan said, stumbling forward as I pressed into his back.

"Why are we whispering in doorways when we can be sitting comfortably at a table with mostly edible food?" Mia asked.

I scanned the picnic tables spread haphazardly throughout the room. All of them had at least one or two campers sitting at them.

"Look, there's nowhere to sit." I frowned.

"What are you talking about? There is plenty of room at that one," Mia said, pointing at one in the far corner.

"There're people already sitting there."

"Okay, let's get on with it," Nolan said, grabbing me and shoving us forward. "Bea, these tables can sit, like, ten people at a time; get used to sharing your personal space." He walked over and unceremoniously dumped our picnic blanket on top of the table we were claiming and stalked toward the buffet. The current residents of the table looked up in confusion, and I hastily followed Nolan to the food.

Now, I wouldn't say that I'm picky, but it might have been mentioned a time or two by an uncharitable relative. I prefer the word "discerning." It means that I'm a little particular, and why shouldn't I be allowed to stick to a food schedule if I want to? My stomach clenched as I walked past rows of mashed potatoes, meat with gravy, more meat with other gravy, and slimy stacks of corn on the cob. As I neared the end of the line, my salvation came as a mound of dinner rolls. I stacked five on my plate, grabbed a few cookies, and followed Nolan and Mia back to our table in the back.

The walk maybe took five seconds, but it still felt like a million eyes were on me, and every little whisper seemed to carry my name. I must be losing my mind. I'd only been here a day or so and I was already as vain as Shelby, thinking nobody had anything better to do with their time than talk about me. I shook my head and marched straight ahead, not making eye contact with any other tables. There was maybe a very specific table that I *especially* did not want to make eye contact with. I wasn't even sure where that table of very specific campers was.

It certainly wasn't in the far corner from ours. Under the poster for *Much Ado about Nothing*, and pictures of some giggling girls holding . . . bunnies? Good lord, did they have wild animals here too?

I slid in next to Nolan, and Mia was already pointing at my tray in disgust before my butt could hit the bench.

"What. Is. That?" She gave me her best mom face.

"That is dinner," I said sweetly.

"No, it is not." She huffed, once again with the mom attitude.

"Prove it," I said, and took a big bite out of roll number one.

She sighed. "Why didn't you get real food, like a normal person?"

"It's Friday. They didn't have mushroom pizza," I said.

They looked at me in confusion, until Nolan pointed in my direction. "No. We are going to ignore that weird and cryptic statement and focus on the matter at hand."

"And what is so important that we can't psychoanalyze Bea's food?"

Nolan leaned forward, sliding his hands all over the table. "This table. Is this it? Is this where we stake our claim and eat our food and have our fascinating conversations for the rest of the summer? These are the issues, ladies. I need to know which table to personalize."

"I am not going to sit at a bedazzled table," I said, tearing into roll number two.

He blinked slowly. "One more smart remark like that, and I am breaking into your cabin and bedazzling the collar on every one of your plain Jane polos."

I snorted.

"Not that I don't love all y'all, because you know that I do," Mia said, placing a hand over her heart, "but have we fully considered merging our group with another?"

"Let me guess." I sighed, my eyes still not drifting to *that* corner.

"They're not all bad," Mia pleaded.

I slid my plate to the side and gave her my best therapist impression. "Shelby is Satan. No offense, Nolan." He held up his hands in surrender. "Nik is an entitled ass, and I'm pretty sure someone in that group yelled out 'Virgin!' while I was up onstage today."

Nolan sputtered, choking on his green beans. I gave his back a few slaps while watching Mia deflate.

"Maybe they aren't *all* bad," I said through clenched teeth. "I doubt we would be able to separate them, though."

"I'm sorry, we're going to have to back this thing up a second. Did somebody accuse our resident Snow White of being pure as the driven snow?" Nolan said, swiveling in place.

"Could this day be any longer?" I shoved roll number three in my mouth in one piece.

"To be fair, you're missing some context here," Mia said. "Mr. G was mentioning how Bea has never done theater, and that it's her first time with the Bard—"

Nolan barked in laughter as Mia shrugged, smiling sheepishly.

"It's not his fault he's surrounded by a bunch of hormonal savages." I sighed. "Why am *I* the resident Snow White?"

Nolan grinned, pulling his hair up into an effortless topknot. "It just stands to reason. If it took that much prodding from your overly extroverted roommate—"

"Hey," Mia interrupted.

"For you to participate in the most basic of social interactions, we're assuming you also shy away from other interactions." He waggled his eyebrows.

"Not that there's anything wrong with that!" Mia added, over a mouthful of mashed potatoes.

"Yeah, yeah," I said, brushing it off. "Bea is the worst teenager in the world. She couldn't care less about dating and would rather spend her time reading than planning devious ways to get people to notice her."

"Couldn't care less, huh?" Nolan said, leaning back. "Well, let's hear it then, Your Highness. Exactly how virginal are you? First base? Second base? Anyone stealing third?"

"I'm going to need you to explain the rules of baseball before we go any further," I said.

Mia blinked in surprise, as if she hadn't considered what it meant when I told her I never hung out with other teenagers.

"So . . . kissing, hand-holding, stolen moments while playing seven minutes in heaven?" she asked, her expression dreamy.

I considered lying. I'm not terribly bad at it, and my parents always believed me when I told them that yes, I did get some exercise today, or that no, I didn't eat just animal crackers all day. There was one problem, though. Lying would mean that I was embarrassed about my lack of experience. That I had regrets, and that these things were important to me. I didn't need boys. I had Oxford.

"*No*," I said, enunciating the word. I paused, still unbalanced from the stage, and barreled forward before I could change my mind. "But I came close once."

Nolan scooted closer to me on the bench, his features shining with interest. "How does one come close?"

It had taken me about six months to tell Dr. Horowitz, and longer still to share parts of it with my parents, but this felt different. I wanted them to know. I wanted them to know *me*. "My parents have always worried about me being too much of a loner, and there are usually a lot of social events within the homeschooling community to give kids more opportunities to make friends."

Mia nodded, swallowing another bite of mashed potatoes. "Makes sense."

I forced another brittle smile across my face. "When I was thirteen, I joined this new group. The rest of the kids had been together forever, and I was new and . . . myself." I shredded roll number four into tiny little pieces. "They all acted so nice, and there was this guy named Bryce Williams. He was blond, tan, and the most popular guy there. The *cutest* guy there."

"Oh, tell us more about hot Bryce," Nolan said, grinning.

I swallowed the lump in my throat. "I was surprised he was interested in me, and I . . . became very interested in him too." I focused on my tray. "I was even more surprised when I found out weeks later that it was all a big joke. They thought I was weird and dorky, and thought it was hilarious to watch me believe that he actually liked me. I guess he got tired of it, because I showed up one day and saw him kissing Jessica Sawyer in the hallway. They just laughed, and he told me how relieved he was to stop pretending." I rolled my shoulders, pinned under the heavy weight of their stares. "I never went back, and now I'm forced to go to theater camp in order to go to college." I tried to smile, the joke falling flat.

"That little shit!" Nolan hissed with a force that had me looking up in surprise. The anger on his face immediately brought me to the brink of tears, and I swallowed down everything I had no idea how to deal with.

Mia snaked her hand across the table and gripped mine hard. "I'm fairly certain we could find his address on the internet. Cali road trip while we can all still be charged as minors?"

A laugh sputtered out of me. "Maybe some other time." Their defense after barely knowing me had both my face and brain on fire. They were nothing like those other kids, and I needed to stop waiting for the other shoe to drop. *Helium. Neon. Argon. Krypton. Xenon. Radon.* "Anyway, can we talk about something else now?"

"Sure, boo," Nolan said, moving us into safer territory, but not before grabbing and squeezing my other hand under the table. "Well, what do you guys think about the casting? They should be posting it soon, so you better get your surprised-yet-gracious facial expressions in order."

Mia moved her food around on her plate. "I dunno. I usually get the comedic roles, but it would be nice to maybe one day get a role that was all romantic and tragic."

Nolan leaned across the table. "You will light up the stage in any role you play, but I hear you, and you deserve to play anything you want to."

She smiled before narrowing her eyes at me. "Speaking of

casting, you wouldn't happen to have inside information, would you? You were talking with Mr. G after class."

I curled my finger around the end of my braid, avoiding eye contact. "Just a little inside information, and only for myself."

She pushed her tray aside and waited for me to continue.

I fidgeted in my seat. "Fine. I begged him to let me be the prompter, and he agreed."

"You what!" she yelped. The cafeteria stilled a bit, and heads turned in our direction. "You what!" she asked, a little quieter this time.

I slid closer to Nolan, flinching under her evaluation, as all my emotions still bubbled too close to the surface.

"This is what I want," I said. "I'm not like you, and I don't want to spend my summer up on a stage."

She glared at me for a moment before speaking. "Fine. I would just like to go on record and say that you made a big mistake. I think if you were able to get out of your head for a second, you would probably be great at it." She went back to pushing her mystery meat around on her plate.

I'm not a quitter. I know a lost cause when I see it, and I didn't appreciate someone indicating that I took the easy way out. "Why? Just because I know the lines? I think we've already established that that's not enough."

Mia narrowed her eyes. "No, because of that right there." She waved her hand in my direction.

I turned to look behind me. "What?"

She rolled her eyes. "*Passion!* If you were as monotone in life as you were on that stage, then I would have thanked the sweet baby Jesus that you made that deal. That's not the case, though, is it? Even the slightest bit of prodding and you're all flushed and filled to the absolute brim with emotions."

I sat there stunned.

"You've wasted your experience here, and you may never have another opportunity to realize these things about yourself, so I'm pissed. Now eat your pitiful dinner before I have another thing to be mad at you about." She pointed at my last roll with a no-nonsense look on her face.

I meekly took a bite of it, caught between surprise and indignation, trying to stomach the rolls and her opinion of me.

"All right, hand it over," Nolan said.

"Hand what over?"

"Your list! I want to see it again."

I dug the crumpled paper out of my pocket and dropped it into his outstretched palm. He smoothed it out on the table before pulling a pen out of his pocket and marking:

9.) *Fli*

I slammed my hand down on the paper. "Wait! What are you doing?"

"Do you want to have a real teenage experience, or this rated-G level shit your parents have put together for you?"

"Do you honestly think I'm looking for rated-R level tasks?"

"I think you'd much prefer checking off certain life experiences in a controlled setting rather than winging it when you get to England."

I paused at that, my fingers curling up into my palm. "Okay. What did you have in mind?"

Mia squealed and leaned in closer as Nolan formed the first sentence:

9.) *Flirt with someone for the sheer hell of it*

"What does that even mean?" I asked.

"It means not everything has to have a purpose or end in true love. Sometimes a person is just cute, and you want to have fun!" Mia said, winking at my stunned expression.

"The practice will be good for you," Nolan said, leaning over with his pen again.

### 10.) *Dance with abandon*

I swallowed a mouthful of dry bread, the edges scraping down my throat. "That didn't really go that well the first time. What else do you have?"

"I thought you'd never ask!" He paused, pen over paper. "Are you interested in physical stuff?"

"Wait, what?" My brain stuttered over images of elegant hands framing my face. Bow-shaped lips moving toward mine. I lunged for the paper, panicking as my face heated up to five thousand degrees.

"I knew it," he said, grinning. He easily moved the paper out of my grasp before scrawling:

### 11.) *Kiss someone*

I leaned back as if struck. "Kiss someone? *Kiss someone?* You expect me to just run up to someone and kiss them?"

"Yep, and I expect you to have a delightful time doing it!" He smiled and leaned down to put his pen to paper again. I finally yanked it out of his grasp and folded it neatly before slipping it back in my pocket.

"I think we've added enough nonsense to my list tonight."

"What are you doing over here?" Shelby said abruptly, sliding in on the other side of Nolan, her question for him alone.

"Lovely to see you too, sister. Did you miss me?"

"Why aren't you sitting over there with us?"

"Because I am sitting over here with these lovely ladies."

"Why? Moving away in a few months isn't enough? You're going to avoid me all summer too?"

Nolan sighed, his gaze dropping to the mystery meat he'd been pushing around on his plate.

Shelby's words and his response were painted with an emotion that felt strangely intimate to witness, and I slid a little farther down the bench. Mia winced, the unspoken question clearly written across her face: *Should we go?*

"Oh, are we moving over here now?" Ben asked, walking up, beaming like the sun. He sat down on the other side of the table with Mia, completely oblivious to the tension.

Mia recovered first. "Well, we're always happy for more company!" Her smile strained as the twins sat in stony silence.

"You know, it's not very nice to move without letting the rest of the group know." Nik eased down onto the bench across from me, his gaze pinning me to my seat like a butterfly under glass. "Although this was an interesting choice."

"You see, sister? The whole gang is here now. No harm, no foul." Nolan turned away from her, giving me a smile that wasn't at all subtle.

I stared at my lap, waiting for some cue that this ritual had finally come to an end. That we could leave. *Helium. Neon. Argon. Krypton. Xenon. Radon.* My fingers curled around the hard plastic tray as I was about to make an executive decision, when Nik leaned forward, his elbows sliding across the table.

"You know, for someone so dead set on being Romeo, you didn't really bring a lot of confidence to your audition." A smug smile played at the corner of his mouth. "That must have been a new acting technique you were using. I can't say I really recognized it." He leaned back, all self-satisfaction, and in that moment I hated him to a degree that left me dizzy. I hated that he saw me fail at something while I saw him excel, and I *hated* that I was trapped here for another four weeks.

"Don't be a jackass, Nik."

Nik raised an eyebrow in Nolan's direction when a flurry of activity spread through the cafeteria and tables of campers got up and ran for the door.

I jumped. "Fire drill?"

Mia grinned. "The cast is posted."

She grabbed my wrist and yanked me to my feet, and we were halfway to the door before my brain caught up with me. We moved into the crush of bodies trying to get outside, and I stiffened at all the unwanted contact. I could feel the panic start to rise as people closed in, arms brushing against mine, and hot breath on the back of my neck. I tried to focus on Mia's hand like a lifeline, and then the space around me cleared enough for me to catch my breath. I knew I was practically panting at this point and tried to pull more air into my lungs.

"Are you okay?"

I looked up into the unreadable face of Nik as he moved in beside me. A single eyebrow went up, and I ducked my head, face burning. Mia dragged me out to the announcement board outside the cafeteria and jumped into the crowd surrounding the lone posted paper as I held back. No matter what Mia said, I knew what my role was going to be this summer, and I was perfectly fine with it. Acting had never been a skill I'd hoped to master. Homeric Greek, yes. Acting, no.

Mia peeled away from the crowd and walked back to where I was waiting.

"Well?" I said, trying to read her expression.

"I'm the Nurse!" she said with a little half smile.

"You know that's a ton of lines, right?" I said.

"It is, isn't it?" she said, smiling a bit wider.

"Yeah, you practically never shut up," I said, encouraged by her increasing enthusiasm. "Who got Juliet?"

We were interrupted by the sound of clapping, and a half circle of groupies had formed around Shelby. She was glowing and was sporting what I assumed was her "false modesty" look.

"I guess that answers that question. If she curtsies, I'm going to vomit."

Mia snorted. "It'd be a better world if she actually sucked. Unfortunately, I think she's probably going to be a decent Juliet."

"Juliet is extremely annoying," I said, turning to look at her in the twilight. "Are you sure you're okay?"

"Yeah, because I know I could do an amazing Juliet, and I know she could never pull off the Nurse." Her smile widened. "I think I'm going to have Nolan make me a fake nose."

The applause grew louder around Nik and his posse, and the crowd moved in tighter around them.

I rolled my eyes, for probably the millionth time today. "And that answers *that* question. Could this place be any more predictable? I've changed my mind; this teenager thing isn't that difficult. I could probably even tell you exactly what is going to happen the rest of the summer."

Mia linked her arm through mine. "Is that so? Well, tell me, do I end up with a hot blond boyfriend?"

"He doesn't stand a chance."

She laughed; all good humor returned. "He got Mercutio, you know?"

I shook my head. "Always a bridesmaid, never a bride."

She nudged me in the ribs. "Maybe he didn't want the spotlight either. Maybe he asked Mr. G to be the prompter, but you had already swooped in with your sad story of acting handicaps."

I forced a smile, Nik's assessment of my skills still hanging over my head. "I have no business on that stage."

"Truer words were never spoken."

I flinched as Shelby's presence frayed what little nerves I had left. She paused in front of us, her face the picture of sweet concern, but not quite pulling it off.

"Have your fans deserted you already?" Mia asked, batting her eyelashes.

She shot Mia a dirty look. "Good job landing the role of the ninety-year-old decrepit woman. I'm sure loads of people wanted it." She smirked at me. "Poor Mr. G, he must not have had a clue what to do with you. I have never heard of anyone being so terrible that he had to make them the prompter."

"Bea asked to be the prompter!" Mia said, the warning clear in her voice.

"Sure, she did," Shelby said. She tossed her hair over her shoulder, immediately dismissing us, and walked back to her group.

I let the comment slide off my back. Old Beatrice may have let people like that get to her, but the new Bea couldn't be bothered by what Shelby thought. Quite honestly, I was proud of her for just attempting to think in general.

"Time to go," I said, steering Mia back to the cafeteria and Nolan. "Let's go make some plans with our costuming friend. I think your version of the Nurse needs a neon-green brocade dress."

# Chapter Nine

"WE'RE GOING TO HAVE SO MUCH FUN!" MIA
pulsed with excitement and pressed herself against the window to
watch the line of campers boarding the bus. I looked across the
aisle and smirked at Nolan. The prospect of getting off campus
had made him even more colorful than usual. He winked over
his bright yellow Ray-Bans, and a turquoise Sharpie slid across his
biceps as he painted on a complicated geometric design.

The idea of shopping and walking around some random
town didn't do it for me, but it was better than the alternative.
No being trapped back in the circle of hell that was going to
be rehearsals. No having to interrupt people when they made
mistakes. No having to listen to Nik and Shelby as they declared
their undying love for each other.

I shoved my ratty messenger bag under the seat. "I'll be
happy if we just get rolling soon. This bus is stifling and smells
like feet."

Mia narrowed her eyes at me. "Mark my words, Bea. I will get
you excited about something before this summer is out. I will cut
through all that smart-girl sarcasm and reach the mushy, sensitive
marshmallow inside."

Nolan snorted, not looking up from his artwork.

"Good luck with that," I said, shoving a pencil through my messy bun for stability.

"Well, here comes something that Mia gets excited about," Nolan said, sliding his sunglasses down his nose.

Ben walked down the aisle with purpose, and my heart sank as he moved closer and closer to our seats at the back of the bus. I swallowed my panic and rose up off the seat trying to see around him. I knew Mia wanted to get to know him better, and I would never begrudge her that, but where he goes—

"He's coming closer," Nolan sang, his full attention on my discomfort.

"Is this seat taken?" Ben smiled hesitantly at Mia, indicating the empty seat in front of us. His collared shirt hung awkwardly on his body, the buttons done up wrong and half of his hair stuck up like he'd just rolled out of bed. I suppressed the instinct to just hold him down and straighten him.

"It is now," she responded, her voice soft and flirty. He grinned and scooted in next to the window. I collapsed into the seat as he sat down alone, and no tall-dark-and-aggressive people followed behind him. It wasn't like I was scared of a certain someone, who would not be named, but it was not unreasonable to want to avoid being near people who inspired sticky, sickly feelings of hatred. The thought of hearing more of his comments on my painful audition would send me into a shame spiral that my confidence might not recover from. I just needed to lie low and get through the next few weeks.

"Incoming!" Nolan hissed. My head snapped up as *he* boarded the bus. Nik scanned the seats, and I faked an interest in my shoes as his gaze passed over me. I looked up again to see Shelby waving her hands, as if she were bringing in an airplane. Of course. He was going to sit with her. That made sense. It was logical, even. Two components who equaled each other in horribleness.

*Romeo and Juliet.*

If you asked me, they deserved each other.

A breathy little sigh leaked past Mia's lips as she leaned forward, her attention fixed on the back of Ben's head.

"I'm surprised he can't feel that," I said.

She bit her lip, teeth scraping riotous fuchsia pink. "Do you think he sat here for a reason?"

"I'm almost positive. Have you seen how short your shorts are today?"

She smiled, leaning back. "Worth every single penny."

The seat in front of us shifted, and I froze, every survival instinct on overdrive. *Helium. Neon. Argon. Krypton. Xenon. Radon.* Blue-black curls fell over the top of the brown vinyl seat, and my fingers twitched.

I peeked around the seat to where Shelby was sitting closer to the front of the bus, her lips pressed tight as she stared at him. *Why would he not sit with her? How was I supposed to relax, when he could be listening to every word?* My nerves danced under my skin as Shelby came barreling down the aisle after him and claimed the seat in front of Nolan.

"Nik!" she said carefully, as if she were talking to a senile elderly person. "Didn't you see me waving? I thought we could practice some of our scenes on the ride there." She pulled her script out of her bag.

*Please sit with her. Please sit with her. Please sit with her.* At least with her, he would be distracted. He paused for a moment but slowly moved across the aisle and into her seat. The air flooded with the dark and heady smell of his cologne. I could taste it on my tongue, and it crawled down my throat as I pressed my lips firmly together. Pine, and something rich and spicy that I usually only found in Christmas puddings. Of course he smelled like a dessert. I licked my lips and tried to ignore the snickering coming from Nolan. I just needed to read the book I brought along and ignore the nerves jangling throughout my body. I wasn't even going to look in that direction. He didn't exist. The space he occupied was just a black hole. A void of nothingness. I forcefully exhaled through my nose, blowing away every trace of him.

Ugh, fine. I would just take a peek.

I just needed to make sure Shelby was claiming all his attention. She was chattering a mile a minute, and he looked across the aisle back at Ben with an apologetic smile. My appraisal traced the slope of his nose and the divot resting above his lips before sliding off his chin. He didn't seem to be participating in Shelby's conversation much, but I assumed that was normal. There probably wasn't a ton going on upstairs. His shirt was twisted up in the back from when he sat down, revealing a golden-brown stretch of skin. I blinked and slowly made my way back up to his profile, following every line and curve up to—only to find a pair of dark eyes on me. I froze as one eyebrow climbed his forehead.

Jerking around, I poured all my attention into looking past Mia and out the window. As if there were something fascinating out there in the parking lot, or somebody whose attention I was dying to grab. Mia laughed quietly with Ben as he hung over the seat, hair flopping carelessly between them. The scene was strangely intimate, but I couldn't look away yet. I never should have looked in his direction, and now he thinks what? Should I tell him that I was only looking over there to make sure he wasn't going to bother me? Was that normal or rude? Honestly, I didn't even know if I could explain the impulse. Maybe I was just searching for something unflattering, like excess body hair, or an ugly lower-back tattoo.

"Honey, we have got to get you a boyfriend."

I stiffened and gave Nolan a glare that should have struck him dead on the spot. "I have no interest in dating. Worry about your own boyfriends."

"Oh, I am *absolutely* worried about leaving poor Sam at home all summer, but your issues seem a little more pressing right now," he said, languidly stretching out across his seat.

I jumped on the possible change in topic like it was a life raft. "Who's Sam? You should tell us every single thing about him."

"Rest assured, you'll be able to pass a detailed examination on the intricacies of Samuel Gonzales before the summer is over," he said, his smile tilting into something softer. "It's my number one TED Talk."

Mia scooted down the seat closer to me. "Stop holding out; give us a few deets now!"

He sighed loudly, expertly drawing out the suspense. "If you insist. He's six foot three, has auburn hair he rarely remembers to brush, and usually has at least one item of food spilled on his clothes at all times."

"Oh," Mia said, the tone of her voice changing pitch. "That seems—"

"—surprising?" I finished, trying to visualize the boy described with the one across from me.

"Bea!" Mia hissed, an elbow shooting out and poking me in the kidney. "That's rude."

Nolan's smirk evolved into a full-on grin. "Oh, leave her alone; she's not wrong." He leaned over, adjusting one of the pencils in my bun as it lurched off to the left. "And Sam would *love* you. He's heading to Brown for aerospace engineering."

"Well, well, well," Mia said, turning up the southern accent. "How convenient that you will somehow both be in Providence, Rhode Island. Why, it's almost as if that was planned."

His reply was cut off as the bus lurched forward, but he pinked up all the way to the tops of his ears.

"Enough about me," he said, clearing his throat and leaning into the aisle. "Let's get back to our fledgling teenager's exciting future love life."

I groaned, resting my head on the seat in front of me as the attention whipped back in my direction.

"He's just messing with you, Bea," Mia said, pulling me back until I looked at her. "Are you really that against the idea, though? I mean, I know things have been difficult in the past, but that's no reason to give up completely."

I shifted next to her as I tried to articulate how the thought of all the effort and drama of dating turned my stomach. How even the possibility of friends had seemed nonexistent until a few days ago, let alone something more intimate. I couldn't even picture it. Or what about the physical aspects of it? What if I was a bad kisser? My very limited exposure to physical contact had made me awkward and uncomfortable in the past, and it wasn't like I'd ever had any opportunities to practice. I bet my inexperience would be pitiful and obvious. Or what if it was Bryce all over again? Just a joke to see if weird Beatrice was dumb enough to think someone could actually like her like that. My throat felt like it was starting to close up. *Helium. Neon. Argon. Krypton. Xenon. Radon. Helium. Neon. Argon. Krypton. Xenon. Radon.*

"It's just not a priority. It's never been a priority, and I don't see the point in trying *now*."

Mia leaned back, her eyebrows raised. I focused on smoothing the wrinkles out of my khaki pants, wishing that the floor would just swallow me up.

"Quit overthinking everything, sweet pea!" Nolan said, smiling encouragingly. "There's nothing wrong with letting life get a little messy!" He yanked off his sunglasses and began loudly scrutinizing the occupants of the bus. "Who should we pick? Who should we pick? What about Andrew, over there? He's filled out quite nicely since last year." He pointed at a boy with spiky black hair, sitting in the second row. His shirt was an unsettling shade of lavender.

Mia shook her head. "I don't know; he seems like he's trying a little too hard." She tilted her head, as if she was trying to determine something, and I squirmed under her gaze. "What's your idea of the perfect love interest?"

I wrinkled my nose. "I have no idea how to answer that." The silence stretched out between us. "Smart? Not deranged? Someone I can talk to about history, literature, and things that interest me."

Mia nodded. "So, we're looking for someone smart, who's most likely not a serial killer?"

"Or we could just not look at all?" I said, shoving my glasses up my nose.

She tapped a finger against her lip. "Who's smart? Who's smart . . ."

"Wait!" Nolan shot up in his seat. "Is anyone wearing a pocket protector?"

They dissolved into laughter, and a small smile tugged at my lips. "If he's not wearing suspenders, don't even think of giving him my number!"

Mia shrieked in delight.

"You only care if they're smart? Why am I not surprised?"

The laughter died in my throat at the interruption as Nik's presence poured into the aisle and he turned around in his seat to face me. I'd thought the auditions had rendered me immune to his voice, but it hit me like a whip. It had to be the accent. That did not bode well for me moving to an entire country of boys with that accent. My face burned as I realized he'd been listening to our entire conversation.

"This is private," I sputtered as he bestowed the full force of his attention in my direction. Shelby's face was cold and hard.

He shrugged. "There's not a lot of personal space in here, and you weren't exactly being quiet. So, do you not think things like physical appearance or humor are important? As long as they're just smart, you're into it?" He leaned in, that mocking smile back in place. "Maybe you're just looking for a good old-fashioned robot."

"Why am I not surprised that *you're* focused on physical appearance?" I pulled at the collar of my polo, my neck warm and sticky. "I'm not talking about this with you."

"Are you calling me shallow?" he asked, his smile biting.

My nails pressed half-moons deeply into my palms, and I forced my body to still and not march up to the front and sit near the chaperone. The violence of that impulse startled me. I was never this volatile, and I struggled for that familiar skin—that Beatrice who had no time to worry about the opinion of her own generation—but it didn't quite fit the way that it used to.

I cleared my throat, hoping I sounded indifferent. "Looks can be fleeting. Would you really want to gamble that your significant other retains an appearance that you will always find attractive, or would you rather be with someone who you respect and could have a meaningful conversation with?" I kept my attention focused on Mia and Nolan, hoping to make the conversation more general and no longer about me.

"You talk in extremes," Nik said, his long legs moving farther into the aisle. "Why does it have to be one or the other? Can't it be both?"

"It's doubtful," I said, sizing him up.

"For someone who's supposedly from California, I would have expected you to be a little more flexible."

"For someone from New York City, I completely expected you to possess that sense of false superiority that allows you to make generalizations about other areas of the country."

His mouth quirked. "I just find it curious that you're so set against the idea of anything but an IQ. No cute boys in your computer clubs?"

Images of golden-blond hair, blue eyes, and a smile that never seemed that sweet flashed across my brain. "Maybe I find a good conversation to be attractive. Unlike this current one."

"Ah, I get it. You don't like people disagreeing with you?"

"I have to respect someone for their opinion to matter to me."

His eyes narrowed, and Shelby grabbed his arm, trying to pull him farther back into the seat. "Nik, I thought we were going to practice?" She smiled at me over the top of her seat, the expression all teeth. "I would ask you to join us, but aren't you just the prompter?"

His eyes were still locked on mine, and I leaned forward. He mirrored my movement and was closer than I expected when I murmured, "You know, I would have loved to be Rosaline instead, but there was some concern I wasn't pretty enough to pull it off."

Surprise flitted across his face, and I refused to look away. He clenched his jaw, and his lips parted for a moment before pressing together tightly. I didn't back down, though, and when Shelby demanded his attention again he turned back around without a word. She threw me one last glare—both vicious and triumphant—but I didn't care. I felt like I had won something important. Maybe the appropriate social interaction would have been to ignore him, or to pretend I never heard him say that, but this new Bea wasn't that polite. I wanted to crawl under his skin the way his barb had crawled under mine. I reached under my feet and pulled a random book out of my bag.

I felt curious looks from Mia and Nolan prickling my skin, but I didn't look at them. I wasn't sure I wanted to see what they saw, so I opened my book and stared at the page until the words swirled together.

# Chapter Ten

**"YOU HAVE GOT TO BE JOKING." I HELD UP THE** lace-edged denim shorts that Mia had thrust into my hands. "These wouldn't even completely cover my butt."

"As if they're supposed to." Mia snorted, inspecting a similar pair in red.

"Are you trying to scare her?" Nolan yanked the shorts out of my hands. "I thought we agreed on easing her into this! She's like a wild baby animal, and any big, sudden movements will have her scampering back off to the mathlete section of The Gap."

"I am *not* a mathlete!" I said. "You make it sound as if I look like the most boring person in the world. I wear normal clothing. Have you ever considered that maybe you're all a little too colorful?" I crossed my arms.

"Look at her, sassing us," Nolan said, narrowing his eyes at me. "I've changed my mind. She's ready for these shorts." He shoved them back in my hands and steered me toward the dressing room.

"You know what? I don't think I'm ready for the shorts. Let's go back to that baby steps idea."

He yanked aside the pink velvet curtain on a dressing room stall and unceremoniously dumped me inside. He pointed a finger at me and said, "Change."

The curtain fell, and I was alone with a pair of shorts and every single one of my insecurities. "Mia! Make him be reasonable!"

"Less talking, more changing!" she replied in a singsong voice.

I pinched the bridge of my nose. I didn't belong in places like this. Everything about this store was vibrant, trendy, and young, and I—wasn't. I was wearing yet another version of my "uniform." Today's polo was a warm brown, and I smoothed the familiar material. I looked clean, neat, and professional.

Boring.

The curtain flung back, and Mia stuck her head inside. "I knew you weren't changing. What's wrong?"

I reached for the words. That maybe I was a wild baby animal and the territory was getting a little too unfamiliar and scary. That maybe I didn't know if I would recognize myself without my uniform. That maybe if these things started becoming important to me now, I really had hidden myself away and wasted the past few years.

"I don't know," I mumbled, studying the swirls in the hot-pink carpet.

She stepped inside. "Bea, look at me."

I dragged my eyes back up to her face and hoped she couldn't see how I was working myself into a full-on freak-out.

"It's only a pair of shorts. It doesn't have anything to do with your past, present, or future. It doesn't have anything to do with your intelligence or Oxford. It does not mean you have to suddenly change your entire personality or wardrobe. It is just a pair of shorts." She squeezed my shoulders and studied me until I gave a small nod.

She was right. One pair of shorts was not going to change my life.

Probably.

I swatted her hands away and gave her a small smile. "Fine, let me try this teenager costume."

She laughed and stepped outside. "Put on the damn shorts, Bea! Let's get some air moving across your poor legs."

"Quick, give her this too!" A phantom hand broke through the curtain and dangled a rose-colored shirt in front of me. It had ruffles.

I sighed, knowing that I was all the way in it now. I peeled off my clothes and yanked the shorts and top on. They fit perfectly, of course.

Might as well get this over with. I took a deep breath before lifting my gaze to the mirror.

I looked—young.

I was showing quite a bit of skin, which I didn't really know how I felt about. The soft pink improved my normal shade, which my mother uncharitably referred to as "blinding," and the ruffles around the neckline seemed to soften everything. I tilted my head, inspecting this new girl with all her sharp edges hidden. She could walk around theater camp without a second glance and would completely blend in. Wasn't this what I had planned to do when I arrived? Study the target group and emulate their behavior? Didn't Mia's lecture on clothes and appearances make me think that blending in more might make all of this easier?

"I know you've changed! I can see your pants on the floor!"

"Shut up, Nolan! She'll come out when she's ready!"

I knew I was lucky. I'd found people who would accept me if I walked out and declared that I was going to dress in Shakespearean costume for the rest of the summer. I could also walk out and say that I didn't want any new clothes and planned to stay the same, and they would accept that too. I pulled my hair out of its lumpy bun and let it fan out across my shoulders. Grimacing at this poseur in a teenager's skin, I weighed my options. I didn't particularly want to change my habits at this point, but the truth of the matter was that this new Bea scared me. The idea of stepping outside that curtain and walking around like this in public was terrifying. Like I'd lost all my armor. It was that feeling right there that had my arm reaching for the curtain. After years of spending all my time alone and everything being familiar and predictable, I wanted to feel something.

*Anything.*

"Look, they do cover the butt," Mia said, wrinkling her nose in disappointment.

"Forget the shorts! Can we talk about how her legs go up to her chin?" Nolan said.

I tugged at the shorts as Mia circled me. "Bea! You look amazing! Not that you didn't before, but we can actually see more of you now!"

Nolan leaned in. "It's like that movie where the hot, smart girl gets a makeover and she's still a hot, smart girl, but people act like they never realized how hot she was before."

"And on that note, I'm going back in the dressing room." I moved past them and let the curtain fall behind me before I smiled.

The rest of the afternoon slipped away from us and became a never-ending line of shops that all blurred together.

"I'm serious, you guys. I cannot carry one more thing!"

Mia grabbed my arm and steered me toward another shoe store. "But look at those little strappy things! They go with that cute skirt you picked up in the last store!"

"Mia! My parents are already going to die from matching heart attacks when they get this bill! I cannot, will not, purchase one more item!" I gave her what I was hoping was a serious, formidable face. Although, if she was paying any attention at all, she knew that she could probably talk me into anything.

"Will the heart attacks be from spending the money, or the fact that you actually bought clothes?" Nolan asked.

"They probably won't even believe it was me. If the bank calls to verify the purchases, they'll think it's a case of identity theft," I said. "Either that or they'll think I've resorted to bribing people to be my friends." I stopped walking and wilted against the closest building. I was hot and sweaty, and my shoulder ached from the number of bags that I'd somehow accumulated.

"Then you really should have bought me those sunglasses I was dying for," Nolan said as he relieved me of some of my purchases.

"I guess you'll just have to like me for me," I said with a grateful smile.

"Don't worry about it, Bea," Mia said, pulling me forward as we headed back to where the bus was parked. "The things you got were necessities. You can't go the entire summer in pants, and you also needed a party dress for the big end-of-summer dance. You can explain all of this to them tomorrow."

Crap. I had forgotten tomorrow was Sunday, and I was really, really not looking forward to explaining my prompting role to my parents. I wasn't 100 percent sure how they were going to take it, and it might be seen as purposefully trying to get out of their big "onstage" culture shock. On the other hand, spending money on clothing is so out-of-character for me that they might see *that* as branching out.

I'd better hedge my bets.

"You know, I think I might need some shoes that can be described as strappy." If I dropped that adjective in conversation, my parents would probably think I'd undergone a brain transplant. At the very least, they might be disoriented enough to not focus on the fact that I'd manipulated myself out of the limelight.

Mia squealed in excitement and steered me back toward the last shoe store. Nolan moaned, dragging himself behind us into the air conditioning.

I slumped down into a chair and waited for them to bring me things to try on. This was the system we worked out in store one, and I wasn't ashamed to admit that I knew they knew better than me. I'd always hated buying new clothes in the past, but I was secretly excited about some of my new purchases. My party dress was dark red and velvet, and although it looked a little old-fashioned, Nolan swore he'd remake it into something spectacular. I'd never even realized that maybe I wanted to own a velvet party dress.

"These are perfect!"

A pair of patent-leather heels were shoved in my face, with rows and rows of straps that had a bit of a bondage feel.

I arched an eyebrow at Nolan. "Hard pass."

Mia sidled up beside him, holding something behind her back. "I bet she likes mine the best!" She presented a pair of gold glitter pumps in triumph.

"They might be just a teeny tiny bit too shiny for me," I said.

"Ha!" Nolan stuck out his tongue.

They walked off to try again, and I relaxed as Mia tried on her own gladiator-looking shoes. I leaned back in the chair, grateful for the chance to rest, and my attention snagged on a pair in the window. They were black, strappy, and had a tiny little bow across the front. They were pretty. Too pretty for *my* feet.

"Can I help you?" A young man wearing a tie appeared at my elbow.

Nolan and Mia were squabbling over a red platform monstrosity in the corner and I probably needed them to sign off on these, but something about them spoke to me. I wanted them for myself, and that realization had me fumbling for my card.

"I'll take those, please. In a seven."

He nodded, pleased, and brought me back another shopping bag to add to my collection. I dragged myself out of the chair and hauled my bags over to Nolan and Mia.

"Okay, I'm done," I said, shaking the new bag.

Nolan and Mia froze.

"You bought something?" Nolan asked, eyeing the bag with suspicion.

I smiled. "If you want something done right, you have to do it for yourself."

He barked in laughter. "This I gotta see." He snatched the bag out of my hand and flipped the lid off the shoe box. His eyebrows shot up.

"Well, well, well. They have bows and a heel. Why, Ms. Quinn, I had no idea you were so girlie."

I blushed a little, pleased that he approved.

"They're adorable," Mia said, beaming at me.

My face was burning, and I grabbed my bag back, shrinking under their attention.

Mia swung an arm across my shoulders. "On that note, I think we are ready to go."

I sagged against her. "Finally! Which way back to the bus?"

Mia's grin grew wider. "Just one thing first," she said, steering me toward the cash register.

"Do y'all have a bathroom we can use?" she asked, her smile sweet like honey. Predictably, they ushered us into a room at the back.

"Do you want me to hold your bags while you pee?" I asked.

"Not quite," she said, her expression innocent as she shoved me inside. She shut the door behind us, pulling the bags off my arms. My brain caught up when she started yanking tags off.

"Isn't it going to look weird if I leave the bus in these clothes and show up in others?" I asked, backing toward the door.

She smiled at me. "Not weird. Noticeable."

"Maybe I don't want to be noticed."

"Then you should have decided to room with Shelby," she said with a wry smile. "You're going to start being an active participant in your own life. I'm still pissed at you for the prompter stunt you pulled, so you're going to let me orchestrate your emergence as a teenager." She handed me the shorts and ruffled top from the first store, a challenging look on her face.

My fingers slowly reached for them, as if moving through molasses. I felt like I was about to walk out naked, or with a big red *A* sewn to my clothes, or like I was wearing a Halloween costume in the middle of March. I was going to look abnormal. I was going to look—

*Helium. Neon. Argon. Krypton. Xenon. Radon—*

"Beatrice."

I winced.

"What are you thinking about?"

I trusted her enough to buy clothes on her whim; I ought to trust her enough to be honest with her. I hesitated for only a second.

"It's easy not to care what other people think of you, when you obviously don't care either."

She nodded. "I get what you're saying. I get that you've only ever made room in your life for school and Oxford. If I thought you didn't want any of this, if you really, truly wanted to stay the same, I would return all of this stuff right now."

I shifted under her gaze.

She grabbed me by the shoulders. "I don't believe that, though. When left alone in a shoe store, you picked out and bought a pair all by yourself. A pair with bows." She grinned at me.

I nodded slowly. She wasn't wrong.

"You're not a beige person. You're brilliant, but you're also funny, snarky, and as ridiculous as the rest of us."

I felt the clothes pressed into my hand, and this time I grabbed them. Before I could lose my nerve, I whipped off my uniform and swiftly changed. As I pulled the shorts on, Mia fished a white pair of flip-flops out of one of my bags and handed them to me.

I slipped them on, and with hands that were only slightly shaking I pulled my hair back out of my bun.

Mia stood next to me, beaming like a proud mama. She dug around in her bag and pulled out a small makeup case. "Might as well go whole hog!"

She smeared some light pink lip gloss on my lips, and I swallowed my nerves and the rest of my protests. Bea was a stranger, but she looked like someone who could walk down the street without a care in the world. I was going to have to borrow some of that confidence now. I shoved my old clothes into my bags and gathered them all up in my arms. I turned to open the door and paused for a moment.

I looked over my shoulder at her. "Thank you."

"For what?"

"Taking an interest. I know it would have been so much easier for you to just run off with Nolan and not have to deal with all of this." I gestured vaguely to myself.

Her smile was so blinding I had to look away. I realized how much her opinion mattered to me. How much I wanted my opinion to matter to her too.

"Aren't you supposed to be smart? Which part of me saying we're friends wasn't clear?" she said, nudging me until I dragged my eyes back up off the floor.

"Well, I don't really have any other friends, so you'll have to let me know if I'm doing it wrong." I worked well with constructive feedback, and I could adjust if I started messing it up. I could change.

"Wait, you don't have any friends other than me?"

I slowly shook my head as delight bloomed across her face.

"Does that mean I'm your *best* friend?" she said, each word pitched higher until she was just squealing.

I laughed, covering my face so she couldn't see how relieved I was. "I guess so, if that's okay?"

"You're being dumb again; let's go tell Nolan so he dies of jealousy."

# Chapter Eleven

"**MOVE, MOVE, MOVE! KNEES TO YOUR CHESTS,** ladies!" Nolan herded us back toward the bus parking lot, but it was clear that I was the weakest link, and they were forced to slow down and wait for me.

"Would they really leave without us?" I gasped, trying to remain upright and keep moving forward at the same time.

"We're only ten minutes late!" Mia said, although I noticed her speed had steadily increased.

"They would definitely miss us," Nolan panted. "Ben would notice his flirt buddy was gone, Nik would notice there was no one there to yell at him, and the whole bus would just be drab and colorless."

I rolled my eyes, which caused me to stumble. "Oh, I see, you bring the color and fun, Mia contributes flirting, and I'm the killjoy that scolds everyone."

"Not everyone!" Nolan yelled over his shoulder as he pulled ahead of me. "Just Nik!"

Mia turned around, jogging backward. "With very good reason!"

"Wait, what's the reason? Are you two holding out on me?"

I didn't really feel like getting into the multitude of reasons why Nik rubbed me the wrong way, or the way he apparently felt I didn't measure up. I focused on putting one foot in front of the other when we raced around the last building and caught sight of the bus parking lot.

"Look! It's still there!" Nolan stopped running almost immediately, and I careened into him.

"You want to give someone a little warning before you just stop like that?"

"Bea, these shoes were obviously not made for running," he chided. "Naturally, I stopped as soon as the threat had passed."

"Those look like sneakers to me."

"I'm sorry to hear that."

Mia ran ahead waving her arms over her head. It looked like everyone else was already waiting on the bus. Troy stepped off just outside the doors and tapped his watch.

"Uh-oh," Nolan mumbled, running up neck and neck with Mia and leaving me behind.

"Sorry, everyone!" Mia said, grinning at Troy. The side of his mouth twitched, and he folded his arms across his broad chest. Nolan mumbled similar apologies as I staggered up to the bus door. I gasped for air, weighed down by my bags and an overall general lack of fitness. Troy reached forward and propped me up by the elbow.

"Hey, are you all right?"

My neck twinged as I looked up at him. "Oh sure, I was actually just getting some exercise in. The shopping bags are helping me add some much-needed muscle tone."

He grinned. "Speaking of shopping bags—didn't you leave this bus looking a little different?" His eyes lingered over my legs, his hand still on my elbow.

I was having a little difficulty getting oxygen, and it wasn't just due to the exercise. "Um, yeah. Apparently, I dress a little too bland for these guys." I nodded toward the bus. "So here I am trying something new."

"I like it. I think it suits you." He grinned wider, his teeth dragging over his bottom lip.

I slowly pulled my elbow out of his hand, but something stopped me from moving to the door. I wasn't used to the attention of others, especially boys, and I wasn't sure what my response was supposed to be, what I even wanted it to be. But this list wasn't going to complete itself, and *make small talk* came to the forefront of my mind as the words tumbled out of my mouth.

"So. Did you buy anything nice?" The warm metal of the bus pressed into my shoulder as I tried to casually lean against it.

He shrugged, mirroring my pose. "I bought some sunglasses. Want to see?"

"Sure."

He reached into the side pocket of his basketball shorts and pulled out a small black case.

"Are you getting on the bus or *not*?"

I spun as Shelby's white-blond hair tumbled out of the bus window.

"Chill, Shelby. We're coming," Troy said with no sense of urgency. He opened the case to show me sunglasses as red as my face must be. I nodded my appreciation and stumbled over the next things to say.

"Um. Okay, well, this interaction is over," I said, moving past him to skip up the stairs. I kept my eyes down and tried to maneuver down the aisle without beaning anyone in the head with my bags. I had a couple of close calls but was too uncomfortable to care. I just kept moving, nearly flying forward when the bus started pulling out of the parking lot. When I got to the back of the bus, I looked up long enough to see that the seat I once shared with Mia now contained Ben too. She smiled at me, a mixture of happiness and sheepishness. I paused for a minute before blindly throwing my bags down into the empty seat in front of them.

The seat Ben once occupied.

The seat across from Shelby and Nik.

I sat down and cringed as my new shorts slid farther up my legs. I tried to adjust them, nearly sliding off the seat.

"Easy there, cowgirl." Nolan leaned forward into the aisle, from his seat behind Shelby and Nik. Troy followed me down the aisle, and Nolan moved aside so Troy could scoot in.

I huffed. "I am so uncomfortable, in so many different, special ways."

Nolan's grin grew wider. "You seemed to have a lot to say to Troy here."

"I was just making *conversation*," I said, emphasizing the word, and blushing as Troy waved from the other side of Nolan. My fingers itched to pull out the list and check off my latest accomplishment.

I peeked over the seat, and Mia's head was close to Ben's. She laughed, her hands fluttering as she spoke, and he'd fixed his buttons in the hours since we parked. What I wouldn't give to be sitting on the inside, with an entire human body shielding my bare thighs from the rest of the bus.

"What is *that* supposed to mean? You and Troy were talking?" Shelby asked, forcing me to acknowledge the seat she was occupying.

"Yeah, so?" I said, hoping she would go back to simpering over Nik.

"Why do you care? You haven't said two words to me since ghosting me last summer," Troy said, leaning over the seat and into her personal space.

"I had no idea you were interested in someone who was trying *this* hard." She leaned around Nik and took my measure. "Did you just stumble into the first store you saw and buy whatever was hanging off the mannequin?"

My face lit on fire as her words stripped me bare.

"I'm pretty sure I've seen you wear something very similar to that, Shelby," Nik said, his tone as lazy as his posture.

My eyes squeezed shut as I willed myself to be anywhere but there. I wasn't sure what was worse—Shelby's poisonous remark or Nik's lukewarm defense. If I were wearing my uniform, I would have snarled back without a second thought. I let my hair swing forward, blocking them out, and tried to resist the impulse to crawl under the seat.

"Stand down, Shelby. Green doesn't look good on you," Nolan barked. "She's just jealous because she thought Troy was still crazy over her, but one look at Bea's perfect legs and there's a new contender in town."

Troy laughed, and I looked back at Nolan in horror. "In what way are you possibly helping?"

Shelby glared but didn't say another word. She tossed her hair and turned to Darla in the seat in front of her.

"So Troy was flirting with you?" Nik asked, his voice pitched low.

I resolutely refused to look across the aisle at him. "Of course not," I said, remembering that hand on my elbow. I was so full of mixed feelings, truths, half-truths, lies, and confusion about whether I was even capable of recognizing those things when faced with them.

He looked back where Nolan was drawing a matching geometric design on Troy's arm, and back at me. Disbelief written clear across his face.

"He was just talking to me."

"That's surprising; Troy doesn't actually have that much to say."

"Isn't he supposed to be a friend of yours?"

"We're camp friends."

I blinked. There were different types of friendships? My research didn't indicate that. To be honest, none of the research prepared me for this. There was a surprising lack of friendship bracelets and secret handshakes, and a lot more talking behind someone's back. How was I supposed to navigate this when everything I thought and felt was broadcasted on my face and tumbled out of my mouth? I settled on pressing my lips tightly together and scooting closer to the window.

"Well? Are you guys going to hook up or something? Have you decided that he is going to be the lucky recipient of your little experiment?"

I glared across the distance. I wasn't naïve enough to not understand the connotations of that. "First of all, there is no experiment. Second, are we friends now? Are we going to braid each other's hair and discuss all of the pros and cons of Troy as a prospective boyfriend?"

This time he laughed. It surprised me. He rubbed his jaw as if he was surprised by it too.

"Fair point. I'm just saying—I know him pretty well. I could give you some pointers, if you'd like." The gleam in his eye told me otherwise.

"I'm sure the pointers you'd give me would be *very* helpful."

"Hey! I'm not one to stand in the way of true love."

"True love is a myth." I yanked on the shorts so hard, I was worried I heard a rip.

"You're showing your robot side again," he said, swiveling brown legs and salmon shorts into the aisle.

I snorted, not bothering to engage.

He leaned forward, sliding his sunglasses up on top of his head. "Troy can sometimes be charming, and it's not unheard of for people to experience love at first sight." A mocking smile spread across his lips. "Especially when they know they have a four-week deadline."

"I find it funny that somehow I'm the weird one for not buying into the love-at-first-sight hype. Take Romeo and Juliet, for example; they're kids and they're willing to ruin their entire lives over a handful of meetings? What if Romeo was incredibly messy, and that ended up being a deal breaker for Juliet? What if Juliet joined some weird cult that believed you could never shower again? Do you think Romeo knew her and loved her enough to get past that? I know it's fiction, but the crazy thing is that people actually believe the plot is possible." I stilled, knowing I was rambling.

I pressed my lips together and slid my hands under my thighs. I risked a glance up at him. He looked amused.

He leaned farther into the aisle. "Okay, let me get this straight. You think love at first sight is impossible, and that people should only get together after a long and thorough vetting process?"

I loudly exhaled, and he held his hands up in surrender. "Don't get so defensive! I'm just trying to understand." His attention wasn't as disturbing when I could talk in generalities, and I'd almost forgotten how much I disliked him. Almost.

*Yeah, but isn't Rosaline supposed to be really hot?*

I swallowed hard and focused on the topic at hand. "Yes, I believe that love at first sight is unrealistic, and what's so wrong with knowing the person you're dating? That way you don't find out terrible things later. Like 'oh hey, honey, I forgot to tell you that I murdered a bunch of hitchhikers in the early nineties.'"

"While that would be useful to know before getting serious with someone, I don't think it happens too often." He smiled that weird, slanted smile that ended with a dimple flourish. "I'm probably partial to love at first sight because I wouldn't be here if nobody believed in it. That's how my parents met."

"Really."

"Yes, *really*. My mum was cast as Ophelia, and my father ended up seeing her play at the last minute. He knew another guy in the play and was able to get backstage, and they've been together ever since."

I shrugged. "Well, I can understand why your family would want to continue on that naïve tradition of hoping for the best."

He narrowed his eyes. "Let me guess. Your parents are academics. They don't hug very often and prefer to keep relationships very tidy and businesslike."

I pushed my glasses up. "Not even close. I'm from Berkeley, remember? My parents are hippies, and I'm pretty sure they would smoke pot if they didn't know how much I'd disapprove."

"Is being a hippy an occupation these days?"

"They're therapists."

"They haven't tried to cure you of your aversion to fun by now?"

"I do not avoid fun!" I said, glaring over the tops of my glasses. "Plus, they aren't *that* kind of therapist." I paused for a moment. "They're sex therapists. I doubt they'd want me for a client."

He blinked slowly. I was so used to their occupation and highly inappropriate dinner conversation that sometimes I forgot it could be unusual for some people. I raised an eyebrow and waited for him to organize his thoughts.

"That's"—he coughed—"interesting."

I sighed. "No, it isn't. I'll hear them discuss some cases and I can't imagine how people could be that obsessed or dependent on others for their own validation. It's just desperation and a fear of being alone."

"Yeah, I can see how you would feel that way. Especially growing up with those examples around you." He reached up, his lean fingers twisting fat curls my mother paid good money to try and re-create. They tumbled down the nape of his neck, and he paused. "You know, you would probably be a pretty good actress if you took it a little more seriously."

I fluffed the ruffles of my top, the material completely foreign to me. "I take it seriously; I just suck."

"Yeah, at the auditions, you definitely sucked."

I scowled at him.

He grinned. "Don't glare at me, Beatrice. You know you did. You also know that you made no effort whatsoever to play any of the characters you were assigned."

I opened my mouth to tell him where to shove those characters. However, a nagging voice in the back of my mind jumped in to agree with him. *You know he's right and you didn't do anything but recite the lines.* I clenched my teeth, no real defense to fall back on. "My name is Bea," I said, crossing my arms and angling away from him.

He snorted. "Maybe to some."

He eyed my new clothes, and I tugged at the shorts again under his lazy perusal. It had seemed like such a harmless idea in the store, but now I just wanted to take all these bags and throw them in a camp bonfire for letting me think that I would be able to pull this off. Beatrice the normal teenager. What a joke.

"What made you change your look like this?"

The words rushed to my tongue, but I clenched my teeth tighter. He didn't deserve my thoughts or fears. Just because we'd been able to carry on a five-minute conversation without arguing didn't mean we were friends. Or that I had forgiven him.

"You don't know me. This could be how I normally look, and maybe I was trying something new the past few days."

"It's not, and you weren't."

"Oh really? Thank goodness you're here to tell me these things."

"You look too nervous and uncomfortable. Plus, you keep trying to yank down those shorts like you haven't yet realized they aren't getting any longer."

If a person could die of embarrassment, I was pretty sure I was in mortal danger.

"Thanks for the insight. I guess you would know all about girls and their various articles of clothing, right?" The words fell flat out of my mouth, and I flamed red as I fumbled over what I was trying to say. "Clearly, you only care about appearances."

He smiled at my nastiness. It was a languid, indulgent smile. My toes curled, and I stretched my feet under the seat in front of me.

"Well, let's hear it, Beatrice. Tell me all about how shallow I am."

Shelby, tired of Darla's company, leaned over and pointedly tapped Nik on the back. "Nik, I'm bored. Let's go over some lines or something."

"In a moment, Shelby. I'm just dying to hear Beatrice's thoughts on my shitty personality."

"Like she can talk about anyone's personality."

"Dial it back, Shelby. Jesus," he said, crushing me with his attention again. "Well?"

*Happily.* I prepared to educate him on my well-developed insight into his character when Nolan slid into my seat, smooshing me against the window.

"Can I help you?" I asked, shifting my clothes back into place and my hair out of my face.

"Nope, but I'm helping you, sweetheart," he murmured.

I kicked bags under the seat in front of me and tried to make space for my body in the tiny area Nolan had allotted me. "How? By squishing me to death?"

He arched an eyebrow. "By stopping you from ruining what had been the cutest conversation up until you decided to show some teeth."

I blinked, realizing that nobody on this bus had any concept of boundaries. I shoved against Nolan. Hard. "You *ass!*" I hissed. "We were just killing time, and I certainly don't need you to censor me! He'd probably benefit from hearing what I think about him."

Nolan tsked, refolding some of my ruffles. "Please. You guys were like a soap opera. Troy and I were wishing we had some popcorn, while Shelby looked like she was casting a curse on you. It was grade-A entertainment." He sighed. "I was hoping you would last the entire bus trip back, but now it looks like we're going to have to focus on something else."

I sputtered, my brain snagged on his comments and stuck on a loop. "Soap opera . . . what . . . I don't . . ." *Helium. Neon. Argon. Krypton. Xenon. Radon.*

"Bea." He leaned down until we were eye to eye. "You guys have chemistry. He was flirting with you. Accept it."

"You're delusional," I said, drawing out the word. "Anyway, shouldn't you be on Shelby's side if she's actually upset by all this?"

He smirked down at me, and I remembered the stony silence that stretched between them in the cafeteria.

I rolled my eyes. "Oh, I see. You refuse to share but expect me to? Is this what friendship is supposed to be like?"

"Fine," he said with a little huff. "Things have been a little difficult at home."

I paused, waiting for him to continue. Listening was at least a conversational tool I was good at.

"Shelby and I have always been close. Very close. Same grade, same friends, same interests, and sometimes even same crushes," he said with a small smile. "We just want different things for our lives, and I don't think she really thought through what was going to happen after high school. So, imagine my surprise when she found out I got into RISD, and considered that a betrayal instead of me following my dreams."

He pressed his lips together, and I reached out and squeezed his arm.

"I don't think I said it before, but it's incredible that you got in."

He shrugged, pink staining his cheeks. "I thought so too. This is going to be the thing that launches my career, but you know how it goes. Our dad isn't the most involved. He's all business and doesn't really have time for the arts, so it's been the Shelby and Nolan team for a long time."

"You two sound really close."

"Two halves of the same person," he said, frowning as he looked across the aisle at her. "She's going through something, though, and I don't know what she's thinking anymore."

"Where's she going in the fall?"

He exhaled, blowing hair out of his face. "She's been waiting for her big break since she was eight. I think she expected to have a CW show or movie deal by now. She didn't bother applying anywhere, and now she's just stuck."

I frowned. I didn't want any information that would humanize Shelby, but a little trickle of pity leaked through.

I risked a look around him and saw Shelby laughing in delight, her hand on Nik's knee. I darted back into my nice hiding spot behind Nolan, ignoring the searching look he was giving me.

"Stop smiling at me like that."

"Oh, don't mind me; I'm just enjoying the heady aroma of a first crush."

"*I don't have a crush on him*," I said, enunciating every word. "He called me ugly, Nolan."

"What?" Every trace of amusement died.

"At the mixer. I made some stupid comment about wanting to be Rosaline and he told Troy I wasn't hot enough," I said, utterly exhausted. I was tired of telling that story, of trying to interpret Nik's dumb facial expressions this whole ride back, and of defending these shorts. I was just depleted.

"Bea, look—"

"I'm fine; I'm just done with this whole *thing*. Okay?"

He nodded, his features grave, and I curled farther into myself. I didn't want to play this game anymore. I just needed everything to stop for a moment.

We arrived back at the camp a short while later. I could feel myself spiraling, my muscles tensed, ready to erupt up off the seat. *Helium. Neon. Argon. Krypton. Xenon. Radon.* Keep it together for just a little while longer. *Helium. Neon. Argon. Krypton. Xenon. Radon.*

"Well, this was certainly a learning experience," Nolan said.

I ignored him, reaching under the seat to grab at my bags. I needed to get off this bus about thirty minutes ago, and I was seconds away from pulling the emergency door open and escaping out the back.

The driver killed the engine, and everyone stood up, bags rustling, quick hugging, and making plans for later. Nolan moved back to his seat to grab his things, and I fidgeted, willing the people in front of me to get their crap together and move.

Every single atom tensed as Nik stood up next to me. "We never got to finish our conversation."

Part of me wanted to tell him what I didn't get a chance to tell him before. Another part of me knew that I was no longer in any shape to be talking to anybody.

I shrugged. "I don't really remember what we were talking about," I said, my tone impassive.

"You don't remember?" Nik interrupted. "Aren't you supposed to have a really good memory?"

I clutched the bags tighter, ignoring the bait.

He cleared his throat. "I think you have some sort of opinion of me, and I'd like to hear it."

I knew I seemed strange, looking anywhere but at him. "Don't remember, sure it was nothing."

I saw a gap in the people in front of me and surged forward. I jostled a few people out of my way, but I got off that bus in record time. I clutched my bags and power walked toward the girls' cabins. Mia would catch up, and I could always explain away my erratic behavior to Nolan later. They'd understand. I focused on my walking. I focused on the path in front of me. I focused on what I would do when I got back to my room, which was crawl into the bed and pull the blanket over my head. I just needed a time-out. Just a few minutes for everything to stop, just so I could catch up.

"Beatrice!"

I heard him call out behind me—and there was no way I could mistake that accent. I kept walking, walking, walking, and hoping he would get the hint. My practical side was telling me that running away meant he might just keep coming and then I would have to explain why I was *literally* fleeing our conversation. However, pausing for any reason would also mean that I would have to continue speaking to him, and I had officially met my quota.

Once I caught sight of the cabin, I allowed myself to ease up a tiny bit. I dragged my purchases up the stairs and through the door and shoved them into the closest corner. I used the last of my energy to stumble over to the bed and drag the covers over my head.

A few minutes later I heard the screen door slam and a familiar tread stopped right next to my bed. "Umm, want to talk about why we're in burrito mode?"

"I don't know what you're talking about," I said with all the dignity I could muster from under the blankets.

"Okay, we can table this for now. Let's talk about how I saw you left one of your bags and Nik snatched it out of my hands to return it to you. But it looked, to the untrained eye, like you ran away from him?"

I peeled the covers away from my face. "He did what, now?"

She raised an eyebrow, holding up the bag in question, and the mattress dipped under her weight as she sat down next to me. "Are you okay? Was today too much?"

I pulled the covers back over my head, shrugging in the darkness. "I just need things to be just a tiny bit predictable for a little while. Just until I catch up."

Her hand squeezed my shoulder through the blanket. "Well, good news, boo bear. We're about to start rehearsals."

# Chapter Twelve

"IT'S A MILLION DEGREES OUT HERE," I MUMBLED as sweat trickled down my back and pooled at the waistband of my khakis. I squinted in the blinding sun, trying to count the number of campers ahead of us filing into the camp director's building. "I'm not even sure this line is moving."

"You'd probably be more comfortable if you were wearing one of the many pairs of shorts you bought yesterday," Mia said.

My face flushed at the thought of that humiliating bus ride and trying to pull those shorts farther down under Nik's watchful gaze. "Yeah, I think I'm done with experimenting for a while. In fact, I don't really need to talk to my parents that badly." I moved to step out of line, and Mia snatched the back of my sweat-drenched polo and yanked me toward her.

She winced and wiped her now damp hand along her own shorts.

"You deserve that for bossing me around," I said.

"I'd respond with something snarky, but I'm pretty sure you're suffering enough. You'd think it wouldn't take this long for people to just grab their phones and move along." She glared at the line in front of us before fixing her attention back on me. "Why don't you want to talk to them? I'm sure they're worried about how you're settling in."

I shrugged, brushing my limp hair out of my face. "They're my parents, and they know this is uncomfortable for me, but I wouldn't say we're that close. They have their interests, I have mine, and we rarely meet in the middle."

Mia frowned. "And what? You guys never attempted to find anything you all like doing together? You just live separately in the same house?"

"Pretty much. I mean, they get along great with each other. Logistically speaking, I'm likely the cause of the strain in our relationship, but I can't change how I am." I squeezed my eyes shut and wished for a cool breeze or for a meteor to fall out of the sky on top of me.

Mia scoffed. "Bullshit. That's it? You act like you're so un-compromising and tough, but I hate to tell you—you're kind of a marshmallow."

I scrunched my face. "What does a marshmallow act like?"

"You know, surprisingly malleable, very huggable, and squishes into a big puddle at the idea of getting onstage."

"Now, *that's* bullshit. I'm just set in my ways and hate the idea of action movies, rock concerts, or vacations to Disneyland."

Mia made a few choking sounds. "Your parents . . . took . . . you to Disneyland?"

I put my hands on my hips. "Yes, *Mia*, they took me to Disneyland. I was nine, and they insisted I hug a variety of sweaty, costumed strangers. I'm not even sure who they were all supposed to be."

She laughed harder. "I'm so sorry! I know . . . that . . . was so traumatic . . . for you!"

At this point we neared the covered porch of the cabin. I

sighed in relief at the shade. "I know it sounds ridiculous. At least after that disaster, they let me plan our family vacations. They've all been indoor and not based on pop culture since then."

She gave me a pitying glance. "Honestly, I'm not sure they did you any favors. They should have taken your butt to a water park the next summer."

"Mia!"

"What?" she said, laughing. "You sound like you were a little nine-year-old tyrant! Just because you were gifted didn't mean you knew best. If they'd done more things to get you out of your comfort zone, you wouldn't be standing in a line in a-hundred-degree heat in a thick polo and pants."

I stood there a little speechless. I'd expected some sort of support from the best friend I'd ever had, even if we'd only known each other for a few days. "I thought we were friends."

Her gaze softened, and she slowly placed her hands on my shoulders, giving me time to get used to the sensation, and gave me a little shake. "Of course we're friends, you ridiculous person. Do you think that friends only agree with each other? You know I think you're great. You're smart, funny, and only a *little* bit neurotic. I'm just telling you to give these people a break. They've clearly rearranged their entire lives to make your life just a little less uncomfortable. Do your part to meet them halfway." She turned, moving up in line, and chuckled to herself. "Girl, if they were my parents and you complained about their Disneyland vacation, you wouldn't have sat right for a week."

My brain stumbled trying to follow her logic. "So, we're friends, but you think I should also try and change my entire personality?"

She sighed, turning back around with her hands on her hips. "Bea, what do you think friendship looks like?"

"Well," I said, thinking of my prior research and trying to put together a list. "I think it's when people like each other and are supportive and nice to each other."

"You don't think that friends can ever have different opinions?"

"I mean, I guess," I said, drawing on my nonexistent experience. "But not about big stuff."

"Honey," she said, stepping closer. "It's disagreeing on the big stuff that lets you know who's actually in your corner, and who's just blowing sunshine up your skirt." She met my gaze head-on. "You also know that I happen to like your personality, but that's separate from me also feeling like you could try to see things from other people's perspective too." She walked up onto the porch of the camp director's cabin.

I frowned, following her, the comments still stinging. "I assume you and your parents have the perfect relationship?"

"Of course not. They're both doctors, and I want to be an actor. Take a minute to imagine how that has gone over the past few years and top it off with me getting into NYU for *acting*," she said, deflating a little. "They keep hoping I'll change my mind, and sometimes I think that maybe I should. The idea of struggling for a big break and maybe not being able to pay my bills is terrifying, and only a few people really make it. Let alone the added challenges of being a Black actress in Hollywood."

"You're definitely going to become a movie star, and I will see all your movies. Even the awful action ones."

She smiled, rolling her eyes and tugging me through the door and into the slightly cooler lobby. We walked up to the table where Ms. Reid sat with a counselor and a pile of envelopes.

"Ms. Reid," I said.

She raised an eyebrow at the damp patch extending across my stomach. "Little warm out there, isn't it?"

"Feels fine to me," I said, twisting my lips into the best smile I could manage.

She rifled through the packets and pulled out one bearing my name. "Listen, Beatrice, your parents are aware of your little prompter maneuver. A move, I might add, I would have stopped if I'd known about it before the casting list went out."

I wilted a little more under her stern gaze and held my hand out. "Well, let's get this over with then."

"You have three hours before you have to return it. If you're late, you lose privileges and will spend next week's call on speakerphone in my office." She handed over my phone and dismissed me.

I gave Mia a little wave as she walked past already squealing into her phone. I made my way back through the crowd and toward our cabin, trying to organize my thoughts. My argument. My parents didn't technically say I had to be on the stage as one of their requirements for me going to Oxford. Maybe they assumed I'd have no other choice. Maybe they thought I'd be so horrible that they didn't even expect me to get a role. Maybe they would just call the entire thing off now.

I swallowed a fresh wave of nausea before punching in my home number. The cabin was quiet, and Shelby was off probably calling her million friends or hiding in the bushes outside Nik's cabin. Nobody else was around to hear what was going to be an extremely well-structured defense.

"Beatrice!" my mom gasped. "We're so happy to hear your voice! Edwin, it's Beatrice!"

"Put her on speakerphone!" I heard him say.

I cleared my throat. "Hey, guys. How are things back home?"

"Oh, great! Same old, same old with work. We saw Nana a few days ago for dinner, and she's doing great too. Enough about us, though! Tell us about camp!"

"Have you made any friends?" my dad chimed in.

"Yes," I said. "I like the girl I'm bunking with. Her name is Mia, and she's very nice. I've also been spending some time with a guy named Nolan."

"Oh!" Mom exclaimed. "Is this Nolan guy cute?"

I rolled my eyes. "I'm sure he would say so."

"Well," Dad said. "It sounds like you're making a bunch of friends. After only a few days!"

I tried not to take the amazement in his voice personally. "Yeah, everyone's been surprisingly nice."

"Why would that be surprising? You're a lovely girl," he said.

A sarcastic reply came to mind, and I swallowed it down, prickly feelings and all. Mia was right. They were trying. This whole camp was trying. The only one not putting in any effort was me.

"Thanks, Dad," I said, smoothing the blanket on my bed.

"That means you've checked off one of the boxes!" Mom said.

"Yeah, two down and only nine to go."

"I thought we only gave you eight tasks?" Dad said.

I winced. "Ah, my friends may have added a few as well." I wasn't even sure I was going to keep the ones that Nolan added. I didn't need them for Oxford, and they might be a little too much for my brain to handle right now.

"Oh really? What did we forget?" Mom asked.

"I don't really remember," I hedged. "Something about dancing?"

"That's great, honey!" Dad said. "We're glad you told them about what you were trying to accomplish, and that they're interested in helping."

I blinked. "Why wouldn't I tell them?"

Now it was his turn to hedge. "Oh, you know. Some people might be a little worried about telling people about— You know what? It doesn't matter at all. You're doing great and we're really happy for you."

"Now, if this doesn't all work out, I don't want you to get disappointed. You've already come so far with just going to camp, and we're already proud," Mom said.

My heart stuttered. "Does that mean that I'm going to Oxford regardless?"

"Well, *no*. I just wanted you to know that if you don't accomplish everything, we're still proud of you."

"You don't think I'm going to be able to do this?"

She exhaled into the phone. "I have no expectations, Beatrice. All of this is so unlike you. I can't even believe you're there."

"Well, I am. I'm here and I'm going to finish this, and I'm going to Oxford in the fall. You *promised*." My breath hitched, and I could taste the cold, brisk English air. The musty smell of ancient books in the Bodleian. I was so close.

"We're not going to back out of the agreement," Dad said quickly. "We just want to make sure you complete the list in the spirit we intended."

"I'm not a cheater."

"Now, I hate to be the one to bring this up, but we heard something about a prompting role?" Mom said.

I jumped up, pacing around the small room. "Being on the stage wasn't on the list. Plus—you guys really don't understand. These kids are professionals, they all have tons of experience, are extremely comfortable on the stage, and I would have ruined the entire thing. No matter how small my role was. I had to take one for the team, and the fact that the director agreed to it just proves my point."

"Well, I suppose now we'll never know, will we?" she replied.

"What's done is done," Dad said. "You're still going to be

at all the rehearsals and working on scenes with other people, right?"

"I think so," I said. "We haven't started all that just yet. We did the auditions, and yesterday we went shopping."

"Shopping?" Mom exclaimed. "They made you go shopping?"

"They didn't make me," I said. "I chose to go."

"Wait. Really?" Dad said.

"Yes, really." I took a deep breath. "And about that, if you see some charges on my emergency card, there is no need to cancel it. I bought a few things."

I braced myself, and after about ten seconds of silence I said, "Are you still there?"

"Umm." Dad cleared his throat. "What kind of charges?"

"You know, some clothes, and a dress for this party we have at the end of the summer," I said as casually as possible.

"What kind of clothes?" Mom asked. "I know you took a bunch of stuff with you."

"I know," I mumbled. "It's other stuff."

"Not your uniform?" she asked, barely concealing her excitement.

"You know I hate it when you call it that."

"Honey, I think what your mom is trying to say is that we're happy you're trying new things. We don't mind the purchases, and we can't wait—"

"Wait, did you say you bought a dress?"

"Yes, Mom. I bought a dress. There is a dance at the end of the summer."

"Edwin, she bought a dress."

"I know; I heard her the first time. Honey, we're really excited for you! Will someone take pictures for us?"

I pressed my fingers into my sternum, the contact grounding me and the damp polo reminding me that despite all the new clothes hidden in bags under my bed, I wasn't even remotely ready to wear them. They were a mistake, and maybe I could still return them when my parents came to pick me up. "I don't know, Dad. I'll look into that."

"I'm just so happy that this is working out so well! I can't wait until Parents' Day to come see you and meet your new friends," Mom said.

"Are you sure you want to come to Parents' Day? It's just so parents can see the play, and I'm only the prompter. You guys could always go take some sort of vacation, and I could just see you back at the house."

"Of course we're coming to Parents' Day! How could you think we would miss that? This is a big deal. Just because you aren't in the play doesn't mean you aren't a big part of this," Dad said, leaving no room for debate.

"Well, I don't feel very connected to it right now, but you know—maybe things will change."

"Bet on it, sweetheart," he said.

"Now, we don't want to keep you on the phone all day, and I know Dr. Horowitz is waiting for your call. Be sure to share all this exciting news with him, and we'll talk to you next week. Love you!"

"Love you guys too."

I flopped back on my bed. A part of me thought that by just boarding the plane I'd be in the clear and practically on my way to Oxford, but Mom's doubt at my finishing just their eight tasks left a stale taste in my mouth. Their list didn't even include kissing. It *should* be easy.

I could do this. I could do this right, and it wouldn't kill me. If they thought I wasn't prepared to undergo all kinds of embarrassment to get to England, they didn't know me very well.

I scrolled through my brief contacts to Dr. Horowitz's office.

He answered on the third ring, and his familiar voice flooded down the phone.

"Hello, Beatrice. How are you?"

I picked at the loose strings on my blanket. "Fine, Doc."

I could almost hear his smile down the phone. *Beatrice, you get so wrapped up in your own mind that sometimes conversations with you are like pulling teeth.*

"Well? Don't keep an old man waiting; what role did you get?"

I paused for only a moment before forcing some excitement into my voice. "I'm actually going to be the prompter! I won't be onstage, but I'm still going to be working with everyone on all the scenes, so it's great."

"How did you end up with that role?" he asked quietly.

I stuck my chin out, even though he wasn't there to see it. "I asked for it."

"I see." He let the silence hang for a moment before I erupted off the bed.

"You don't understand! I literally almost passed out onstage during auditions. There was no way I was going to make it through a summer of that."

"Was it the anxiety? Did you recite the noble gases?"

"It was *everything*. Having to be in front of everyone, having to be on display when I was clearly awful at something. And there was this group that were laughing and enjoying how terrible I was." My voice trailed off, and in the heavy silence that followed I knew he was thinking of Bryce.

"We're not always excellent at everything we try, and sometimes it takes time to be proficient. We also don't always enjoy when we're struggling at something new, but don't you usually enjoy it when you defeat a particularly difficult problem?"

"It's not the same," I said, chewing my nails bloody.

"Have you met anyone there that you're getting along with?" he asked, switching gears.

"Actually, I have," I said, feeling weirdly proud and wanting to show him how far I'd come. "My roommate is really nice, but I'm not sure if we just had an argument or not."

"Well, arguments can be pretty normal, especially with people who are spending a lot of time together. What was it about?"

I shrugged, everything wilting under the humidity and his expectations. "I don't know. I think she thinks I could do more to spend time with Mom and Dad."

He paused, the silence dragging out between us. "And how do you feel about that?"

"I thought she understood me and liked me for me."

I could just picture him, sitting in his favorite chair in his office and carefully cleaning his glasses to give me a little more time to think. "She said that real friends can disagree, and that I should give them a break."

"I believe she's right."

I tried to swallow the words clogged in my throat. "What am I supposed to do with that?"

"I think you have to decide if you're happier about having real friends or more upset that they don't think you're perfect."

I sat there on the bed while dappled sunlight moved across the floor, and turned everything over and over in my brain.

"Either way, I'm glad you're branching out. Have you shared with them the details of this experiment?"

"Yeah, it all came tumbling out, and they're trying to help me with it."

"Well, that's great!"

I paused for just a moment. "It's probably not like the last time, right? I would know if it was?"

"You mean with Bryce and the rest of those little monsters?"

I blinked at his harsh tone. "Beatrice, growing up can be hard, and young people can often be cruel, but you should know that that sort of trick or joke is unusual. Most people spend time with other people because they like them and they want to develop a relationship with them. Not everything is a trick, and not everybody has an ulterior motive."

"Sure, Doc," I said, trying to keep my voice light. "I know that."

"Do you?" he said, doubt trickling down the phone.

I sighed. "For the most part. There are some other people here that I've had some weird interactions with and I'm not really sure how to interpret them."

"Well, have you just tried asking them?"

I thought of the gleam in Nik's eye as he told me he'd *help* me with Troy. I doubted I'd ever get a serious answer out of him. No, I was on my own, and the best course of action was to just ignore him and avoid any more of these conversations in the future. There, that solved everything. The matter was officially settled, and I wasn't going to spend another second thinking about it anymore.

"I'll keep that in mind, Doc," I said brightly.

# Chapter Thirteen

**BRRRIIINNNGGGGGG.**

"Turn it off, Bea!" Mia moaned from under a pile of blankets.

I sat up, swatting at the alarm clock. "Don't fall back asleep. You're the reason I never get breakfast anymore."

"As if you eat anything substantial anyway," Mia mumbled, swinging her long legs out of bed and stumbling toward the bathroom.

A sharp spike of fear stabbed me in the stomach at the thought of our first actual rehearsal today. The cramping worsened as I imagined scenarios where Mr. G would have me participating in every scene and interrupting people. Maybe, if I was lucky, he would forget about me and I could run off and read in the corner. He'd never had a prompter before. Maybe he wouldn't even know what to do with me. I pulled myself out of bed and stumbled over a shopping bag peeking out from under the bed. Grabbing it off the floor, I rifled through the contents. My fingers brushed the gauzy white tank top inside, and I recoiled like I'd been bitten. What had I been thinking? Did I honestly think I could go to sleep as one person and then suddenly become another? To wear new clothes, new makeup, a new skin, and somehow become "Bea"? She was a confident girl who knew when to smile and how to talk to people. She was a lie.

*Helium. Neon. Argon. Krypton. Xenon. Radon.*

"Get out of your head," Mia said, slouching in the doorway.

"Hmm?" I said, innocence washing over my features.

She walked over, peeling the balled-up bag out of my hands, and put it gently on the bed. "You are under no obligation to wear anything new or do anything you don't want to do. This stuff is just supposed to be fun, right?" That deep little crease was back between her eyebrows.

"Sure," I said, my lips curling into what I hoped looked like a smile.

"Speaking of fun, I actually have a present for you!" She grinned, jumping up and down.

"What?"

I couldn't remember ever receiving a gift from anyone other than my parents.

"Oh, stop looking so spooked! It's just a little something I picked up while we were out." She rifled through her bags and sprang back up with a neon-pink enamel brooch of a book.

I froze as she walked over, placing it in my hands. "You got me a book brooch? A *pink* book brooch?"

"Yeah, you know. Since you like books so much." She stood there with that teasing smile playing across her lips and I scrambled around in my brain for the right response.

"Calm down, Bea! I can see you freaking out," she said, her smile full of forgiveness. "I have no expectations; feel free to wear it or not. I just wanted you to have it."

"Of course I'm going to wear it. I love it!" I clenched it tight in my fist, feeling uncertain ever since my conversation with Dr. Horowitz. "Look, I know I'm a tedious person—"

"Shut up," she said, blowing me a kiss. She headed back to the bathroom with her makeup bag and usual swagger.

I placed the pin carefully on top of my dresser as its shiny pink surface reflected the surprise on my face.

We made it to the auditorium and plopped into some seats along the back row just in time. I unfolded my legs over the seat in front of me and my teeth were already set on edge by the day ahead.

"Okay, okay, listen up." Mr. G clapped his hands until everybody looked up. "I'm thinking that a change of scenery would ease us all into this. We're going to practice down by the lake and break off into small groups to try and cover most of the big scenes today."

"Oh, I would have worn a bathing suit under this if I'd known," Mia said, pouting and grabbing her bag.

I smirked, picking up my messenger bag. Reading quietly and not being forced to listen to rehearsals seemed like a much more pleasant way to spend my day. It was a testament to my new thrill-seeking personality that this would take place next to a body of water.

We shuffled out of the auditorium, down toward the boathouse and dock, when I heard Mr. G calling my name.

"Bea! Hold up a second!"

I reluctantly stepped off to the side and watched him navigate through the throng to make his way over to me. He fumbled with a stack of scripts and had a pencil tucked behind each ear.

"I wanted to talk logistics of how you could best help with the prompting while we have all of these small groups."

I deflated. "Oh sure. What did you have in mind?"

If he noticed my lack of enthusiasm, he blazed right past it. "Well, a lot of our bigger scenes include the same characters, so we'll need you to step in and play a few roles while some of these core characters are off practicing other scenes."

I stiffened, running through a multitude of scenarios in my mind where I was the center of attention, or where people would be watching me and expecting me to be something I wasn't.

"Relax, Bea," he said, smiling. "It's really informal, and everyone will be busy doing their own thing."

My right ring finger was the only nail that hadn't yet been worn down into nothing. I ripped the jagged edge off with my teeth. "Of course. It'll be fine."

He placed a warm hand on my shoulder, guiding me as we followed the group down to the lake. "We'll start off small and have you do a two-person scene, while I get some of the more complicated scenes set up. How does Juliet sound?"

I stumbled, my bag sliding off my slumped shoulder into the dirt. "Um, that's pretty much the most difficult role for me in this entire play. Maybe I can work with Shelby and do Romeo?" I was just picking the lesser of two evils at this point.

He reached down and picked up my bag. "I need to get a start on this scene with Juliet, Nurse, and Lady Capulet. I'm sure we can do that later in the day. Don't worry. Nik is a pro and will walk you through everything."

I sighed as he handed over the bag and jogged ahead without a backward glance.

The group congregated under a grove of trees, and I power walked over to Mia.

She raised an eyebrow. "What was that about? You look like he's given you the lead role."

"Almost," I said. "I'm supposed to run lines with Nik while the rest of you are doing other scenes." I fumbled around in my bag, jamming an extra pencil into my bun just to keep it upright.

Amusement lit up her entire face. "The Juliet to his Romeo? Oh, this is going to be amazing."

"Hardly. Do me a favor and try and speed through your scene, so we can all move on."

She nodded to where Shelby and Nik were talking to Mr. G. Shelby was arguing and gesturing between her and Nik, while Mr. G held his hands up in protest. "I have a feeling that Shelby will be doing everything in her power to hurry through every scene that doesn't include Nik."

It said something unflattering about me that I was pleased somebody else was as irritated with today's configuration as me.

Mr. G herded the small groups scattered along the edge of the lake, and I wandered down to the shore. Tapping the placid water with the toe of my loafer, I racked my brain for the number of times in my life when I'd swam in a natural body of water. Maybe a few times when I was a kid, but the beach was never at the top of my list for fun. I walked to the dock and followed its long expanse into the lake. The breeze ruffled my hair, and I massaged the knot of tension at the base of my neck.

Someone cleared their throat and I spun around.

Nik. Of course.

I shifted under his gaze. "Ah. You're ready to start?"

His dimple winked at me before disappearing. "Don't sound so excited."

"You know I'm not excited."

He rolled his eyes. "I'm not exactly thrilled about this either. How about we get this over with as painlessly as possible?"

I nodded back toward the shore where the groups were starting to practice. "Should we go back?"

He shook his head. "No, I'd rather stay out here."

I shrugged, already resigned.

"Okay, let's start with act two, scene two."

I shuffled around in my head until I found what he wanted. My stomach roiled with the selection. *Stop it.* I was the prompter, and there was no reason to be nervous. I wasn't acting in these little exercises.

He studied me, frowning at my defeated posture, before tossing his script down.

"How about we break the ice a little bit before starting? Move around a bit, Beatrice." He took my bag off my shoulder, placed it on the dock, and started jogging in place. He nodded toward me to start as well, his hair tumbling into his eyes. His long legs moved in an easy rhythm, and I hesitated a moment before joining.

"What exactly is this accomplishing?"

He sighed, exasperation bleeding into the sound. "You're too wound up and already fixating on how miserable you intend to feel. Maybe this will help you focus on other things." He switched it up, breaking into jumping jacks, and I followed with clumsy movements.

"I'm not an athletic girl, you know."

He smiled, but the shape of his mouth was sharp and not at all comforting. "You don't seem to be a theater nerd either, but here we are."

The sun warmed me, and I felt the first prickles of sweat start to bead. I pressed my hand into my side, my breath coming in gasps. "Okay, that's enough."

He nodded, finding his place in the script. I studied him as he rolled his shoulders and paced in front of me. One minute he was the prickly boy who hurt my feelings, and in the next minute his entire demeanor changed. The lines of his body became more graceful, his posture shifted. He held his head high—an indolent prince. As this stranger emerged in front of me, I wasn't sure if it made things easier or not. He stopped pacing and turned, his eyes fixed on my movements. The hairs on my arms stood on edge.

"*But soft!*" he murmured. "*What light through yonder window breaks?*

*It is the east, and Juliet is the sun.*

*Arise, fair sun, and kill the envious moon.*"

He stalked around me as if to get a better look.

"*Who is already sick and pale with grief,*

*That thou, her maid, art far more fair than she.*"

I was ten shades of red, and I forced my hands to stop from touching my face. As a rational person, I knew he wasn't talking about me. But, god, the way he spoke, I *believed* it. The words crawled under my skin, and I stared at the ground. I wasn't sure what he'd see on my face if I let him. Instead, I focused on the old, cracked wood of the dock and traced the whorls with my shoe as his words tumbled over me.

"*. . . Oh, that I were a glove upon that hand,*

*That I might touch that cheek!*"

"*Ay me,*" I said, risking a glance as he moved closer.

"*She speaks.*" He grinned. "*O, speak again, bright angel! For thou art*

*As glorious to this night, being o'er my head,*

*As is a winged messenger of heaven.*"

His voice was pitched low, intimate.

I cleared my throat and stumbled over the words. "*O Romeo, Romeo. Wherefore art thou Romeo? Deny thy father and refuse thy name—*"

"Beatrice," he said cutting off my rushed speech. "It's not a race to see who can finish their lines the fastest."

I bristled. "I am just filling in so you can practice your lines. I don't require any acting advice, as *I* am not acting."

He tapped the script against his leg. "Would it really be so bad? Whatever brought you here, you're in the acting concentration at a theater camp. A little effort isn't unreasonable."

I bit my lip and alternated between wanting to explain to him and wanting to shove the play—and the entire summer—down his throat. I settled on silence.

He rubbed his jaw and took a deep breath. "It can be a little difficult when you first start."

He moved closer, and I remained stiff as a board. He paused for a moment and gave me an evaluating look.

"Can we try something?"

I shrugged, and he extended his hands out to my shoulders, giving me plenty of time to move away. When I didn't, he grabbed my shoulders and propelled me around to face the water. His fingertips pressed into my clavicles, and he quickly released me.

"You're a young woman who had an encounter with a fascinating guy. You're a little sheltered, and probably more than a little bored, and fancy yourself in love with him. You're just looking out onto the world, alone with your thoughts, and whispering things you're not brave enough to say to anyone." I could hear him retreating behind me. "I'm not here; I'm not watching. Just try and see if you can find some common ground with this character who suddenly finds herself out of her depth."

I took a shallow breath as a mantle of responsibility settled heavy on my shoulders. This notion that I was obligated to give an honest effort to this experiment I had taken on. He was almost trying, I reasoned. I could maybe offer the same in return. I ignored the slick fear of failure and started again.

"*O Romeo,*" I said in hushed tones, "*Romeo. Wherefore art thou Romeo?*

*Deny thy father and refuse thy name.*

*Or, if thou wilt not, be but sworn my love,*

*And I'll no longer be a Capulet."*

I finished stronger, and louder, my tongue tripping over the strangeness of her speech. I imagined I was the type of girl who talked to the moon.

*"Shall I hear more, or shall I speak at this?"* he said. A lover's whisper. A prayer murmured in the dark.

I turned back to see him watching me, his expression unreadable. I turned away again, pretending I was alone again on the banks of the lake.

*"'Tis but thy name that is my enemy,"* I reasoned.

*"Thy art thyself, though not a Montague.*

*What's Montague?"*

I walked closer to the edge of the dock, casting my thoughts out onto the water's still surface.

*"It is nor hand, nor foot,*

*Nor arm, nor face, nor any other part*

*Belonging to a man. O, be some other name!"*

I warmed up, getting into it as if I were in a spirited debate.

*"Romeo!"* I finished louder. *"Doff thy name,*

*And for that name, which is no part of thee,*

*Take all myself!"*

I turned, smiling, hands on my hips and chin thrust in the air. I'd met his challenge, and although I may not have been a starry-eyed young girl madly in love, I was Juliet who reasoned. Juliet who acknowledged the danger and disaster that was falling for the son of her family's worst enemy, but who was able to talk herself into believing for a moment that it would be possible.

That loving just the boy alone would be enough.

I barely had time to recover as he moved around me. Haughty. Master of everyone and everything he touched, and so sure of his place in the world. Even more so now that the one girl he wanted was just caught talking about him.

*"I'll take thee at thy word,"* he said. A promise.

*"Call me but love, and I'll be new baptized:*

*Henceforth I never will be Romeo."* He spreads his arms wide, smirking.

A rush of indignation burned through me. I felt the pressing need to take him down a peg or two.

*"What man are thou that, thus bescreened in night,*

*So stumbles on my council?"* I said, glaring at him as if he were the lowest of the low.

He winced, bowing beautifully, but not sincere. He held the form and peeked up at me and winked.

*"By a name I know not how to tell thee who I am."* He straightened and brushed imaginary lint off his shirt. *"My name, dear saint, is hateful to myself."*

He closed the gap between us.

*"Because it is an enemy to thee."* He murmured the last word softy and reached up, catching one of the errant curls trying to escape my bun between his fingers. His voice pitched low, and I leaned closer as the lines of reality blurred.

*"Had I it written, I would tear the word."*

A peal of laughter rang out back on land, and I jolted backward. My face burned as the spell was broken and reality rushed back at me. He remained very still, watching my progress as I took several more steps backward and reestablished a clear barrier. *Helium. Neon. Argon. Krypton. Xenon. Radon. This isn't real. You weren't hot enough to play Rosaline, and he is the sort of guy who thought he had every right to comment on your appearance. To judge you.* I smoothed my hair back from my face and bent down and picked up my messenger bag. I felt more comfortable slinging it across my body, the weight familiar. "You know, I'm not sure how much practice you need running lines.

If I'm not mistaken, you haven't looked at your script either." I nodded at it, still closed in his hand.

He snorted, looking out across the lake—his profile bathed in sunlight. "I'm the product of Shakespearean actors. You think just because I don't spend all my time studying I don't know *this* play?"

"No," I said, tripping over myself, "I was just saying that this is pointless if you already know the scene."

He still wouldn't look at me but nodded before chuckling to himself. "You're absolutely right."

I held my breath as he walked past me back toward the small groups, feeling as if we were each having a different conversation.

He paused and my breath caught in my throat before he turned back. "You know, for a moment there, I thought you were really Juliet." The comment felt like it was aimed to hurt.

He didn't wait for my reply and approached Mr. G before being swallowed back into another scene. He didn't turn back around, and all the feelings I recognized and some that I didn't jangled around inside me. I beat down the more disturbing ones that kicked me for shutting down before the scene ended and, perhaps the most disturbing one of all—how often he made me forget that I disliked him.

# Chapter Fourteen

"**WHAT ARE YOU DOING SULKING OVER HERE?**"
A shadow blocked out the sun, and I smiled and turned toward the exasperated voice.

"Sulking? It took a lot of effort and bad acting on my part to be able to sit over here quietly and read my book," I said from my place sitting out on the dock. I looked around Mia to see campers walking back up toward the auditorium.

Mia bent down and swiped the book out of my hand before shoving it in my bag. She stuck out her hand. "Up you go; he's letting us go early today, and it's time to grab bathing suits!"

"What, now?" The sun hung high in the sky, and I glanced at my watch, surprised at how much time had passed.

She pulled me upright. "I'm melting here, and we're all going to cool off in the lake."

I brushed my clothes off and frowned at the murky water. "You can't see the bottom."

"I feel you could use a hearty dose of mystery in your life. You can swim, right?"

I slung my bag over my shoulder and matched her pace as we walked back toward our cabin. "Ish? I'm not going to be winning any races, but I doubt I'd drown if left to my own devices."

She slapped me on the back. "That's the spirit!"

I dragged my body down the path, my legs feeling heavier and heavier with each step.

"Is it just going to be us two?" I asked.

She tossed a smile over her shoulder. "We're in the middle of the woods with a bunch of other teenagers and nothing else to do. What do you think?"

I wilted a little more and pulled my limp ponytail off my neck. "Well, how did practice go?"

"Really good! I think I'm getting the feel for this character and putting my own shine on her! I'm excited for my parents to see it!" she said, floating down the path to our cabin. She turned her face up to the sun, not a care in the world, before skipping up the stairs of our porch.

A smile tugged on my lips. "That's sweet that you're close."

Her smile wavered a little. "We are, but I think I can do something really special with this role, and I want to reassure them I'm not wasting my time with all this." She pulled open the door and I followed her into our room.

"I'm sure they don't think that."

"They've always been my biggest supporters, but things have been a little strained since I declared my major," she said, throwing her bag down. "Now, they would love you, Ms. Mathematics and Statistics."

"Because of my sparkling personality?"

"Exactly right." She pulled out a bunch of bikinis and started mixing and matching, while I eased open my top drawer and pulled out my old one-piece.

"What do you think?" she asked, holding up a bright coral top and sparkling gold bottoms.

"I think you're asking for a wardrobe malfunction."

She laughed. "I'm going to take that as a yes."

I pulled on my old suit, the black shiny material dulled to gray, and ignored the evaluation from across the room. She didn't say a word as I changed into it, but I felt her circle around me as I dug around for a large T-shirt to throw on over it.

"I take it back."

"Hmm?" I said, distracted.

"When did you get that suit?" she asked, picking up a bag of towels.

"Umm, a few years ago? I don't swim that often."

"The suit and you are both classic, in all the best ways."

I flushed, pulling a baggy shirt over my body. "Well, that settles it; I'm going to sit on the dock completely covered."

"Oh, I'm just teasing you. Come on, Bea." She pulled me toward the door, and I bounced off Nolan's chest as he burst into the room.

"About time! What was taking so long?" He yanked the bag of towels out of Mia's hand and threw it over his shoulder as he herded us out the door.

I frowned. "Do you all still have your cell phones? How'd you know we were going to the lake?"

"What else is there to do? All us regulars have an established routine for the summer," he said.

I smoothed out the shapeless fabric covering me as Nolan swung an arm around my shoulders, putting me in a headlock. "Whatcha got on under there, boo?"

"None of your business," I said tartly, giving him a small smile to take the sting out of it.

He pulled the loose neck of the shirt open and peered down. "Okay, okay, girl. You can work with that."

I yanked the material out of his hands and pressed it close to my body. "I'm just going to be relaxing on the dock, thank you very much."

"We'll see about that."

By the time we got back to the lake, it was clear that everyone else had the same bright idea. Groups from every concentration splashed in the water and milled around on the shore.

"Looks like Shel is already holding court out on the Island," Nolan said, striding up to the water's edge.

A shriek pierced the air, and I looked up to where one of the nameless, faceless tan guys in the acting group threw Darla off a wooden platform floating in the middle of the lake. The remaining people on the large raft screamed in laughter as she came up sputtering.

"How'd they get out there?" I asked, frowning at the distance.

Mia shrugged. "It's not that far, and pretty shallow most of the way out."

Nolan guided me down the dock. "Don't worry, Bea; I'll carry you when you get tired of doggy-paddling."

I snatched the towel bag and sat down, swinging my legs over the edge of the dock. "I'm going to stay here on dry land. You two go enjoy your noisy games out there."

I dug my book out and sighed happily, finding my spot from earlier.

"Fine," Mia said. "But try not to get horribly sunburnt. I'm betting you'll join us once it gets to be a million degrees out here." She dropped her shoes and cover-up next to me and with a giant "Whoop" cannonballed off the dock.

I fell back, laughing, and tried to protect my book the best I could. Nolan followed Mia's lead, and cool water sprayed the end of the dock.

"Thanks for nothing!" I yelled. With one last wave from Nolan, they swam out toward the platform. I picked at the giant loose shirt that was now clinging to my body. I peeled it off before abandoning it in a wet pile. A breeze whipped through the trees, ruffling my hair, and goose bumps prickled across my skin despite the sun. I closed my book and inhaled the experience of being outside. Fresh grass, bleached wood, and pure, distilled sunshine flooded my senses. I took a deep breath, filling my lungs to the brim.

I was enjoying something new, and I didn't think I could surprise myself like this anymore.

I wiped my book along my thigh, and it fell open to the list that I was using as a bookmark. I pulled a pen out of my bag and made a bold check next to number five: *Do an outdoor activity.* The ink stretched across the paper with relish.

"You're going to burn if you stay out here like this," said an annoyingly perfect English voice.

I slammed the book closed. Squinting against the blinding sun, I made out the outline of Nik and Ben. "Noted," I said, ignoring them and flipping back to my page, the list briskly folded and tucked in the back.

"I'm serious, Beatrice; you're really pale," Nik said. "Did you even put on sunscreen?"

"I'm not a child," I snapped. I didn't need his help to function in the world. If anything, I functioned much better if I didn't have to interact with him at all. I angled my body away from them, dangling my legs in the cool water. The skin across my shoulders pulled tightly, and I clenched my jaw. I would rather drown myself in this lake before acknowledging he had a point. I could always look for some sunscreen in the bags next to me once he left.

Ben shifted, glancing between the two of us. "Umm, so is everyone else out on the Island?"

"Yep, Mia's out there," I said, opening to my page again.

Nik coughed, and I looked up.

Ben was bright red. "I was just . . . trying to see where people . . . might be." He rubbed the back of his neck before pulling off his shirt and shoes and jumping into the water.

I watched him as he waded out to the platform, and raised an eyebrow at Nik.

"That was a little direct for him," he said, answering my unspoken question. "He's shy."

"He already knows she likes him; why bother being shy?" I shrugged. "I knew what he was asking, and I answered it for him."

"I know you find us regular humans confusing, but he was probably hoping we'd all pretend that we didn't know, while he was still finding the courage to ask her out."

I slammed the book shut. "I'm not a robot," I said. "Forgive me for not wanting to play stupid games that insult everyone's intelligence."

"Stand down, Beatrice. I'm just telling you how things are."

I smiled, dripping with insincerity. "Thank you so much for your help. Have fun out there!" I glanced toward the platform and back at him.

A hint of a smile flitted across his features. "You know, it's kinda nice here on the dock. I think I'll stay for a while." He yanked his shirt off, revealing a wide expanse of skin. I froze as he eased himself down next to me and dangled his legs in the water.

*Don't look at him, don't look at him,* I chanted to myself.

All of my muscles tensed, and I breathed in little huffs as I tried to talk myself off the edge. *Helium. Neon. Argon. Krypton. Xenon. Radon. Just breathe. There's no reason for your body to be experiencing a fight-or-flight response; he's just a stupid boy.* I struggled for indifference. I risked a glance, and he was evaluating me under long, dark lashes. His head tilted to the side, and I squirmed.

"I could always go somewhere else if I'm bothering you that much," he said.

"Bothering me? You can sit wherever you want; I couldn't care less," I said, clearing my throat. I could see the lean lines of his form in my periphery. It was an awful lot of skin.

"Okay." He turned his head, and I could see the hint of a dimple. "So, Beatrice—"

"Bea," I interrupted reflexively.

"Beatrice," he continued as if I hadn't spoken. "Are you willing to tell me what brought you here yet?"

"Nope," I grumbled. Realizing that he was going to stick around and irritate me for the foreseeable future, I rifled around in Nolan's bag looking for sunscreen. Finding a tube, I methodically applied it. I scowled as he raised a smug eyebrow.

"Fine, I'll play along. What brought you here this summer?" I asked.

"Why, Beatrice, are you trying to have a conversation with me?"

"Forget it," I said, rubbing lotion onto my knees.

He held his hands up in mock surrender. "I'm just playing with you. You want to know my deepest, darkest secrets? I'll spill. It all began about eighteen years ago on a rainy evening in West London."

I snorted while trying to swipe sunscreen on my back. "You're even more dramatic than Mia."

He laughed, loud and genuine. I bit my lip hard as a traitorous smile tried to surface.

"Somehow I doubt that. Do you need help getting your back?"

"Nope!" I yelped. "I'm sure everything is covered." I shoved the tube back in Nolan's bag and turned to him, trying to recall all the articles I read about thoughtful listening and the art of conversation. "So, Nikhil, you were—telling me about your childhood?"

The strange look was back. "Not really. I know you've heard that my parents helped start this camp. Pretty sure you've used that against me on at least one occasion," he said. "This is their baby, so of course I would go all of the years I was able." That pinched look softened into something almost sweet.

I flushed but couldn't apologize. He'd said some unflattering things about me as well. I dug deep for my calm, conversant personality. "How nice to have parents so involved. One would hope you also enjoy the time you spend here, and that it wasn't all for their benefit."

"Of course I enjoy it; I love acting. I mean, when I was a kid it took me a while to realize that it wasn't normal for families to recite *King Lear* over waffles or have Monologue Mondays where we all presented a piece we were currently working on." He paused, giving me another weird look. "What's going on here?" He waved his hand in my direction.

"What do you mean?" I asked, blinking rapidly.

"You. You've gotten all weird and formal," he said. "Go back to ignoring me or yelling at me, but this is like talking to a teacher or a friend of my parents."

"Excuse me?" I snapped. "I will have you know that I am displaying textbook listening skills and asking excellent leading questions."

He tensed; his lips pressed so tightly together they blanched. I got the strange sensation he was trying not to laugh, and I knew that if he did I would have no choice but to throw myself off the dock.

He leaned in my direction as one of his renegade black curls tumbled over his forehead. "Beatrice, did you read a book on how to talk to people?"

I pulled away and fought the urge to fidget under his gaze. Refusing to answer the question would make me a coward, but admitting it also seemed pathetic. I settled for somewhere in the middle. "We all know our skill set."

This time he did smile. No anger or condescension—just pleasure. "We certainly do."

My stomach dropped a bit, almost like I was in free fall. We'd go from arguments, like earlier on this same dock, to moments like this. I couldn't even keep up with him if I wanted to, and I didn't. I definitely didn't.

"Look, Beatrice, maybe we should clear the air or—"

"Nik!" a shrill voice blasted from the water. We both turned toward the platform to see Shelby waving her hands over her head. *"Nik!"*

"I'm not sure if you realize, but I think Shelby has something important she wants to share with you," I whispered.

*Like mono*, I thought.

"I noticed," he said.

"Nik!"

"I wonder if she thinks you haven't seen her yet," I said, squinting at her flapping form.

"Hard to tell," he said. "How many more 'Nik's do you think she'll yell before coming over here?"

"Don't you dare bring her over here!" I said. "Go out there and be with your own kind."

He leaned back, placing his hands behind his head, and smiled. "Nah, I like it over here. I think I'll stay."

I sputtered, blinded by abdominal muscles.

*"Nik!"*

"That's it," I declared, flinging myself into the cool water. My head went under, and my feet squished into something soft on the bottom. I rocketed to the surface gasping.

"Beatrice! Are you okay? Can you swim?" he demanded, his face tight.

I swiped my hair out of my eyes. "Don't be ridiculous; of course I can swim. I was just surprised. I wasn't expecting the bottom of the lake to feel like the inside of a creature's mouth."

He exhaled sharply, leaning back. "What's your plan now?"

"To leave you to your fate," I said as regally as I could muster. I turned, making my way out to the platform little by little. I knew Nolan was joking about the doggy paddle, but it was a perfectly usable form of swimming. I was almost halfway there when a long body sliced through the water and overtook me. Nik paused long enough to give me a wink before continuing.

"Ass," I mumbled, continuing my slow pace.

Mia and Nolan were whooping and shouting encouragements by the time I made it out to the Island. Nolan swung an arm out and fished me out of the lake, and I collapsed on my back staring up at a brilliant blue sky.

"You okay there, muffin? Not big on the cardio?" Nolan leaned over, blocking out the sun.

"You're carrying me back," I gasped.

"Oh, I'm sure we could find someone to volunteer for the job." He nodded over to where Shelby was practically sitting on top of Nik.

"Your sister is taking me back? How nice, I wasn't aware she liked me."

Mia walked up, joining the huddle over me. "What are we talking about?" she whispered.

"How all of you are dripping on me," I moaned, rubbing my face.

"Should we tell her what Shelby was saying when she spotted the two of them over there?" Mia asked, wiggling her eyebrows.

"I don't think I want to know."

Nolan sighed. "I promise you, if I'd had my phone I could have live-tweeted the entire thing. I would have gone viral."

I sat up, forcing them to scatter. "Enough of that, what's the point of being out here?"

Mia shrugged. "We sit; we talk; we throw each other off the edge."

I nodded. "I don't know why I keep looking for a reason in any of the things we do."

"Learn to relax, dollface," Nolan said, pulling me to my feet.

"It's fun!" Mia said, looking over her shoulder at Ben.

I winced, thinking of my misstep with him earlier. "Hey, Mia. I should probably tell you—"

Nolan promptly scooped me up and threw me into the lake.

I'm pretty sure I was still screaming as I went underwater, and I reemerged furiously paddling and sputtering. The whole raft was still laughing as I reached out and clutched the side.

Nik crossed the platform to meet me as I struggled to climb back up.

"Need a hand there, killer?" he said, extending his own.

I considered it, but Shelby ran up and curled a hand around his arm. Like contact between them was the most natural thing.

"Hey, Nik, we should practice some of our scenes while we're out here," she said.

Having a good idea which scenes she wanted to work on, I rolled my eyes so hard I almost lost hold of the raft. Ignoring his still-outstretched hand, I ungracefully shimmied my way back onto dry land. Glaring daggers at Nolan, I promised revenge, but he didn't even have the decency to look concerned.

After a moment, I realized the conversation behind me now *involved* me.

"I'm sure you remember most of your part," Shelby said. "If not, we have the prompter girl here, and she can remind you."

"Sorry, I'm off the clock," I said. Shelby turned away in a

huff, but seeing Nik's relieved smile, I had to interject, "Don't be modest, Nik. Based on our practice earlier, I'd say you know the play as well as I do."

He narrowed his eyes. "Oh, I wouldn't say that. If we practiced, you'd *definitely* have to participate to help us out."

"Don't be silly!" I exclaimed, dismissing his concerns and enjoying myself immensely.

Mia laughed. "You know, I wonder who knows it better! Our resident genius or the guy whose parents created a Shakespearean summer camp."

Nik rolled his eyes. "I have read plenty of Shakespeare, regardless who my parents are."

Ben came up beside him, nodding. "I've seen Shakespearean-themed movies with Nik, and he knows them backward and forward." He inched closer to Mia, the words for her alone.

"No way," Nolan said. "Our girl would murder him."

"What do you say, Beatrice?" Nik asked, a cocky smile and my name on his lips.

At the slightest whiff of a challenge, my vicious competitive tendencies perked up. "I wouldn't want to hurt your feelings. . . ."

"Try me," he said, eyes flashing.

"All right then," I said. "Rules?"

We paused as the group tried to figure out the best way to measure our abilities.

"What about quotes? Any of Shakespeare's plays, and the other person has to guess where it came from?" Ben said.

I nodded. "Okay, that sounds reasonable. Any play, and any line at all?"

"Whatever you think you can come up with," Nik said, grinning.

"Terms?" I raised an eyebrow at Nik.

"You don't want to do this for satisfaction's sake?"

I shook my head. "If I'm putting forth some effort, I want to win something."

"Okay," he said, crossing his arms. "What do you want if you win?"

I bit my lip and turned back to my friends for advice. Mia shrugged, and Nolan was too busy smiling smugly to be of much use. I racked my brain and realized that there was no scenario where Nik could take over my prompting duties. He had his own leading role to worry about. The only other alternative was embarrassment.

"Nolan, what's the heaviest, most cumbersome costume in the play?" I asked, a smile stretching across my lips as Nik's eyes narrowed.

"Definitely the Nurse's," Nolan said. "There's padding, a wig, and we're experimenting with the idea of a nose prosthetic."

"Sounds perfect," I said, delighted. "If I win, you'll have to wear the Nurse's full costume for a day. Including the prosthetic and old-lady makeup."

The raft erupted in laughter, and Nik flushed a bit. He shook out his raven-black curls and nodded. "It's like that, huh? Okay, then I guess I'm going to have to pick something equally awkward for you."

"Bring it on," I said with false bravado as Nolan squeezed my shoulders. My stomach spiked with fear, and I tilted my chin up. I imagined it was a lot easier for Nik to make me uncomfortable than vice versa. Scenarios of him making me take over his role for an entire day, or walk around in a bathing suit during practice, or any number of nightmares raced through my head.

"It won't be that bad," he promised. "In fact, it's the smallest thing in the world."

I leaned forward, waiting to hear what fresh hell he'd come up with.

He smiled. "A kiss."

The only thing that could have possibly shaken me from the stupor those two words created was the choking sound that emanated from Shelby.

"Why would you want to kiss her?" she demanded, slapping his arm.

"Maybe I should clarify; *she* would be the one who'd choose to kiss *me*," he said, his expression mirroring our practice from earlier. "An active participant."

He was watching me carefully, but I'd pretty much frozen. My chest was too tight to pull in air, and my knees had locked rigidly into place.

"If it's too high a price to pay, we can just declare me the winner and forget about it," he said quickly, something I couldn't name flickering across his face.

"Nope, those terms sound perfect," Nolan interjected, spinning me around and pulling me into a huddle with Mia.

"Breathe, baby," Mia said, her eyes sparkling.

"I—I—I don't know why," I sputtered, trying to process the situation and come up with a rational path forward. *Helium. Neon. Argon. Krypton. Xenon. Radon.*

"I do!" Mia crooned.

"Shhh!" Nolan hissed. "We all know why; she's just going to take a little more time to get there." He put his hands on my shoulders and crouched down until we were eye level.

"Do you think you'd lose?" he asked, squeezing my shoulders until he came into focus.

I thought for a moment, finding clarity in a problem I could work through. "No. He knew Romeo's part very well, but I know some pretty obscure Shakespeare."

"Well, there you go!" he said. "There's no chance of you losing, so no reason to freak out! Also, I'm going to take this opportunity to deploy number seven on your list."

"Wait, what?"

"I double-dog dare you to do this."

"You're using the list on me?"

"I'm using this situation to help you check some shit off! You already told me there was no chance of him winning, so get over there and embarrass him in front of all of us!" He paused, waiting to make sure I was okay, until I gave him a shaky nod.

With that settled, he spun me back around and marched me to the center of the raft. Keeping an arm around my shoulders for support, he declared, "Our champion has agreed to the terms. Let the great Shakespeare-off commence!"

I nodded, my breath coming in little spurts. He was right. This could check off my fourth task. I would be 36 percent done with the list. That made this all worth it.

Shelby was rapidly whispering in his ear, but Nik studied me and raised a mocking eyebrow. "You're sure about this? I'm happy with us just declaring my superiority in all things Shakespeare."

"Oh, I'm sure," I said as Mia came up on my other side and gave my arm a squeeze. "Since you're so confident, why don't you start?"

"I'd be delighted to," he said, strolling up to me in the middle of the raft. He tapped his chin for a moment before saying, "Let's start a little easy, shall we?"

"Don't start easy on my account," I said, faking confidence I absolutely did not have.

He smiled. *"You are the sweetest flower of all the field."*

My mind lurched as I processed the line and tried to ignore the snickering of the other people on the raft. I tilted my face up at him, and if his hard smile was any indicator—he was *not* going to play fair. He was going to unnerve me and win because I was too flustered to think. I straightened my spine and glared at him. Not today, Satan.

"You're right; that was too easy. *Romeo and Juliet*," I scoffed. "I've got one for you: *Let's meet as little as we can.*

*I do desire we may be better strangers.*"

My side of the raft cackled in amusement as he winced.

*It's all an act*, I chanted in my head.

"Ouch," he said. "That is, of course, *As You Like It*."

My stomach dropped. He would not be easily beaten, and I was forced to reevaluate some of my previous opinions of him.

He took a few steps closer. "*Why, now I see there's mettle in thee, and even from*

*this instant do build on thee a better opinion than*

*ever before.*"

"*Othello*." I moved around him, trying to maintain the distance. I scrolled through all the quotes ferreted away in my brain. "*I think thou art an ass.*"

He barked in laughter. "*The Comedy of Errors*, and a little heavy-handed, don't you think?"

I shrugged.

He took a step closer. "*Thou art so lovely fair and smell'st so sweet*

*That the sense aches at thee.*"

Nolan reached out and squeezed my shoulder, and about 90 percent of my body was having difficulty performing basic tasks.

"*Othello*—" My voice cracked. "Apparently you have a thing for one of his more psychotic works."

He shrugged. "I was inspired."

"Me too," I said, teeth bared. "*What rubbish and what offal!*"

Surprise flitted across his features. He thought for a moment.

"Almost got me with that one. The longer quotes are easier. I'm going to go with *Julius Caesar*?"

I nodded, my shoulders drooping. Shelby gave up her position as a silent bystander and marched up to where we were standing. "It's almost time to go back and get ready for dinner," she announced, her voice pitched higher than normal.

He grinned. "We can all go back, but not until I take my turn. If Beatrice gets this right, we can call it the end of round one, and we'll just have to pick it up again later."

I ignored the sounds of snickering behind me and nodded. He gave me a beautifully wicked smile that I felt deep in my gut, and I knew it was going to be bad.

He chuckled. "Since you tried to get me with a short quote, I will repay you the same way."

I braced myself as he came closer. I stared straight ahead as he stopped right in front of me, my eyes fixed on the little divot between his clavicles.

"*I will call you my mouse,*" he murmured.

My face caught fire as I imagined how he saw me. All skittering, nervous, awkward Bea. Always hiding in corners, and always running. I pulled my gaze up solidly to his face and glared as he stared down at me, his expression always unreadable. I'll show him *mouse*.

"*Hamlet,*" I barked before turning my back on him and walking into the arms of my cheering friends.

# Chapter Fifteen

THE NEXT MORNING I DRAGGED THE STACK OF
shopping bags out into our cramped little living room, pulling out tops and shorts, and two dresses I must have had heatstroke to agree to. Mia's soft snoring paused for a moment, and I eased the door closed behind me.

I'd slept badly the night before, with visions of that raft and stumbling over quotes from Shakespeare. A little mouse running in circles reciting *Hamlet*, *The Tempest*, and *Macbeth* like the world's worst fever dream. I had to have been out of my mind to agree to that competition. In hindsight it felt like some elaborate prank on weird, awkward Beatrice. *Flirt with the nerdy home-schooled girl who doesn't do well with social cues. Pretend like you want to kiss her after telling people that you didn't think she was pretty enough to be Rosaline. It's just like Bryce all over again.* I squeezed my eyes shut until the world paused. It didn't matter. None of it mattered, and I wasn't doing this for *them*. I had an entire life ahead of me at Oxford.

That was, after all, what I wanted.

I was out of bed before the dawn, having officially given up on sleep, and ready to take a few moments to myself before the whirlwind of another day started. No screaming through bathroom doors, no lukewarm showers or scrambling to get out the door always running late. It was here, sitting in our dingy common area and sipping on weak coffee, that I could finally find some threads of myself again. There were parts of me that were changing whether I intended for them to or not, but the familiarity of old habits was soothing.

The weak rays of early morning flickered through the window and cast a bleak light on all the shopping bags that were supposed to make me a normal person. I'd avoided them since their purchase, and Mia and Nolan had been careful not to comment on the fact that I was still walking around business casual as usual. I was chalking this impulse up to just another bad decision made over the past few days. I was never going to be that girl who ran around camp in a skirt or clothes in a color that wasn't routinely found in nature. I didn't like a lot of synthetic material, and I was hopeless with patterns. I was, however, practical. The practical side of me knew that I'd spent an embarrassing amount of money on clothes I could probably no longer return, but maybe there was something I could salvage from this. I tossed back the rest of my coffee and slowly stacked shirts with the pants and shorts that they were bought with. While the resulting outfits looked trendy and youthful, they were also not necessarily me. I rubbed my fingertips against a gauzy tank top with riotous splashes of dark pink and navy blue and smiled to myself at the over-the-top reactions Mia and Nolan had had every time I tried on one of their suggestions. Maybe they weren't the exact same as me, or the type of serious, studious people I'd envisioned when I thought of Oxford and finally being understood. I'd put my foot in my mouth more than once and I made everything way more difficult than it needed to be, but there was no denying that they seemed to want what was best for me. That they wanted me for me alone.

I straightened my plain white short-sleeved button-down shirt, and before I'd registered what was happening my fingers unraveled the buttons. I tossed it aside and pulled the frivolous pink concoction over my head. Feeling emboldened, I rifled through the bags until I found the tan ankle pants that while so similar to my trusty khakis were tailored and fit me correctly. I ripped off tags in a frenzy, pausing only to sneak back into our room to grab my loafers and a navy tweed vest I'd packed while thinking this was a camp that would require papers to be presented. Pausing for a moment, I grabbed the brooch that Mia had bought me off the dresser.

I pulled the tweed vest on over the colorful blouse and added the finishing touch: my large pink book. The early morning light winked across its surface and pulled a smile across my lips. I knew the navy tweed and geeky pin clashed, but it also seemed to blend with my normal teenager outfit. Something about the whole thing was jarring, but I loved it.

Maybe this new Bea didn't sacrifice her previous self but was able to find out how to bridge the two people who now seemed to live in her skin.

By the time Mia emerged, I was sitting at the kitchen table, my second cup of coffee warming my hands. I'd painstakingly applied a rose-colored lipstick I'd found in the bathroom, which I was hoping was Mia's, and relished her dropped jaw with a raised eyebrow.

"Something wrong?" I took a sip.

"Yeah, I see you sitting there playing it cool," she said. "I thought I would die from not asking when you'd get into all this stuff!" She ran over, flicking my vest and brooch. "And look at you mixing it up, and getting a little weird with it!"

She sauntered back to the bathroom and smiled over her shoulder. "You look killer, girl. Very original."

A warmth rolled through me to my toes. It was probably the coffee, I thought, and took another sip.

My good mood persisted through Mia and Shelby's morning squabble over the bathroom, then breakfast, but promptly died upon entering the auditorium.

"All right, everybody!" Mr. G clapped, the sound rippling throughout the room. I braced myself for the inevitable announcement of how I would "help" him today and whose abrasive acting was going to invade my personal space.

"I know we've been taking it a bit slow and breaking it up into small groups, but we've got to get a move on from this point forward! We only have three weeks before we need to have a functioning play, and there's a lot of work to do with the lighting and directing groups too. I just want to remind you that the people in these groups are my right-hand men and women. I want you to take their direction and pointers as you would take my own." He grinned, slapping a tall blond guy on the back. He was dressed all in black, his fingers curled over a clipboard.

Mia wiggled her eyebrows, and I smothered a laugh, reclining back in my seat.

"I need you all to focus really hard on learning your lines. I want you running them in the daytime, at night with your friends, and pretty much in your sleep. If you guys are having some trouble, be sure to seek out Bea, and she'll go over it with you." Mr. G nodded in my direction and I slouched down farther in my seat.

"You're not giving off a very helpful air," Mia whispered.

"Turns out I'm an extremely unhelpful person. Every man for himself out there."

"Even for your amazing roommate?" she asked, her bottom lip quivering.

"Please, you memorized your lines within the first few days."

She preened. "I know; I just wanted to make sure you knew I was special."

I laughed, slouching farther down as heads turned back toward me again. "Of course you're special. I've seen the notes you've scribbled in your script, and I hear you practicing your old-lady voice in the shower."

"I take it seriously, Bea," she said, straightening in her seat. "This is what I want to do with my life."

"I know," I said, reaching over and awkwardly gripping her hand. "And you're amazing at it, so we're all lucky we get to watch you for the rest of your life."

"This play just has to be perfect, you know?" she said, squeezing my hand back. "It's the last play they'll see before I head to NYU and I just want them to see what other people see when I perform."

"Your parents?" I asked, my voice low.

She nodded, tightening her grip on my hand.

"Now, I want us all to start from the beginning," Mr. G said, clapping his hands as his team of clipboard holders dispersed. "We're going to go through the entire play, and we're going to start with some very basic blocking. If you're not onstage, the directing squad will be walking around and putting you in small groups to continue running lines while we work up here. I want the chorus and our Capulet and Montague entourages up here now!"

I ignored the flurry of activity as everyone started dividing up, rushing onstage. I turned to Mia, finally releasing her. "Want to go over some of your lines?"

She nudged my arm. "As much as I appreciate your offer, I have a pretty good feeling they're not going to let us just sit back here and hang out." She nodded at the aisle as Mr. G slowly made his way toward us. "Speak of the devil."

I tensed a little, still struggling with all these forced interactions that people just kept flinging me toward. I tried to plaster a somewhat acceptable smile on my face. I think I failed, because his steps faltered a little when I turned the full force of it on him.

"Mr. G, what can we do for you?" I asked.

He scanned his clipboard. "All right, ladies. I'm setting up this big run-through of act four, when they discover Juliet is dead. Mia needs to head over there and steal the show."

"Why, I would be delighted, Mr. G," she said, turning her accent up a few levels. She tossed a sassy smile over her shoulder and waltzed over to where a group was starting to form in the wings.

I cleared my throat as he continued flipping through papers. "Did you want me to watch what's going on up on the stage and help them?"

"No. I've got something special in mind for you, Beatrice."

"Okay," I said, hesitant. "Sure."

"That's the spirit!" he said. I unfolded my legs and followed him down the aisle. He nodded toward the front of the auditorium where Shelby and Nik were huddled together. My knees locked in protest, and I stumbled. Mr. G's hand shot out and propped me upright.

"You okay?" he asked, fumbling his clipboard.

"I'm fine," I stammered. "What exactly do I need to help Nik and Shelby with?"

"Well, they have quite a few powerful scenes to pull off, and both of them are almost off book, but we need you to monitor them to make sure they're getting it perfect."

My nails cut into my palms and my feet dragged toward their circle of metal chairs set up off to the side of the stage. Nik's gaze was alternating between Mr. G and me, his expression unreadable. "Are you sure it wouldn't be better if I worked with the actors on the stage, or that scene you're trying to set up with Mia?" I asked.

Mr. G nodded toward two people who did not seem to welcome my arrival. "The directing kids have the stage, and I'll take care of Mia's group, so we need you to work with our two stars. I know you'll be a great help to them."

I buttoned my vest before quickly unbuttoning it again. "Okay. Fine."

"You're the best, Bea."

"Um. Thank you," I mumbled, using the only response I could think of.

We paused at the edge of their circle. "Nik, Shelby, I asked Bea to watch your rehearsal and help you out as needed. Keep an eye out for where we are onstage so you know when to jump in."

Nik's gaze traveled down to my toes, and then up again. He kicked out a long leg and snagged a chair with his foot and pulled it in front of him. "Pull up a chair, Mouse. Don't be shy."

I glowered at him. "Don't call me that. The game is on hold right now."

Mr. G looked between us, his brow furrowed. "Is everything okay? I feel like I'm missing something."

"Nik imagines himself to be a psychotic prince; it's fine." I smiled, baring teeth.

"We were discussing *Hamlet* yesterday," Nik said. "You had to be there."

Shelby glared at me as if I'd started any of this. "I feel we already have enough distractions. We're fine on our own."

"Fine by me," I said, spinning around to go back to my seat.

Mr. G grabbed my arm and turned me back around. "Regardless what Shelby might think, she's not actually in charge here, and this is the grouping that makes the most sense at this time." He frowned at Shelby until she looked away. "Have a good rehearsal; I'll be over there if you need anything." He walked over to join the large group waiting for him.

"Well, what a coincidence," Shelby said. "Did you ask him to set up this little arrangement for you?"

I grabbed a chair and loudly dragged it far from either of them. "Why in the world do you think I would want to be sitting here right now?"

"Ouch," Nik said, his mouth turning up. Always in on some joke I didn't get. "We've started act two, scene two—try and keep up."

I frowned, and he turned his attention to Shelby and settled into his character. Shelby stared back at him; her smile turned sickly sweet.

"*My ears have not yet drunk a hundred words*
*Of that tongue's uttering, yet I know the sound.*

*Art thou not Romeo, and a Montague?*" she started, biting her lip.

I fought the urge to roll my eyes.

"*Neither, fair maid, if either thee dislike,*" Nik said, his breath hitched.

She scooted a little closer, her eyes wide and fluttering. "*How camest thou hither, tell me, and wherefore?*
*The orchard walls are high and hard to climb,*
*And the place death, considering who thou art,*
*If any of my kinsmen find thee here.*"

Nik smiled at her, his palm pressed against his heart.

"*With love's light wings did I o'erperch these walls,*
*For stony limits cannot hold love out,*
*And what love can do, that dares love attempt.*
*Therefore your kinsmen are no stop to me.*"

She grabbed his arm, panting. "*If they do see thee they will murder thee.*"

I coughed, and she bowed her head before turning to glare at me. "What?"

I hesitated for a moment. It was stupid. The smallest mistake in the world, but he was *wrong*, and that tiny word grated against my brain. "His last line, he said 'therefore *your* kinsmen' instead of '*thy* kinsmen.'"

"Are you serious? Are you that determined to insert yourself into this? How could that possibly matter?"

Nik shifted and pulled his arm out of her grasp in one fluid motion. "Beatrice can't help it, Shelby. She's just determined to prove she knows her Shakespeare better than me."

"Believe it or not, Shah, I don't worry about you all that much. I will admit you lasted longer than I thought you would, but I already know I know my Shakespeare better than you."

He shrugged. "I guess you'll just have to prove it at the rematch."

I jammed my glasses up my nose. "When exactly is that happening?" My palms felt damp, and I wiped them on my pants.

He pretended to think for a second, every action overdramatized. Then he snapped his fingers and pointed at me. "Tomorrow night. We're having movie night. We'll resolve it then."

"Can't wait!" Shelby said, an octave higher. "Now if Beatrice is done ruining our progress, can we please continue?"

"Sorry, ladies, we're almost at my cue onstage. I'm going to head over there and wait my turn. Catch you later." He leapt up onto the stage and disappeared into the wings.

"Exactly what do you think you're doing?" Shelby demanded, ripping my attention back to her.

"I'm the prompter," I said slowly.

"Not that, this ridiculous thing with Nik."

"I mean, he was wrong, and I thought he'd want to know how the line really went."

"Are you acting stupid on purpose? I mean with changing your clothes and throwing yourself at Nik! This whole ridiculous pretense of you 'beating him' at Shakespeare quotes?" she demanded, with air quotes. "The whole thing *stinks* of desperation."

Her words slashed against the easy confidence I had found this morning, almost as if she knew which wounds would bleed the most. I wasn't sure which cut the deepest: the insults themselves or the surprise that maybe it mattered to me. The realization that maybe I actually wanted to be part of this world I'd spent my whole life avoiding. That I wasn't as impervious to how other people saw me as I thought.

That I looked ridiculous in this borrowed skin of a normal girl.

"I don't know what you're talking about. I'm not throwing myself at anyone," I said, hating the stammer that slipped through.

"If you think Nik actually wants you, you're delusional. He's mine. Guys like that date girls like me. We like the same stuff; we're friends with the same people; we live in the same city. They don't date awkward losers that spout off a bunch of random facts and buy new clothes thinking they can hide what they are." She leaned in, her breath hot against my ear. "Besides—he told us all he didn't think you were very pretty. That first night, you remember? You wanted to be Rosaline? Well, he didn't think you measured up."

I stood there frozen, my mind oddly wandering to a turn of phrase that I had stumbled across reading once. The protagonist of that book mentioned that he was hit "in the solar plexus." The term seemed made-up, and upon further research I learned it was referring to a complex of ganglia and radiating nerves of the sympathetic system at the pit of the stomach. I felt an odd kinship with that old character now, because I was hollowed out. Shelby had shoved her prettily manicured hand through my stomach with a handful of words. Of *facts*.

It didn't matter that I already knew he said that and had willfully ignored it in our interactions since. Maybe the shock came from the very tiny part of me that thought that maybe Nolan was right and that there was a small chance Nik liked me. I had no idea what I would have done with that information, but some part of me must have thought it was a possibility.

She was right, though. I didn't belong here, with any of them, and I was just fooling myself. Honestly, it was a kindness, and a reminder I could have dearly used the last time I thought this sort of thing was happening.

I stepped back, my expression grim. "I'm aware. I heard it when he said it."

Her smile wavered for a moment, but she was determined to produce some sort of reaction out of me. "So, you understand, then? Just give it up, Bea. We don't need you interrupting, and nobody needs your help here."

"I'm thrilled to hear that," I said, trying to tamp down on the bubbling feelings threatening to spill out. *Helium. Neon. Argon. Krypton. Xenon. Radon. Helium. Neon. Argon. Krypton. Xenon. Radon. Helium. Neon. Argon. Krypton. Xenon. Radon.* I took a few deep breaths, trying to pull more oxygen into my lungs.

Nik eased himself down onto the edge of the stage. "Looks like they aren't quite ready for me yet." His attention sharpened as he looked at my face.

"Everything okay here?" He glanced over at Shelby, his brow raised.

I didn't stick around to hear her response. I spun around and started walking for the double doors and freedom. I heard him call out my name, but I had to get as far away from all of them as possible. As soon as I cleared the doors, I made a run for it and didn't stop until I was winded and climbing the steps to our cabin. I peeled off all the shiny new clothes that tried to dress up this awkward duck into a swan, and I sank onto my bed, telling myself that I hadn't cried since I was thirteen and I wasn't going to start now.

I just sat there with my heart aching for Oxford.

# Chapter Sixteen

**THE COVERS WERE YANKED FROM MY BED, AND** I bolted upright as I was ripped from sleep. Mia stood over me, holding my bedding in her arms. Her look was thunderous, and I fought the urge to scoot away.

I cleared my throat. "Morning, Mia."

"Don't you 'morning, Mia' me!" she said. "You're lucky I have enough respect for sleep to have waited until morning to rip these off of you! I considered doing it last night when I got back from dinner and you were all wrapped up and probably *fake* sleeping."

I scrubbed a hand over my face. I *had* been fake sleeping. I just wasn't up for explaining what had made me run out on practice.

"Thank you for your restraint?"

She threw the blanket at me and put her hands on her hips. "Is that all I'm going to get? You ghosted me! You never came back to practice and were nowhere to be found when it was time for dinner! Where did you go all day?"

I shoved the blanket off me. "I was here reading for most of it. Then I took a walk in the evening." I shrugged, omitting that my walk was purposefully chosen to be around the time people would be going to dinner. "At that point, I was tired and just went to bed early. I'm sorry for making you worry."

She didn't soften at all. "You think I can't smell that bullshit, Bea? You're going to tell me exactly what was going on between you and Shelby before you ran out of that auditorium like a bat out of hell."

I moaned, flinging myself back on the bed. "I don't want to talk about it. It's stupid and makes me feel stupid for even bringing it up."

Mia sat down on the foot of the bed. "If it made you disappear for almost a day, it's not stupid, and it's something that needs to be dealt with," she said, frowning. "You want to really be friends, Bea? Not just for some checklist, but for real? This is what that entails. You share these moments with the people that care about you. Now, you can hem and haw for as long as you want, but neither one of us is leaving this room until you spill." She settled in, making herself comfortable.

"You're going to forcibly keep me here?" I grabbed my glasses off the nightstand, her frown coming into sharper focus.

"Oh, I'm not joking around here, sweetie. I'll kick your ass until you tell me, and then I'll go next door and kick Shelby's ass for whatever terrible thing she pulled."

I shifted under her serious expression. "I don't doubt that for a second."

"That's because you're a smart girl," she said. "Now, *spill*."

I leaned back, pressing a pillow to my face. "Fine," I said, muffled. It was easier if I didn't have to look at her while I said the words. "Mr. G made me babysit Nik and Shelby and monitor their lines yesterday, which was never going to go well."

"Yeah, I saw that part."

I hugged the pillow closer, overwhelmed with all the feelings

I didn't want to closely look at. "Anyway, things were as awkward as you can imagine and Nik brought up the quote game again and said we would rematch at movie night." I swallowed, dreading the next part. "Then Nik left, and she laid into me. She said that I was delusional for thinking Nik could like me, and it's *not* like I was even thinking that!"

I flung the pillow across the room and stared up at the lop-sided ceiling fan. I squeezed my eyes shut as the last part spilled out. "She said I was ridiculous, because of trying to dress differently. Then she mentioned what Nik said about me that first night. You know, the Rosaline thing." I didn't want to mention how she'd shattered what little confidence in socializing that I had built up here and how close I was to just "ghosting" the rest of the summer. Mia came into view as she leaned over me, and she placed her hands on my face. Her touch was gentle, and I leaned into it.

"I know you're new to this, and sometimes people need time alone to process stuff, but let your friends know what's happening to you before you disappear again."

I felt impossibly small. "It was stupid. I should be able to just ignore her. I don't know why it bothered me so much."

She exhaled and sat heavily next to me. "She didn't just try and hurt your feelings, Bea. She dug as deep as she could, and she attacked the most sensitive part of you that she thought she could find."

I looked down at my feet.

"That wasn't just irritation at you interrupting her extremely clumsy attempts to seduce Nik. That was her trying to eliminate a threat."

I looked up at her. "Don't be ridiculous. I'm no threat. They're going to end up together—it's inevitable."

She looked at me like I had grown a second head. "He started to run after you yesterday, until Shelby clung to him like some sort of strangling vine. It looked like he really laid into her after that. Not that that changes a single thing, and he's still on my shit list for that ridiculous Rosaline comment, but he doesn't seem to be on her side either."

I dismissed that visual and gave Mia a wobbly smile. "She's probably right. I was just playing pretend with all this stuff. I don't know who I was kidding."

She frowned and I thought for a second that I was going to have to tackle her to stop her from storming into Shelby's room, but she stepped forward and enveloped me into a hard hug.

"Beatrice Quinn, I'm going to tell you something I learned a long time ago." She released me, her expression serious. "I grew up in a small southern town. I'm talking *small* small. Like, I like to say I'm from Atlanta, because nobody would recognize this town unless they were actually from it. It didn't help that I went to a tiny, conservative—although they tried to pretend they were apolitical— private school. I was told for most of my life to stop being too loud, too colorful, too dramatic, too queer, too flirtatious, too opinionated, too *everything*. For a while, even though I hate to admit it, I even tried. Then once I had become some dampened, muted version of myself and they still weren't happy, I realized something."

Her grip on my shoulders tightened.

"I realized that they didn't get to decide what sort of person I was, and I could change at a moment's notice if I damn well wanted to. I could be thoughtful and studious, and then go out to the movies in the tiniest miniskirt I could find. I could sing and dance my way through life and spend an entire weekend in the same stained pajamas and not want to hang out with anyone. Do you see what I am saying? Nobody has the right to tell you who you're supposed to be and how you're supposed to look or act. *You* decide, not some frigid, uppity bitch."

I blinked. "You know, one of my favorite quotes is about something like that. It's by this poet named Walt Whitman. He said, '*Do I contradict myself?*

*Very well, then I contradict myself.*

*(I am large, I contain multitudes.)*'"

She grinned. "Yeah, well, he knew what he was talking about. With that motto blazing in your mind, I want you to shake off that poison Shelby tried to throw at you and continue being the Bea we all know and love."

"Painfully awkward, and slightly hostile?"

"That's the one!" she said, laughing. She reached into her dresser, pulling out clothes for the day.

"Thank you," I said, trying to keep the mood light. "I don't want to burden you or force you to be my babysitter or life coach."

She paused and gave me a look that highlighted how dumb I could be for someone that was supposed to be smart. "Did you not listen to anything I just said? I do things because I *want* to, and I'll have you know I'd be a damn fine life coach."

I smiled at the accuracy of that, knowing I would listen to her and walk into lava if she asked me to. I dug around in my own drawers, pushing past piles of silky, colorful fabric. My fingertips found the reassuring texture of thick cotton, and I pulled a gray polo out of the drawer. "What is this movie night people keep mentioning?"

"We usually try and screen a film version of the play we are performing, so we can see different interpretations. This year, of course, we're watching the DiCaprio *Romeo and Juliet*. A little different, what with the gangs and all, but still pretty exciting!" Her smile wavered as I pulled on a pair of khakis.

"Is there a movie theater in this place that I've somehow missed?"

"Not so much. They have this old projector, and we aim it at the side of the auditorium. We all drag a bunch of blankets and pillows out there and build a giant nest."

"That doesn't sound like fun at all."

"I'm just going to ignore that response, per usual." She pulled a canary-yellow blouse over her head. "It's especially fun if there's someone you wouldn't mind snuggling up to under the stars."

I adjusted my glasses. "Speaking of that, how are things going with Ben?"

She swung an arm around my shoulders as we walked out the door. "Why, I thought you'd never ask. He's almost as hard to pull out of his shell as you were, but I'm content to let the wistful looks continue until he finds the nerve."

"You should put him out of his misery."

"There's no fun in that."

# Chapter Seventeen

**I MANAGED TO KEEP A LOW PROFILE AT REHEARSALS** that day, sticking to Mr. G like glue and helping him with the formal run-through happening onstage. We worked through lunch, and by the time dinner came around I was exhausted and more than a little sick of Shakespeare.

I dropped my tray onto the table as Nolan frowned at my sad little collection of cookies.

"How your massive brain runs on all that garbage is beyond me." He waved his fork in my direction as I slid onto the picnic table bench across from him.

I unwrapped a delicious-looking chocolate chip cookie and was too delighted to bother rolling my eyes at him. "This is me roughing it. This camp has disrupted all of my normal habits, so I'm a bit at a loss with what to feed myself." I took a large bite in his direction. "I decided to go with the most comfort-inducing items."

Mia stabbed her lasagna, and that crease reappeared between her eyebrows. "You mean in the real world you don't eat rolls and cookies for every meal?"

I shrugged. "I'm a creature of habit."

They all waited patiently until I sighed in exasperation. "Fine, yes, I eat the same thing on specific days of the week, and the next week I repeat the entire thing over. It's easy, comforting, and I've done it since childhood."

The silence was broken by plaintive little snorts coming from Nolan as he attempted to hold in his laugh. I waved a hand in his direction. "Oh, just let it out already. I know it sounds nuts."

"But what if you end up going out? Or what about what your parents make for dinner?" Mia sputtered.

I pushed my remaining cookies around. "It hasn't really been an issue. If we eat together, I just eat what I want, or they go out by themselves." Mia's frown deepened, and I knew we were on the precipice of another lecture on how I needed to try more with my parents. She was right, I knew that, and somehow after all this time Dr. Horowitz's voice actually sank in. I did live too much in my own head, and I was going down the path of not maintaining a single relationship that was important to me.

I felt a twinge of regret at sobering what was once a normal, lighthearted conversation and decided enough was enough. I'd let Shelby drag me down, but I wasn't going to expend any more effort feeling sorry for myself.

I firmly pushed up my glasses before nodding at Nolan. "Give me all the dirt on this movie night."

He arched an eyebrow. "And why do you ask?"

I flushed. "I just want to know what might be expected of me."

Nolan brushed his hair out of his eyes. "I was wondering if you were perhaps trying to get the lay of the land in order to put the moves on one of the resident hotties."

I scrunched my face up. "No, thank you. I don't intend to share my blanket nest with anyone."

He nodded, all seriousness. "DiCaprio *Romeo and Juliet* is a special experience, and not to be shared with just anyone. Especially not assholes that despite a very romantic Shakespearean quote game gesture are still in the doghouse for douchebaggery at the mixer."

Mia tensed next to me, and I placed a cooling hand against my throat.

"I . . ." I cleared my throat and tried again. "I don't want to keep talking about him. He's with Shelby, and I'm not interested in any of that drama."

Mia kept her eyes riveted to her plate, and Nolan glanced back and forth between us. "Something's weird. Mia, your stunning face is scrunched up like a goblin. Explain."

She winced and took another bite of lasagna.

Nolan threw his fork down. "You can't keep secrets at the table of truth." He stabbed the table with his finger.

"That's not an actual thing." I took a big bite of cookie to try and pull off a casual air. "It's no big deal. Shelby just tore into me during rehearsal the other day. She made a variety of things quite clear."

"Is that why you didn't show up for dinner last night?" Nolan asked, narrowing his eyes at me.

"Just drop it, Nolan," Mia said, and I squeezed her hand under the table. After the fact, I was a little stunned at how easily that gesture had come to me.

Nolan spun around on the bench and looked across the cafeteria to where Shelby sat with her little crew. "What exactly did my loving sister say to you?"

I paused, afraid I'd have another emotional response to the retelling. "Oh, you know, the usual. 'You're a giant loser that nobody likes, and you're delusional if you think a few new clothes will make people way out of your league take notice.'"

Mia frowned, her gaze dancing over my polo shirt.

Nolan turned back around, his face tight. "That's what desperate creatures do when they're threatened, cupcake. They lash out as hard as they can and hope they don't get their snobby little asses kicked." He stood, his tray rattling as his hip bumped the table. "I'll be right back."

"Don't do anything," I said, panic staining my words.

His lips were a flat line. "I think she just needs a little reminder about a few things."

"Nolan. Please," I begged.

He wavered for a moment before returning to his seat. "I have no idea what's going on with her," he said, strained, before turning the full blast of his attention on me. "Any clue why she said those things to you, Little Miss Genius?"

I shrugged. "I think maybe my existence was just irritating her that day."

"I wouldn't say that," he said. "I think she has eyes in her head and she realized that the resident Romeo might lean more toward brunette bookworms."

"For *God's sake!*" I sputtered. "People saying nonsense like that is why she's so evil!"

He chewed on his lip. "Shelby's had a—difficult year. None of this is any excuse, and she can definitely be a bitch, but she isn't usually vicious."

"I find that hard to believe."

"I know what it looks like, and I'm not sure if she's really that into Nik, or if she's trying to lash out because of me, or all of the above. Ever since I heard about RISD, it's like there has been this wall between us, and I have no idea what is going on with her and it's like I barely recognize her anymore."

Mia stretched her fingers across the table, squeezing his wrist. "You got into the best design school in the country, and she's not allowed to take any part of that away from you. You should be thrilled, and she'll have to come to terms with her own shit."

He flushed; the expression fit strangely on him. "With her being stuck at home, I haven't really wanted to make that big a deal about it, but I'm so excited to start, I can barely focus on anything else. I'm going to learn things I've only dreamed of, and all of you will be wearing my clothes in ten years." He pointed his fork at Mia. "Especially you; you're not allowed to do any red carpets unless it's my dresses."

She laughed. "I'll have that written into my contracts."

He smiled lopsided, his white oxford pulling across his chest. "I don't know what to do about Shelby. I think part of the reason she's been avoiding me is that she's trying to hide how much she's freaking out, but I miss her almost as much as I'm mad at her."

"Have you tried talking to her?" Mia asked, worrying her bottom lip with her teeth.

"Of course I have," he said, stabbing his lasagna forcefully with his fork.

"Then just give her some time," Mia said, giving his arm another squeeze.

"I don't know how to stop her from unraveling or attacking Bea."

"It's not your job to protect me from people being mean to me, Nolan."

"The hell it's not," he said, uncharacteristically serious. I forced cookie down past the tightness in my throat.

"I'd be more sympathetic if she wasn't trying to take other people down with her," Mia said. "Also, I *maybe* would have scaled back on talking about how excited I am to be heading to NYU in the fall around her."

I frowned. "You shouldn't have to do that either. You should both be proud of your accomplishments."

Nolan nodded. "She hasn't said anything to me, but I'm guessing she just needed a win, to feel wanted by something or somebody, and she's randomly decided that's Nik. She dumped Troy for him, and they hooked up a little last year before the end of the summer. I think she thought they would just pick right back up where they left off."

My heart tripped over his words. If they'd already been together, there was no reason for her to waste her time yelling at me. "That settles that."

"He created a Shakespeare bet where his prize for winning was a *kiss* from *you*," Mia said.

"That was so hot," Nolan said, fanning himself with his napkins. "I'm still mad at him," he said, quickly clarifying. "But damn, that was hot."

"It was just to throw me off my game!" I trapped my hands under my armpits, so they'd stop moving. "He knows how I get a little flustered with all of . . . that."

Nolan grinned. "With all what, dear heart?"

"With all of the drama involved in being forced to interact with raging hormones."

"Hey!" Mia laughed, throwing her napkin at me. "I've been on my best behavior!"

Nolan grinned. "So that little lamb is just trailing behind you solely on the promise of what's to come?"

Mia choked on her iced tea. "If you mean because of my incredible wit and personality, then yes."

He grinned before nodding in my direction. "All right, hand it over."

"What am I handing over?"

"The list! I want to see where we stand!"

"Where *we* stand?"

"Yes! I double-dog dared you, and now number seven is complete."

I shoved the list across the table, and he eagerly unfolded it. "Four down, seven to go. That's pretty good progress with three weeks left."

"I still haven't decided if I'm going to do your additions yet."

"Bea! You have to! They're officially part of the list now," Mia said.

"Are you worried about the kissing one? Don't fret, love. I'll help you out." He leaned over his lasagna, pulling me across the table by my polo. Mia shrieked as I ducked my head, swatting him away.

"This must be where the party's at!" Ben hovered at the edge of our table, his expression open and earnest.

"Ben!" Mia exclaimed, scooting over. "Sit! Have you eaten yet?"

He pinked up at her offer, sliding onto the bench. "Yeah, I finished a little while ago. Everyone's talking about where they're all going to set up for the movie. I just wanted to see what you guys were up to and if you were all planning on heading out there?"

Nolan snickered, depositing me back on my bench and slipping me the list. I kicked him hard under the table.

"We were just going to head over there and find a good spot! Do you already know where you're sitting? I'm sure we could find a cozy place to all sit together," Mia said.

Ben nodded, scooting closer. "The more the merrier, right?"

"I couldn't have said it better myself," Nik said, sliding onto the bench next to Nolan.

I dropped my cookie in surprise and tried to look casual.

"Why, Nik, if you wanted us to watch the movie together, you should have just said so," Nolan said, laying his head on Nik's shoulder.

Nik smirked. "I'll keep that in mind, Nolan."

"Wait, I'm mad at you; you're not allowed to share my blanket fort anymore," Nolan said, narrowing his eyes.

"What have I done now?"

"You know."

I flushed and aimed a kick in Nolan's general direction again.

Nik leaned across the table, the wood tugging on his black tee. Black tee, black hair, black eyes. Black heart. "Long time, no see, Mouse," he said, his tone almost accusatory.

"Don't call me that," I said. "Also, I literally see you every day."

He worked his fingernail under a jagged shard of wood and pulled it free from the table. "Call me crazy, but I have a weird feeling you've been avoiding me."

"I haven't been avoiding you, but I also have no reason to look for you." My gaze flickered beyond him to the people at his old table frowning in our direction.

"Ouch, that hurts." He clutched his chest.

"I doubt that. Find someone else to play with. I'm not interested." My gaze dropped to my lap, and I fidgeted with the hem of my polo. The sooner he went back to Shelby and she stopped sending hateful glares in my direction, the better for everyone. As the silence dragged on, I risked a glance up at him.

"You don't want to play anymore, Beatrice? Well, we all know what the price of forfeit is," he murmured. Sharp brows furrowed over eyes that had gone strangely soft.

My spine stiffened. "You and this game."

He shrugged. "Don't act like I created this all on my own. You're the one who was strutting around the Island telling everyone that she was the Queen of Shakespeare."

I could feel my heartbeat in my ears, and I fought to remain sitting. I pointed a finger straight at his face. "Now, listen here, you—" The words died on my tongue as I realized the rest of the table had stopped talking and all eyes were on us. Nolan smiled delightedly and cradled his chin in his hand. I took a shaky breath and tucked the accusing finger under my thigh. It took several cleansing breaths to let the fire die down.

Shelby slid in next to Nik, unapologetically forcing Nolan down the bench. She looked through me like I was a ghost before turning a thousand-watt smile on Nik. As someone with a history of questionable retainer use, I found it really was an impressive thing to behold.

"Have you guys finished slumming it over here yet? It's almost time for the movie, and those backstage losers are going to steal all the best spots."

"As always, my darling sister, you say the sweetest things."

"Bite me."

"Well, I'm definitely done now," I said, standing up as Shelby continued to ignore my existence. "Mia?"

"Absolutely!" Mia sang, grabbing her tray and beaming as Ben took it from her and went to dispose of it. She glanced over at our end of the table. "Everyone get some blankets and pillows and we'll meet out on the quad. Except you, Shelby; you can fly your ass back to hell."

Shelby picked at her manicure, completely unbothered.

With one last smile at Ben, full of promise, Mia grabbed ahold of my hand and dragged me back in the direction of our cabin. I was almost certain she was going to bring up yet another public argument with Nik, but she didn't say a word. We grabbed blankets, pillows, and couch cushions and hurried back to the quad. Nolan and Mia fashioned a giant, squishy nest from pillows and blankets, and I sank gratefully into the fabric.

"What is this?" I asked, batting away some itchy material from my face.

"Tulle," Nolan said. "Costume department prerogative." He continued fluffing pillows before sprawling out in front of me. Mia sat on the other side of our haven, leaning against a tree and leaving a giant space open for Ben. I wiggled down, trying to get comfortable and hoping to enjoy what was going to be one of the very few dramas I'd ever seen. The outer lights all switched off, plunging us into an inky darkness. A darkness that was only ever possible out in the woods. A brief exclamation of protest went up amongst the campers, but I wiggled down even farther, the anonymity of it all curling around me. Stars spilled out across the velvet sky, and my eyes gobbled up every single one. The projector whirred to life, and the story blossomed across the side of the building in flickers and streaks of colors. I was spellbound. Those familiar characters and language came to life as the chaos, passion, and violence that was infused in every line unfolded before me. I wiped away a stray tear as a young Juliet, who carried an innocence that Shelby would never be able to replicate, watched in devastation as she realized the boy she had just fallen in love with was one of her most bitter enemies.

I felt the blankets shift, and I tore my attention away from the screen long enough to see Nik recline next to me. My skin sat tight and uncomfortable on my bones. Waiting on pins and needles for some snarky comment was almost worse than the words themselves.

"That's how it's supposed to be done, isn't it?" he murmured, nodding toward the screen.

I bit my lip, ignoring him, trying to once again find the magic that had been broken by his presence.

He shifted again. "I don't want to make you uncomfortable, Beatrice. If you'd rather I go, I can go." He moved, poised to get up.

I paused at his use of my actual name and snuck another glance at him. In the dim lighting, his eyes were the same hard obsidian as the world beyond our little nest. He remained still, allowing my evaluation, and ready to leave at my word. I tasted the dismissal on the edge of my tongue. The one that would banish him back to Shelby so I could burrow under mountains of tulle and clutch this movie to myself. To experience every nuance as if I was in a vacuum. The same way I always watched movies. The same way I always did everything.

I bit my lip, the silence dragging out. Maybe for once I wanted someone else's opinion. Someone else's commentary on parts that I found interesting, or dumb. To have a shared experience. He clenched his jaw and nodded once at my lack of a response. He sat up, pulling a blanket aside. I felt a twinge of guilt deep in my gut and cleared my throat. It wasn't his fault I was a human cactus.

"You're fine," I said.

I felt the blankets move again as he settled back down. I waited about two minutes before the words tumbled from my lips. "Hiding from your fan club?"

He made a small sound of amusement. "You have no idea."

"Everyone has a pretty good idea."

He turned toward me, and I saw a flash of white in the darkness. "You know, I once saw Shelby beat a mugger down in Central Park with a Prada shoe. Not a hint of fear, just pure domination. Now, stick her in the woods at a completely safe camp, and the slightest hint of violence in a movie had her almost smother me because she got *scared*. Strange how that goes."

"Yeah, strange," I murmured. I tried to get back into the movie, but images of Nik and Shelby hanging out in NYC together kept running through my head. They were going to shows, and eating brunch, and doing other ridiculous things that young, beautiful people did. I bit my lip, trying to avoid saying anything stupid, but I wanted answers more than anything else.

"So, you two spend a lot of time together out in the real world?" As soon as the words left my mouth, I cringed.

He paused for a moment before murmuring, "Some. We have friends in common."

"Yeah, she mentioned something about that."

He rolled over on his side, facing me. "Listen, Mouse. I would take anything she says to you with a grain of salt. Something about you sets her off in a weird way."

"Stop calling me that, and I'm *so* sorry that my mere existence is so troubling to Shelby. I'll just hide out the rest of the summer in my cabin; would that be okay? Or would she prefer if I just drowned myself in the lake?"

His hand snaked out and grabbed my wrist as I struggled to get up and stalk off. "I was warning you that she isn't reasonable when it comes to you. Not because I care in the slightest if she's irritated. I just wanted to make sure you don't let her get to you."

I stilled, the pressure of his hand on my wrist pulling me down like an anchor. My already-impaired social filter couldn't stop the next words from leaving my mouth. "If she's so awful, why are you friends with her?"

He sighed, the sound more intimate in the darkness. I touched my newly released wrist, flopping onto my back, and shook off the feeling of his fingertips.

"She's been through a rough few years, but she wasn't always like this." I felt his arm drop down into the tulle, next to mine. "Don't you have any old friends that you might not have much in common with anymore, but you still spend time with them because of your history?"

"No, who has time for friends?" I said, folding my arms across my abdomen.

His pause hung heavy over us. "I know I tease you, but you know I'm just playing, right? My intention has never been to hurt you," he said. "Even though I know you witnessed a particularly stupid moment of mine." He coughed; his voice strained. "I'm still dying to know why the hell you came to a theater camp."

I stiffened in horror as I felt my lower lip wobble a bit. *You will not cry in public, Beatrice Quinn. You have already wasted enough time on this nonsense.* I stomped those feelings down and swallowed until it no longer felt like I had a knot in my throat.

"I don't have many friends, Nik. I never had time for them, and I wasn't willing to make a place for them in my life and schedule. I was interested in my projects and books. It's been all about getting away from California, and getting to Oxford, where I thought I truly belonged."

He twitched and his arm moved against mine. "And all that work paid off. You got in and you're going in the fall."

"Maybe."

"Maybe? What do you mean, maybe?" he said, sitting up.

"My parents are concerned that I'll go off to school and not let anybody in my life. That I will become one of those people that die at home, who nobody discovers for months because nobody misses them."

"I think *I'm* still missing something."

"They sent me here to learn to be a real teenager, Nik. I'm here to socialize and learn to make friends. If I can't pull it off, I'm stuck in Berkeley for at least another year."

"I think . . ." He paused, and I tried not to lean in his direction. "I think you're one of the realest people I know."

That statement seared through me. No commentary on how I should do this, say this, look like this. I cleared my throat, unsure how to even remotely navigate a response to that. "I don't think I ever heard about your plans for the fall."

His chuckle trickled through the inky darkness. "Well, that's kind of a funny story—"

"Nik!" Shelby's sharp whisper cut through the night and Nik tensed beside me before burrowing down in the blankets. I froze before grabbing a handful of tulle and piling it on top of him. I stared straight ahead while Shelby marched past, irritation bleeding into every step. His head peeked out from underneath the baby-pink pile, and it was all so ridiculous the laughter just burst out of me.

He grinned before looking up in concern. "Mouse, shhhhh! You're going to bring her back!"

I was beyond help at that point, tears pooling behind my glasses, and he shoved some of the tulle over my head.

"I thought you were trying to help me," he said, his amusement surrounding me like our bubble.

"I think you can fight your own battles, Shah," I said, suddenly shy. I pulled the scratchy material down from my face and tried to find the threads of our conversation.

"What were you saying you were going to be when you grow up?" I cleared my throat. "I mean, if you grow up."

"Ouch, another sick burn from Beatrice Quinn." He pulled the material off and turned his head toward me. "I'm going to act, Mouse."

I could see him, moving across the stage in a way that made it impossible to tear your eyes off him. He belonged there, and it made as much sense as me sitting in a lab. I didn't know how to say it, so I settled on "Good."

The word felt heavy between us, and I felt the hard half-moon of his nail as his pinkie finger pressed against mine. I froze, not moving an inch.

"Why did you bet a kiss?" If I could have grabbed the words and shoved them back deep down into my stomach, I would have.

He sighed, the sound long and drawn-out. "Oh, I don't know. I figured it'd motivate you to try really hard not to lose."

"It has," I said simply.

His laugh swelled above the sounds of the movie. "God, you pull no punches."

I pressed my lips together, but it didn't feel like a criticism. I could hear his soft breathing in the lulls of the dialogue, and my entire existence was narrowed down to that single millimeter where his finger met mine. I turned his answer over in my mind. "I don't think I can handle the game tonight."

"Don't fret, Mouse. When I beat you, it's going to be in a really public way," he murmured. His voice was pitched low and rough, scraping across my skin.

"Why do you insist on that ridiculous nickname?"

"Come on, you know your Hamlet."

"And?"

"And it's an endearment."

"Why won't you just call me Bea like everyone else?"

"Because I want you to notice when I'm around." A streak of white teeth shone through the darkness, and then he was gone.

# Chapter Eighteen

"CUT! STOP! MERCUTIO, YOU KEEP STEPPING on Romeo's lines!" Mr. G clawed his hand through his thinning curls. "Bea! Where's Bea?"

I dragged myself up to the stage where Mr. G paced.

"You bellowed?"

He spun around. "Bea! I need you to fix this! The costume design group is about to come in and start fitting everyone. I have to work on the final scene, Friar Lawrence still has stage fright, and I just need you to—*fix* this." He waved blindly at the stage before storming off.

"Well, he seems tense," I said, adjusting my glasses. "Who exactly needs fixing?"

Ben coughed, and hesitantly raised his hand. "I believe that would be me."

"Cool," I said. "What's your problem?"

Nik rolled his eyes. "He doesn't have a problem. Mr. G is always like this as we get closer to opening night."

"Awesome. In that case, I'm just going to go sit down again." I spun around, thrilled to find another dark corner to ignore people from. I'd been casually avoiding Nik for the past few days and was still a little raw from the intimacy of movie night. That fingernail seemed way too solid to be anything but purposeful.

"Wait!"

I turned, and Ben shifted in place. "Do you think you could maybe watch? I keep tripping up on some of my lines and cutting off Nik. I'm worried I'm going to mess this up, and there's only two weeks left, and I just . . ."

My frown softened as his voice echoed the same sentiment that had me begging for my prompter position. The very least I could do was sit here and maybe give him a little confidence. I sighed, sliding into one of the front-row seats, and gave Ben a weak smile as they got back into position.

Nik slouched and shuffled his feet as he walked, his head bent and his mood sullen. Ben walked up next to him and clapped him on the back.

*"And to sink in it, should you burthen love—*
*Too great oppression for a tender thing."*

Nik shrugged Ben's hand off his shoulder and gave him an incredulous look.

*"Is love a tender thing? It is too rough,*
*Too rude, too boisterous, and it pricks like a thorn."*

He spit the words out with anger, and I frowned, squashing down the traitorous butterflies rising with the cadence of his voice.

Ben nodded, and haltingly replied:

*"If love be rough with you, be rough with love.*
*Prick love for pricking, and you beat love down.—*
*Give me a case to put my visage in!"*

Ben fumbled as he tied a plain black mask onto his face, and I grimaced. The problem was obvious, even for someone who didn't really have the best track record with identifying and interpreting emotion.

I cleared my throat, and the scene ground to a halt.

"Okay, so the problem is that Ben—"

"Beatrice," Nik cut me off, his tone sharp as a knife. "I want you to make sure that your feedback is constructive."

Ben waved him off. "Don't stop her, Nik. I asked for her help, and I want the truth."

I bit my lip, the weight of Nik's stare crushing the words on the tip of my tongue. The words that would have said Ben just wasn't as good as Nik and Nik's talent just made that *extremely* obvious. I suppose that wasn't constructive, although it was the truth.

"Let me try this again," I started as Ben turned his hopeful, puppy-dog gaze on me. "Ben, are parties fun?"

"Umm, I'm sorry, what?"

"*Are parties fun?*" I clipped, enunciating each word.

He looked to Nik for help, an instinct that seemed like habit. "Sure? I mean, they're supposed to be."

I nodded. "Okay. What would you typically do at them?"

He shrugged. "I don't know. Hang out with my friends, have a few drinks, maybe dance some."

"Okay. What do you think Romeo and Mercutio are going to do at *this* party?"

Nik ducked his head, my brain marking the smile that spread across his lips before he turned.

Ben nodded. "I guess they will probably hang out with their friends, have a few drinks, and maybe dance some."

"That seems to be the plan, so I'm asking you if parties are fun because it doesn't seem like you're very excited to go to one. I imagine if we told Mia that we were all going to a party, she would be bouncing along next to me, talking about all the things we were going to do, and her happiness would be visible to everyone."

He smiled with a sweetness that made me think their relationship was further along than I thought. "I can see that, and that's actually pretty helpful."

Nik shoved his hands in the pockets of his jeans as they strained against his hipbones. "Now that all that's out of the way, are you telling us that you've *never* been to a party?"

I folded my arms across my chest, shrinking into myself as the spotlight turned in my direction.

A pile of brocade fabric was thrown into the seat next to me. "Did someone say party? I got here as soon as I could." Nolan brushed his hair out of his eyes and winked down at me.

Nik laughed, his posture relaxing with Nolan's arrival. "Talking about parties? That's your bat signal?"

"Naturally."

"Bea was just helping me get into the mind-set of my character as he prepares for a party," Ben piped up.

I smiled as he tried to divert the attention away from me. He was kind. I scolded myself for always discounting him because he was quiet and shy.

"Actually, we'd moved past that, and Mouse was about to tell us how it's possible that she's never been to a party."

Nolan whipped around to face me. "Never? As in never ever?"

I ignored him, rubbing one of the brocade dresses between my fingers as he swatted me away.

I rolled my eyes and pitched my voice low. "You'd think at some point you would all stop being surprised by these things."

"You're right, boo. This is all completely in line with your character." Nolan looked up at Nik. "Spread the word, we're doing it tonight. Let's do A *Midsummer Night's Dream*."

Nik saluted. "I'll spread the word." He nodded at Ben, who just smiled at me.

"Wait, what's going on?" I asked as Nik hopped down off the stage and walked toward a large group off to the side.

He spun around, casually ambling backward. "What's happening, Mouse, is that you're going to get some firsthand knowledge on what a party is like." He spun back around.

I blinked rapidly, shoving my glasses back up my nose. "What the hell just happened? Did you all just pull a party out of thin air?"

"Not that I couldn't do that if I wanted to, but we typically throw a big party each year. We just hadn't decided when yet." Nolan wiggled his eyebrows. "It's a secret party, so keep it to yourself."

My hands started to sweat. Was I supposed to dress up? I only had the one dress for the end-of-summer party. Was I going to be expected to dance? That wasn't happening. Would I have to carry casual conversations with people I didn't know very well? *Helium. Neon. Argon. Krypton. Xenon. Radon. Helium. Neon. Argon. Krypton. Xenon. Radon.*

"I see that look. Just breathe. You're going to love it!" He leaned over, pulling me into an embrace that only partially smothered me with petticoats.

"Is it going to be another movie?" I asked, my stomach in knots. "You said *A Midsummer Night's Dream*?"

"Every good party planner knows that a party has to have a theme, and ours are always Shakespearean." He leaned in. "I may have been taking an inventory of our costume closet and found a bunch of wings that are begging to be let out."

"Wings?" The word got stuck in my throat.

"Don't even worry about your costume; I'll come over later and fix you right up!" he said before spinning away. "Lady Capulet, let's see if you can actually stand still during a fitting for once in your life."

I watched his retreating back, my mind struggling to process, as Mia ran up. "I heard the party is tonight!" She bounced from side to side.

I pulled her in close and hissed, "This escalated after everyone basically found out that I've never been to one!"

"Don't be silly," she said, rubbing my arm. "We do this every year. Nobody will be judging you or expecting anything from you! You can participate as little or as much as you want." She pulled me into a half hug and squeezed my arm. "Last year was so much fun! Our theme was *The Tempest*, and I went as Miranda. I was all wild hair and bloodred lips. I fashioned a cape out of a sheet."

"You guys don't do anything normal." I covered my face, trying not to imagine what costume Nolan was going to come up with for me.

She laughed and poked me in the ribs. "You're one to talk. These things are pretty standard. Maybe not the costumes, but all the usual teenager stuff happens at these things."

I peeked out from behind my fingers. "What exactly do we consider normal teenager stuff?"

She grinned. "I wouldn't dream of spoiling the surprise." She headed back over to her rehearsal group and blew me a kiss. "Don't worry; I'll be with you the whole time."

I stared dumbly after her. I could pump the brakes. I could say no and spend the evening tucked under the blanket. Burrito-mode, and safe. My hand grazed over the bulge in my pocket, the list that hadn't even been halfway completed. Safe wasn't going to get me to Oxford, and I had to pick up the pace. The deadline was in two weeks, and Mom wasn't giving me an inch. I pulled out my list and paused over *Accept an invitation you don't want to.* Pushing my pen into the paper so hard it almost tore, I checked it off.

# Chapter Nineteen

**"PSST. BEA! ARE YOU AWAKE?"**

I rolled over, my brain cloudy with sleep. "I'm up. I'm up. What's wrong?"

"It's party time!" Mia said, her voice slicing through the darkness.

I sat straight up in bed. "The party? I thought the party was off!"

"Why on earth would you think that?"

"Because you all refused to talk about it! I tried to bring it up at dinner and was completely shut down!"

Mia's tinkling laugh wrapped around me. "This is a super-top-secret party. No talking about it, no acknowledging it in public, and no getting caught! This camp is pretty indulgent with us, but this would not be something they would be able to turn a blind eye to, and I'm not about to fly home in shame!"

I clutched my blanket to me. "We could get expelled? That's it; I'm out." I flopped back in bed and rolled away from her.

She laughed again, creeping across the room and ripping the blankets off me. "What are you so *afraid* of?"

"All of this!" I exclaimed. "Your secret parties and rules. What if I get sent home? I'm supposed to go to Oxford in the fall, Mia!"

"Bea, what was the point of you coming to this camp? To act in a play, or to make friends? I'm just thinking that if you got expelled for having too much fun, they'd probably send you on to Oxford early and you wouldn't have to be a prompter for the next two weeks."

"That's a hell of a chance to take."

"Well, what about the list?"

"What about it?" I rubbed the sleep out of my eyes.

"I bet we could check off a box or two tonight."

I groaned. "I should have never shown you two that thing."

"You showed it to us because you knew we would help you make the most of your time here! That includes a party! You don't want to roll up to Oxford with no idea what to expect."

I paused. I knew she was right. The chance to observe this sort of thing amongst people who would have my back was more than I could hope for over there. I swallowed my numerous objections and swung my legs out of bed. "*Fine.* Let's get this over with then."

"That's the spirit!"

I reached over to turn on the lamp, and she grabbed my hand. "No lights! It would be weird if one of the counselors saw a bunch of lights turn on around this time. I think Nolan is outside by now, and I'm going to smuggle him in." She slipped into the darkness, and I took a deep breath as my stomach fluttered.

The door burst open as Nolan hustled into the room with piles of fabric and wings clutched to his chest. Mia followed behind him, closing the door softly.

"Pull the curtains!" Nolan hissed as he pulled out a small candle and matches.

I did as he said, and a small anemic light filled the room. Nolan had tiny little horns sticking out of his tousled hair, green board shorts, and a sash of ivy across his chest. His skin sparkled like diamonds.

"Let me guess," I said, my lips curling into a smile. "Puck?"

He gave me a jaunty bow. "In the flesh."

"You're shedding glitter all over our room."

He shrugged. "Small price to pay, my queen."

"What's that now?"

Mia picked up a gauzy white slip and a pair of delicate gold wings. Her eyes sparkled in the candlelight. "You're the guest of honor and going as Titania!"

"The queen of the fairies?" I asked dumbly.

"The very one!" Nolan thrust the dress into my hands and shoved me out of the room and into the bathroom. I pulled on the dress, and the silk slip was cold as it slid across my skin. Rhinestones sparkled across the gauze overlay as moonlight filtered in through the window. I'd never touched, let alone worn, anything as delicate or whimsical as this in my life.

I blindly felt my way back into the bedroom, suddenly shy under their stares. Nolan walked up to me and pulled the hairband out of my hair. The heavy weight tumbled loosely onto my shoulders as he smiled.

"Perfect," he murmured, slipping a harness for golden wings over my shoulders. Mia grinned at me as she walked up and placed a crown of gold ivy leaves on my head. I shivered as electricity shot through my body under their ministrations.

"Who are you supposed to be?" I asked, nodding at the flowing toga draping her body. A gold braided belt cinched the waist, and a matching gold headband was threaded through her curls.

"Hermia," she replied, giving me a spin. "It was my costume from last year, and I was feeling nostalgic."

Nolan leaned toward me. "I may have dropped another toga off at Ben's cabin so he could be Lysander."

I grinned at our horned matchmaker. "You romantic, you."

He shrugged. "I'm just trying to nudge fate in the right direction." He stepped closer to me and gently smeared glitter across my cheeks, like war paint. His hands lingered on my face, and he leaned in. "You are the queen of all the damn fairies, and you don't avert your eyes or bow to anyone."

My knees trembled a little as I thought of all the possibilities the night could hold, but I met his gaze and gave him a firm nod. The crown heavy, yet comforting, on my head.

"That's my girl." He squeezed my shoulder before turning around and clapping in Mia's direction. "The party express is rolling out of here in about five minutes, so I'm going to need everyone to pull themselves together. My minions should be done setting up by now, and it's just about time for me to make a fashionably late arrival."

"You have minions?" I asked.

He rolled his eyes and spread his arms out so I could take in the full impact of his glittering appearance.

I shrugged, conceding the point. "Fair enough."

Mia picked up the small candle and extinguished the light. We stumbled into the living room over each other and almost made it to the front door when Shelby's door flew open.

"Are you all done waking up the entire camp?" she hissed, stepping out into the moonlight as the light winked across a small silver crown on her head. Her attention snapped to the golden ivy nestled in my curls.

"Are you kidding me?" She stepped forward, and I stumbled

back into Nolan's warm presence. "I hate to break it to you, but there is only one queen here."

"Seriously, Nolan, you're going to have to do a DNA test. There is no way you two are related," Mia said.

Nolan's hands moved to my shoulders and gently squeezed. "That's all right, Bea. I have another toga here, and you'd make a beautiful Helena. It'd actually be a little cute for you to end up being the peanut butter to Nik's jam tonight."

I froze at the thought, but Shelby's eyes narrowed.

"Nik is going as Demetrius?"

Nolan shrugged. "He didn't feel like dressing up that much. A toga seemed a good choice for him."

Shelby's face scrunched up and she paused for only a moment before ripping the crown off her head and holding her hand out. "Fine, I'll be the bigger person and change. Give me the toga."

Nolan pulled out another white dress from his bag and placed it in her outstretched hand. Her fingers closed around it, but as she tried to pull it toward her she was yanked forward into Nolan's personal space. "Be nicer, sister. Be the person I know you can be."

She grimaced, pulling the material free. Spinning on her heel, she shut her door behind her. Nolan ushered us out and we stepped off the path and into the woods. Silver filtered in through the trees, and Mia slipped her warm hand into mine as we raced into the night. I brushed aside branches grasping at my dress and swallowed the laugh bubbling up my throat. Nolan moved up beside us, righting my crown.

He smiled, glittering and fey under starlight.

"I don't want to get between you and your sister," I murmured.

He cut his eyes toward me. "The problems between us have nothing to do with you, but don't think I wouldn't defend you if it came down to it."

"I can fight my own battles," I said, finding his hand in the darkness and giving it a squeeze. Words I didn't know how to say clogged in my throat.

Mia squeezed my other hand. "We know, but nobody is allowed to pick on you but us."

Nolan laughed, the sound floating up into the trees. "I have a feeling we are going to have so much teasing material by the time this evening is over."

"I doubt that." A small twig snarled in my hair, and I stumbled. "Could we please move to the normal path to go wherever the hell we're going? Why are we creeping through the trees?"

Mia giggled, slapping her hand over her mouth as the sound ricocheted around us.

"We can walk on the path if you want to get caught!" Nolan hissed as he moved ahead. "It's not too much further; we're just going to the Globe."

"The Globe?" I blurted as they shushed me. I'd almost forgotten about our mysterious replica playhouse that was situated out in the woods. This theater that we would not move our rehearsals to until the very last week.

"There it is!" Mia whispered, squeezing my arm, as a structure loomed up out of the darkness. We stepped out of the woods and stepped into the shadow of a round whitewashed building. I grinned at the authenticity of it, sliding my hand down the heavy double doors that Nolan had already reached.

He smiled back at me before swinging them inward and giving me a dramatic bow. "My queen, may I present your kingdom."

I was too stunned to offer a sarcastic reply. I stepped over the threshold, my eyes drifting toward the stars sparkling through the open ceiling and finally landing on the giant stage sitting foremost in front of me. Large clusters of thick white candles were peppered across the stage and down the aisle between the pews. I was pushed forward as Nolan steered me up toward the stage, where two large gilt thrones were sitting center stage.

"Make way for our queen, you peasants," Nolan announced, and I blushed at the looks from the other campers.

"I think you're taking this costume thing too far," I said, turning my head to hide behind my hair as he pushed me up the stairs to the stage.

"No such thing as too far, my sweet." He spun me around, my dress billowing out like starlight. The backs of my knees hit the throne, and I sank down onto red velvet. My knuckles blanched and I gripped the armrests as if my life depended on it. He shared a secret smile with Mia, and the hairs on my arms stood up.

"What's going on here?" I asked, butterflies swarming in my stomach and threatening to choke me.

"My queen, so glad you could join me."

My eyes shuttered closed. I opened them to glare at Nolan before acknowledging the figure now leaning against the throne next to me. He was wearing black board shorts, while gold glitter sparkled across his broad chest and a golden ivy crown nestled in his black curls. As candlelight flickered over his skin, I was glad I was already sitting.

I fixed my gaze on a random spot over his head. "A little birdie told me that you were going as Demetrius," I said flatly.

"That wasn't very nice of him. Especially since he was thoughtful enough to drop off this crown and a surprising amount of glitter," Nik said, dropping onto the throne next to me.

"If you need help reapplying later, you let me know!" Nolan said, not an ounce of apology in his smile. "Play nice, you two!" He ambled back to Mia, who gave me a little wave before locating Ben in the crowd. She grinned at his toga and bashful stare, and I knew no rescue would be coming from her.

I exhaled a long-suffering sigh. Horned matchmaker all right.

"Oh, don't be that way, Mouse." Nik laughed at my visible discomfort. "You'd rather be paired with a different king?"

"Shhh," I whispered. "Titania and Oberon are estranged."

"Then it's perfect for us," he whispered back. "You asked to postpone the game during the movie, and being the gentleman I am, I conceded. Tonight's the night to finish this, though." He waved at the candlelit stage and the small groups milling around. "Perfect setting, huh?"

He smiled at me, a mix of amusement and something I couldn't quite put my finger on. I once again felt like I was missing something important. Some social cue that was always slipping out of my grasp.

"Why do you want to play this so badly?" I asked.

"Why are you trying so hard to avoid this? I remember you starting this, and you seemed very enthusiastic when we first started."

On the tip of my tongue were questions I had no idea how to answer: *You picked a kiss just to motivate me not to lose? Wouldn't it be punishment for you, too, if you won? Since I wasn't pretty enough to be believable as Romeo's first girlfriend?* As my mouth moved to form the words, I couldn't bring myself to say them. *What if it was a joke I wasn't getting? What if it was just a normal teenage thing and I was taking it too seriously? What if he was just making fun of me? What if this was history repeating itself all over again?*

I swallowed the knot in my throat. "Fine. If you want to be humiliated in front of your peers, I'd be happy to help." I glared at him as the memory of Nolan's words stiffened my spine. I averted my eyes to nobody.

"I should probably warn you that I love a challenge," he murmured, every inch a fairy king.

The heavy wooden doors slammed closed, and a toga-clad

Shelby marched up the aisle like a drill sergeant. I pinched the bridge of my nose, wondering who up there had it in for me.

Nik smiled at her as she stomped up onto the stage. "Nice toga. Helena or Hermia?"

"It couldn't *possibly* matter. I can see that you are clearly not Demetrius," she said, turning her attention to me. "And look here! Little Bea as queen of the fairies. How ironic is that?"

I silently thanked Nolan for this new argument that Shelby and I could share as understanding dawned on Nik's face. I could not face another person defending me to her as I looked on in silence, so I shot off the throne, a manic smile straining my lips. "Be my guest." I gestured to the throne, and maybe Nik as well, and walked off without a second glance.

I milled through the crowd, searching for my friends. Nolan was easy to find, reclining on a pew as a gaggle of people surrounded him and were clearly hanging on his every word. He waved his hands in the air, his gestures becoming more extravagant as the crowd leaned in a little closer. Mia's white toga fluttered in my periphery and disappeared into the wings. I followed her, moving around the curtain as she stepped closer to Ben and her hand reached out, trailing down his arm. He laughed, moving closer to her, and I turned away, blushing. I didn't belong here, but I didn't want to make anyone feel like they had to save me because I was too awkward to function in public. I pushed my glasses up, weighing the options of hiding or attempting to escape only to have them run after me in concern. I sighed, the gauzy material sliding across the tops of my thighs.

I was here for the long haul.

Moving off to the side, I felt impossibly alone as people I kind of knew but didn't really know drifted around me. Off in the corner a bench peeked out from behind a curtain, and I moved toward it—stopping short when I realized it already had an occupant—the guy playing Tybalt. The guy who had stopped me outside the bus on our shopping trip. The one Shelby had apparently dumped for Nik last summer. *Troy.* The candlelight winked over his bare chest as he leaned over and pressed a bottle to his lips. A pair of brown shorts hugged his hips, and a donkey head rested on the bench next to him. I could still see the two thrones and the backs of Shelby's and Nik's heads. They were close together, and my stomach lurched. My feet were moving before my brain had made a decision. It was time to dip my toes in. All in.

### 9.) *Flirt with someone for the sheer hell of it*

I stopped in front of him. "What are you doing hiding over here?" The question sounded sharp. Accusatory. I tried to soften it with a smile, but it felt lopsided.

He looked me over, his eyes lingering on my hem as he brought the bottle back to his lips.

"Also, why is nobody here wearing a shirt?" I said, shifting in front of him.

He flexed, moving the donkey mask and gesturing to the space next to him. "Why? See something that you like?" He reclined on the little bench, taking up more space than strictly necessary.

I wrinkled my nose and stared at him until he looked away. He flushed, and I rolled my eyes before joining him and moving my wings to accommodate the space. "So, what made you choose Bottom for tonight?"

"Who?" he asked, angling his body toward me.

I frowned, nodding at his donkey head. "Bottom? The character in A *Midsummer Night's Dream* that gets turned into a donkey?"

He shrugged. "I don't know the play that well."

"Oh. Okay then." I grasped for conversational material. "During the play, Titania the queen of the fairies has a spell cast on her that makes her fall in love with the donkey guy."

He grinned, sliding closer to me. "Oh yeah? You're dressed as the queen, right?"

I paused. This was the desired reaction, right? He says something complimentary, and then I say something complimentary? We were supposed to go back and forth until what? What was the end point when it's just "for the sheer hell of it"?

I adjusted my glasses, trying not to fall off the bench. "Something like that," I said, his eyes still on my crown.

"You know, you're pretty cute. I'm Troy, in case you forgot."

I flushed, pulling my hem down as I shifted onto more of the bench. "I know who you are. You can call me Bea."

"I know who you are too." He leaned a little closer. "It's cute that you're shy."

I leaned back, maintaining the distance between us. *Take a compliment, give a compliment.* "I'm not actually that shy." The silence crawled up my spine. "Your tan is very symmetric."

He blinked. "Umm—okay. Thanks?" He lifted his bottle, taking a healthy swig.

"Is that alcohol?" I asked, inspecting the label.

He snorted before taking another swig. "Barely. We all smuggle in what we can for this party, but I got stuck with the peach schnapps."

I glanced over to where Nik and Shelby were still talking. "Everyone?"

He followed my gaze and chuckled softly to himself. "Are you talking about Golden Boy over there? Pretty sure he brought something pretentious like wine."

He rolled his eyes at my shocked expression. "It's not that big a deal, Bea."

He held the bottle in my direction, and I frowned.

"I doubt this stuff could make anyone drunk," he muttered.

I weighed the importance of alcohol exposure prior to going to Oxford. I knew that wine was available with dinner and some academics considered themselves collectors or purveyors of this type of thing. I could consider broadening my education to these topics if only for the conversational aspect they could provide. I felt my hand close around the cold bottle as Troy's eyebrows shot up. I inspected the lip of the bottle and considered his cleanliness in general before closing my eyes and taking a large gulp.

The liquid poured into my mouth, and the thick, cloying taste of fake peaches overwhelmed me. I roughly swallowed it down, coughing a bit.

He laughed. "Your face is priceless. I can't believe you did that."

"It's not the worst decision I've made tonight," I said, taking another swig to try and differentiate the flavors I was tasting. "Is there vanilla in this? Or is that lemon?"

He grinned. I tried to hand the bottle back to him, but he waved me off. "No, that's all you now. I don't think I've ever seen anyone approach schnapps so seriously before, and I'm dying to see what you figure out."

I shrugged, taking another swig. "It doesn't seem like there's any alcohol in it."

He nodded in agreement. "You know, I've been saying the same thing all night."

# Chapter Twenty

**"WHAT THE *FUCK* IS GOING ON HERE?"**

I was laughing so hard, I was gasping for air. Troy grabbed the bottle out of my hand and ripped off his donkey mask before saluting Nik and taking a hearty swig.

I turned around, nearly falling off the bench, as Troy reached out to support me. Nik's face was thunderous, and I felt fluttering in my belly. I slapped Troy in the chest. "This here is my friend Troy. I'm teaching him some scenes from *Midsummer Night's . . . Dream.*" I snickered.

Troy winked provocatively at me. "She was telling me how the queen falls madly in love with the donkey." His arm wrapped tightly around my waist as he kept me from toppling off the bench.

"I think you mean 'jackass,'" Nik barked. "Did you get her drunk?"

Troy held up a hand in surrender, and I almost tumbled to the floor. "Oh, she did that all on her own. She was determined to identify every flavor in peach schnapps."

I shrugged out of his embrace and stumbled forward as another wave of warmth flooded my system. "Nik, did you know that three hundred different varieties of peaches can be found in the United States?" I wobbled a little, and he stepped closer, catching me, his large hands resting lightly on my waist. "There are over two thousand varieties globally," I finished, a little out of breath.

"Is that so?" he murmured, the words caressing the side of my neck. "You can tell me more about that as I walk you home."

Troy jumped up. "You're not her dad! She can decide what she wants to do. We were having a great time before you stormed over here. Just go back to Shelby."

My eyes narrowed, and I pushed at Nik's chest, escaping his arms. "Oh yeah, you should go back to Shelby."

Nik rolled his eyes. "Be reasonable, Mouse; I just want what's best for you."

"You don't get to pick what is best for me. I decide. *I'm* the decider." I gestured at myself.

He sighed, looking for someone in the crowd. "You're right; you're the decider. What would you like to do?"

"You know you can always tell him to go away and we can continue where we left off?" Troy said, patting his lap. The smug smile on his lips for Nik alone. I rolled my eyes and dragged Nik away, his witch-black eyes darkening. My stomach flipped with excitement at the snarl on his lips, and his anger was more intoxicating than anything I'd found in that bottle. I stepped closer, breathing him in. My body was making decisions that my brain hadn't completely vetted, and I realized my hand was still on his arm. I snatched it back, curling my fingers into my palm. Gold glitter marking where we'd touched.

Nik turned to the crowd and waved someone over. I poked him hard in the stomach, wanting all his focus again. "I thought you were ready to settle this . . . thing."

He looked down at me. "What *thing* are you talking about, Mouse?"

"The game?"

He frowned. "No, not tonight. You're drunk."

I glared, taking a mental inventory of my faculties. My limbs felt a little heavy, my body felt flushed and warm, and I might have been a little less graceful than normal, but I felt . . . okay. He was just being overdramatic. "Troy is right. I don't need another dad." I folded my arms.

He laughed in disbelief. "You're agreeing with Troy now? What has gotten into you?"

"What's wrong, Nik? You don't like it when the little mouse talks back and isn't all quiet, nervous, and does whatever you say?"

He yanked the crown off his head, curls tumbling. He stepped closer. "If you think that's how I see you, you aren't as smart as you think you are."

I scoffed, and someone pulled me into a headlock that was barely disguised as a hug.

"Everything okay over here, children?" Nolan drawled. He sized Nik up and down and raised an eyebrow at my flushed appearance as I pulled myself free. "I assume you flagged me over here for a reason?"

I scowled. "Everything is fine, Nolan. Nik is just being more protective than he has any right to be. Go back to your group."

"I found her with half a bottle of peach schnapps in her system, and in Troy's lap." He frowned as Nolan started choking.

"I was not in his lap! I slipped!"

"The events that led you to that point are not relevant."

"Okay! *Enough!*" Nolan looked back and forth between the two of us before focusing on me. "Are you feeling all right, Bea?"

I nodded, hugging myself as embarrassment washed over me.

He winked, the promise of all the things he was going to say when we were finally alone. "Let's go get you a little water before you get back out there," he said as Nik sputtered.

"That's it? Aren't you going to take her home?"

Nolan turned slowly, the only guy in camp who didn't have to physically look up to him. "She's not a child that I'm going to send to her room for naughty behavior. She had a little bit to drink, and we're going to give her some water and time to sober up."

Nik clenched his jaw, tossing his crown across the stage. "Come on. You're serious? It was Troy!"

Nolan shrugged. "Yeah, he's a mimbo, but who of us hasn't made a few blond and tan mistakes?" He straightened my wings. "I'm going to go try and find you a bottle of water, love."

I looked around his retreating figure, and Troy saluted me with his bottle, a knowing smile on his lips. I wrenched my attention back to Nik as he struggled to master his features.

He swiped a hand raggedly across his face, trying to wipe the scowl from his lips. "I'm an idiot. I keep messing this up."

I met his gaze, not looking away and not giving an inch. The candlelight flickered over him as thousands of little diamonds winked across his skin.

"I . . . I don't know why I reacted that way. I was worried he might be taking advantage of you. Do you want to go back over there?"

I considered saying yes just to spite him, but then I'd have to spend more time with Troy. I shook my head, organizing my thoughts. "No. I told him I was moving to Oxford in the fall, and he thought I meant in Florida."

Nik choked on a laugh. "Yeah, probably no real future there."

I frowned. "Try not to look so superior about it." I took another step back as embarrassment did more to sober me up than water probably could.

He broke into a grin. "Sorry, Mouse. If I knew you were that hard up, I would have suggested we just finish the game and your inevitable loss already."

I froze as the implications of his casual statement seared my brain. I took another step back but stopped myself. This game was just hanging over my head, and the sooner I could be done with it the better. "You know, you're right; let's just get this over with."

He frowned. "Get this over with?"

"Yeah, once I beat you, we can finally stop talking about it and just go our separate ways."

"You're so sure I will lose?" he asked, raising an eyebrow.

"Absolutely," I said, tilting my chin up and trying to make myself as big as his presence.

"Oh, I wouldn't discount me that quickly, Mouse," he murmured. "Although I don't think I'll be collecting my winnings tonight while you're full of peach schnapps."

My face flamed red. "Not that it will even be an issue, but I am in complete possession of all of my faculties."

He gave me a look that seared me to my toes. "Whatever you say, Beatrice."

He turned away from me, clapping loudly. "Can I get everybody's attention? For the entertainment portion of this evening, you all are about to witness the second and final round of the great Shakespeare-off!"

He waved all the small groups in until they were scattered around the stage. I saw Mia and Ben walk up holding hands. Her lipstick was smudged, and she threw me an ecstatic smile.

"The contestants tonight are myself, of course . . ." He paused as whistles and cheers broke out amongst the other campers. He gave a beautiful bow and pointed in my direction. "And in the other corner, we have the brilliant, and sometimes scary, Miss Beatrice Quinn!"

A piercing whistle from Nolan broke through the murmurs. "Scary?" I asked, joining him in the makeshift circle.

A beautiful smile stretched across his lips. "A little terrifying sometimes."

"What are the terms again?" I heard Nolan's voice break through the crowd, and I shot him a glare promising a swift and memorable end.

"Ah yes, the terms," Nik said. "In the extremely unlikely scenario that Beatrice wins, I will be wearing Mia's costume around camp all day, old-lady makeup and all." The group dissolved into laughter and he waved his hands, quieting them down. "Now, if I win, which is our most likely outcome, Beatrice will be bestowing a kiss on me." He smiled at them all, with not an ounce of shame, and I felt my face alight.

"Well, that was quite a performance," I murmured.

He shrugged. "All in a day's work. I believe the first turn belongs to me." He paced slowly around me. "What to choose, what to choose . . ."

I stood ramrod straight, missing the warm glow of the schnapps.

*"I'll give thee fairies to attend on thee,*
*And they shall fetch thee jewels from the deep,*
*And sing while thou on pressed flowers dost sleep."*

I tried not to react at his voice, or the words tumbling out of him. I shot him a surprised look as the origin of the words came to me. "Been brushing up on your *Midsummer Night's Dream?*"

He smirked. "We're not all you, Mouse. I don't remember it innately. Now hit me with your best shot."

I met him at the center of our circle.

*"Asses are made to bear, and so are you."* I smiled sweetly at him as he barked in laughter and the crowd whooped.

*"Taming of the Shrew,* and rather appropriate at the moment."

He moved toward me, his eyes dancing. *"The lady doth protest too much, methinks,"* he murmured.

"Hamlet," I blurted out, not breaking his gaze.

*"You do blaspheme the good in mocking me,"* I fired back, my face on fire.

He circled me. *"Measure for Measure."* His hand snaked out and claimed a curl, rubbing it loosely between his fingers. *"Wherefore was I to this keen mockery born? When at your hands did I deserve this scorn?"* he said.

I pulled out of his reach, keeping a safe distance on the other side of the circle. "A *Midsummer Night's Dream* again. You need to branch out more if you're going to win this thing." I gave him a speculative glance. *"Why, this is very midsummer madness."*

"Madness, huh?" He smiled and stalked toward me. I backed up a step as he stopped right in front of me.

*"Twelfth Night.* Don't think I didn't see you trying to trip me up," he said.

I blushed; all bets were off at this point and I was trying to end this as soon as possible. I looked up at him bathed in candlelight, every ounce of his attention riveted on me, and every part of me briefly hoped, just for a moment, that this meant something. Anything.

*"You haunt me in every place,"* he murmured.

A million thoughts roared in my head, barely audible over the murmurs of the crowd. I felt riveted to the floor, and the sensible part of my brain insisted that I put my foot down and demand he tell me what was and wasn't real. The traitorous part thought that if a boy was ever going to kiss me it should be *this* moment.

In the end, none of those things happened. I ripped my gaze from his and choked out, *"Othello.*

"*My lord, I will take my leave of you.*

*You cannot, sir, take from me anything that I will not more willingly part withal.*" My voice cracked.

His jaw tightened and he arched an eyebrow at me. "*Hamlet.* Still enjoying this game, Mouse?"

I nodded, swallowing a million unspoken questions.

He sighed, pinning me in place. "*Sweet, bid me hold my tongue,*

*For in this rapture I shall surely speak*

*The thing I shall repent,*" he said.

The words tumbled around in my brain, and I stumbled, no longer feeling any warmth from the schnapps.

"Umm . . . that would be . . ." I paused, racking my brain and coming up empty. My breathing hitched, and I fumbled for the answer. "That would be . . . No, I know this. Hold on a second." A very self-satisfied smile slid across his face as my palms grew damp.

"The answer is . . ." I looked out at the crowd and Nolan was clutching the guy next to him. Mia's hand was pressed across her mouth, her eyes darting back and forth between me and Nik. I spun back to Nik. My mind was an absolute blank, and panic rose inside me like a wave. *No no no no no no. I'm sure I know the answer, I just need to focus. Focus focus focus. Helium. Neon. Argon. Krypton. Xenon. Radon.*

"I . . . I don't know."

He bit his lip, as if holding back a laugh, and nodded. "I picked a hard one. I hoped you didn't know it."

Surprise curdled into defiance. "Well, what's the answer then? Is it even Shakespeare?"

He arched an eyebrow at me. "Yes, it's Shakespeare, and I didn't peg you for a sore loser."

I couldn't even remember the last time I'd lost a game.

"*Troilus and Cressida*," he said, and I deflated.

The whistles and clapping from the crowd roared in my blood, and every ounce of my attention was riveted on the boy slowly approaching me. I felt like I couldn't get enough oxygen to fill my lungs. The edges of my vision started to darken, and I stumbled forward. He was there in an instant, supporting me. There was no way he couldn't feel my heart threatening to burst out of my chest.

I dragged my eyes up to his and swallowed thickly.

This was going to happen. I'd read about it, seen it in public and in movies. Plenty of people do it, and I'd familiarized myself with the science behind it. Kissing involves five of the twelve cranial nerves and causes a release of a neurotransmitter called dopamine, which can mimic the same response people get when they take drugs. I suppose as long as it's done correctly.

I froze as he looked down, searching my face. I imagined that like most skills, there would be a learning curve to kissing, and I could anticipate poor performance until given the opportunity to receive some instruction.

I tore my eyes away from his and scanned the crowd scattered amongst the candlelight—all laughing and looking up at us. Laughing at *me*. Despite the warm, bubbly feeling that came along with my liquid courage, all the reasons I was avoiding Nik came back to me. I was still that same awkward, glasses-wearing, socially stunted girl, and he was still the guy who turned heads everywhere. The guy who hung out with Shelby in Central Park and who had a movie star smile and actual movie star parents. I took a step back, pulling myself out of his reach. There was not a hint of logic in this, and my wretched heart stumbled as my trajectory moved me farther from him.

"Mouse," he murmured, with an eyebrow arched. "What's going on in there? I already told you I have no intention of settling this bet tonight."

I numbly shook my head, my focus tunneling on him until the rest of the audience faded and it was just him and me in the barely lit darkness. "I don't understand this."

I gestured between the two of us.

"I think you do."

"No!" I hissed. "I have no idea how we got to this point. We argue more often than not, I feel like you're laughing at me most of the time, and you didn't even think I was pretty enough to play Rosaline. If this is a joke, you should tell me now."

"Beatrice, you're being ridiculous. Maybe when you're sober—"

I felt the terrifying prick of tears, as he didn't even bother addressing any of my fears. "Do not discount me, Nikhil. We're done here."

With that I fled.

I raced to the side of the stage and down the stairs toward the door. *Helium.* I felt the stares of the audience burning into my back, and Shelby's peal of laughter rose above the murmurs. *Neon.* I burst through the doors, trying to orient myself, and plunged back through the woods we'd come through. *Argon.* Branches raked against me, pulling at my hair and my wings. *Krypton.* I raced forward, warm rivulets sliding down my face. *Xenon.* I paused, my fingers scrambling over the rough bark of a large tree as I tried to remember the direction we came from. *Radon.* I couldn't even remember the last time I'd cried.

Spying a break in the trees, I lunged toward it and stumbled out onto the public path. Mia's warnings about being caught rattled around in my brain, but at this point I wasn't sure if I could make it until the performance. Being sent back home, where nothing unpleasant or surprising ever happened, would be a relief. I took deep, gasping breaths, trying to center myself, as I walked back toward the cabin.

I swiped at my face; my hands streaked with grime. What was I thinking? I wasn't this kind of girl. I couldn't just walk up to a guy and *flirt*. Or kiss someone onstage in front of a crowd of people. At this point I wasn't even sure I could kiss someone at all.

Mia crashed out of the bushes behind me. "Thank God, there you are! These woods are dark!" She leaned over, her hands on her knees as she caught her breath.

I sniffed, my vision blurring, and willed the tears to stop falling. *Stop. Crying.*

She stood up, her eyes softening, and she slipped an arm around my shoulders. We walked in silence until our cabin came into view.

"Thank you," I mumbled, unable to meet her gaze. "For coming after me."

Her arm tightened. "Of course I came after you. I made Nolan stay and hold Nik back."

I froze, imagining *that* possibility. She nudged me, and we staggered up onto the front porch.

Her concern hung heavy in the air between us. "Do you want to talk about it? About what happened up there with Nik?"

I felt a million years old. "Maybe. I'll see you in there." I nodded toward our bedroom and slipped into the bathroom. My heart sank as I saw the tears in my dress and the beautiful golden wings. My hair was wild, with small twigs tangled in it. My eyes were large and overwhelmed as tear tracks cut through grime on my cheeks. Dread hung heavy in my stomach as I thought of

Nik so beautiful in the candlelight, and his refusal to answer my questions. What were the rules? Why couldn't I figure out this problem?

I tugged the crown off my head and tossed it in the sink.

# Chapter Twenty-One

**I PINCHED THE BRIDGE OF MY NOSE. THE BRIGHT** lights of the auditorium pierced my brain, and I whimpered as Mr. G bellowed next to me.

"What is going on with all of you today? It's like two weeks of progress were just flushed down the toilet!" Mr. G slammed his script down as Mr. and Mrs. Capulet hurried offstage, their heads bent in embarrassment. I shifted next to him, feeling my pulse behind my eyes.

I resisted the urge to pull my hands over my ears. The not-so-subtle reminder of how many poor decisions I made last night was just the wake-up call I needed to keep my head down and ride out the rest of the summer without any more drama. Agreeing to stand near the front with Mr. G and help him with today's rehearsal was another poor choice, and it was all Mia's fault. I was prepared to sulk in the back and lick my wounds, if it weren't for her reminder that the list was only halfway done and I was running out of time. I couldn't let all these *emotions* cloud my judgment and ruin Oxford.

"We're moving on to the next scene!" Mr. G said, beating his leg with his script, his blood pressure rising in front of me. I felt a small twinge of pity at the retreating forms of the Capulets, but he wasn't wrong. We were all too wooden, too stiff with each other. It was almost as if all these delicate little strings of attraction, these impossibly complicated relationship dynamics, had exploded during our illicit party. Now everybody was on their very best behavior. Nobody wanted to look stupid or vulnerable in front of each other, so everyone was reciting their lines without the fervor or enthusiasm to believe them.

"I didn't honestly think we could get worse."

I turned to where Mia perched in the front row—her poor attempt at a whisper garnering glares from the people around her.

She looked effortless in her oversized Jackie O sunglasses, which were an accessory made necessary by either some alcohol ingestion that I wasn't aware of or the long night we had as we talked through everything that had happened up there on that stage. Or, most importantly, what had not happened up there.

"I have an idea." Nik's voice cut through the crowd. "We could play the truth game."

I flinched, inching behind Mr. G.

Murmurs broke out amongst the crowd, and Mr. G stopped scowling for a moment at the suggestion. "That can sometimes be an effective tool, but it can be a lot to ask from those who are relatively new to acting."

This produced a riot of protests and exclamations, and all I could think of was how predictable my generation was.

As Nik's voice once again rose above the murmurs, I still refused to turn around.

"Maybe if I explain? The truth game is where for an entire twenty-four hours you have to tell the absolute truth to any question posed to you. It makes us *all* vulnerable, and we all put ourselves out there. It can make it a little easier to act foolish or become another character afterwards without fear of being judged."

The insistence on trying the game seemed a little less enthusiastic this time, but overall, most of the group was determined to try it.

Drama-hungry teenagers.

"Beatrice, perhaps this is the type of exercise you needed all along," Mr. G said, patting me on the shoulder. "It can do wonders for stage fright."

I wrinkled my nose. "Oh well, maybe next time. I'm just the prompter, so I don't think I will really need to participate."

Sorry, not sorry.

"Then it's settled," Nik concluded. "For the next twenty-four hours, the truth game is in effect. You're not allowed to hold the truth against anyone, and whatever you ask somebody you better want to actually know."

The audience clapped in enthusiasm, and I wondered how many of them would still be talking to each other by tomorrow. Mia slid up next to me and poked me in the ribs. "You should play! It sounds insane, but there's something very liberating about it. No masks or hiding anything, just being your one hundred percent authentic self."

"I'm pretty certain my authentic self would burn so many bridges that I'd be packed up and put on a plane before the twenty-four hours was up."

She pulled the sunglasses off. "Or you could be the smart girl that I know you are, and use this opportunity to maybe answer some of the questions you were so confused about last night?"

I winced as the memory of my tipsy rants to Mia from the previous night came flooding back. Even in the light of day, there were things that I didn't understand. Did he honestly expect me to kiss him in front of all of those people? What does that say about him? What would I have done if he'd moved just a little faster than my brain and it had actually happened?

I shook my head. "There is no point in going down that road."

She frowned before leaning in and squeezing my hand. "Try and spend less time locked away in your own brain. Now, if you will excuse me, I'm going to go over and stand next to Ben and make him *very* nervous."

I laughed as she skipped away, but my attention was snagged as the boy in question made a beeline straight for me.

He walked up, his hair tumbled like he'd just rolled out of bed and his eyes always unreadable. "How's your head this morning?"

I wanted to die just a tiny bit as I remembered his face when he stumbled across me and Troy. "None of your business."

"Yeah, you've made yourself quite clear on that, when you literally ran away from me last night. It's kind of a habit of yours."

"I didn't run." I scowled. "I just didn't see the point in—being there anymore."

"Ouch."

I rolled my eyes. "Don't pretend you're hurt. I'm sure you went right back to being the life of the party and barely remember any of it."

"My memory is fine. I wasn't the one trashed on peach schnapps. Also, don't pretend to know what I'm feeling. If you want to know, you're going to have to play the game."

I shook my head and physically forced myself not to take a step back.

"What's the matter? Scared?" He cocked his head to the side.

I bristled, indignation almost choking me. He was just playing with me. Again. He expected me to refuse, to not commit. To be honest, all of them did, even Mr. G with his little sympathetic smile. They didn't see me as a participant in this camp, this game, this life. Just a bystander looking in.

"Fine," I snarled, with confidence I didn't feel. I was going to experience something even if it killed me. I turned my back on him and walked quickly back into Mr. G's protective orbit. If I was going to experience something, I wanted it to be on my terms. I knew Nik wasn't going to make it easy on me, and I could feel the pricks of his attention on the back of my neck the rest of the morning. I tried to focus on the scenes unfolding in front of me, but I was hyperaware of every movement. He would walk toward me, and I would scoot closer to Mr. G or strike up a conversation with Mia. All it would take was one moment. One second where I wasn't paying attention and Nik would corner me. By the time we broke for lunch, I was about to fall over.

I dropped my tray in exhaustion and slid into my normal seat across from Nolan. My head was still aching from the party the night before, but it had taken on a new sharpness with the additional stress. I yanked open my container of yogurt as I realized he wasn't talking. For once.

I looked up and swallowed abruptly as his eyes pinned me to my seat.

"What?"

"Go ahead, Bea. Just keep enjoying that little yogurt. Nothing to see here, nothing to talk about or share with your friends," Nolan said.

I rolled my eyes. "Fine, let's get this thing over with."

Mia dropped her tray next to mine. "This whole thing would be a lot more interesting if Bea had agreed to participate in our little experiment."

Nolan's gaze darted back and forth between us. "I'm not sure which story I want to hear first. Bea, you go. Wait! No, Mia, you go first!"

I sighed in relief, until his gaze snapped to mine. "Don't

think we're not going to get every detail out of you before this is all said and done." He turned back to Mia and nodded.

"Well—" Mia drawled out. "Everyone was terrible this morning. Either hung over, or just bad at baseline, and Mr. G was having one of his little hissy fits, when guess who rode in on his white horse to suggest a little game to help the actors loosen up."

They turned to me, and I poked at my turkey sandwich, ignoring all of them.

"What is this shining solution that our Prince Charming came up with?" Nolan asked.

"It's this ice-breaking activity that some directors have a thing for," Mia continued, ignoring me. "You basically put yourself completely out there for twenty-four hours. You say nothing but the truth, and through the vulnerability and awkwardness you really bond with your castmates."

Nolan's eyebrows shot up. "I could ask you anything right now, and you would tell me the truth?"

Mia shrugged. "My life is an open book."

"Have you kissed that blond love muffin that follows you around like you're the second coming?" Nolan said, pointing a fork in her direction.

"Like our plane was going down," Mia said, her smile smug.

Some of my yogurt went down the wrong pathway.

Nolan swung his attention back to me. "Ah, I see, and our little genius decided that she wasn't ready to give up all her secrets just yet?"

"She deflected by saying that she was just the prompter."

I sighed. "Well, about that—"

She grinned. "Oh my stars! I saw him go up to you after, but I didn't think he would convince you."

I flushed. "He didn't convince me. I decided for myself that I might want to be a little more approachable."

Nolan flung down his own sandwich and rubbed his hands together. "Are you ready to play twenty questions?"

I felt sick. "Go easy on me, Nolan."

"Oh, *relax*. I'm just going to ask a few select questions that will get us all caught up."

I braced myself as he grinned. "Were you sitting in Troy's lap in an effort to make Nik insanely jealous?"

Mia covered her mouth while she chewed. "You know, I didn't think of it like that. Pure genius."

I put my head on the table and mumbled, "No. I accidentally ended up there. The schnapps were stronger than I calculated."

"Ah," he murmured. "It was just a happy coincidence then. Did you make the connection that all of the lines he said to you in the contest were basically a love letter?"

My head shot up. "That was to throw me off my game. He was just playing with me."

Nolan met Mia's gaze before landing back on mine. "Do you realize that you are the only one who believes that?"

I looked at Mia for support as she busied herself with her sandwich. "I don't think—"

"Why did you run away?" Nolan asked, the tips of his fingers brushing mine.

I stared at my plate. "I wasn't sure what he was going to do or what I was supposed to do, and I wasn't sure I wanted to stay there to find out." I shifted awkwardly on the bench. "This whole thing just doesn't make any sense."

Nolan chewed on his lip as he examined me before slipping his hand into mine. "Does it have to?"

I shook my head, at a loss for words. "For me? Yes."

He nodded and shot me a brilliant smile. "Okay, boo, that's enough then. Now for the most important question, who do you think is the most handsome man in this entire camp?"

I laughed, my hands shaking under the table. "The rules are that I have to tell the truth, not inflate your ego."

"Rude."

"Incoming!" Mia whispered next to me, her smile bright.

Nik and Ben ambled over from their table, and Nik slid in next to Nolan again as Mia squished up next to me to make room for Ben.

"Why didn't Troy come over?" Nolan asked, smiling at Nik.

I resisted the urge to crawl under the table as Nik narrowed his eyes at me. "Is there a reason why Troy needs to come over?" he asked, his tone as even as glass.

I ignored him, peeling the crust off my sandwich.

"Bea, quit playing with your food," Nolan chided. "No reason, we were just talking about some of the highlights of the party last night."

Nik snorted. "Troy was a highlight?"

Nolan waved him off. "Maybe not for you. Tell us, Nik, what was the highlight of your night last night?"

Nik hid a smile. "I'm guessing you know about the game we're all playing? That's fine, Nolan; I'll go along with it." He tapped his chin. "I would have to say that the highlight of my evening was beating Beatrice pretty soundly at our Shakespeare-off."

I glared daggers at him. "Beating me by one point doesn't really qualify as 'soundly,'" I said, using air quotations. "Plus, you studied beforehand."

"You had every opportunity to do so, if you chose. Maybe a part of you was secretly hoping to lose."

"Oh sure, the same part of me that literally fled from you collecting your prize."

"I made myself perfectly clear last night that you would be sober when I collected that prize."

My heart stuttered and I turned toward Mia, panic bleeding

into my voice. "Didn't Mr. G say we had to be back by noon? We should get out of here."

She frowned, looking between Ben and me.

Nolan leaned across the table. "Hey, Ben, have you asked Mia to be your girlfriend yet?"

His ears turned a brilliant shade of red. "Umm, I don't think we've discussed any of that yet."

"But you want to, right?"

Ben looked helplessly at us before turning to Mia. He nodded. "Yes."

Mia grinned and gave him a kiss on the cheek. "Nolan, remind me to punish you later. You don't get to take advantage of the game anymore unless you play yourself."

He pulled his hair up into a bun. "I was just tidying up loose ends so Bea could get back to work."

# Chapter Twenty-Two

**THE REST OF THE AFTERNOON EVOLVED INTO** an elaborate dance I didn't know the steps to. I was unsettled, always on the wrong foot, the offbeat. Balanced on a knife's edge, with no instructions. I could sit Nik down and outline all the questions and inconsistencies, and he would be obligated to answer to my satisfaction. I could finally understand. It would finally make sense. On the other hand, what if I opened myself up to a conversation that didn't result in the answers I needed? What if I walked away worse off than before, and also had to undergo a similar interrogation? A microscopic examination of thoughts and feelings I had no idea what to do with? It was better to balance. To both play and not play. Schrödinger's scaredy-cat.

Nik was determined to make it difficult. Like everything else.

I sank deep in my chair as Nik leaned over me, helping himself to some of Mr. G's peanuts. His white T-shirt sliding tightly against his shoulders. He would insist on walking the long way to get up to the stage with each scene—his arm brushing past me, ruffling the hairs on my neck. That tiny smile tugging on his lips.

My stomach had hopelessly tangled into knots by the time

we broke for the day, and I had to call a time-out for myself. Mia didn't even bother arguing with me—my jangling restlessness was setting everyone's teeth on edge. She skipped along, her hand tightly wound in Ben's on the way to dinner, and I slipped out the side door. I had protein bars in my room, and my presence at that table would just open up more potential opportunities for embarrassment. A person might call it cowardly, but I preferred to think of it as having a highly developed survival instinct. I refused to be the gazelle at the edge of the lake who waded in blindly.

It was that instinct that reared its ugly head later that night as I read my book, lulled into a false sense of security by the sounds of the dryer. The rest of the camp were at dinner, and the sound of the laundry room door swinging closed had my stomach dropping into my shoes.

I *knew* it was him. He couldn't just leave well enough alone. No crowds, no buffer, nobody else to take over the conversation when the words turned to dust in my mouth. I glanced at the machine. Six minutes and thirty-four seconds left. I could probably live without these clothes. I slammed my book closed, balanced on the balls of my feet, and wavered between fight and flight. I was always running. That was what I was basically known for, right? Someone insults my clothes? Run. Someone makes a stupid bet and expects you to kiss him in front of a roomful of people? Run.

Run. Run. Run.

*Helium. Neon. Argon. Krypton. Xenon. Radon.*

A skittering little mouse.

I knew he was moving closer, and even the silence was predatory. I pressed the jagged edges of my fingernails into my palms as my clothes tumbled over and over. I wasn't running anymore. He was such an asshole to come in here. He knew I didn't want to talk to him, and maybe I shouldn't have agreed to this stupid game, but I was not about to be intimidated.

Not anymore. Not by anybody.

He moved past, not saying a word, and started unloading his clothes into the machine next to mine. I walked over to a bench a few feet away and sat down. Five minutes and forty-eight seconds.

"So, tell me," he said, not bothering to turn around. "Just a burning desire to do laundry at this time, or are we trying to avoid something?" He briskly dropped the lid on the washer. "Or someone?"

He was so hard to read. The magic that scrolled across his face onstage, where every emotion and thought was served up on a perfect silver platter, was gone in real life. At least with me. All I got was furrowed brows, mocking smiles, and encounters that left me with a bigger headache than the peach schnapps.

He spun the dial, and the machine whirred to life. My own machine continued to toss my clothes around, the rhythmic rumble previously soothing. Five minutes and twenty-two seconds. They had to be dry enough at this point, right? I stiffened as he waltzed over to me and sat down on the bench—his leg brushing against mine as if he didn't have a care in the world.

He was too close, and I tried to slow my breathing.

"Is this your plan? Refuse to talk to me, and pretend that you're still technically playing the game?"

I racked my brain for any scrap of conversation. Anything to place us back in safe territory. "Did you know that *Hamlet* has the longest speaking part in any of Shakespeare's plays, at one thousand five hundred and thirty lines? I assume you do, since I remember you saying that you played Hamlet once. Maybe you didn't count them, though." My voice strained to sound normal.

"That's what you want to talk about? How many lines Hamlet has?" he asked, finally looking at me. The corner of his mouth twitched as I jumped up. Forget it. They could be wringing wet and I would still throw them in my basket as if that were the most natural thing in the world. My hand reached out to lift the lid as he reached out from behind me. His palm splayed across the scuffed metal, and my heart sank.

"Beatrice."

"If I don't want to talk to you, shouldn't you maybe take that as a hint?"

He sighed, close enough for his breath to ruffle my hair. "I think you do want to talk to me. You had plenty to say to me last night before you ran away from me. *Ask me.*"

I swallowed the concrete lump in my throat. I did not want to get into it. His dismissal was answer enough, and I needed to get out of here. I tried to lift the lid of the dryer, straining against the weight from his hand.

He stepped back, disappointment coloring every word. "Nothing? It's not until you're drunk on peach schnapps that you want to settle this?"

I spun around, stretching my spine as he loomed over me. "The alcohol activated some neurotransmitters that impaired me long enough to think discussing any of this would make any sort of difference. Now that I'm no longer handicapped by that, I don't see the point." I tried to shrug nonchalantly, my shoulders jerking upright like a marionette's.

"This is what you do," he said, his eyes dark as midnight. "You hide behind your facts and words to avoid being a real person. Tell me, Mouse, do you even feel anything at all?" He took a step closer, and my retreat trapped me between him and the machine.

"Of course I feel things, you *asshole!*" I said, the word thrown down like a weapon. This emotion was at least familiar.

He placed his hands on the machine behind me. Not touching me, but still a cage. "Then tell me something real. Right here, right now." His breath felt hot against my ear, and I locked my knees to prevent the sway of my body. Like a sunflower toward sunshine.

I pressed back into the warm metal of the machine. "I don't know what to say in this type of situation."

"There is no rote response to this, Beatrice," he said, stepping closer.

I could feel the long lines of his body, and I ducked my head so he couldn't see my face. I was drowning. He was so silent as his fingers curled around a strand of hair that had escaped my bun. "If you want me to take control of the conversation, I can." My brain was barely able to continue basic respiratory function, let alone interrogate him on every interaction we'd ever had. He tensed, as if he'd finally made a decision, and he leaned down.

"Have you fantasized about kissing me?" The whisper fluttered against my neck.

I couldn't catch my breath and he was waiting for an answer, but he wasn't giving me any room to think. I could lie. Oh, I could lie and be cold and indignant, and I doubt he'd ever bother me again. The words settled behind my teeth, ready to cut through the tension and that mask that always seemed to be in place.

He was right, though. I did want something real, even if I only ever got this one time. Even if it blew up in my face afterwards. Like before.

"That's the only question you want to ask me?"

He hesitated for the briefest of seconds. "Yes."

No going back now.

"Yes," I choked out.

He exhaled and took a step back. I felt as if my strings had been cut, and I focused on his shoes. They were scuffed and still muddy from last night. I pushed my glasses up, waiting to see them retreat.

"*Look* at me, Beatrice."

I didn't want to look at him, but simply refusing just seemed childish. I clenched my jaw and dragged my eyes up. Like jumping off the dock. All in. He was so heartbreakingly beautiful, and everything was too close to the surface.

"What are you feeling?" he asked.

*Hate. Anger. Lust. Sadness. Happiness. Embarrassment.* "I don't know." *Helium. Neon. Argon. Krypton. Xenon. Radon.*

He nodded, and that impassive control was no longer written across his features. Just wide-eyed focus as he drank in every ounce of me. I felt like an ant under a magnifying glass. Some tiny creature he was analyzing as I slowly caught on fire. I was dying for him to do or say anything. To kiss me, crush me against him, or proclaim he couldn't live another second without me.

He just stared, looking as unsettled as I felt. "Christ, Beatrice. We've wasted you on the sidelines."

He paused a moment more before he turned and slipped out the door.

I managed to remain standing until the screen door slammed, but then I crumpled to my knees. There was a giant wound in my chest, and I couldn't seem to keep anything in. The very root of me was slipping right through my fingers, and all over the tiles.

The buzzer sounded.

# Chapter Twenty-Three

"THERE'S A GUY," I BLURTED OUT, INSTANTLY regretting it. I was sprawled across my bed wearing an actual pair of shorts and an old chess club tournament shirt. The smothering humidity hung heavy in our room, while the ceiling fan just swirled it around my head.

"Oh?" I could practically hear Dr. Horowitz's eyebrows crawl up his forehead. "What about this guy?"

"Forget it," I said, cringing.

"Beatrice," he said gently. "Out with it."

I pinched the bridge of my nose, trying to focus. "There's a guy and I don't know what I'm supposed to do with him."

"Well, he's not a houseplant, Beatrice. I don't think you *have* to do anything with him."

I sprang up off the bed, walking off the jittery energy. "I feel that I do. It's like he's circling and things are leading up to some point, but I don't know to what end or what to expect."

He made a nonspecific sound, and I paused, ready to finally hear the answer. The solution to what would have been a whiteboard full of red.

"Well," he said. "I think before we go any further, only one thing matters."

I strained, holding the phone as close as it would go. "Yes?"

"Do you like him?"

I blinked. "That's it? That's all you got?"

"It's a simple enough question, Beatrice," he said, his voice soft with amusement.

I turned the question over in my mind, realizing a little belatedly that I'd spent so much time thinking about Nik's intentions that I'd resolutely ignored mine. I opened my mouth to answer, but the words were stuck. I guess the problem would just be solved if I said no, but what if I said yes? How could I say yes? It was impossible to forget the past, or to ignore the fact that last time I'd brought up a guy to Dr. Horowitz I'd been sobbing so hard I could barely get the words out. He'd knelt down near my chair, concern radiating off him, but he waited until I'd spilled the entire story about Bryce at his feet. He'd helped me find a way to put myself back together that felt safe to me, that made sense to me. After all that, after all the work we'd done, he only wanted to know if I *liked* Nik?

"I don't think that has anything to do with this," I said stiffly.

"Beatrice."

"Dr. Horowitz."

"If you like him, it's okay."

"It most certainly is *not*," I said, panic bleeding into my words.

"Okay, let's do it your way," he said. "The problem at hand is there is a boy who exists and you may or may not have feelings of some kind about him?"

I cleared my throat. "Undetermined, yes."

"Now we're getting somewhere. And the concern is that he may not like you in return?"

I frowned. "Well, not exactly."

"The concern is that he may like you in return?"

My frown deepened. "Also yes."

"Okay, well, what evidence do you have that he doesn't like you?"

I nodded, cataloging my thoughts as scientifically as I could. "Well, he said something mean about me the first night we met. I'd been rude to him too, but his comment was worse. He used to scowl at me a lot, but he mostly teases me now, and refuses to call me by my new nickname."

"Beatrice, I don't know if I'm that fond of this young man."

"Agreed," I said, chewing on the end of my ponytail.

"Let's hear the evidence that he may like you," he said, disapproval lightly staining his words.

I couldn't help but smile at his gruff tone. "My friends seem to think he might, he's always trying to seek me out and include me, and there's something about the way he looks at me sometimes that I can't really put my finger on."

He cleared his throat. "I see."

"Do you? Because I can't see anything, and I don't know what I'm supposed to do about any of this." I flopped back on the bed limp as a noodle. I'd been waiting all week for this call, and he was supposed to have all the answers.

"Beatrice, I know you want a clear-cut plan and solution, but human beings aren't like that, not even yourself."

I sat up as I heard the screen door slam. "I think I'd like it better if he was a manageable houseplant."

He laughed. "And I think this is the most teenage conversation we've ever had. I don't know what you're doing over there, but things are changing, and I'm very interested to see what you decide."

Mia stepped through the doorway, her eyes lighting up at the phone in my hand. "Are you talking to your parents?"

"No, I'm talking to my therapist," I said, smiling at the way her face fell. "You'll meet the parents in a week."

She walked over and flounced on the bed next to me. "Well, you tell your therapist that we have things well in hand over here, and not to worry."

"Dr. Horowitz—"

"I heard, Beatrice," he said, the smile in his voice coming through and wrapping around me. "I believe it."

# Chapter Twenty-Four

**"I'M GOING TO NEED YOU TO STOP BREATHING**
if I'm going to get this fitting correct." Nolan gave Darla's dress a
yank as she shot him a nasty glance.

I ignored them both and continued my efforts to be as useless
and unseen as possible.

"I can't help it; it's a million degrees here. I don't know why
we can't just stay at the air-conditioned theater until opening
night," Darla whined as she shifted under Nolan's uncompro-
mising gaze.

"Are you willing to suffer for your art or not?" he snapped, his
usually bouncy hair and personality flattened by the humidity.
"We're one week out, and the Globe blocking is still garbage."

I shifted on the hard pew, which was painstakingly authentic
but left no room for comfort. The midday sun beat down through
the hole in the ceiling, and trickles of sweat streaked down my
back. I'd reluctantly put on a cotton tank top this morning and
was slowly coming around to the benefits of lighter materials.

"Nik! Where's Nik? I need you onstage now!" Mr. G bellowed.

I ducked my head and scooted down lower in my pew. I'd
avoided Nik over the past week, and we hadn't exactly talked

since that night in the laundry room. All the things I wanted to say to him or ask him just seemed—impossible. A ravine too wide to cross.

"Nik, you have five seconds to get on this stage!"

With that last declaration I felt my chances of avoiding him were probably better off backstage and trying to stay out of the way of the set designers. I groaned as I sat up, my damp hair sticking to my back, and I piled it haphazardly on top of my head.

"I'm heading backstage." I patted Nolan's shoulder as I moved around him.

"I'm sure you'll never run into him back there," he responded tartly.

I stuck my tongue out and slipped up the stairs and behind Juliet's balcony. I moved through the crew as they bustled around, fixing costumes, sliding sets around, and adjusting lights. It was easy to blend into the crowd and just disappear. I felt myself slipping more and more into old habits. Maybe it was silly to think that things were going to change. That *I* could change. I barely even knew this new Bea, so why did it feel like a loss? Like a book I'd just started but never got the chance to finish?

"Beatrice," Nik said.

I stopped short at the low murmur. I debated pretending I hadn't heard him, but at that point I'd paused too long. I turned, and there he was backlit against the stage.

"Nik. I didn't see you there."

"I can imagine," he said, his lips pressed tight. "Every time I think I see you over the past week, you vanish into thin air."

I shrugged. "I've been busy. Opening night is almost here, and then we'll all go our separate ways. Lots of things to accomplish before then." I winced as I stammered.

"Nikhil Shah! Get on this stage now!"

Irritation colored Nik's face. "Can you just wait here a moment? I'd really like to talk to you."

I glanced behind me at the trusty bench I'd found during our party. I'd come back here to avoid this conversation specifically.

"Please, Beatrice? Just give me a moment."

I nodded. There was no graceful way to avoid it if he asked like that. I still felt so raw whenever he looked at me. Like a wound with salt rubbed in.

He disappeared onto the stage and I exhaled. If I could just stand there during our conversation and refrain from admitting something else humiliatingly personal, I'd consider it a success. I rubbed my face, trying to find some remnant of the girl who arrived here almost three weeks earlier.

"What are you doing back here?" Shelby asked, her words sharp as a whip.

I ignored her, turning my body and watching the scene unfold onstage. Nik laughed, his lines carrying backstage and filling the silence.

"Are you ignoring me?" she huffed, tapping her shoe.

"I don't owe you a response," I said.

"You know, I really don't get why my brother likes you so much."

I briefly looked back. "Same."

"Can't you go wait somewhere else? I have to stand here. I'm going onstage soon."

"I'm not stopping you from standing here. And no, I can't move. I'm waiting for someone."

She stood next to me, looking out on the stage as Nik slung an arm around Ben's neck. The two of them strutting across the length of the stage.

"What's going on with the two of you?"

"Nothing," I said, the word catching in my throat. An impossible weight settled on my shoulders. Going back home and leaving this behind me was for the best. I could finish picking out my classes, maybe even move a little earlier and get settled at school. How could I feel loss when I had Oxford to look forward to? Well, provided that I finished my last five tasks. The lump in my pocket reminding me all I had to lose.

"Is *he* the reason you're waiting here?"

I swallowed a nasty retort as I fought to find the high road. "What do you want, Shelby? Do you want to go over a scene or something?"

"No, I don't need you to go over a scene with me," she said, each word dripping with disdain. "I want to know what it is about you that has everyone just falling over themselves this summer. 'Oh, poor Beatrice! Be nice to Beatrice! We all have to protect Beatrice!'"

I blinked, the polished marble exterior crumbling in front of me. Her hair was snarled, and beads of sweat pooled on her upper lip.

"Look, Shelby, I'm sorry to hear about your plans for next year, but maybe you could—"

"Do not pretend to know anything about me!" she said, each word rising in pitch. "I don't need your help. I'm *fine.*"

She spun on her heel, leaving me frozen in her wake. She walked out to where Nik and Mr. G were working through some blocking and announced that they were now going to work on her part of the masked ball scene. I rolled my eyes as everyone fell in line to accommodate her.

I stood in the wings of the stage as she turned to Nik and nodded at him to begin.

He looked at her like she was everything he'd ever wanted

and had never realized until that moment. He took her hand gently in his.

*"If I profane with my unworthiest hand*
*This holy shrine, the gentle sin is this:*
*My lips, two blushing pilgrims, ready stand*
*To smooth that rough touch with a tender kiss."*

He pressed a kiss in the palm of her hand, and her performance was colored by a hint of triumph:

*"Good pilgrim, you do wrong your hand too much,*
*Which mannerly devotion shows in this,*
*For saints have hands that pilgrims' hands do touch,*
*And palm to palm is holy palmers' kiss."*

Their fingers entwined as they glided in a circle, lazily moving through the steps of a dance. My stomach clenched, and there it was. The ugly realization that I wanted this.

That I wanted him.

All that time trying not to look too closely at that simple little question Dr. Horowitz asked, as if it was too blinding, like the sun, and the answer found me anyway.

*"Have not saints lips, and holy palmers too?"* His hands circled her waist.

*"Ay, pilgrim, lips that they must use in prayer,"* she teased, pulling out of his reach.

*"O, then, dear saint, let lips do what hands do.*

*They pray; grant thou, lest faith turn to despair."* He approached her with the confidence of a prince.

*"Saints do not move, though grant for prayers' sake."* She let him catch her this time, and a hand slid behind her back, pulling her to him. His other hand tangled in her white-blond hair.

*"Then move not, while my prayer's effect I take."*

He kissed her.

I knew it was coming. I knew it was coming the second she started this specific scene, but seeing it still made my knees weak. I don't know how I'd been able to avoid witnessing this over the past few weeks, but here on the stage that I'd previously shared with him and thinking of the kiss that was supposed to be mine, I felt like I'd truly lost something.

Her arms twined around his neck, and she put everything into that kiss as he gripped her arms.

Mr. G cleared his throat. "Umm, this kiss is supposed to be relatively chaste, but I appreciate the enthusiasm to the scene."

Shelby finally pulled herself away, her words breathless. "Sorry, Mr. G. I guess we've just had a lot of practice." She turned slightly in my direction, her smile for me alone. At this point she might as well have just pissed in a circle around him.

I swallowed down a wave of hurt, and Nik's confused gaze finally landed on me. He took a half step in my direction before Shelby grabbed his biceps. "Nik? We're in the middle of this scene!"

I took several wobbly steps backward before turning and walking back around to the front of the theater. I thought about continuing straight through the doors to the outside, but I'd said I was done running away and I meant it. I went back to where Nolan was still pinning Darla into her dress. Sliding into the pew next to him, I ignored the worried glance he threw my way. Nik and Shelby continued the steps of their dance, and I took a deep, cleansing breath. The lines of what was acting and what was real blurred over and over again at this camp, and I'd reached the end of my rope. I wasn't made for this type of drama or confusion. I was finally done.

"What's that, love?" Nolan asked carefully.

I hadn't realized I'd said that last part out loud.

"I'm done," I whispered again.

# Chapter Twenty-Five

"ARE YOU OKAY?" MIA ASKED, PAUSING BRIEFLY while brushing her teeth. White foam collected at the corners of her mouth, and she leaned against the doorjamb.

I snuggled deeper into the bed, pulling at the loose seam of my NASA T-shirt. "Yes, I'm okay; it's my favorite time of day."

"Bedtime should not be your favorite time of day," she tossed over her shoulder, going back into the bathroom.

All I knew was that I couldn't spend another second trying to unravel these feelings, and not having to deal with them for eight hours was amazing.

She walked back into the room, her hands on her hips, and her oversized sleep shirt slipped off her shoulder.

"I know what this is about."

"You do? Then please tell me."

She sighed before crawling over me into bed. Nudging me upright, she threaded her fingers through my hair. My throat tightened as I was suddenly eight again, my mother attempting to reach me. To find some common ground. Mia separated pieces near my hairline, weaving a French braid down the side of my head.

"Nolan was there when Nik and Shelby kissed onstage. He saw your face."

I shrugged, my back moving against her chest.

"It's just a play. That doesn't mean anything. It definitely didn't mean that he likes her." She pulled a hairband off her wrist, securing the end of the braid, and moved to the other side.

"I know it's a play, Mia. Let's just say that I realized multiple things during that scene, and it's for the best if I just lie low for the next week. Then we all go back to our normal lives."

She tugged on my hair. "That's it? These four weeks get filed away somewhere in that big brain of yours and you just move on as if we never existed?"

"I don't know." I tripped over the next words. "Do you think—do you think you might want to talk on the phone every now and then?"

This time she tugged hard. "Are you sure you're smart, because that was the dumbest shit I've ever heard. Of course we're going to talk on the phone."

My lip wobbled, and I was glad she was sitting behind me. "Good. I'm glad that's settled." I sat up straighter as something dawned on me. "What's going to happen to you and Ben?"

"Funny you should ask. Guess who also got into NYU?"

I whipped around, and she yelped trying to hold on to the end of my new braid. "Stop moving!"

"He's going to NYU too?"

A self-satisfied smile spread across her lips. "Isn't that an exciting coincidence?"

"Acting too?"

"God, no. Bless his heart. Business."

I nodded, the braid unraveling underneath her fingers. She

turned me back around. As she redid her work, I leaned back into her.

"Don't think I'm not going to visit you in England. I'll expect you to show me a good time."

My chest tightened. "What if I don't make it? I have five tasks left to do. Five tasks in one week."

Mia secured the end of my new braid. "Don't worry; we'll get to them all."

"It took me three weeks to do six."

"Okay, let's take a look at what we have left."

I leaned over, plucking the list off my nightstand. I tossed it behind me, my fingers smoothing the heavy ropes now tumbling down my shoulders.

"Okay, I have an idea. We're going to cross one off right now." She scooted around me and ran into the bathroom. I grabbed the discarded paper while she slammed cabinets. I wrinkled my nose, scanning the remaining items. None of them required toiletries.

Mia ran back into the room, several rolls of toilet paper bundled in her arms. She tossed me a roll, and it bounced off my chest. I adjusted my glasses, my brain struggling to follow her logic.

"Toilet paper? Are you sure you read the list right?"

"I'm sure. Get your shoes on, girl."

I pulled my sleep shorts farther down. "I'm going outside? In my pajamas?"

"Yep! Let's go! Let's go!"

I slipped on my loafers, and she stacked several rolls into my arms. As she pulled on my arm, we hurried down the porch stairs and jogged toward the main campus.

"Where are we going?" I asked, my breaths coming in little huffs.

"Shhhh!" she hissed. "This is a rite of passage. If there's one prank every teenager knows how to do, it's this one."

I stumbled, grasping for a roll that bounced into the dirt. She nudged me toward the path behind the director's cabin.

I pulled her into the shadows of the eaves. "Are you crazy? We can't get caught by the boys' cabins!"

"We better not get caught then!" Her eyes danced, and she turned and jogged down the path. I was going to kill her.

"Are we going to prank Nolan?"

"Sure," she said, her smile sweet as sugar.

"What are we supposed to do? String this across the door so he trips?"

"Well, that's one tactic, but let's try and think on a larger scale."

We neared the first cabin, snorting as we tried to hustle down the path without making any noise. She carefully counted, stopping as we approached number six. She leaned in, her breath hot against my ear. "Now watch this." She spun the roll, unraveling a pool of paper at her feet before throwing the roll high in the air. It arced toward the roof, catching on a branch, and careened back toward the ground. Paper waved in the cool breeze, and I bit my lip to stop from laughing. She nodded, her teeth gleaming in the moonlight, and I unraveled one of my rolls. I threw it through the beams of the porch, and a streak of white rippled across their front door. She bent over; silent laughter caught in her throat. I grinned at my handiwork. Cool air kissed my legs as I picked up the roll and raced around the cabin, the paper twining around like a ribbon on a present. Mia tossed her roll up into the old oak stretching over the roof, the paper hanging in wide swaths. A snort slipped past my lips as I rested my hands on my knees.

"Nolan is going to *kill* us when he sees this." My heart swelled as I imagined his glare from across the cafeteria table.

"Did I say we were pranking Nolan?" She wiggled her eye-brows as I pulled myself up.

"Wait."

"I don't remember saying exactly who we were pranking."

"Mia."

"Who knows who lives here at cabin number six?"

"What have you done—" I was cut off as the screen door slammed open and Nik and Ben ran out onto the porch. I swallowed as Nik stepped into the moonlight.

"Shit."

I took off, the path disappearing under my legs. I barely registered the curse that went up behind me. I focused on the last of the cabins and where the path spilled out from the woods and onto the open stretch of grass of the quad. As I neared the exit, unyielding arms circled my waist and yanked me back into the shadows of the woods. I was spun and deposited against the trunk of a large oak, the bark biting into my back. Nik stood over me, bare chest heaving, sweatpants slouched across his hips.

"Look—"

One hand rested by my ear, and he held up a finger as he worked on catching his breath.

I bit my lip as his abs rippled with every raspy inhale.

"Why the hell did you TP my cabin?" He straightened and stepped closer.

I swallowed, focused on his Adam's apple. "Am I allowed to talk now?"

"Dammit, Beatrice! What am I supposed to think? Are you mad at me? Are you flirting with me? I don't know what I'm getting from you!"

"Is this how people typically flirt?"

He looked up as if asking for help, before stepping closer.

He tilted my chin up closer to him and licked his lips. "If you wanted to see me, you could have just said so."

I placed my palms on his chest, both hungry for space and unwilling to push him away. I could feel his heart pounding under my fingertips. "I had no idea this was your cabin. I just had to check something off my list," I murmured, his lips so close I could smell his toothpaste.

I felt the muscles tense under my hands. "What list?"

"Don't worry about it." Being so close to him almost felt like I'd drank more peach schnapps. I tilted my head up for easier access.

"What list, Beatrice?" He grabbed my wrists but let my palms stay on his chest. I curled my hands into fists.

### 2.) *Share a secret*

I didn't feel so strongly about keeping things from him anymore; in fact, despite seeing him on that stage with Shelby, I still wanted him to know everything. I wanted him to know me. "Remember when I told you my parents sent me to camp to become a real teenager? Well, it wasn't just that I had to come to camp. I had to check off certain activities before my parents would agree to Oxford. One of the tasks was to pull a prank." I waved weakly at the paper-strewn cabin behind us.

"What else?" He dropped my wrists. "What were the other tasks?" He stepped away, and I shivered at the loss of his body heat. A muscle twitched along his jaw, and I straightened my T-shirt.

"Um, well, I had to make friends, and do an outdoor activity. I accepted an invitation I didn't want to and flirted with someone for the hell of it." I rattled off the boxes I'd accomplished as he took several steps farther back.

"So, these were all 'tasks,' huh?" He forced the words out

through his teeth, and I felt the vacuum of space left between us in my bones. "What about our game? The quote contest?"

I blinked at the anger written into his features. "I mean, there was a task about executing a dare, and Nolan dared me to participate, but—"

"Of course there was." He turned away from me and stalked back down the path to his cabin.

"Wait. Nik! Are you *mad* at me?"

He spun around. "Yes, Beatrice. Yes, *I am mad at you.*" He enunciated each word as if I were a child. He turned back around, and I jogged to catch up with him.

"I don't see what the big deal is. I'm sorry about the toilet paper, but this feels a little bit like an overreaction."

"An overreaction?" I tensed as his shout splintered through the woods. "I've just learned that every interaction I've had with you has been you checking off a fucking list. Is that why you ran away during the party? Why you've been avoiding me? Was kissing not on your precious itinerary? No need to force yourself to check that box off?"

"No, it's on the list."

A number of emotions I couldn't pinpoint splashed across his face, but I could taste his anger in the air between us. An ugly part of me reveled in the fact that I could produce any kind of strong reaction from him. Even if I didn't understand it.

"I don't know why I'm surprised," he said. "I should have known."

"Should have known what?" I didn't know if I wanted to hear his answer, but I asked anyway.

"That all this is a game to you, and we're all just little lab rats running around in your experiment." He stepped closer, shaking his head. "That it doesn't matter what I might want, because none of this even matters to you."

I wanted to rip him to pieces. "You think you have me all figured out?" I stretched up on my toes, making myself as big as the anger bubbling up in my throat. "You want to talk about playing with people? I heard you call me ugly during our first meeting! Then you develop this ridiculous game where the prize is kissing me? Then I see you making out with Shelby onstage, right after you ask me to wait for you?" I laughed, the sound harsh under starlight.

"Wait, is that why you didn't wait for me? You thought I was kissing Shelby?"

"I saw you kissing Shelby with the eyes in my head."

"That was the play!"

"I've studied the play, Nik! I know the context and the blocking of that scene! There's usually no tongue!"

"Why would you even care? I could kiss every girl in this camp and it would be all the same to you!"

"Then do it," I said before spinning on my heel and leaving him on the path.

"So that's it?" he called from behind me. "None of this matters, and it's all been a misunderstanding on my part?" His tone was harsh and scraped against every exposed nerve our fight had laid open. I spun around, ready to end this farce once and for all, when he stepped forward into the silvery light.

I'd stumbled around all these different relationships these past three weeks and I'd been frequently wrong and confused by what people wanted from me, but not now. This facial expression I recognized. It was on Ben's face every time he looked at Mia. It ran through Nolan's features when he laughed about RISD and talked about Sam. It was in Mia's eyes whenever she said she wished her parents were excited about her plans to be a professional actress.

It was *want*, and I had no idea what to do about it. If there was anything to even do about it with us leaving in a week and this graveyard of unresolved arguments between us.

Mia appeared at my elbow. "We have to get out of here. I think some of the other cabins have woken up."

I nodded, and with one last look we turned and disappeared into the darkness.

# Chapter Twenty-Six

**"MIA, IF YOU POKE ME IN THE EYE ONE MORE** time, we're going to have to stop," I said, my eyelids spasming as she leaned in again with the mascara wand.

"You're fluttering your eyelashes like Shelby whenever she looks at Nik. I can't get anywhere near you!"

At the mention of the two of them, my stomach dropped, and Mia took a quick step back. "I'm so sorry, honey. It was stupid for me to bring them up."

I grimaced at the gnawing pain in my stomach that I felt whenever someone mentioned his name. I wasn't sure if the stress of this summer had given me an ulcer or if I had an actual hunger for him that my body was furious at not getting to indulge in. Like tacos, or birthday cake.

I shook my head. "No, it's stupid of me to still be thinking about all that." Every time I squeezed my eyes closed, it was always him and his lips a whisper away before I ruined it. Before he ruined it.

"It's not stupid, honey. You had feelings for him; those don't just disappear at the snap of a finger."

I shrugged. "I'm not sure what I felt for him." Mia pursed

her lips, and I rolled my eyes. "Fine, I am willing to admit to the *tiniest* crush in the world, which received a fatal blow when I saw Shelby stick her tongue down his throat and died completely when he threw his temper tantrum in the woods."

"I was there too, you know," she murmured. "To be honest, it kind of looked like he was just concerned that you didn't feel anything for him. I think that would be an easy enough thing to fix."

I shot to my feet, smoothing out the wrinkles in the dark burgundy velvet of my party dress. "It's done now, Mia. The summer is almost over, and I am going to a party tonight with the best friends I've ever had, in the prettiest dress I've ever worn."

Her eyes watered a bit before she pulled me into a bone-crushing hug. "I don't even know if I can explain to you how important you are to me now."

"I'm pretty sure I know exactly how you're feeling," I said, laughing.

She took a step back, dabbing at her eyes. "Now shut up before you ruin my makeup." She turned all business as she inspected my appearance. She'd pinned my hair so it tumbled down over one shoulder and kissed the sweetheart neckline of my dress. The stuffy formal boatneck of the original tailoring long gone under Nolan's clever hands. I blotted the dark red lipstick staining my lips and squirmed under her inspection. "I don't think it's going to get any better. We should probably head over there."

She shook her head in amusement. "You're heart-stoppingly beautiful."

I adjusted my glasses, still unable to accept a compliment with any grace. "You're one to talk." I nodded at her gold sequined minidress. "You look like an Oscar, so I'm sure everyone in the camp is going to be hovering around you all night."

She clapped her hands in delight. "I'm a big fan of the moth-to-a-flame effect."

I linked her arm in mine and felt a giddy rush of satisfaction all the way down to my toes. My toes, which were encased in beautiful, bow-adorned shoes that I had picked out for myself.

On the way out the door we passed Shelby in the bathroom. She was wearing a delicate silver dress with thin straps. I paused, torn by the feeling that the correct societal response would be to invite her to walk with us, but she stared at us for a moment before leaning over and closing the door.

"Hag," Mia coughed as we stepped out into the night.

The walk to the cafeteria mirrored our first evening at camp together. The moonlight still lit up the path, and the cool breeze rustling through the trees made my dress flare out. The same, but yet so different. This time, as I entered the cafeteria, I was enchanted at the twinkly lights, fake trees, and other set remnants that were peppered throughout the room.

"I knew that dress would be a showstopper!" Nolan swooped up behind me and spun me in a wild circle.

"It's perfect since you tinkered with it," I said, smoothing out the skirt.

"Now you can tell people you own a Nolan Walsh original, back from before he was famous."

"I'll treasure it." I smiled up at him before looking around in wonder. "Who did all of this?"

"The set design kids, of course!" he said before giving Mia a spin herself.

"Are you wearing a tux?" I asked as he preened.

"It's a miracle he was able to refrain from wearing it all summer!" Mia said, petting the rich black velvet.

I grinned at her. "So, can I have cupcakes whenever I want this time, or do I have to socialize with strangers again?"

Mia scrunched up her nose. "I think we've probably done enough socializing this summer. We've already met all the important people." Her smile widened as Ben broke through the crowd, wearing a beautiful blue suit. He staggered a little as he saw Mia, and I had to turn away from the look in his eyes.

"All right, love, are we ready to check off *dance with abandon*?" Nolan asked as he tucked me into his side.

"You know, this is one task that just might not happen. I've only ever danced with my dad, and that's been at weddings I couldn't get out of. It never worked out well for either one of us."

Nolan laughed out loud, pushing us into the crowd. "As it happens, I'm an excellent instructor."

"Yeah, I think we're going to have to chalk this up to something that my body just does not do."

Nolan shook my shoulders until he held my attention again. "I know your reflex is be all Negative Nancy about new stuff, but I want you to focus that impressive brainpower on the task at hand."

I straightened, giving him a determined nod. He slowly stepped side to side, back and forth, in a linear pattern. I paused, waiting for more to happen, before slowly moving my feet in rhythm with his.

We continued like this until I arched an eyebrow. "Are you sure you're a good dancer?"

"So sassy, and you come in here pretending you're not a normal teenager."

I snorted, pointing at Mia and Ben dancing. Her long limbs were moving with the tempo as he laughingly tried to keep up. "When do I get to do that?"

"Fine, we'll accelerate your lessons. Let's start moving your arms now." He moved his upper body as he stepped side to side. His shoulders bouncing to the beat as he raised an eyebrow in my direction.

I faltered a step as I tried to take in all the components of his movement. He smiled as he moved behind me, placing his hands on my shoulders. "You're thinking about it too much; I want you to close your eyes."

I sighed in resignation. "I'm not sure if this is really—"

"Do it, woman!"

"Okay, okay." I closed my eyes, letting my other senses overwhelm me. The bass of the music reached into my bones, and my head moved along with the raspy lyrics. The musky bite of Nolan's cologne tickled my nose, and he squeezed my shoulders.

"That's it; now loosen up a bit. Just focus on the music and move however you want to."

I continued doing the back-and-forth step that he showed me, but this time the rest of me didn't remain completely still. I was awkward, a little stiff, but I was at least moving to the music. I opened my eyes and looked back at him laughing. He grinned, spinning me around until I was breathless. I looked up, and the laughter died in my throat.

Across the room, staring at me, was Nik. He was wearing a suit that must have been made for him, with a crisp white shirt that was open at the collar. I froze, and Nolan kept me from toppling over. Nik turned away as Shelby stepped in front of him, refocusing his attention.

I tilted my chin up at Nolan. "Spin me again."

With his firm hands on my waist, we moved through the room and from song to song. A thin sheen of sweat broke out across my skin, and I laughed loud and clear as he swept me into a dip. Mia danced around me, her hair a halo backlit against lights from the DJ booth, and I stretched my arms out to the ceiling and spun—my dress billowing around me. Other people moved in and out of our orbit—a handsy Troy, who was quickly banished, a girl named Carla from set design who dipped me even lower than Nolan, and a boy with a soft smile who spun me again until the world blurred. I bent over as a stitch in my side spasmed, and waved Mia off as I stumbled through the crowd toward the cupcake table. I pulled my glasses off, the edges starting to fog, and cleaned them with the hem of my skirt. Pulling my damp hair off my neck, I leaned over to evaluate my choices.

"That's way too serious a face for cupcakes," Nik said.

I would likely never get used to his accent.

I shrugged, not able to look at him. "It depends on how seriously you take baked goods."

He cleared his throat. "It looked like you were having fun out there."

"Nolan is making it his mission to teach me all the life skills he thinks I'm missing."

He nodded. "Right. The list."

I froze, waiting for that same anger that rolled off him in the woods, but he just nodded and turned to walk away.

"I'm not a robot."

"What?" he asked, turning back.

I cleared my throat. "I'm not a robot."

He sighed and fiddled with his cup of punch. "I know you're not a robot, Beatrice."

"Good," I said, relieved. "So, you understand? About the list?"

"No, Beatrice, I don't understand. I've wanted to all summer, but I just don't understand anything about you, or what you want, or *this*," he said, his voice rising to be heard over the music.

"I'm not a machine that just took a list of tasks or instructions and mindlessly processed them," I said, frustration building in every word. "How can you know me so little to think that?" *How could he be so blind to have not seen me?*

"I know you; I just . . ." He roughly rubbed his face. "I messed things up so badly in the beginning, and then I tried to fix it, and then I tried to fix it for other reasons. I thought I was clear and you understood what I was trying to tell you, and I just—"

"Let's just enjoy the party, Nik," I said gently. There was so much to unravel and yelling over the music in front of a cupcake tower wasn't the way to resolve any of this.

He nodded slowly and tossed back the rest of his punch. "Well, I'm glad you're having fun."

I winced at the stiffness of our conversation and his posture. Everything was so stilted, like we were smothered under all the things that had happened over the summer.

I snagged the chocolate before letting my eyes slide over him one more time. "Thanks."

I turned and made a beeline for the door and the promise of fresh air.

The night was cool on my flushed skin, and I took a deep, cleansing breath in. I'd been having a great time before that brief, weird conversation, and I just needed a quick reset before I went back in. I walked down a bit, out of the way of the door, and leaned against the scratchy wood of the building's exterior. Taking a big bite of the cupcake, I looked up at the millions of stars dotting the skies.

They winked at me, like old friends. I knew their names, their origin and evolution. Cassiopeia. Ursa Major. Hercules. Sagittarius. Things were different now, though. *I* was different. I now had memories of nights sitting under them, and whispered conversations during movies, and racing through the woods laughing with friends while golden wings rippled behind me. Despite some of the more frustrating or confusing aspects of this summer, I knew deep down that something had irrevocably changed.

"You're going to get chocolate all over that dress," Shelby

said, stepping outside, the music flaring brightly before cutting off with the closing door.

I scraped the chocolate off my bottom lip with my teeth, briefly hoping I hadn't smeared my lipstick. "What do you want, Shelby?"

Her mouth was thin as a blade, and she looked like she wanted to be literally anywhere else. "Look, Nik is really mad at me right now, so is Nolan, and I may have been acting a little crazy, so I just wanted to say—"

"Are you actually trying to apologize to me right now?"

Her nostrils flared. "I mean, some people think I may have been a little hard on you, and—"

"You've been awful. *Awful.* Awful with extremely specific and brutal purpose."

She took a deep breath, her eyes locked on the rough gravel she carefully tried to navigate over. Her icicle-thin heels sinking into the dirt. "Look, Beatrice, I heard you'd been homeschooled, so you might not understand how some of this works."

"If you think that my being homeschooled prevents me from understanding or recognizing your insults, you're gravely mistaken."

She stopped her gradual approach, arms folding tightly across her body. "I'm just trying to apologize, okay?"

"Apology not accepted." I tossed the remainder of the cupcake into the black leaching out from the woods.

"Why are you being so difficult? Is this because of Nik and the kiss?"

I moved back toward the door. "As surprising as it is for everyone to understand, including Nik, not everything I do is because of him."

She stumbled forward, blocking my path. "Look," she said, screwing her mouth up in a distasteful moue. "I was a bitch. I was a giant bitch. I was just jealous of you, and everything was coming so easily for you, and I may have reacted poorly."

I walked a few more steps before my brain registered the comment. "Wait, what? Jealous? If this is because of Nik . . ."

She tottered over to the side of the building, her dress like liquid moonlight, and leaned against the rough wood. She turned her face up toward the night sky, uncomfortable under my appraisal. Cassiopeia personified.

"No, not because of Nik. Are you sure you're smart?" I moved to step around her, and an arm shot out, blocking my path.

"Sorry, it's hard to turn off. No, it's because you have all this shit lined up in front of you. You got into your dream university, and you don't even care about this stupid camp. It's all I've been looking forward to for *months*. A few seconds up on a stage with only parents in the audience. It's pathetic."

I swallowed the consolatory words that reflexively bubbled to my lips and the small physical acts of intimacy that I'd learned through Mia. An arm around the shoulder, a squeeze of the hand. I stood there, stock-still and half hidden in shadow as Shelby wilted in front of me. "Nik isn't even talking to me right now. Nolan either, and it's hard to figure out how I got here."

I raised an eyebrow, and she had the decency to blush.

"I mean, I do get it, but Nik's face when he realized I'd kissed him like that because you were there. It was like he didn't even recognize me, and *I* didn't even recognize me."

"I know you're in love with him, but—"

She laughed, the sound strained. "I'm not in love with him, Bea. I mean, maybe a tiny bit, the way everyone's a little in love with him." She cleared her throat, adjusting the silver bangles cheerfully jangling on her wrist. "No, I wanted a fling. A perfect Romeo, because I was finally Juliet."

"Why are you telling me this?"

The door eased open a bit, and Mia peeked out. A deep divot carved between her eyebrows. "Hey, Bea? Something is going on in here. Can you come?"

I was there in an instant, my hand clasped firmly in hers and Shelby forgotten. We hurried toward the dance floor where Ms. Reid was talking with Ben and Nik. Nik's expression was grave as he gripped Ben's shoulder. Ms. Reid leaned toward them, her words low and inaudible over the music.

"What's happening?" Mia asked, her fingers tightening around mine.

Ben looked up at our approach, fear splashed across his features. "It's Bianca. She's been in an accident. I have to go home. My parents booked the red-eye for me tonight."

Nik gently moved him toward the door. "I'll help you pack."

Ben nodded before squeezing Mia's hand. "I'll find you before I leave."

"Go, go!" she said, blinking rapidly.

I stepped closer to her. "It's his sister," she said in response to my unasked question.

"Oh my god," I whispered. "I hope she's okay."

"Me too. They're really close."

I nodded, putting my arm around her. "I'm so sorry the summer is ending on this note."

She smiled at me, her bottom lip trembling. "Thanks, Bea. Do you want to get out of here?"

I nodded in relief. "You took the words right out of my mouth."

We moved toward the door before she froze.

I looked around in alarm. "What now?"

She turned to me. "Ben's leaving."

I rubbed her arm. "I know, honey." The endearment tasted strange on my tongue.

"No!" she exclaimed, her eyes wide. "Bea, he's *leaving*, and you're the only understudy!"

My stomach plummeted into my shoes.

"You're going to be Mercutio!"

# Chapter Twenty-Seven

"BABY, I'M GOING TO NEED YOU TO STOP WIG-gling. You're about half the size of Ben, and I'd like you to not look like you're wearing a giant brocade trash bag."

I took a deep breath, willing myself to remain still as Nolan furiously pinned me into Ben's old costume. A wave of nausea crawled up my throat, and I beat it back down as sweat beaded across my brow.

"Bea, I know you at least have the lines down, thank God, but we only have a few hours for you to nail down the blocking. The show is tomorrow, and I need you to pay attention." I refocused on Mr. G as he stabbed the script in front of my face. "I need you to cross to stage left after this line or Benvolio is going to run right into you!"

I nodded, my palms slick with sweat.

"Nobody is going to run into her," Nik said, his voice tight with irritation. "We all know she's stepping into this role at the last minute, and we'll keep an eye on her."

The fear abated a slight amount. "Are we sure nobody else can do this?" My voice wavered.

Mr. G squeezed my shoulder. "There's nobody else who even

knows a fraction of his lines. You're here, Bea! Your parents paid the tuition, you know the part, and it's just going to be great!"

His strained smile did nothing to boost my confidence. Another cold sweat broke out across my body, and I pulled out of Nolan's grasp, mumbling a quick apology as I rushed off the stage. I barely made it to a trash can before the small quantity of water I was able to force past my lips this morning came back up. I sank to my knees, clutching the can, as I felt my heavy, damp hair being lifted off my back.

"Leave it." I halfheartedly waved him off. "It's all sweaty and gross."

Nik scoffed. "I couldn't care less. You've been put in an impossible situation, and I want to make sure you're okay." The melodic rhythm of his accent soothed me.

My fingers tightened on the rim of the can. "I don't know how they expect me to do this. I'm going to ruin this entire thing."

I felt a reassuring pressure on my back as he rubbed circles. "You're not going to ruin anything. You've seen Troy act, right? We'd be going down whether Ben was here or not."

A broken laugh escaped me as I raggedly wiped my lips and sat back. "I don't think I can do this."

He shrugged. "I happen to disagree."

"I'm sure. You just want a body to fill this role, but I am telling you that I don't think that this is going to happen. We just have to call it off."

"Mouse," he murmured, pausing until I looked up. "You think I care that much about this play? I've been in more than I can count, and in roles I like *a lot* better than Romeo. I show up here every summer because I love Shakespeare and my parents, and want to support them, but we could shut the whole thing down today and I wouldn't think twice."

My heart lifted as salvation came into sight.

"But"—and with that word my hopes came crashing down—"do I think that you aren't capable of doing this? Not for a second."

"Just because I know the lines doesn't mean that I'm capable, or that I would pull it off."

He shook his head, his hand moving up to the back of my neck. "It has nothing to do with the lines and everything to do with you. You're one of the most mesmerizing and expressive people I have ever met. I think the second you stepped out onto that stage the entire audience would fall madly in love with you."

Goose bumps broke out across my arms, and I struggled to meet his gaze. "You think so?" I turned my head away, pulling out of his reach and trying to gain some distance. "Maybe even pretty enough to play Rosaline next time?" I needed space from him. I needed him to storm off so I could try and pull all these messy pieces back together into some semblance of a person.

He turned my chin back to look at him. "I know you heard that asinine comment, and I've been trying to say something about it for a long time. All of my attempts to fix this have been clumsy and somehow made worse by my own stupid blundering." He tilted my chin up higher. "Beatrice, I'm sorry. I need you to know that. I was embarrassed and angry and said a stupid comeback to my stupid friends thinking it would make me feel better. When I realized you heard it, I knew I would spend every second of this summer trying to convince you that I wasn't normally such a dumbass. You *have* to know. It was a ridiculous comment that even in the heat of the moment, when I was upset, I still didn't believe."

Butterflies raced through my belly, and his teeth flashed white in the dim lighting. "But pretty? I don't know if I could ever call you something as simple and insignificant as that."

I wiped my damp hair away from my face, unable to hold his gaze anymore. "Thank you for saying that. I suppose I should apologize for implying you were such a bad actor that only your parents' camp would cast you."

He snorted. "Look, I know now isn't the best time, but there are some things that we need to talk about." He stood up and helped me shakily to my feet. "Things I need to tell you," he corrected himself.

I nodded. "I think I'm dealing with just about all I can handle at the moment." I wiped my hands on my pants before wincing at damp streaks staining the suede.

He nodded back, disappointment evident. "Of course, but soon."

"Soon," I agreed, bile threatening to come up again. I wasn't sure what things he would want to say to me at this point, but I had no reserve to take another hit. It was all I could do to remain upright with everything that had been happening.

I gave him a wobbly smile. "Go ahead; I'll meet you back there. I want to clean up first."

I made my way into the bathroom and stared at the ghost in the mirror. Her hair was sweaty and plastered to her, her skin pale and her upper lip beaded with sweat. I looked like I was about to pass out at any second. I splashed cold water across my face and neck as Shelby walked in.

She eyed me up and down. "You look like shit."

I laughed, despite myself. "I know."

She chewed her lip before appearing to make a decision. "Are you . . . okay?"

I pressed a paper towel so hard against my face I saw stars. "No, I'm not. Not as if you would care."

"I was just asking. You don't have to be all dramatic."

I didn't respond and wrapped my hair up into a bun.

She shifted in place. "Okay, look. I know we're not really friends."

I raised an eyebrow at that understatement.

She rolled her eyes. "Come on, Bea. I'm trying, and I do appreciate you stepping in so we can continue the play. I've never had the lead before, and I'd hate for it to end like this." She frowned as I dry heaved again. "Come on, it's going to be fine."

I adjusted my glasses back on my face. "What part of this looks like it's going to be fine?"

"You're the genius who got into Oxford and has everything in the world go perfectly for her. Let's try rising to the occasion, yeah?"

"What in my life is going perfectly? I'm soaked in sweat, I have vomit on my breath, and I'm about to make a fool of myself in front of a ton of people."

She shrugged. "Yeah, and then you get to move away to freakin' England and start a completely new life. Sounds awful. Way worse than staying at home while all your friends leave for college and move on with their lives."

I paused as she fiddled with her hair. "I know Nolan going to RISD must be tough."

She picked at her nail polish, not looking up. "Not just him. Everybody. Maybe a few will be at NYU, but they'll all be obsessed with their new lives. I'm the only one stuck in limbo."

I should have just left her in there, but I wasn't ready to go back onstage yet and a small part of me felt sorry for her. I didn't forgive her, but I understood desperation when I saw it. I understood what seeing your future slip through your fingers felt like.

"You know, there is still a small chance I'm not going to go. I might be stuck in Berkeley for another year."

She frowned. "What are you talking about?"

I sighed, the story falling easily from my lips at this point. "My parents are worried that I'm not emotionally equipped to handle going away to college. They sent me here with a list of tasks to accomplish to learn how to make friends and socialize."

"You don't know how to make friends?"

"I find it weird that you're surprised by this."

"So, you think they might not let you go?"

I shrugged. "I've accomplished most of the tasks, but I'm just worried they're going to look at what I've done and think it's not enough. There's only one left that they came up with, and I'm pretty sure I can pull it off. Your crazy brother added another one, but I'm going to ignore it."

She pulled herself up on the counter, legs dangling. "Oh my god, I can't even imagine what he would have come up with." She wrinkled her nose. "Scratch that, I can *totally* imagine what he would pick."

"It involves kissing, which he felt I could somehow knock out while I was here."

She leaned back, her head resting against the mirror. "You could have. Wasn't that the bet you lost to Nik?"

I raised an eyebrow. "You know very well that was the bet I lost, and you were thrilled to death I didn't collect."

"Why didn't you?"

Shelby had been awful to me, by her own admission, but there in the dim lighting and close quarters of the bathroom I felt the words bubbling up.

"Because I didn't want my first kiss to be the result of a bet. Or a joke."

She slid off the counter, frowning. "I don't believe it was a joke. Nik's a good guy. He wouldn't do something like that just to make fun of somebody."

"Yeah, I think you're a little biased when it comes to Nik."

"Look," she groaned, massaging her temples. "I know I've pointed out some of his more questionable behavior to you, but I've honestly never seen him like this with anyone else. I've never seen him look at anyone the way he looks at you."

I didn't have the ability to do a single thing with that comment as I stood there barely keeping it together with vomit on my breath. "Is that why you hate me so much?"

"Look. I know what it looks like, but I told you I'm not in love with him." She looked at me directly, unapologetically. "And I don't hate you."

I pushed my glasses up my nose. "Could have fooled me."

She paced around me, her skirts brushing against my legs in the small space. "I already told you I just wanted a perfect summer with a perfect Romeo." She paused, her back to me. "I messed everything up. Nolan and Nik are still barely talking to me, and it's not like I'm even heartbroken. I was mostly irritated that he wouldn't just fall into line where I was trying to place him."

I bit my lip, unsure how to respond.

"I'm sorry," she said, turning in the small space. She forced the words out through her teeth, but they rang sincere. "I know I'm selfish, and petty, and was a giant bitch to you when I was really just angry with myself."

"Does this mean we're best friends now?"

She laughed, the sound pained but present. The lines of her body relaxed a fraction. "You're such a dork."

"Probably so, but I'm a dork that you clearly want to be best friends with."

"Forget I said anything," she tossed over her shoulder as she moved to the door. The smile she tried to hide reflecting in the mirror.

She paused before tugging the handle and turned back to me. "I used to have stage fright."

I blinked in disbelief.

"It's true." She wrinkled her nose. "The thing I found that worked best was that I made up a stage persona when I was acting. When I'm her, I can be brave, fierce, and I don't have to worry about anything." This time as the smile broke out across her face, she didn't try and smother it. "Her name is Britney Foxx, and she's really excited about her first leading role."

I laughed as I imagined the inspiration for that name.

She shrugged. "You should try it."

With that she was gone.

# Chapter Twenty-Eight

"SAY YOUR LINE, WAIT FOR TYBALT, MOVE around Romeo, draw your sword, stab, stab, die," I murmured. I'd been running the blocking cues for my fight scene late into the night, and I wasn't sure it was going to be enough. My legs swung off the stage, and campers and parents were milling around, touring the Globe before our big performance tonight.

"Move around Romeo, stab, stab, die," I said, trying to remember if Tybalt was to my left or right.

"Who's dying?"

I looked up as Mia laughed, and two older, attractive people who could only be her parents smiled up at me. "Bea, these are my parents: Dr. Mary Parker and Dr. Kenneth Parker."

I jumped down, pulling at my shorts, and stuck a hand out. "Beatrice Quinn, lovely to meet you."

Mia's mom came forward and folded me into a tight hug. "Mia has told us so much about you, and I'm so glad you ended up coming this year." With her coral lipstick, fuchsia dress, and riotous curls that matched her daughter's, I could see that the apple didn't fall far from the tree. I turned to Mia's dad, who was wearing a suit that was absolutely made for him and had soft brown eyes and a smile that warmed up the room like sunshine. He bypassed my hand as well, coming in for another hug.

"Have your parents arrived yet?" he asked after he released me.

I looked around them toward the door. "I haven't seen them, but they're notoriously late."

Mia giggled. "I can't imagine how that irritated you growing up."

I squinted at the new reason for my continuous lateness. "It could be challenging at times."

"Mia told us that this is your first play, and you must be excited about having such a big role," her dad said.

"I'm extremely nervous, but luckily I know there are actors like Mia in the show that are talented enough to make me look good," I said, smiling at her. I barreled ahead before they had a chance to respond. "In fact, she's so incredible that I'm very relieved that she's majoring in acting, so she gets to share her talent with more of the world."

Her parents shared an amused look, and her mom slipped an arm around her shoulder. "We're well aware how talented she is, and we're very excited to see her performance tonight."

Mia smiled, her heart in her eyes, and she blew me a kiss. "I'm going to show them the sets in the back! Let me know when your parents get here; I am literally dying to meet them."

"Figuratively!"

"Nope! I'm literally *literally* dying," she said, grasping at her throat as her parents led her away.

I fidgeted, trying to yank my shorts down more again. My parents hadn't seen my bare legs in ages, and I was secretly hoping to shock them so badly that they'd pull out their cell phones and order my plane ticket right there. I smoothed the white tiered tank top down and couldn't help the butterflies in my stomach. It felt like it had been years since I last saw them, and I wasn't sure how this new person would fit into my old life. Would everything be different? Back in the carefully structured isolation of my life in Berkeley would I just slide back into place?

A smile broke out across my face as two familiar figures came through the door and looked around in wonder at the wooden pews and the sunlight dancing in from the open ceiling. My mom was dressed in her usual maximalist style, all colorful layers and bangles up both of her forearms. My dad was wearing a blue seersucker suit with a pink bow tie. My heart swelled at how normal it felt. I raced down the aisle, and Dad looked up just in time for me to crash into him.

"Oh! Excuse me!" He released a handful of ruffles and jumped back.

"Very funny, Dad," I said as his jaw dropped open in recognition.

He froze as Mom recovered first and crushed me to her.

"We missed you so much." She pulled away and inspected me from head to foot. "Look at you—I don't think we would have noticed you if we passed you in the street." She rubbed the thin layers of my ruffled top before spinning me around. "What size is this? I love it!"

I danced out of her reach. "Hands off, Mom! It's mine!"

Dad laughed, staring at me in amazement. "You look so comfortable."

I shrugged. "Yeah, who knew that shorts in the summer were a good idea? Weren't you guys the ones that were supposed to be teaching me these things?"

"You look happy, sweetheart." He pulled me in for another hug. "I hid the credit card bill from your mother," he whispered.

I winced. "Oh yeah, sorry about that . . ."

His eyes danced. "I figured it made up for about sixteen years of extremely responsible behavior."

"I'm so glad you see it that way."

Mom clasped her hands in front of her, bangles jangling. "Are you excited about the play tonight? Will you be behind the scenes with the director, or can you sit in the audience with us?"

I cleared my throat. "Oh yeah, there have been some changes since we last spoke. One of our actors had to go home because of a family emergency, and I'm in the play now. Surprise!" I said, my voice cracking.

"Oh. Well, that's wonderful, honey," Mom said, her eyes wide. "What part are you going to be playing?"

"Umm—Mercutio?" I said.

Dad coughed. "Mercutio? The most outgoing and exuberant member of the cast?"

"Yep!" I said, my voice pitched higher. "That's the one."

They nodded in unison.

"Well, we're so excited to watch you, sweetie!" Mom said.

I nodded, a plastic smile on my face.

"Beatrice, do you have a moment? I'd like you to meet my parents," Nik murmured from behind me.

I turned and looked up at him as his aftershave wrapped around me, dropping my IQ at least thirty points.

"Really? Why?"

He rolled his eyes. "I'm not going to bother answering that." He looked up, noticing my mom fidgeting with my ruffles and curls. His brow furrowed as he glanced between my parents and me, and I know he had half expected to see a couple with pocket protectors and briefcases.

"Nik, these are my parents, Sophia and Edwin Quinn. Mom and Dad, this is Nik. He's our resident Romeo."

Nik cleared his throat and stuck out his hand. "She means in the play, you know, not . . . in regular life or anything."

I'd never seen him so awkward before, and I bit my lip to stop from snorting.

My mom gave him a knowing smile. "I'm sure."

She turned and arched an eyebrow at me.

*Stop it,* I mouthed.

"Um, Nik?" I coughed. "Didn't you say something about meeting your parents?"

"Nice to meet you, Mr. and Mrs. Quinn." He nodded at my parents, grabbed me by the elbow, and guided me over to a big group before I could protest.

"Are you sure you want to do this? They look pretty busy," I faltered, trying to pull down my shorts more.

"I'm sure they'd much rather talk to you."

"I don't know about that. They'll probably send me an additional bill for ruining the play tonight for everyone."

"You're going to kill it." With that he pushed through the crowd and pulled me in front of a striking couple. The woman had flame-red hair and green eyes and was wearing a stunning royal-blue dress. The man was ridiculously handsome, with the same golden-brown skin as Nik, and clearly where he got his great bone structure from. They both smiled as Nik made introductions.

"Mum, Dad, this is Beatrice Quinn. It's her first time acting, and she is the one that had to step in at the last minute for Ben. Beatrice, these are my parents, Miranda and Rishi."

"Beatrice!" Miranda said, beaming. "We've heard so much about you and are so happy to finally meet you. I only wish it was under happier circumstances."

His dad stepped forward and shook my hand. "So nice to meet you, Beatrice. We stopped by the hospital to see Bianca before we flew out here. Thank God she's stable."

"I'm so glad," I said, haunted by the look on Ben's face when he first heard the news.

Nik slung an arm around my shoulders. "Beatrice here is going to be heading off to Oxford in the fall."

His parents took quick note of his body language, and his dad broke into a smile. "I was an Oxford man myself. If you'd said Cambridge this conversation might not have stayed so friendly!"

"All bark and no bite," Nik said, the most at ease I'd seen him all summer.

"In fact, Nik here—"

"Why don't you tell them what you plan on studying, Beatrice?" Nik said, interrupting.

I raised an eyebrow. "Statistical genetics. Although I'll probably start off just trying to take all the classes that seem interesting to me."

Nik looked down at me fondly. "Don't they have a limit to the number of classes they'll let you take in a semester?"

I frowned, remembering my admissions packet. "Yes."

I peeked over Nik's shoulder, making sure my parents were okay, and saw Mia hugging my dad.

I smiled at Nik's parents. "It was really nice to meet you both, but my friends are randomly embracing my parents and I should go provide some context."

Miranda's smile widened. "Break a leg tonight. I'm sure we'll be seeing a lot of you."

I hurried through the crowd and got there right as Mia released my dad.

"Hey! I see you've met Mia?"

Mia bounced next to me. "I'm sorry; I couldn't wait! I knew we were going to have so many fun Beatrice stories to share!"

"Ha. Ha."

She laughed, squeezing me into a hug like I was her favorite teddy bear. "You know I'm just playing." She held her hand up to her ear like a phone and winked at my parents.

I was still in Mia's arms, and Mom's eyebrows looked like they were going to disappear up into her hair. "Mia's my roommate."

"And her best friend," she said, tightening her grip until I wheezed.

"And my best friend."

"Who is going to come visit her in England on spring break."

I looked up at her and smiled, my poor heart stretching into a million different directions. "Who's going to come visit me during spring break."

"Okay, guys, I left the parents with Nolan and have to get back before they're either scandalized or end up adopting him." She flashed a brilliant smile at my starstruck parents and skipped away.

I straightened my shirt. "As you can see, I have made a few friends, and I've almost completed the list."

"Almost?" Mom asked, frowning.

I pulled it out of my pocket, and Mom plucked the stained, smeared paper out of my hand. Unfolding it, she and Dad scanned the page, and his eyebrows lifted as they got to Nolan's additions. "You been flirting and dancing with abandon?" he asked, his voice strained.

Mom smiled, all her teeth on display. "I see that the kiss task is still unchecked. As is the one we wrote about hugs?"

I swallowed thickly. "Don't hold your breath on the kissing, and I expect to get all the hugs checked off tonight, don't you worry. There will be nothing holding me back from going to Oxford."

She sighed, folding the paper back up. "I know you wanted to accomplish everything to get to Oxford, but I hope you had fun doing it as well. I hope . . . I hope that Oxford is no longer the only thing in your life that you're looking forward to?"

A wave of anxiety and regret rose in my throat, and I pressed my lips together. The thought of not laughing with Nolan every day, of not feeling like every nerve ending I had was on fire whenever Nik walked past me, of not whispering sleepy thoughts to Mia every evening—it all threatened to undo me. I settled for shaking my head until I trusted myself to speak. "It's extremely important to me, but no—it's not everything anymore."

Her eyes watered, and she grasped Dad's hand. "Okay." They shared a secret look, and she took my hand with her other. "You'll have to show us the classes you're planning to take when we get home."

# Chapter Twenty-Nine

"**DO YOU THINK SWEAT STAINS WILL SHOW** through this doublet?" I lifted my arms in concern while Nolan and Mia evaluated the finished product.

"Are you sure you're all right?" Mia asked with her hands on her overpadded hips, the deep crease between her eyebrows emphasized with makeup.

"That doublet is perfection and could withstand any stress response," Nolan said, pulling the garment back into place.

"I'm fine," I said breezily. "I've only vomited twice, and I've dragged a trash can behind that curtain, so I can vomit at will from the wings."

Mia's face pinched, and she grasped Nolan's arm. "This is too much. We shouldn't have asked her to do this."

I forced a smile, which was probably more teeth than anything at this point. "You've worked so hard, and you think I would ruin the opportunity for you to show your parents how incredible you are?"

Her lip wobbled, and she smoothed back the wisps that broke free from my braid crown.

"The audience is filling up, everyone is ready to go, and

there's nothing to do about it now. This is happening." I collapsed back into a chair and stuck my head between my legs as my vision started to go dark. "This is happening." *Helium. Neon. Argon. Krypton. Xenon. Radon.*

"Is she okay?" Shelby's voice filtered in from far away. It sounded like my ears were stuffed with cotton.

"Okay, that's it," Nolan said. His voice sounded garbled, and Shelby's feet disappeared from my periphery. He crouched down, bringing himself eye level with me. "What is the worst thing that you think could happen?"

I sucked in a mouthful of air, my lungs struggling to expand. "That I ruin the play? That everyone worked so hard, and the only thing people will be able to see or remember is how horrible I was?"

Mia snorted. "You are not going to ruin the play, and honestly, some people didn't work that hard. Troy scrawled a lot of his lines on the palms of his hands."

Nolan nodded in agreement. "Bea, how many American students get into Oxford every year?"

I frowned as I ran the numbers. "I'm not sure. A few dozen?"

"Out of that supertiny group, how many of them do you think were homeschooled?"

I shrugged. "Realistically? One?"

He nodded. "We already know you're a unicorn. That you have talents and abilities that we can only guess at. Are you telling me that you don't think you can walk out there and have a conversation that you already know the words to?"

I sat upright. "It's not that simple."

He spread his hands wide. "It could be."

I cradled my face in my hands and mumbled, "Shelby told me she invented an alter ego to combat her stage fright."

Mia laughed. "Beyoncé does that too!"

Nolan clapped. "All right, we'll create your alter ego, and then all this pressure can rest on her instead."

I grimaced. "I don't know; it sounds really silly."

"Nonsense. Now tell me about your character. What would it take for you, or this imaginary person, to do a great job out there tonight?"

I slumped in my chair. "I'm not sure. Be confident? Outgoing? Funny? Be the life of the party?"

Nolan turned to Mia. "How on earth did Ben get this part?"

A smile tugged at her lips. "Oh hush, he has other strengths."

Nolan walked behind me, massaging my shoulders. "Okay, I want you to close your eyes."

I did what I was told.

"You are extremely beloved. Your entire life has been a string of parties and conquests, and everybody wants to be your friend. You're so popular that you can get invitations to the parties of your enemies, and they even hope you come! Life has been one big joke, and every time anybody sees you, they are instantly happier and charmed."

I rolled my shoulders as Mercutio came to the forefront of my mind. His mischievousness, his lack of conscience and desperation for a good time. I exhaled. I knew his words, I knew his mind, and I knew his end.

I tilted my head up. "How am I supposed to act that careless? That free?"

Nolan smiled down on me. "Who says it has to be you?"

Mia crouched in front of me, her hands resting on my knees. "Let's talk about your alter ego. What characteristics do you think she has that you lack?"

"Confidence?"

Nolan pshawed. "I've seen you speak your mind in the heat of the moment with not an ounce of fear. Just terrifying conviction."

"The alter ego also has to be very outgoing and funny."

"You're hilarious, just in a smart and dry way." Mia squeezed my knees. "Maybe we can make the alter ego a little more willingly social?"

I shrugged. "The life of the party?"

"Well, you've only been to one so far; give it a little time," Nolan joked. "I think we can say that your alter ego is just this older, more worldly version of you. She knows what she wants, she fears nobody and nothing, and people are helplessly drawn to her."

I flushed as Shelby ran back up to us. "I got it!" She bent over, trying to catch her breath in a corset.

"You've got what?"

She pulled a plastic glass of red wine out from behind her. "Reinforcements!"

My stomach clenched, remembering my morning after the peach schnapps.

"It's really filling up out there," she added.

I blanched and held out my hand. Nolan passed me the glass, and I tossed the contents back. My mouth stained red, I exhaled shakily.

"This is just one little hurdle and then Oxford, right?" Shelby asked, her cheeks pink from exertion. "You finished the list, right?"

I pulled myself out of the chair. "Almost. I'm going to ignore the kissing, but I still have to hug three people."

"Well, why didn't you say so?" Nolan asked, lifting me into a bone-crushing hug. I swayed when he set me back on my feet.

Mia crushed me into her arms next, the padding making her shape unfamiliar.

Suddenly Shelby was in front of me. She tentatively put her arms around me, and we shared the briefest of hugs. She stepped away, her cheeks even pinker.

"What's your alter ego's name?" Mia asked, nudging me.

"Oh, good point!" Nolan paced around me. "It has to be a name of strength and power, and something that resonates with you."

I paused for a second before breathing out. "Athena." They all turned to look at me. "Athena Ruth Bader Ginsburg."

"Of course it is," Nolan and Shelby said in unison. They looked at each other in surprise before Shelby reached out and grabbed his hand tightly. He pulled her in and gave her a kiss on her forehead before turning to me and adjusting my doublet.

I took a deep breath and stood up straighter. I could do this. *Helium. Neon. Argon. Krypton. Xenon. Radon.*

I kept my calm as the bell rang to let us know that we had five minutes to curtain call. I casually wiped the sweat from my upper lip and cleaned my glasses during the first scene. I counted down each second until my entrance. I didn't come in until the last part of act one, and I watched as my castmates finally came into their own. They became more confident with every murmur of the crowd, and I laughed along with them.

Then of course, there was him. He could have been in the chorus and every eye would have still been drawn to him. However, in the lead role, with his black-and-gold doublet shining in the light, he was mesmerizing. He sulked around the stage, his obsession with Rosaline still coloring every decision he made. I drank him in, every line perfect and every move graceful. I blushed as he moved off the stage and into the wings with me. He grinned, a little out of breath, as Lady Capulet and Mia moved past us.

"Break a leg!" I whispered after her.

He nudged me. "Are you ready? After this scene, we're going out together."

I nodded. "I know."

He squeezed my arm. "I'm going to grab some water." He slipped off, and I closed my eyes.

This would all be over soon, and I would be heading back to normal life. The studying, research, and projects, which I did enjoy—*sometimes*. I would probably never be in a situation like this again. It would just be one moment, one blip in time, and I could be somebody completely different. Somebody who never winced when she realized she'd said the wrong thing at a gathering. Somebody who put herself out there, and who'd broken hearts and had hers broken in return. Who'd tried the weird food that didn't fit her weekly schedule, and who'd laughed and cried and relished and wallowed in mistakes. That life that I had been so terrified and dismissive of the past few years. I wanted it all now, and I wouldn't be satisfied until I tasted every drop.

The audience laughed, and I grinned as Mia hammed it up onstage. Shelby looked on with wide eyes, as if she didn't understand the joke. She was the picture of innocence, and I remembered her triumphant look as she announced her alter ego. A smile tugged along my lips.

"Almost time to go." Nik swiped his lips and tossed his water bottle to the side. He looked down at me as if he expected me to run at any second.

I inched forward and got into position with the group as we

prepared to leave the wings. One step and the Bea who looked down on acting fell away. One step and the Bea who took herself too seriously slid off my shoulders. One step and the Bea who was willing to stay on the sidelines just *disappeared.*

I stepped out, clean and new under blinding lights that lit me up from within. I swaggered around as Benvolio and Romeo hotly debated our excuse to get into the party.

"*Give me a torch. I am not for this ambling.*

*Being but heavy, I will bear the light,*" Romeo barked out in disgust as he held his hand out expectantly to one of the torch-bearers.

I ran to his side, slid my hand into his outstretched one, and gave him a spin.

"*Nay, gentle Romeo, we must have you dance!*" I said, laughing.

He stumbled and looked at me in surprise. He straightened his clothing and replied:

"*Not I, believe me. You have dancing shoes*

*With nimble soles. I have a soul of lead*

*So stakes me to the ground I cannot move.*"

I shook my finger in his face and gave him an exaggerated pout.

"*You are a lover. Borrow Cupid's wings*

*And soar with them above a common bound!*"

He smirked and clasped me on the shoulder.

"*I am too sore enpierced with his shaft*

*To soar with his light feathers, and so bound,*

*I cannot pitch above dull woe.*

*Under love's heavy burden I do sink.*"

He leaned heavily against me until I staggered under his weight. I laughed, shoving him off me.

"*And to sink it, should you burthen love—*

*Too great oppression for a tender thing."*

He slid to the floor and reclined, smiling up at me. My heart skipped a beat.

*"Is love a tender thing? It is too rough,*

*Too rude, too boisterous, and it pricks like thorn."* He flung his arm over his face.

I put my hands on my hips as I looked down on him in exasperation.

*"If love be rough with you, be rough with love."*

I leaned over and gave him a playful kick in the ribs.

*"Prick love for pricking, and you beat love down.—"*

I swung back to kick him again, and his arm snaked out and grabbed my leg, pulling me down next to him. I shrieked, laughing, and snapped at one of our comrades from the floor:

*"Give me a case to put my visage in!"*

They slipped a mask into my hand and I slipped it over my face as Benvolio helped me off the ground.

*"A visor for a visor.—What care I*

*What curious eye doth cote deformities?*

*Here are the beetle brows shall blush for me."*

I finished and looked over at my Romeo challengingly. His features were mostly hidden by the mask, but his eyes were wide in amazement. A powerful feeling coursed through me and I turned to the audience and gave them a saucy wink.

He moved close to me and reprimanded me:

*"And we mean well in going to this mask,*

*But 'tis no wit to go."*

I rolled my eyes and walked past him.

*"Why, may one ask?"* I tossed over my shoulder.

He grabbed my arm, spinning me around before I could get too far away from him. He looked down at me meaningfully.

*"I dreamt a dream tonight,"* he said, biting his lip.

"*And so did I,*" I murmured.

"*Well?*" He smiled and raised an eyebrow. "*What was yours?*"

My smile was strained, and his hand was still on my arm. "*That dreamers often lie.*"

He released me, and Benvolio cleared his throat, reminding us that we were not alone onstage. I skipped, snaking through all the merrymakers, taunting Romeo from a much safer distance. I moved through my monologue with manic eyes and breathless observations until Romeo pulled me toward him laughing.

"*Peace, peace, Mercutio, peace!
Thou talk'st of nothing.*"

He tucked me under his arm as we wrapped up the scene, and we walked offstage together. We'd barely cleared the wings before he turned toward me and lifted me off the floor. He spun me around, burying his face in my neck. I swallowed a shriek as the next scene started, and he slid me to the floor before ripping my mask off.

"Where the *hell* was that hiding?"

I laughed, embarrassed. "I'm not really sure."

He cradled my face in his hands. "You were incredible, Beatrice. You *are* incredible."

I leaned into his hands as the stage manager came up to us.

"Romeo, you're on in a moment."

He nodded, not taking his eyes off me. I gave him a small smile and slipped out of his embrace. I moved back toward the dressing rooms until I saw Nolan and Mia sitting off to the side.

Nolan slow clapped, grinning like a maniac.

I covered my face with my hands. "I know, I know, it was too much."

Mia ripped my hands from my face. "Are you kidding me?

You were absolutely unbelievable! I have goose bumps all over my body!"

Nolan gave me a tight hug. "I have to admit I'm really enjoying you and Nik's specific interpretation."

I frowned in confusion. "What do you mean?"

He grinned. "You know, the one where Romeo and Mercutio are more in love with each other than with all the ladies they're chasing."

Mia snorted in agreement, and I rolled my eyes. "Whatever you guys say. I'm going to go spend some time in the back."

Nolan raised an eyebrow. "Not trying to see Shelby make out with your man again?"

I winced but acknowledged that hiding was pointless and a little bit risky when I was due back onstage shortly after that.

"On second thought," I said. "I wouldn't miss this scene for the world. It's pretty iconic." It was also a nice realistic reminder for me. The lines of what was real and not real were muddled again.

I stood in the wings as Romeo pulled Juliet aside, her white-and-gold gown glittering in the lights. She looked up at him, her face shining bright.

"*Saints do not move, though grant for prayers' sake.*" She smiled.

"*Then move not, while my prayer's effect I take,*" he said.

I prepared myself for the blow. He looked up, past her, and his eyes caught mine. He leaned in and, turning his head at the last moment, he kissed her on the cheek.

Never skipping a beat, he continued, "*Thus from my lips, by thine, my sin is purged.*"

Shelby was stunned for a moment and responded accusingly, "*Then have my lips the sin that they have took.*"

Nik grinned down at her.

"*Sin from thy lips? O trespass sweetly urged!*
*Give me my sin again.*"

He once again moved quickly and placed a peck on her cheek.

I bit my lip to stop from smiling and chided myself that I was being ridiculous.

# Chapter Thirty

MY HAIR WAS PLASTERED TO MY HEAD AS rivulets of sweat poured down my back. I raced around the stage, with my sword drawn, as Troy and I came to blows.

He smirked at me and pointed his sword in my direction.

*"I am for you."*

I smiled back at him, promising violence.

Romeo's panicked voice cut through the tension. *"Gentle Mercutio, put thy rapier up!"*

At his insistence, I pulled my sword up and gave him a jaunty salute. Romeo barked orders in the background as I went over the blocking in my head one last time. Stab, stab, die. Stab, stab, die.

Tybalt lunged toward me, and I danced away. Only one more, and then die. I moved fluidly, and Romeo grasped me by the shoulders.

*"Hold, Tybalt! Good Mercutio!"*

I looked up at him, smiling. My sword arm faltered and dropped. Then under Romeo's arm, Tybalt plunged his blunt plastic sword into my belly. I pitched forward, my hands clutching Romeo's doublet. I felt the betrayal of getting caught between the Capulets and the Montagues, and the unfairness that it was my death that was paid during their war.

Stab, stab, die.

I clutched my belly and slid down onto the floor.

*"Help me into some house, Benvolio,*
*Or I shall faint. A plague o' both your houses!"*

I coughed weakly.

*"They have made worms' meat of me. I have it,*
*And soundly too. Your houses!"*

Benvolio pulled me to my feet and dragged me off the stage, and I sank to my knees in the wings. I ripped the doublet off me, revealing a thin tank top underneath. The cool air kissed my sweat-slicked skin, and I sat there breathing heavily.

I was done. I had done it.

I had no more scenes to worry about, and my contribution to this play was complete. A laugh escaped my lips as I pulled myself to my feet and pulled loose the braid that had been wrapped around the crown of my head. Nik raced off the stage behind me and grabbed me by the hand. He pulled me through the maze of sets in the darkness until we reached the platform for Juliet's bedroom. He hopped up and pulled me up next to him, grinning.

"What are we doing?" I murmured.

"I wanted to talk to you. To congratulate you, without somebody coming up and interrupting or telling me I have to be on the stage soon."

"Well, you can't blame them; you are onstage a *lot.*"

He stepped closer to me, his fingers sliding behind my neck. "You were magnificent tonight. You outshined everybody, and I couldn't take my eyes off you."

I swallowed, balanced on the edge of something I couldn't describe. My hand reached out, and the scratchy material of his costume scraped against my palm. He leaned down, his breath intermingling with mine.

"Why didn't you kiss Shelby?"

He grinned, his eyes shining. "Because I only wanted to kiss one person on this stage tonight."

My breath caught, and he was so beautiful I was dizzy just standing next to him. "Are you sure? Still trying to collect on your bet?"

He groaned, pressing his damp forehead against mine. "I was such an idiot, in literally every situation. There in the dark, during that movie, all I wanted in the world was to tell you that I picked a kiss because it was all I could think about—all day every day. I was so worried if I made a move on you, you'd run away and never talk to me again."

I chuckled, the air thick. "I probably would have run away."

"Every word, every stupid action, was my bumbling way of trying to convince you to want me too."

I wasn't sure who moved first, but from one second to the next his hands were threaded in my hair and his lips were on mine.

And I burst into flames.

My heart was beating so fast, and as he gently moved against my mouth the scientific part of my brain was attempting to remember the signs and symptoms of a heart attack. As his tongue slipped past my lips, I pulled him closer and decided that if I was currently dying, I could think of no better way.

His lean body pressed me into the side of the set as every nerve ending exploded, and all I could think was that I was spinning, spinning, spinning, and I never wanted it to stop.

"Nik! Beatrice!"

Nik froze against me, and as things came back into focus I prayed that the heart attack would go ahead and finish me off. Shelby's furious face slowly came into focus, and I blinked against the blinding light as Nik shuddered against me, trying to stop laughing. I peeked around him, and the dumbstruck audience stared up at us.

"Did you notice the set was turning around?" I rasped.

He raggedly rubbed his face. "Not even a little bit."

"I thought everything was spinning because you were a good kisser," I confessed wistfully.

He looked down at me, the heat in his eyes warming me another fifty degrees.

"Get *off* the stage!" Shelby hissed, pausing her monologue.

He grinned at me. "One last thing to do." He spun us around and gave an elegant bow as the audience began to laugh and clap. I hid my face behind my hand, my cheeks bright red, and gave a clumsy little bow before Nik dragged us both offstage. We collapsed into each other.

"I can't believe my parents saw that," I moaned, my head shooting up in horror. "Oh my god. *Your* parents saw that too!"

He grinned. "Try not to freak out too much; they'll all get over it. I don't regret a second of it." He pulled me toward him and gave me another searing kiss that made my toes numb. "I have to get back out there soon," he said. "I'll see you at curtain call."

I nodded, my heart in my eyes, as he ran back into the darkness.

I wandered off in a daze, and the rest of the play floated past me. I ducked out of the way of sets, passed out water bottles, and congratulated my costars as they stumbled off the stage with triumph in their eyes.

Mia's comforting hand hugged my waist, and Nolan stood on my other side, arm linked in mine. We all watched the final scene as our star-crossed lovers were lying in their tomb and their families were coming together for the last time. Seeing the amazing thing we all created was one of the most overwhelming and important moments of my life. A single tear streaked across my cheek as the mark of this experience, these *people*, seared into my heart.

"I can't believe Rishi and Miranda Shah saw you stick your tongue down their son's throat," Nolan said, his shoulders shaking.

I pinched him, my face burning. "Some friends you are! You couldn't warn us that the set was turning around?"

Mia snickered. "You guys were too sneaky! We had no idea until . . . well, until everybody knew."

I groaned, and she gave me a little squeeze.

"I can't wait to tell Ben; he will just die when he hears!"

I smiled at that. "So, things are still—"

She grinned. "Oh yeah, things are very much still on. No plans yet, but we'll see how things go."

I leaned into her as I registered where we were in the play. "Oh, here we go!"

The Prince stepped toward the audience, his face somber.

"A *glooming peace this morning with it brings.*

*The sun, for sorrow, will not show his head.*

*Go hence, to have more talk of these sad things.*

*Some shall be pardoned, and some punished.*

*For never was a story of more woe*

*Than this of Juliet and her Romeo.*"

The breath whooshed out of me as the curtain fell.

In a scramble, all the sets were moved back, and everybody got into place for curtain call. We took our bows separately, and the whistles and claps that I received had my face flaming. By the time the company all took a bow together, the audience was on their feet. Yeah, it was mostly our parents, but we'd done a hell of a job, and we knew it.

The curtain came down again, and this time it would stay down. Everyone hugged and congratulated each other, and I was swept up in it all. Then Nik appeared in front of me, and I couldn't stop crying. I wasn't sure if it was happiness or sadness at the root of it, and he cupped my face as if I was his most precious possession.

"It's an amazing feeling, isn't it?"

I nodded, fat tears still sliding down my face. "I don't know if I will ever feel normal again."

He wiped my cheeks and grinned. "There is nothing normal about it."

I reached out to pinch him when Shelby approached, hesitating on the edge of our little bubble.

"Hey, Bea? Can I talk to you for a second?"

Nik's arm tightened around me, but I slipped out of his grasp. "I'll be right back."

We moved away from the crowd and she gave me an appraising glance.

"You did pretty good tonight."

I smiled at her. "You weren't so bad yourself."

"Did Athena do all the heavy lifting for you?"

I wrinkled my nose. "Surprisingly enough, it was Beatrice who wanted to be the center of attention for once."

She nodded. "That's an interesting development. Well, I've heard they know their Shakespearean theater over there at Oxford."

"I'm probably going to focus on the books, but I might check out a play or two." I hesitated before extending the smallest of olive branches. "You know, Mia's coming for spring break, and I was going to invite Nolan too. You could always come with him, if you'd like."

She blinked, her features tight. "You want me to come?"

"I mean, I know how desolate you're going to be without me."

A laugh slipped out, sharp as her expression. Her armor snapped back in place, and the only crack was the small smile still on her face. "Maybe that would be okay. I'd have to check my calendar."

"You do that."

She nodded, moving backward. "Take care of yourself, Bea."

"You too," I murmured, but she was already gone.

I felt arms wrap around me. "Everything okay?"

I leaned back against Nik's chest, basking in his warmth. "We were just fighting over you. We've decided to duel at dawn."

He snorted, ruffling the hairs on the back of my neck. "You're pretty good with that sword. I'd think twice if I was her."

I turned, grinning up at him, as chaos continued to erupt around us. Parents began to wander backstage, shrieks of excitement carried up over the house music, and I stood there leaning into the most satisfying feeling I'd ever known.

"Beatrice Joanna Quinn!"

I spun around as my parents stood across from me with jaws you could have swept off the floor.

I jerked out of the reassuring circle of Nik's arms. "I didn't see you both there," I said, my voice two octaves too high to pull off normal. "How did you—how did you like the play?"

They squished me into another group hug before Mom pulled away, smoothing the plastered hair back from my sweaty, tear-stained face. "After a lifetime of you doing extraordinary things, I didn't think I could still be this surprised by your abilities. It was like I'd never even met that girl from the stage before." Her lip wobbled a little. "I would really like to know her better, though."

I grinned, a few more tears squeezing out. "I don't think I'd met her before either, but we both have plenty of time to figure her out."

"Let me get in here too," Dad said, scooting Mom over and

pressing a kiss onto my forehead. "You were the most incredible thing I'd ever seen, but I could have probably done without the scene you and Romeo added."

I felt the heat spread across my face like wildfire, and Nik walked forward, the two of us a united front.

"We were performing one of those new contemporary versions," Nik said, his crooked smile for me alone.

"I'm sure," Dad deadpanned, his gaze stuck on Nik's arm slung across my shoulders.

"Well, we need to clean up, return these costumes, and I still need to pack for tomorrow," I said, strung entirely too tight after all that had happened that night. All that had happened over the entire summer.

Mom smiled, guiding Dad back to the exit. "We're so proud of you, sweetie, and we'll see you tomorrow. We'll have plenty of time to talk on the plane."

"Love you," Dad said, smiling at what I'm sure was an extremely pained expression.

"Love you both," I said before burying my burning face in Nik's doublet. I could feel the rumbles of his laugh as I pulled my face away and looked up.

"Do you want to get out of here?"

He slipped his hand in mine, and we raced out the back.

# Chapter Thirty-One

WE STRETCHED OUT ON THE VELVET CAPE OF his costume, and I didn't relish the thought of explaining the grass stains to Nolan. I snuggled in the crook of Nik's arm, and he pressed a kiss onto the top of my head. It was such a new and foreign sensation to me. Human contact like this. My fingers danced across his stomach as I marveled at the fact that I could touch him whenever I wanted to.

"I'm glad we have a chance to talk, because I have something I need to tell you." His chest rumbled under me.

I froze. "Oh my god, please don't tell me you have a girlfriend back home."

I felt the vibrations of his laughter.

I shot up and swatted at him. "Or your fancy European parents have betrothed you to somebody?"

He yanked me down and kissed me senseless as his clever fingers tangled in my hair.

"Oh no you don't; I will not be distracted!" I leapt off the cape, towering over him. I put my hands on my hips for added intimidation.

He threw an arm behind his head and smiled lazily at me. "I like it when you're irritated with me."

"Then you should be thrilled right now."

He laughed. "I should have told you sooner, but then things got so confusing between us that I thought if I told you then you would think it meant something weird. Then it didn't seem like there was ever going to be a good time, and then we kissed, and now this seems like a *really* awkward time." He pressed his lips together, stopping the deluge of concerning information.

I stepped back, my heart hammering beneath my thin tank top. "Oh god. You only have six months to live, don't you?"

"Mouse."

"Your parents are secret agents and have been reassigned somewhere where you'll have to take on a completely new identity and leave all this behind?"

"Mouse."

My breath huffed out in little gasps, and my glasses fogged up, masking his amused face. "You're actually a serial killer, and you're going to murder me and bury my body on the quad."

I felt his presence before I could clearly see him, and he slid my glasses off before wiping them on his T-shirt. He gently placed them back on my face before breathing the words into my lungs. "I'm going to Oxford too. I got in for acting."

My heart stuttered. "Wait, what?"

He shrugged, ducking his head. "You heard my dad; it's his alma mater. I've been planning to go since I was a kid."

"Why didn't you tell me that first night?" I asked, sinking back down onto the black velvet, shock numbing me.

He eased himself down next to me. "Well, we did start arguing almost immediately."

"I guess you have a point there." I leaned back on my heels

and looked at him with new eyes. The possibility of continuing this—whatever this was—past the summer scorched me.

I bit my lip. "Is this just a warning that I might see you around campus at some point, and to not be too surprised?"

He frowned. "You only want to see me in passing?"

"I don't know what the normal protocol is," I stuttered, gesturing between us. "I don't know how this typically goes?"

He leaned back and snaked a hand around my wrist, yanking me toward him. I sprawled across his chest. "I intend to see you *a lot*, Mouse. I'm going to walk you to your five thousand classes, make you eat dinner when I know you've forgotten, push around a wheelbarrow to transport all your books, and kiss you at every possible moment."

My chest tightened, as if my heart was too big to comfortably fit inside there anymore.

"So, this is a thing now?" I asked, my chin propped up on his chest.

"One of the most important things," he said, his voice raspy.

I rolled off him, finding my spot in the crook of his arm again, so he wouldn't see my eyes water. "You know that I'm probably going to freak out about a lot of things, right? This summer was only a fraction of new experiences, and if anything, I'm only going to get more awkward."

"I don't know if that's possible."

I pinched his side. Hard. "I'm serious!"

He moved quickly, flipping me onto my back and hovering over me. His eyes bright. "I can take whatever you throw at me."

I sniffed. "Are you sure you don't want to just find a less awkward girl who will be able to impress all your friends with her shiny hair and normal conversation?"

He hovered over my lips. "Sounds awful."

I snorted, the sound cut off as he took my ability to speak, and my mind quieted as I devoted myself to my latest skill.

I was always a very attentive student.

As he tucked me back into his arms, I clutched the soft material of his shirt and tried to pinpoint the moment that led me here. The specific thing that changed the trajectory of my life—probably forever. Was it Mia and her easy laugh cutting through the velvety dark of our bedroom? Her gentle prodding for me to try something new and embrace change and the accompanying fear? Or maybe Nolan and the traitorous blush he would coax out of me at every turn? Perhaps it was the impossibly beautiful boy lying next to me, whose infuriating actions and gentle declarations unmade me several times over. Or maybe it was a combination of all of the above?

Maybe I saved myself and found the courage to realize and demand the life I truly wanted. Whatever the reason, whatever the cause, my heart swelled in gratitude and I breathed out into the night sky.

*"I can no other answer make, but thanks, and thanks, and ever thanks."*

# Acknowledgments

The first person I want to thank for all of this is *you*. There are so many beautiful books and incredible authors out there, and it means everything to me that you took a chance on Bea and Nik's story. Getting to share this with you, talk to you about it, and scream about certain scenes is absolutely why I want to do this.

I'd be nowhere without agent extraordinaire Jim McCarthy, who has shown unwavering support and excitement about this book ever since I blazed into his inbox, promising theater kid shenanigans. He's helped me navigate this emotional and confusing process and can somehow sense whenever I need someone to check in or offer gentle encouragement. I am beyond excited to see what else we can send into the world together.

To my editor, Jennie Conway. I remember being so nervous for our first call, and you instantly put me at ease with talk of *Pride and Prejudice* tattoos and Nik and Darcy comparisons. I hung up feeling like I'd just talked to an old friend, and I knew this book was in the perfect hands. I felt like I had edited this book for ages, and there was nothing left to change about it, but you unlocked depths in a way that can only be magic. Thank you, for changing my life, and for believing in me and these kids.

A huge thank-you to the entire team at Wednesday Books, for taking a chance on me and this book. I bought a Wednesday tote at Yallfest in 2019 and used it every day for work until I retired it in the fall of 2020 with the signing of my deal. You were always my dream imprint (a fact I told Jim often) and I am beyond proud to be a part of the incredible stories you are putting into the hands of readers everywhere. A huge thank-you to Rivka Holler, Meghan Harrington, and the entire Wednesday marketing and publicity team for helping get this book into those hands. Special thanks to Kayla, for sensitivity reading and providing such thoughtful feedback. Thank you all from the bottom of my heart.

Thank you to Kerri Resnick, Katie Smith, and the Wednesday design team, for giving me the most perfect pink cover of my dreams. I will be dyeing my hair to match it for decades to come, and I am so grateful that something this beautiful is mine.

Thank you to Bel Romain, Jennifer Kelly, and Krissy Parnell Baccaro. You were the first people to ever see the very first version of this book, and your unwavering support and encouragement is the only reason I got to the finish line.

Thank you to Megan Lally, for teaching me more about writing than any college course I've ever taken. I had so many ideas, and you gently took me by the hand and showed me how garbage my grammar was, and you were right to do so! Your encouragement talks should be bottled and sold, and I can't thank you enough.

Sophie Gonzales, how can I thank you enough for your mentorship? You helped me take this book from a meandering stroll through six weeks at camp into something with purpose. I love your honesty, your passion, your friendship, and most important—your hair. I'm hoping to crash many more industry parties with you, and maybe I'll actually be invited this time.

Big thanks to Author Mentor Match, for helping me find Sophie and a community. Writing was a pretty isolating experience until I found myself welcomed into so many groups and DMs. It truly is a family.

Thank you to Sophie, Emily Wibberley, and Austin Siegemund-Broka for taking the time to read and blurb this book. I am such a huge fan of all of your work and am so very grateful.

How can I ever thank you, Julia Foster? This book took shape in a series of Monday submissions between our inboxes. The fact that we even found each other, two needles in a giant haystack, is a miracle. Thank you for your encouragement, your friendship, and your hilarious edit notes.

Thank you to Jo Fenning and Jenna Voris, for being two of my favorite people/writers on the planet and our daily group chat that gives me life. Jenna, from stumbling across each other on the internet to late-night wine in my kitchen—I am so thankful for your incredible spirit and unmatched support in my life. Jojo, you popped into my DMs when I needed you most, and I have refused to let you go ever since. I would be lucky to have a third of your strength, and I am in awe of you daily.

Thank you to the Bull City Squad (TJ Duckworth, Katie Perkinson, and Paige Ladisic) for welcoming an awkward outsider in. You went from my first real-life writer friends to some of my actual best friends of all time. I want to meet you all at Panera every Sunday for the rest of our lives.

Thank you so much to everyone else who read early versions of this book (across its long life span) and offered encouragement along the way: Brittany Borshell, Emily Miner, Jenna Giuffrida, Allison Saft, and everyone else I yeeted a few chapters at. You all helped a very nervous woman reconcile herself to sharing her words with the world.

Thank you to Jordan Bishop, author assistant of my dreams, whose patience and skill have helped keep a very ADD woman on track. You're the absolute best.

Huge thank-you and congratulations to the #22Debuts!! Y'all! We're doing it!!!

As mentioned above, this book is dedicated to my parents: David and Dee Thompson. They raised two little girls out on the edge of a swamp in small-town North Carolina and made an adventure of going to the library every Saturday. I am who I am because of you both. Thank you and love you.

To my sisters: Leora Thompson and Krystalyn Drown. You both know me, as only sisters can, and your support means the world. Thank you for your love and your championing of this book.

To the rest of my overwhelmingly supportive family: thank you so much to all of the Thompson and Kaylor clans. You're all so kind and encouraging, and always quick to ask for updates. Thank you for all of your love. Shout-out to Aaron Scheib, who is family regardless of his last name, and my incredible aunt Cheryl, who is my second mother in every sense of that word.

To Austin: thank you for listening to me talk about this for years and for every time I lock myself in my office for days at a time. I don't deserve your love and understanding, but I am thankful for it every day.

Thank you to Melissa Dixon and Juliet Norman. You've been supporting me since we were sipping vodka cranberries in too-loud clubs in undergrad, and you still get excited about my weird ideas . . . like writing a book.

Thank you to the people in my life blessedly removed from this industry, who don't understand why this is taking so long but support me anyway. Thank you to Gaea McCaig, Kassandra Spiller, Rayleen Jones, Kathleen Claus, Vanessa Taylor, Carlee Komoroski, Anna Frank, Rebecca Slate, Hannah Crosby, William Reed, and the crews at Granville and Duke. Special thank-you to Dehra McGuire, whose real-time reading of this book added five years to my life.

Thank you to Dr. Kelli Rachel Brooks for frequently cornering me at work and asking about my writing. You taught me everything I know about medicine, and your unwavering support of this has made me feel like I can truly do both. I promise I'll be brave enough to send the book to you . . . soon.

Last but not least, special thank-you to Panera Bread for their unlimited refills and a place to squat for hours at a time. Shout-out to Sunday Panera, Tabby Panera, No-refill-left-behind Panera, and even Worst-Wi-Fi-ever Panera.